With the tragic early death of Robert Rankin during the millennial celebrations, it seemed that the world had lost forever its leading exponent of Far-Fetched Fiction. But happily this was not the case. Within days of Rankin's demise, Brentford medium Madame Lorretta Rune received an urgent spirit communication from him. 'Purchase twenty-three exercise books and two hundred biros and prepare to take dictation of my final novel,' she was told. The result was this techno-gothic masterpiece, the first ever posthumously written novel. It pro_____d doubt that for Rankin, as f_____h was a good caree_____

Robert _____ of the *Operator*, *W_____ex and Drugs and S_____, The Dance of the _____rout Mask Replica, Nostradamus A___ly Hamster*, *A Dog Called Demolition, The Garden of Unearthly Delights, The Most Amazing Man Who Ever Lived, The Greatest Show Off Earth, Raiders of the Lost Car Park, The Book of Ultimate Truths*, the *Armageddon* quartet (three books), and the *Brentford* trilogy (five books) which are all published by Corgi Books.

For more information on Robert Rankin and his books, see his website at:
www.lostcarpark.com/sproutlore

THE FANDOM OF THE OPERATOR

Robert Rankin

CORGI BOOKS

THE FANDOM OF THE OPERATOR
A CORGI BOOK: 0 552 148970

Originally published in Great Britain by Doubleday,
a division of Transworld Publishers

PRINTING HISTORY
Doubleday edition published 2001
Corgi edition published 2002

5 7 9 10 8 6 4

Set in 11/13 pt Bembo by
Falcon Oast Graphic Art Ltd.

Corgi Books are published by Transworld Publishers,
61–63 Uxbridge Road, London W5 5SA,
a division of The Random House Group Ltd,
in Australia by Random House Australia (Pty) Ltd,
20 Alfred Street, Milsons Point, Sydney, NSW 2061, Australia,
in New Zealand by Random House New Zealand Ltd,
18 Poland Road, Glenfield, Auckland 10, New Zealand
and in South Africa by Random House (Pty) Ltd,
Endulini, 5a Jubilee Road, Parktown 2193, South Africa.

Printed and bound in Great Britain by
Cox & Wyman Ltd, Reading, Berkshire.

Book about death
to celebrate a new life,
the birth of
Summer Dawn Patricia:
may you know love and happiness

1

It was a Thursday and once again there was rancour in our back parlour.

I never cared for Thursdays, because I cared nothing for rancour. I liked things quiet. Quiet and peaceful. Wednesdays I loved, because my father went out, and Sundays because they were Sundays. But Thursdays, they were noisy and filled with rowdy rancour. Because on Thursdays my Uncle Jon came to visit.

Uncle Jon was lean and long and loud and looked a lot like a lizard. There's a bit of an animal in each of us. Or a reptile, or a bird, or an insect. Or even a tree or a turnip. None of us are one hundred per cent human; it's something to do with partial reincarnation, according to a book I once read. But, whether it's true or not, I'm sure that Uncle Jon had much of the lizard in him. He could, for instance, turn his eyes in different directions at the same time. Chameleons do that. People don't. Mind you, Uncle Jon's eyes were made of glass. I never looked too much at his tongue, but I bet it was long and black and pointy at the end.

Uncle Jon was all curled up, all lizard-like, in the visitors' chair, which stood to the east of the chalky-drawn line that bisected our back parlour. The line was an attempt, upon the part of my father, to maintain some sort of order. Visitors were required to remain to the east of the line, whilst residents kept to the west. On this particular Thursday, Uncle Jon was holding forth from his side of the line about pilgrims and parsons and things of a religious nature, which were mostly unintelligible to my ears. Me being so young and ignorant and all.

My father, or 'the Daddy', as I knew and loved him then, chewed upon sweet cheese and spat the rinds into the fire that lick-lick-licked away in the small, but adequate, hearth.

I perched upon the coal-box, beside the brass companion set that lacked for the tongs, which had been broken in a fight between my father and my Uncle Jon following some long-past piece of rancour. I was attentive. Listening. My pose was that of a Notre Dame gargoyle. It was a studied pose. I had studied it.

'Thousands of them,' rancoured my Uncle Jon, voice all high and hoarse and glass eyes rolling in their fleshy sockets.

'Thousands of parsons, with their lych gates and their pine pews and their cloth-bound hymnals and their pulpits for elbow-leaning and their embroidered mats that you are obliged to put your knees upon whilst praying. And what do any of them really know? I ask you. What?'

The Daddy didn't reply. I didn't reply. My mother, who lathered sprouts in the stone pot by the sink in our kitchen, didn't reply either.

Nobody replied.

There wasn't time.

'Nothing,' my Uncle Jon rancoured on. 'Charlie is gone, and to where?' There was no pause. No space for reply. 'I'll tell you to where. To none knows where. Wherever that is. And none knows.'

My father, the Daddy, glared at Uncle Jon.

'Don't glare at me,' said the Uncle.

My father opened his mouth to speak. But pushed further cheese into it instead.

'And don't talk to me with your mouth full. They don't know. None of them. Clerics, parsons, bishops, archbishops, pilgrims and popes. Pilgrims know nothing anyway, but popes know a lot. But even *they* don't know. None of them. None. None. None. Do *you* know? Do you?'

I knew that *I* didn't know. But then the question probably hadn't been addressed to me. Uncle Jon had been looking at me, sort of, with one of his glass eyes, but that didn't mean he was actually speaking to me. He'd probably been speaking to the Daddy. I looked towards that man. If anybody knew an answer to the Uncle's question, it would probably be the Daddy. He knew about all sorts of interesting things. He knew how to defuse a V1 flying bomb. He'd done that for a living in the war. And he knew all about religion and poetry. He hated both. And he knew how to concentrate his will upon the cat while it slept and make it wee-wee itself.

I never quite understood the worth of that particular piece of knowledge. But it always made me laugh when he did it. So, if there were anyone to answer

Uncle Jon's question, that person would, in my limited opinion, be the Daddy.

I looked towards him.

The Daddy looked towards Uncle Jon.

Uncle Jon looked towards the both of us.

I really wanted the Daddy to speak.

But he didn't. He just chewed upon cheese.

My daddy hated Uncle Jon. I knew that he did. I knew that he knew that I knew that he did. And Uncle Jon knew that he did. And I suppose Uncle Jon knew that I knew that he did and probably knew that I knew that he knew that I did. So to speak.

'You *don't* know,' said my Uncle Jon.

I looked quite hard at my uncle. As hard as I possibly could look. I was young and I hadn't learned how to hate properly as yet. But as best as I possibly could hate, I hated Uncle Jon.

It wasn't just his eyes that I hated. Although they were quite enough. They were horrible, those eyes. They didn't even match. Not that it was Uncle Jon's fault. It wasn't. My daddy had explained the situation to me. He told me all about glass eyes and how opto-something-ists (the fellows who dealt with this sort of thing) matched up eyes. They matched up a glass replacement eye to its living counterpart. Both of Uncle Jon's eyes had left his head when a bomb from Hitler had blown up in his back yard. My daddy hadn't had a chance to defuse that one. He'd been down at the pub fighting with American servicemen. These opto-something-ist fellows had bunged my uncle a couple of odd eyes, because they knew he wouldn't notice. They looked horrible, those odd glass eyes. I hated them.

Being blind didn't bother Uncle Jon, though. He'd learned how to see with his ears. He could ride his bike without bumping into people and do all the things he'd done before that needed eyes to do them. There was a special name, at that time, for being able to see without having eyes, as my Uncle Jon was able to do. Derma-optical perception, it was. There used to be a lot of it about, back in the days when people believed in that sort of thing. Back then in the nineteen fifties. People don't believe in that sort of thing nowadays, so blind people have to go without seeing.

Uncle Jon travelled a lot with the circus, where he did a knife-throwing act that involved several midgets and a large stetson hat. The crowds loved him.

The Daddy and I didn't.

The Daddy worried at the medals on his chest with cheese-free fingers and finally stirred some words from his mouth. 'Cease the rancour,' were these words. 'You're frightening wee Gary.'

'I'm brave enough,' said I, for I was. 'But who is this Charlie of whom my uncle speaks?'

'Yes,' said my daddy, 'who *is* this Charlie? I know not of any dead Charlies.'

'Charlie Penrose, you craven buffoon.' My uncle rolled his mismatched peepers and rapped his white stick – which he carried to get himself first in bus queues – smartly on the floor, raising little chalky clouds from the carpet and frightening me slightly.

'Charlie Penrose is *dead*?' My father stiffened, as if struck between the shoulder blades by a Zulu chieftain's spear. 'Young Charlie dead and never called me mother.'

'And never called *me* sweetheart,' said my Uncle Jon. 'And I have written to the Pope regarding the matter.'

My daddy opened his mouth once more to speak. But he didn't ask 'why?' as many would. Uncle Jon was always writing to the Pope about one thing or another.

'I am shocked,' said my father, the Daddy. 'I am deeply shocked by this revelation. I was fighting with Charlie only the last week.'

'I was fighting with him only the last yesterday and now he is no more.'

'*So!*' cried the Daddy. '*You* murdered him! Hand me the poker from the brass companion set that lacks for the tongs, son. And I will set about your uncle something fierce.'

I hastened to comply with this request.

'Hold hard,' said my uncle, raising his blind-man's stick. 'I am innocent of this outlandish charge. Charlie died in a bizarre vacuum-cleaning accident. He was all alone at the time. I was in the Royal Borough of Orton Goldhay, performing with Count Otto Black's Circus Fantastique. To rapturous applause and a standing ovation, even from those who had to remain sitting, due to lack of legs.'

'Charlie was my closest friend,' said the Daddy. 'I loved him like the brother I never had.'

'I never had that brother too,' said my uncle. 'I only had yourself, which is no compensation.'

'Do you still require the poker, Daddy?' I asked.

'Not yet, son, but keep it handy.'

'That I will,' said I, keeping it handy.

'I am appalled,' my daddy said. 'Appalled, dismayed and distraught.'

'And so you should be.' Uncle Jon turned his glassy eyes to heaven. 'And so should we all be. And I have had enough of it. Charlie is dead and there will be a funeral and a burying and words will be spoken over him and what for and why? Nobody knows where he's bound for. Whether to a sun-kissed realm above, or just to the bellies of the worms beneath. No one, not even the Pope. And I think it's a disgrace. The Government spends our tax money putting up Belisha beacons and painting telephone boxes the colour of blood, but do they put a penny into things that really matter? Like finding out what happens to people after they die, and if it's bad, then doing something about it? Do they? I think not!'

'Daddy,' said I. 'This Charlie Penrose, who you claim was your closest friend. Why did he never come round here?'

'Too busy,' said my father. 'He was a great sporting man. Sportsmanship was everything to him. And when he wasn't engaged in some piece of sportsmanship, then he was busy writing. He was a very famous writer. A writer of many, many books.'

'Poetry books?' I enquired.

My father smote me in passing. 'Not poetry!' he shouted. 'Never use that word in this house. He was the writer of great novels. He was the best best-selling author of this century so far. He was the man who wrote the Lazlo Woodbine thrillers. And also the Adam Earth science-fiction novels. Although they were, in my opinion, rubbish, and it's Woodbine he'll be remembered for.'

'Surely that is *P. P.* Penrose,' said I with difficulty, clicking my jawbone back into place. 'P. P. Penrose. But this is terrible. Mr Penrose is my favourite author. Are you certain that this Charlie is really the same dead fellow?'

'Same chap,' said Daddy. 'He changed his name from Charlie to P.P. because it gave him more class.'

'We have more class at my school, when no one's off sick with diphtheria,' I said.

'Same sort of thing,' said my daddy.

'No, it's not,' said my Uncle. 'Don't just humour the boy, tell him all of the truth.'

My daddy nodded. 'It's nothing like that at all, son,' he said, smiting me once again.

I considered the poker. A boy at our school had done for his daddy with a poker. He'd done for his mummy too. And all because he wanted to go to the orphans' picnic in Gunnersbury Park. I wouldn't have dreamed of doing anything as horrid as that. But it did occur to me that if I smote the Daddy just the once, but *hard*, it might put him off smiting me further in the future. It would be the work of a moment, but would take quite a lot of nerve. It was worth thinking about, though.

'There'll be a wake,' said my Uncle Jon, derailing my train of thought. 'There's always a wake.'

'What's a wake?' I asked, pretending that I didn't know, and edging myself beyond my daddy's smiting range.

'It's a kind of party,' said my Uncle Jon, lizarding all around and about in the visitors' chair. 'Folk like your

14

daddy drink a very great deal of beer at such functions at the expense of the dead man's family and rattle on and on about how the dead man was their bestest friend.'

'Is there jelly and balloons?' I asked, because I greatly favoured both.

'Go and play in the yard,' said the Daddy.

'We don't have a yard,' I informed him.

'Then go and help your mummy lather sprouts.'

'That's women's work,' I said. 'If I do women's work I might well grow up to be a homo.'

'True enough,' said my uncle. 'I've seen that happen time and again. Show me a window-dresser and I'll show you a boy who lathered sprouts.'

My father made a grunting noise with his trick knee. 'Much as I hate your uncle,' he said, 'he might well have a point on this occasion. He knows more than most about homos.'

'I'll take that as a compliment,' said my uncle, 'although it wasn't meant as one. But let the lad stay. He should be told about these things. He'll never learn to walk upon ceilings, just by standing on his hands.'

'There's truth in that too,' said my daddy.

'What?' said I.

'What indeed!' said my daddy. 'But tell me, young Gary, what do you know about death?'

'Well,' said I, toying with the poker, 'I've heard that good boys go to heaven and that brutal fathers burn for ever in the fires of hell.'

My uncle laughed. 'I've heard that too,' said he. 'But what do you actually know about death?'

I shook my head in answer to the question.

'Nothing,' I said. In truth I knew quite a lot about death. It was a particular interest of mine. But I had learned early on in my childhood that adults responded favourably to ignorance in children. They thrived on it. It made them feel superior.

'What *is* death, Uncle Jonny?' I asked.

Uncle 'Jonny' pursed his lizard lips. 'Now that *is* a question,' he said. 'And it's one to which no satis-factory answer really exists. You see, it's all down to definitions. It is generally agreed amongst members of the medical profession that a subject is dead when they have suffered "brain-stem death". Which is to say, when all cerebral activity – that is, brain activity – has ceased. This is referred to as clinical death. Although, I am reliably informed, certain techniques exist that are capable of keeping the body of a dead person "alive" in a hospital by electronically manipulating the heart muscle and pumping air into the lungs.'

'Why would anyone want to do that?' asked my father.

'I don't know,' said my uncle. 'For use in spare-part surgery, I suppose, or possibly for the recreational activities of some deviant doctor.'

'Go and lather sprouts!' my father told me. 'I'll risk you becoming a homo.'

'I want to listen,' I said. 'Or I'll never learn how to walk upon the ceiling.'

'You know enough,' said my father.

'I don't,' I said. 'When is this wake, Uncle Jonny? Can I come to it?'

'No, you can't,' said my daddy.

'It's not really for children,' said my uncle. 'The body

will be in an open casket. Have you ever seen a dead corpse, young Gary?'

I had in fact seen several, but I wasn't going to let on. 'Never,' said I. 'But I'd like to pay my respects. I've read most of Mr Penrose's novels.'

'Have you?' asked my father. 'I didn't know you could read.'

'Yes, and write too. And do sums.'

'That infant school is teaching you well.'

'I'm at the juniors now – I'm ten years of age – but P. P. Penrose is my favourite author.'

'*Was*,' said my father.

'Still is,' said I. 'And I'd like to pay my last respects to him.'

'That's the ticket,' said my uncle.

'No, it's not,' said my daddy. 'You're a child. Death isn't your business. It's something for adults. Like . . .'

'Cunnilingus?' my uncle suggested.

'Like *what*?' I asked.

'Go to your room!'

'I don't have a room!'

'Then go to your cupboard.'

'I don't want to go to my cupboard,' I said. 'I want to know things. I want to know about all sorts of things. Every sort of thing. I want to know all about death and what happens after you die . . .'

'So do I,' said Uncle Jon.

'Shut up, you,' said my daddy.

'We have to know,' said my uncle. 'It's important. We *have* to know.'

'It's *not* important!' My father's voice was well and truly raised. 'It happens. Everybody dies. We're born,

17

we live, we die. That's how it is. The boy's a boy. Let him be a boy. He'll be a man soon enough and he can think on these things then. Get out of my house now, Jon. Let me be alone with my grief.'

'Your grief for Charlie? You old fraud, what do you care?'

'I care enough. I do care. He was my bestest friend.'

'You never had a bestest friend in your life.'

'I did and I did. You cur, you low, driven cur.'

'You foul and filthy fiend!'

'You wretch!'

'You cretin!'

And there was further rancour.

I never cared for rancour at all.

So I slipped away to play in the yard.

2

I would have played in *our* yard. If we'd had one. But as we didn't have one, I didn't.

I went to play in the graveyard instead.

The graveyard was really big back then. Before the council divided it up and sold all the best bits. All the best bits were the Victorian bits, with their wonderful tombs and memorials. All those weather-worn angels shrouded by ivy and all those vaults that, if you were little enough and possessed of sufficient bravery, you could crawl into.

I *was* little enough and had plenty of bravery. I could worm my way in under the rusted grilles and view the coffins of the Victorian dead at my pleasure.

You might consider me to have been a morbid little soul. But that was not how I considered myself. I considered myself to be an explorer. An adventurer. An archaeologist. If it was acceptable for adults to excavate the long-buried corpses of the Pharaohs, then why shouldn't it have been all right for me to have a little peep at the bodies of my own forefathers?

On this particular Thursday, I didn't worm my way under any of the iron grilles. I just lay in the sunshine upon my favourite tomb. It was a truly monumental affair. A great fat opulent Victorian fusspot of a tomb, wrought into the semblance of a gigantic four-poster bed, mounted upon a complicated network of remarkable cogs. The whole fashioned from the finest Carrara marble.

It was the tomb of one David Aloysius Doveston, purveyor of steam conveyances to the gentry. 'Born 27th July 1802, died 27th July 1902.' A good innings for a Victorian; a grand century, in fact.

I'd taken the trouble to look up Mr Doveston in the Memorial Library. I'd wondered why it was that a purveyor of steam conveyances had chosen to have his tomb constructed in the manner of a fantastic bed.

In amongst the parish records, housed in the restricted section, I located a big fat file on Mr Doveston, who, it appeared, had been something of an inventor. I uncovered a pamphlet advertising what appeared to be his most marvellous creation: 'the Doveston patent steam-driven homeopathic wonder-bed'. This incredible boon to mankind had been displayed at the Great Exhibition and was presented as being 'the universal panacea and most excellent restorer to health, efficacious in the cures of many ills, pestilences and dreadful agues that do torment mankind to mortification'. These included 'milliner's sniffle, ploughman's hunch, blains which pain the privy member, rat pox, cacky ear, trouser mite, the curly worms that worry from within' and sundry other terrible afflictions.

I must suppose that the homeopathic wonder-bed proved equal to the claims of its inventor, for not only had he lived to be one hundred years of age but also, as far as I knew, ploughman's hunch and the curly worms that worried from within no longer plagued the general public.

In fact, as I could find no trace of any of these ghastly maladies listed in any medical dictionary, I remain of the firm conviction that Mr Doveston's invaluable invention effected their complete eradication.

I was surprised, therefore, that he hadn't, at the very least, had a local street named after him.

I lay upon the marble replica of Mr Doveston's beneficial bed, all curly-wormless and thinking a lot about the death of P. P. Penrose and all my uncle's rancour.

Although I hadn't let on to my father, or to Uncle Jon, I felt very bad about the passing of the Penrose. Very bad indeed. I loved that man's books. I was a member of the now official P. P. Penrose fan club. I'd saved up, sent away for and received the special enamel badge and everything. I had the Lazlo Woodbine, private-eye secret codebook, the pen with the invisible ink, the unique plastic replica of Laz's trusty Smith & Wesson (that was *not* a toy, but a collectable) and the complete set of *Death Wears a Turquoise Homburg**** trading cards. I was saving up for the Manhattan *Scenes of Woodbine* diorama playset, a scaled-down section of New York City, where you could *be* Woodbine (if you were very, very small).

Lazlo Woodbine was the classic 1950s genre

*A Lazlos Woodbine thriller.

21

detective. He wore a trenchcoat and a fedora and worked only in the first person. And, no matter how tricky the case might be, he only ever needed four locations to get the job done. His office, where women-who-would-do-him-wrong came to call, a bar where he talked a lot of old toot with his best friend, Fangio, the fat boy barman, an alleyway where he got into sticky situations, and a rooftop, where he had his final confrontation with the bad guy. According to Laz, no great genre detective ever needed more than these four locations. And I was saving up for the complete set. And it all came in a cardboard footlocker.*

None of this will mean very much to anyone who hasn't read a Lazlo Woodbine thriller. But as most of you will realize, this was special stuff, which if it was still extant and found its way into an auction room today would command incredible prices.

I was a fan. I admit it. A big fan. Still am. I loved and still love those books. All those stylish slayings, all the Woodbine catchphrases. All the toot he talked in bars, the women who did him wrong, the bottomless pits of whirling oblivion that he always fell into at the end of the second chapter when he got bopped on the head. The whole kit and genre caboodle and the Holy Guardian Sprout inside his head.

I loved the stuff. I did and do. I loved it.

Which is why I mention it here.

I *was* miffed. I'm telling you. I felt well and truly cheated. My favourite author dead and never called my

---

*Remember those? No? Well, please yourself, then.

father mother. And my father had actually known him. And I never knew that he did. I could have met the man. Had him autograph my books. Talked to him. But no. He was dead. Defunct. Gone and would write no more.

That seemed really unfair. Really stupid. Really pointless. I felt really bad.

I mean, and give me a minute here while I get deep, I mean, what is the point of death? Does anybody know? Being alive has a point, it has a purpose. If people weren't alive, weren't aware, then what would be the point of the universe? It might exist, but if there was no one in it to know it existed, it might as well not exist. You had to have people in the universe to be aware that there was a universe. You didn't actually need God, who it was claimed created the universe, He was completely unnecessary. You could just assume that the universe had always been there, always would be there, for ever. But without people to see it was there, what was the point of it being there? No point! That's an original concept, you know: *I* thought of that. That was what being alive was about.

But dying, what was the point of that? You spent your life being aware, taking in information, creating things, like P. P. Penrose created Woodbine, or Mr Doveston his wonderful bed. And then you died. And that was it. No more awareness, no more creativity, no more anything. What on Earth, or off it, was the point of dying?

It's a big question, you know. A really big question.

I won't labour it too much here, because I don't want you getting bored and closing the book, especially as it does get really exciting as it goes along. But it's important that I do address the issues that led me to take the course of action that I took.

You see, even though I was young, I did have this thing about death. It bothered me, it upset me, it annoyed me. And even way back then, when I was so young and all, I felt that there had to be a point to it. It couldn't be that you just appeared out of nowhere, into the universe, lived for a short while, then were just snuffed out and were gone for ever more. That seemed utterly absurd. Utterly wasteful. Utterly pointless. There had to be something more. Something beyond life. Something we weren't being told about.

But then, of course, we *were* being told about it. We were being told about it all the time. I was being brought up in a Christian society. I was being told what would happen to me when I died. If I was good, I'd go to heaven; if not, then down below to the bad place. For ever.

Now *that* didn't make any sense to me. The proportions were all wrong. You only got sixty, seventy, eighty years alive, then your creator decided your eternal future. That certainly wasn't fair. That was ludicrous. So what *did* happen after you died? Did anyone know? My conclusion was, no, they didn't. They were only guessing.

People believed that they knew. But that was all it amounted to, belief. No one really knew for sure. It was all very well having faith in a religious hereafter, but having faith in a belief didn't mean it was correct. I'm sorry if I'm going on about this, but it is important. I personally believe that the whole God thing was invented by some clever blighter, because he knew that it was the best way to keep society behaving in a decent fashion. And, more than that, he realized that without some belief in the hereafter, with rewards for the good people and punishment for the bad, society would go all to pieces.

I think that whoever that person was, he (or she) was probably right. I mean, imagine if it was proved conclusively that there was no life beyond death. Imagine if all those Christians and Muslims and Hindus and Jews suddenly found out for certain that the whole thing was a hoax. I'll bet they'd be really upset. I'll bet a lot of them would go down to the nearest pub, get commode-hugging drunk and then go looking for a vicar or a priest to punch.

They would, they really would.

I'd been brought up as a Christian, but at that time in my life I didn't believe in a hereafter. It didn't make any sense to me. I remember my Uncle Tony dying. He'd had Alzheimer's, although they hadn't had a name for it back then. All that *was* Uncle Tony had died before his body did. His personality, along with his understanding, his memories, his recognition, gone. So *what* of Uncle Tony was going to the afterlife? In my opinion, nothing. The way I saw it, when you were dead, you were dead. Gone, finished, goodbye.

But I was torn, you see, because I could understand the point of being alive (I thought) but I couldn't understand the point of being dead. And I felt sure that there had to be a point. That's been my problem all along, I suppose, thinking that there *has* to be a point. It's been tricky for me.

Difficult.

Difficult times. Difficult thoughts.

But I was young then, so I can forgive myself.

'Wotchadoin'?'

I opened my eyes and beheld my bestest friend. His name was David Rodway. Answering to Dave. Dave was short and dark and dodgy. A born criminal. I know there are lots of arguments, the nature-versus-nurture stuff. I know all that and I don't know the answer. But Dave was dodgy, dodgy from young, from the very first day I met him back in the infant school. But dodgy is compelling, dodgy is glamorous – don't ask me why, but it is. I liked Dave, liked him a lot. I was his bestest friend.

'Hello, Dave,' said I.

'I've just been round your house,' said Dave. 'Your daddy was fighting with your Uncle Jon.'

'Was he winning?' I asked.

'No. Your uncle had him down and was belabouring him with his blind-man's stick.'

'Good,' said I. 'My daddy clicked my jaw out once again.'

'Never mind,' said Dave. 'One day you will be big and your daddy will be old and frail and then you can bash him about at your leisure. You could even lock him in a trunk in the cellar, feeding him dead mice through a hole and giving him no toilet paper at all.'

'That's a comforting thought,' said I. 'And offers some happy prospects for the future.'

'Glad to be of assistance.' Dave climbed onto the Doveston marble bed and lay down next to me. 'I figured you'd be here,' he said. 'You being so morbid and everything. You always come here when there's fighting in your house.'

'There's usually fighting in my house,' I said. 'If it's not my dad and my uncle, then it's my dad and my mum.'

'What about your brother?'

'He's gone to prison again.'

'For fighting?'

'Yes,' I said.

'I never fight,' said Dave. 'Don't see the fun in it. You know my funny uncle?'

'Uncle Ivor? The one who's a homo?'

'That's him. I said to Uncle Ivor, "Do you like all-in wrestling?" And do you know what he said?'

I shook my head.

'He said, "If it's all in, why wrestle?"'

I shook my head once more. 'P. P. Penrose is dead,' I said.

'No?' said Dave. 'You're joking. It's not true.'

'It is.'

'But he's my favourite writer.'

'Mine too.'

'I know, you introduced me to his books.'

'He's the greatest.'

'*Was* the greatest, now.'

'Still is and always will be.'

'This is really bad news,' said Dave, taking out his hankie and burying his face in it.

'I've seen that trick before,' I said. 'Give me one of those humbugs.'

'What humbugs?' said Dave, with one cheek bulging.

'You just slipped a humbug in your mouth. Give me one.'

'It was my last.'

'You are so a liar.'

'There'll be no more Adam Earth books, although they were rubbish. But there'll be no more Lazlo Woodbine books.' Dave rooted in his trouser pocket and brought out a fluffy-looking humbug. 'Imagine that, no more Lazlo Woodbine thrillers.'

I took the fluffy-looking humbug, spat upon in and cleaned it on my jersey sleeve. 'There's going to be a wake,' I said. 'For P. P. Penrose. And my daddy and my uncle will be going to it. They knew him.'

'They never.'

'They did. My daddy said that Mr Penrose was a great sportsman. That he thought sportsmanship was everything. Or something like that.'

'I've never cared much for sportsmanship,' said Dave, chewing ruefully upon his humbug. 'But we should go to this wake. Do you think the coffin will be open and the dead corpse on display?'

I popped the still rather fluffy humbug into my mouth and nodded.

'We could get something,' said Dave.

'Get something? What do you mean?'

Dave grinned me a toothy smile. 'Something to remember him by.'

'We have his books to remember him by.'

'No, I mean something more personal than that. Something of his. Some personal possession.'

'Steal something from a dead man? That's not nice.'

'You've done it before.'

'Only coffin handles and stuff. Not from someone newly dead.'

'Relics,' said Dave. 'We could take relics. After all, that man was a saint amongst writers and there's nothing wrong with owning the relics of a saint. It's something you do out of respect. It's not really stealing.'

'What sort of relics?' I asked.

'I don't know. His little finger or something.'

'We can't do *that*!'

'Why not?'

'Because we'd get caught. Someone would see us.'

'All right,' said Dave. 'Then we go to the funeral, see where they bury him, come back the same night and dig him up. We could choose the bits we want at our leisure.' Dave liked doing things at his leisure.

'Now you're talking sense,' said I. 'In fact . . .' And I set to thinking.

'What have you set to thinking about?' Dave asked.

'Something big,' said I. 'Something *very* big.'

'Do you want to tell me what it is?'

'No, I don't,' said I, rising from the marble bed of the Doveston. 'I have a really big idea, but it will need work. I have to go to the library and do a bit of research.'

'I was just going that way myself.'

'No, you weren't. But I'll meet you later and tell you all about it. This big idea of mine will take at least the two of us to bring it to fruition.'

'Speak English,' said Dave.

'I'll meet you at six o'clock at the launderette.'

'Now you're speaking my language. I love that launderette.'

'I know,' I said. 'Goodbye.'

'Goodbye, then,' said Dave.

I left Dave and the graveyard behind and took myself off to the library. I often visited the library on Thursday afternoons. I did this for two reasons. Firstly, to get away from all the inevitable rancour in our house, and, secondly, because the library was closed on Thursday afternoons. You might have wondered how it was that a ten-year-old child could gain access to the library's restricted section in order to look up information on Mr Doveston. The answer is, of course, that under normal circumstances, he wouldn't be allowed to. Which is why I always visited the place when it was closed. Me being so slim and scrawny and all that I was capable of slipping under the iron grilles that protected the Victorian mausoleums in the graveyard, I was also sufficiently slim and scrawny and all to slip in through the cat flap in the caretaker's lodge, borrow his keys and let myself into the library. I do not consider that this was a criminal activity. I was only engaged in research. Where could be the harm in that?

However, the way fate cast the dice, there *was* harm in that.

But how was I to know it then?

I thought I was engaging in research. And research to bring to fruition a big idea that I'd had. Because it was a very good idea. One that could benefit everyone. Well, at least everyone who enjoyed reading P. P. Penrose. Which was an awful lot of people.

I'll let you into my big idea now, because I can't see any reason to keep it a secret. It was Dave who inspired the idea. With his one about digging up Penrose to take a few relics. My idea was that if we were going to dig up Mr Penrose, then why not go one better than simply taking a few relics? Why not take *all* of Mr Penrose? Why not take Mr Penrose's body and do something useful with it? Something that I had read a bit about in the restricted section of the library one Thursday afternoon. In a book called *Magic Island* written by a certain Mr William Seabrook.★ The book was all about Mr Seabrook's experiences in Haiti during the early years of the twentieth century. Mr Seabrook had met voodoo priestesses. He had also seen real zombies.

My reasoning, youthful as it was, was this. If we were going to go to all the trouble of digging up Mr Penrose, why not try to bring him back to life?

To my young mind it was a blinder of an idea and I couldn't see why any adult would find it less than admirable and enterprising. There they were, the adults, willing to consign this great writer with his great mind to the worms, when, if he was reanimated, he might have years and years left in him to write more and more wonderful best-selling books. Who could possibly find anything wrong with my reasoning? In my opinion, no one.

So I went off to the library.

★This book is hard to come by, but if you can find a copy it's well worth a read. Seabrook was a pioneer of rubber fetishism back in the 1920s and also a chum of Aleister Crowley. Credentials enough, I think.

3

Captain Runstone was drunk. He was always drunk on Thursday afternoons. After he locked up the library at one o'clock he took himself off to the Flying Swan and got himself all drunk. He left the Flying Swan at three-fifteen, purchased a bottle of Balthazar's Barnett Cream sherry from the off-licence, returned to his Lodge, hung his keys upon the hook beside the door, removed himself to his bedroom, consumed the cream sherry and by six o'clock was thoroughly stupefied.

I never knew exactly why it was that Captain Runstone drunk himself into oblivion every Thursday afternoon. I was very glad that he did, of course, because it allowed me access to the library. But I never knew why. It was probably something to do with the war. Most things were, back in the nineteen fifties. Most things that were bad were blamed upon the war. Which was a good thing in a way, because people never like to blame themselves for the trouble they're in. And if they don't have something really big to blame, like a war, or a depression, or a recession, or a bad government, they only start blaming each other.

Captain Runstone had bits missing – his left hand

and also, I'd been told, his left foot, which accounted for his curious gait. Which is not to be confused with a curious gate. Like the one belonging to my Aunty May. Which had hinges on both sides and so had to open in the middle.

My Uncle Jon told me that Captain Runstone had been tortured by the Japs in Singapore. And, in fact, went into great detail regarding the specifics. And I knew that the captain cried out in a foreign tongue in his drunken sleep, because I'd heard him at it. But I didn't know for sure what the truth was and I didn't care too much. He wasn't a relative, and as I didn't even care too much about my own relatives I could think of no good reason to care at all about Captain Runstone.

I slipped in through the cat flap and nicked his keys, slipped out again and let myself in through the rear and secluded door of the Memorial Library.

I loved that library.

I did. I really did.

I loved the smell of it. And the utter silence. Libraries are always quiet, but they're rarely silent. You have to be all alone in them to experience their silence. And when you're all alone in a library, you experience so much more.

And I do mean when you're *really* alone. Just you and the library. Just you and all those books and those millions and millions of words. Those words that were the thoughts of their authors. The lives of their authors. It's special, really special. The restricted section held some most remarkable tomes. Books of Victorian pornography. Books on forbidden subjects.

The inevitable *Necronomicon*, which every library has and every librarian is obliged, by law, to deny all knowledge of. Books upon freaks and evil medical experiments. And guidebooks to lead you on the left-hand path. Which is to say, Black Magic. Most people don't really believe in Black Magic. It's the stuff of horror films and the occasional psycho. It's not *real*. It's like fairies and Bigfoot. It makes for an entertaining read, it's a bit naughty, but it's not *real*.

This runs somewhat contrary to the beliefs of those who wrote about the subject and knew of what they wrote. Those whose books are only to be found in the restricted sections of libraries. The restricted sections that *you* can't get into.

You can try if you like. You can apply for access. You can fill in forms and you might get into 'a' restricted section. But you won't get into the real one. The real one downstairs. In the basement. The one with the triple locks on the door. They won't let you in there. Only government officials with high security clearance can get into those.

And do you know why?

No, you don't.

I'll tell you. But later, not now. Now I'm telling you all about this bit. And this particular bit is particularly pertinent to the telling of this tale, because it contains one of those special life-changing kind of moments.

I never told Dave about me getting into the restricted section. Dave didn't even know that the library closed on Thursday afternoons. Libraries were of no interest to Dave. If Dave wanted a book, such as an Ian Allen train-spotters' book for instance, he simply stole it from W. H. Smith's. Dave had no need for libraries.

I undid the triple locks, swung open the iron door, switched on the lights, closed the door behind me and descended into the restricted section.

It smelled bad. It always did. These books weren't like the ones upstairs. Some of these books were deathly cold to the touch. Some of them had to be forcibly dragged from the bookshelves and prised open. They actually resisted you reading them. It was hard to concentrate upon a single sentence. Your thoughts kept wandering. There was one tiny green book with a lumpy binding that I never managed to get down from the shelf. I always wondered just what might be in that one.

On this particular Thursday afternoon I didn't bother with my usual assault upon it. I hastened to the voodoo section. Mr Seabrook had referred in his book to a tome called *Voodoo in Theory and Practice*, which had apparently contained the complete instructions for reanimating the dead, and I felt certain that a copy of this would be found somewhere here.

It was.

A greasy little black book with complicated symbols wrought in silver upon its spine. It gave itself up to me without a fight. It seemed almost eager to fall into my hands.

I leafed through it. The actual ceremony involved seemed straightforward enough. But, and there was a big but, it required a great many herbs and difficult-to-acquire items all being stewed up in a human skull and fed to the corpse. This, I considered, might be problematic. This was Brentford, after all, not Haiti. Where, for instance, was I going to find powdered Mandragora? Not at the chemist in the high street. But, and this reduced the big but to a smaller but, I was the bestest friend of Dave and if anything could be found and nicked, then Dave would be the boy to find and nick it.

It would have taken me ages to copy out the list of ingredients and all the details of the ceremony, so I slipped the copy of *Voodoo in Theory and Practice* into my pocket and prepared to take my leave.

I was almost at the top of the stairs when I heard the noise. It was the noise of the rear and secluded door being unlocked.

The noise caught me somewhat off-guard, because I was sure that the captain slept. So, who might this be? Well, whoever it was, I wouldn't let them find me. I would wait, very quietly, until they had passed by the iron door and then I would slip out and be away smartly on my toes.

'The restricted section is just down there,' I heard a voice say.

I fled back down the stairs and ducked under them, bunched myself up in a corner and waited.

'The door's unlocked,' I heard another voice say. 'Security around here is a joke. And look, the light's on too.'

'Hello,' the first voice called down the stairs. 'Is someone down there? Captain Runstone, is that you?'

'Of course it isn't him,' said the other voice. 'He's drunk in his bed. He's always drunk in his bed at this time on a Thursday. I've done my research.'

'Hello,' called the first voice again. 'Hello, down there.'

'Stop all that. Come on, follow me.'

'I'll wait here. You go down.'

'Don't be such a sissy.'

I heard a scuffle and the first voice saying, 'All right, I'm going. There's no need to push.'

Down the stairs the two of them came. I saw the heels of their shoes through a crack. Shiny and black, those shoes. Then the trousers. They were black as well. And then, when they were both at the foot of the stairs and standing under the light, I could see all of them. Two young men in black suits, with short-cropped hair and pasty pale faces. They looked rather ill and I wondered whether perchance they were suffering from the curly worms that worried from within. I certainly felt as if I was.

'It smells horrible down here,' said the owner of the first voice, the taller – and also the thinner – of the two young men.

The other man said, 'Shut up, Ralph.'

The thinner man's name was Ralph.

'Don't tell me to shut up, Nigel.'

The other man's name was Nigel.

'Smells like something's died in here,' said Ralph.

'It's the smell of magic,' said Nigel. 'Magic always smells like this. It smells a lot worse when it's being worked; this stuff's only idling.'

'I should never have taken this job,' said Ralph. 'I should have stayed in the drawing office.'

'You wanted action and adventure and now you've got it.'

Nigel was nosing about the bookshelves. 'There's some great stuff here. I think I might take one or two of these home to add to my private collection.'

'Mr Boothy would know if you did. He knows everything, you know that.'

'It's tempting, though, isn't it?'

'It doesn't tempt me at all.'

'Well, let's just get what we've come here for and then we'll leave.'

'Yes, please, let's do that. What have we come here for anyway?'

Nigel rooted about in his jacket pockets and brought out a slip of paper. '*Alondriel's Trajectories*,' he said, 'Arkham, 1705.'

'Bound, no doubt, in human skin.'

'Just red cloth. I'm sorry to disappoint you.'

'I'm not disappointed at all. So what is to be found in *Alondriel's Trajectories* and what does the old man want it for?'

'Old man Boothy doesn't confide in me. Perhaps it's something to do with the communications project.'

'Oh, *that*,' said Ralph, scuffing his heels and hunching his shoulders. 'I don't think I believe in all that.'

'No?' Nigel asked, as he ran his fingers over book spines and peeped and peered and poked. 'You know better, do you? You know better than the experts? All the boffins? All the ministers? All the brains behind these projects? You know better than all of them?'

'I'm not saying that I know *better*. I just said that I don't think I believe in it.'

'It's only a theory so far, but I think it makes a lot of sense,' said Nigel, still peering and prodding and poking. 'And if it's true, then it answers a whole lot of big questions and opens up a lot of opportunities.'

'Receivers,' said Ralph, with contempt in his voice. 'That we're all just, what? Radio receivers?'

Nigel turned upon him. 'Receivers and communicators,' he said. 'But what we really are is not up here.' He tapped at his temple. 'It's out there somewhere.' He pointed towards out there generally. 'It works through us, but it's bigger than us.'

'All right,' said Ralph. 'Now, correct me if I'm wrong, but this is the theory in essence. The theory is that human beings – that's you and me and everybody else – are not really thinking, sentient life forms. We *are* alive – we eat, we breathe, we reproduce – but we don't actually think.'

'In essence,' said Nigel. 'It's a bit like television sets. You sit and watch them, you see the pictures, you hear the sounds, but they're being broadcast from somewhere else. The TVs are only receivers that pass on information.

'And the theory is that human beings are like that. Our brains don't actually do our thinking. Our thinking is done somewhere else, by something other than us, then broadcast to our brains.

'And the brains send messages to our muscles and make our bodies function. Move our eyes about, make our voices work, make our willies get a stiffy when we want a shag.'

'So I'm not actually *me*,' said Ralph. 'I'm a sort of puppet being moved by invisible strings by something that I have no knowledge of?'

'That's the theory.'

'Well, it's a duff theory. If it were true, then I'd know, wouldn't I? The "I" that is pulling the invisible strings, I'd be aware that I was doing it. I'd know where I really was.'

'The theory is just a theory, so far. That something that is nonhuman is experiencing life on Earth through us. How can you actually prove that the thinking you do really goes on in your head and not somewhere else?'

'Oh, don't talk daft. Hit yourself on the head with a hammer, you'll feel the pain.'

'The sensory apparatus housed in my body will feel the pain. Look, Ralph, you can't actually feel with your brain, can you? You see through your eyes, but where is the actual image you're seeing? The image is being projected through the lenses of your eyes into your head and processed in your brain *somehow*. And it's somewhere in your head. Is it? Can you be sure? How would you know if it wasn't? And the sounds you hear through your ears, where are those sounds? Inside your head somewhere? They could be in your armpit – you wouldn't know any different, you'd just register that you're "hearing" sounds. If in fact what you're hearing is *actually* what's really there to be heard. Human ears have a somewhat limited range. There's a lot more noise going around us than we can actually hear.'

'I don't know what you're talking about,' said Ralph. '*Actually!* And I don't think you know either. My thoughts are my thoughts. They're inside *my* head. They're not somewhere else in the universe being beamed to me. I can feel myself.'

'Please don't do it in front of me!'

'You know what I mean. I'm *me*. I don't believe all this stuff. It's mad. And if my thoughts are coming from elsewhere, and your thoughts are coming from elsewhere, then the thoughts of the expert who came up with this theory are coming from elsewhere too. So, if whatever it is that's pulling these invisible strings is really pulling these invisible strings, it wouldn't let him have those thoughts. If it didn't want to be found out, it wouldn't, would it?'

'Perhaps it does want to be found out. Or perhaps it thinks that it can't be found out. We don't know, do we? What is the point of the communications project? To find out. And if it's there, to find out what it is, why it's doing what it's doing, what it intends for the future. Everything.'

'The theory's full of holes,' said Ralph.

'Ralph, you and I only know a bit of the theory. A hint. What we've overheard when we shouldn't have been listening. What we've been told, which is bound to be not all of the truth. What we'd like to believe; what we don't want to believe. If it's true and the communications project works, then we'll be on the inside of something really incredible. Something that will change everything on Earth. Certainly the way we "think" about everything. You joined the team because you wanted action and adventure. You wanted to get out of the office.'

'I thought it would be like spying. Or undercover work.'

'It *is* undercover work. It doesn't come much more undercover than this.'

'I thought it would be like, you know, like *him*.'

'Like Lazlo Woodbine? You fancied yourself as a private eye?'

'Who doesn't?' said Ralph.

'Help me find the book,' said Nigel. 'Let's find the book and get out of here and then we'll go down the pub.'

'I didn't think it would be stealing, either.'

'The book will be returned. The books are always returned.'

'Yes,' said Ralph. 'But what I don't understand is this, the department is a branch of the Government, right? A secret branch that even the Prime Minister doesn't know about, but it's really big and powerful. So how come, if the department has so much clout, it doesn't have its own copies of these books? Why do we have to keep creeping into public libraries to borrow them?'

Nigel sighed. 'How many books do you think there are down here?' he asked.

'Thousands,' said Ralph, looking all around and about.

'Thousands. And there's further thousands in every other library. And that adds up to millions. They're safer here in these little suburban libraries, where no one would ever think of looking for them, than all together in some top-secret library at the Ministry, where some Russian spy would be bound to find them.'

'How could he find them if the library was top-secret?'

'Because it would be such a huge top-secret library

that it would take up half of London. You are such a twonk, Ralph. Perhaps you should just go back to the drawing office.'

'It's dull in the drawing office.'

'Then just help me find the book.'

'What's this book about, then?'

'How should I know? Help me find it and we'll have a look inside.'

Ralph shrugged and scuffed his heels a bit more. And then he helped Nigel to search for the book. And after a while, which seemed a long time to me, as I cowered in the shadows under the stairs, they found it.

'There,' said Nigel. 'We have it.'

'So go on, open it up.'

I ducked my head. I had learned from the occasional bitter experience that certain of these books were better opened with care.

Nigel apparently hadn't, so Nigel swung open the book with a flourish.

I couldn't quite see what happened from where I was cowering, but I registered a sort of bang and a flash and there was a very bad smell, far worse than the one there already was. And Nigel took to coughing and Ralph took to gagging into his hands. And Nigel dropped the book and there was another sort of bang. And then Nigel gathered up the book and tucked it under his arm and the two of them scuttled up the stairs and hurried away on their toes.

I crept out from my hiding place and stretched and clicked my shoulders. I knew that I had just heard and seen something that I wasn't supposed to have heard and seen. Something secret.

Something big.

Bigger than the something big I was up to.

Something *really* big.

I didn't quite understand what I'd heard. But then it was clear that Ralph and Nigel didn't quite understand it either. But looking back on it now, from where I am now and after all that happened to me, I suppose that I am quite impressed by myself. By the myself that was me back then. Because I seemed to know instinctively that what I had heard was in some way going to shape my future. I had a sort of a future already planned for myself – I hoped to enter the undertaking trade – but I knew that the conversation between Nigel and Ralph meant something to me personally. It was almost as if it was meant for my ears. As if it had been no coincidence that I was there to hear it.

And now, all these years later, knowing what I know and having done all the things I have done, I know that it wasn't.

So, with my purloined book in my pocket, I climbed the stairs, switched off the light and left the restricted section, locking it behind me. Then I left the library, locking that behind me, returned the keys to Captain Runstone's lodge and headed home for my tea.

4

Tea at my house was sombre and quiet. I liked that in a tea. My mother said grace and served up the sprouts. My father sat soberly, though he was bloody and bruised.

'Uncle Jon gone, then?' I asked, when my mother was done with the grace and we had said our amens.

'Quiet, you,' said my father. 'Just eat up your sprouts.'

'I am no lover of sprouts,' said I. 'They make my poo-poo green.'

'Don't talk toilet at the table,' said my mother.

'Nor anywhere else, for that matter,' said my father.

'Sprouts are full of vitamins,' my mother said.

'They will put hairs on your chest,' said my father.

'I don't want hairs on my chest,' said I. 'I am only ten years of age. Hairs upon my chest would be an embarrassment.'

'I'm too tired to smite him,' said my daddy. 'You do it, Mother. Use the sprout server. Clock him one in the gob.'

My mother, harassed creature that she was, ignored

my father's command. 'Have you done your home-work, Gary?' she asked.

'I'm going over to Dave's after tea. It's a project we're working on together.'

'That's nice,' said my mother. 'You work hard at your studies and then you'll pass your eleven-plus and go to the grammar school like your brother.'

'My brother didn't go to grammar school, Mother,' said I. 'My brother went off to prison.'

My daddy glared at me pointy knives. My mother took up her napkin and snivelled softly into it.

'You'll be the death of your mother, son,' said my father. 'It's wise that I am to keep her so well insured.'

'Daddy,' said I. 'You know a lot about most things, don't you?'

'More than a lot,' my daddy said, stuffing his face with his sprouts. 'But you're right that it's most things I know.'

'We're doing a project about sacred herbs.' I toyed with my dinner and diddled at spuds with my fork. 'I have to collect a number of different ones, and I was wondering if you might know where they might be found.'

'Herbs?' said my father, thoughtfully. 'There's parsley and sage, Rosemary Clooney and *Time* magazine.'

'These are a tad more exotic.'

'Rosemary Clooney *is* exotic, or am I thinking of Carmen Miranda?'

My mother ceased with her snivelling. 'What sort of herbs do you need?' she asked.

'Mandragora,' said I. 'And Bilewort and Gashflower.'

'Cripes,' said my father. 'If it isn't toilet talk, it's sexual deviation.'

'They're herbs,' I said. 'Surely you've heard of them?'

'Oh yes,' said my father. 'Of course I have, yes.'

My mother, always polite, smiled thinly at my father. 'Your father has a lot on his mind,' she said. 'What with his bestest friend dying so tragically and everything. If you want to know about herbs, Gary, then go and see Mother Demdike in Moby Dick Terrace.'

'I've heard folk say that Mother Demdike is a witch,' I said.

'Wise woman,' said my mother.

'Surely that's a euphemism,' said I.

'No, carrot,' said my father; 'no, motorbike. Am I close?'

'Sorry?' said I.

'Oh, excuse me,' said my father. 'I thought it was one of those word-association tests.'

'One of those *what*?'

'I did these tests,' said my father. 'A psychologist chap came down to our GPO works and wanted volunteers to do these tests. You got paid five pounds if you took part, so I took part.'

'Your father will do almost anything for science and a fiver,' said my mother.

'Yes,' said my father. 'So this psychologist showed me this series of inkblots and he said, "Tell me what each one looks like." He showed me the first one and I said it looked like two people having sex. Then he showed me another and I said it looked like a man having sex with a donkey. And then he showed me another one and I said that it looked like a lady having sex with a tractor. And so on and so forth. And do you know what the psychologist said?'

I shook my head.

'He said that I was obsessed with sex.'

I shook my head again.

'And do you know what I said to him?'

I shook my head once again.

'I said, "*Me* obsessed with sex? You're the one who's got all the filthy pictures!"'

The sun went behind a cloud and a dog howled in the distance.

'I have to go now,' I said. 'I'll call in on Mother Demdike. If I'm not home by midnight, direct the policemen to her hut and tell them to look in her cauldron for body parts.'

'Won't you stay for pudding?' asked my mother. 'It's sprouts and custard.'

I declined politely and once more took my leave.

I had an hour to waste before I met up with Dave, so I decided not to waste it at all and instead wandered over to Moby Dick Terrace and the hut of Mother Demdike.

Now, it has to be said that Mother Demdike had something of a reputation in our neighbourhood. She lived all alone in a little hut at the end of the terrace. She was said to eke out a living by casting horoscopes and selling gloves that she knitted from spaniel hair. She smelled dreadful and looked appalling. She was really ugly.

Now, I've never seen the point of ugly people. I

suppose I was born with a heightened sense of aesthetics. I enjoy beauty and abhor ugliness. Mother Demdike was undoubtedly ugly; in fact, she was probably the rankest hag that had ever troubled daylight. It pained me greatly to gaze upon her, but the seeker after truth must endure hardships and, if I was to re-animate Mr Penrose, I required the necessary herbs. So if Mother Demdike could furnish me with those herbs, having to look at her ugly gob for half an hour was a small enough price to pay.

I had never actually spoken to Mother Demdike. I'd seen her out and about. A tiny ragged creature, all in dirty black, befouling the streets with her ugliness, trailing a ferret on a string. She cursed all and sundry, puffed on a short clay pipe and spat copiously into the kerb. Children feared her and adults crossed the street, and also themselves, at her approach. People, it seemed, really feared this old wretch. She could put the evil eye on you, they said. She could turn milk sour and wither your willy with a single glance. I have no idea who actually ever went round to her place to have their horoscopes cast or to purchase a pair of her spaniel-hair gloves.

For myself I couldn't see what all the fuss was about. As far as I was concerned, Mother Demdike was just an ugly old woman who fancied herself as a bit of a character. A studied eccentric. I mean, a ferret on a string? Come on!

Around her hut was a low black Neuburg fence, of a type that you just don't see any more. The gateposts were of the Hirsig design, possibly the very last pair of such gateposts in the district or indeed anywhere else outside the Victoria and Albert Museum. Although they were common enough in their day. Which was a day when Hansom cabs rattled cobblestones and Jack the Ripper had it down upon 'hooers'. The gate that hung between these posts was a Regardie, with a Mudd cantilever catch and a Miramar double coil spring. The path that led to the hut was of Cefalu stone slabs pointed with a three-to-one cement and silver-sand mix. These details may appear irrelevant. And perhaps they are.

The hut was a dank little, dark little, horrid little hovel, with sulphurous smoke curling up from a single chimney. Bottle-glass windows showed the wan light of a meagre fire. I hesitated for just a moment before knocking with the goat's-head knocker. Not for fear or for any such whimsy, but to rebutton my fly, which had come undone.

Knock, knock, knock, went I with the knocker.

'Enter,' called an old voice from within.

I pushed upon the door and entered. Sniffed the air and marvelled at the pong.

'Gary Cheese,' said Mother Demdike.

'Mother Demdike,' I replied. 'Good evening.'

The hag sat at her fireside. The hut boasted a single room, which served her as everything it should and could. There was an iron fireplace. A rocking chair in which the crone sat. A lot of herby-looking things dangled down from all over the low ceiling. A ragged rag rug sprawled upon the packed-earth floor and a great deal of magical paraphernalia lay all around and about.

I cast my eye around and about. I viewed the

paraphernalia. It all fitted so well. If you were going to adopt the persona of a witch woman you had to do the job properly. You'd need the scrimble stone and the alhambric and the mandragles and the postuleniums and also the fractible buckets.

Mother Demdike had the lot. She also had a great many ancient-looking tomes, several of which appeared to have the stamp of the Memorial Library's Restricted Section upon their spines. I raised my eyebrows at this. This dishonest woman was helping herself to my reading material.

'Come closer, my dear,' said Mother Demdike.

'If I come any closer,' I said, 'I'll be behind you. Which, considering your pong, is no place I wish to be.'

'You're a rather rude little boy. Do you know what I do with rude little boys?'

'Cook them up in your cauldron?' I asked, stifling a yawn.

'Cook 'em up for my dinner.' And the hag cackled. Cak-cak-cak-cak-cackle, she went.

'That's a horrid cough you have there,' I observed. 'You should take some linctus.'

'Come and sit beside me.' The crone extended a wrinkled claw and beckoned to me with it.

'Do you mind if I just stand here with the door open?' I asked. 'I mean, I understand about the ambience and atmosphere and everything and I respect your right to behave like an old weirdo, but, well, you know.'

'Bugger off,' said Mother Demdike. 'Bugger off or I'll cast a hex on you.'

I scratched at my head. I'd got off on the wrong foot here. I should be polite. 'I'm sorry,' I said. 'I'm a bit nervous.'

'And so you should be. Don't you know I'm a witch?'

'Wise woman,' I said.

'That's just a euphemism,' said Mother Demdike. 'I'm a black-hearted witch who's kissed the Devil's arse and suckles her familiars at her supernumerary nipples.' She stroked something bundled up in rags upon her lap. Her ferret, I presumed.

'Do you know anything about herbs?' I enquired. 'Only, we're doing this project at school and I need some special herbs.'

'Come a little closer,' said Mother Demdike. 'Let me have a sniff at your aura.'

'My aura?' I said.

'Indulge me,' said the ancient.

I took a small step forward. 'Sniff away,' I told her. 'But I think your pong will overwhelm mine.'

Mother Demdike sniffed. 'Oh dear, oh dear,' she said.

I lifted an arm and sniffed my armpit. 'I had a bath last week,' I told her. 'And I used soap and everything.'

'I think I've been waiting for you,' said Mother Demdike. 'Tell me about these herbs that you need.'

So I told her.

Mother Demdike looked me up and down. 'You're a bad'n,' she said.

'I'm not so bad. I get most of my homework in on time.'

'You have bad intentions.'

'I have only good intentions. Do you know where I can get these herbs?'

'I have all of them.'

'Oh, good,' I said. 'Now, as I'm doing this as a school project I'm sure you won't want to charge me any money for them, so—'

'I won't,' said Mother Demdike.

'You won't? Oh, good.'

'All I want to do is to read your palm.'

'That's fair enough.'

'So stick your hand out and let me take a peep.'

'Could I have the herbs first, before you do?'

'Why would you want to do that?'

'Well,' I said, 'can I be completely honest with you?'

The hag cocked her head on one side, whereupon a spider ran out of her right ear-hole. She snatched it from her cheek, popped it into her mouth and munched upon it. 'Go on,' she said, spitting out a couple of legs.

'It's a rather funny thing,' I began. 'You see, I woke up today . . . Or, rather, I think I did. But perhaps I didn't.'

'You didn't?' said Mother Demdike.

'Well, I'm beginning to wonder. Because everything today has been so absurd. My father claims that his bestest friend has just died. This bestest friend turns out to be my favourite author. I'm sure my father never knew this man at all. I went to the library and over-heard these two men talking about a secret project. About how human beings are just receivers of mental waves sent from somewhere else in the universe. And now I'm in a witch's house. Oh, and I've been

53

thinking about reanimating this famous author. Bringing him back to life through voodoo, which is why I need the herbs. Now, you tell me, does this sound like normality to you, or is something really weird going on?'

Mother Demdike looked me up and down once more. 'Oh yes,' she said. 'You're going to be trouble. You're going to be big trouble.'

'Big trouble? What do you mean?'

'People sleepwalk,' said the ancient. 'People drift through their lives, rarely paying attention to the fact that they are alive. Rarely, if ever, marvelling at their very existence. At the miracle of life, of awareness. That for a brief moment in time and space they exist.'

'I was only thinking that myself earlier,' I said.

'Life is incredible,' said Mother Demdike. 'It's unbelievable. It's beyond belief. In a universe otherwise dead, we live. And what do people do with their lives? Waste them on everyday trivialities. On being part of a society. A little cog in a great big impersonal engine. But once in a while someone appears, out of nowhere, or so it seems, someone who's different. These special someones add something to society. They give it something special. And this takes humanity forward. Towards what, I don't know. Towards something, though, towards finding something out about itself and its ultimate purpose. Because everything must have a purpose. It wouldn't, couldn't, exist if it didn't. It may well be that you are one of these special someones, Gary. That you have something very special to give to humankind. If this is true you will be *aware*. And if you are *aware*, you will experience life

54

differently from the rest of humankind. To you it will seem unreal, as if you are in a dream. How could it be any other way for someone who is different from the rest?'

I stood there in the doorway of the little hut and I didn't know what to say.

'Look at me,' said Mother Demdike. 'Look at me and look at this little hut of mine. It's an anachronism, a hangover from another time. Another century. I'm a piece of history. You will grow up and tell your children that, some time in the past, when you were young, an old witch woman used to live down the road from you. And you'll point to the place where my hut once stood and there'll be a block of flats or something here. And your children won't believe you and even you will begin to doubt your memories, because how could you have really met an old witch woman in the nineteen fifties? That doesn't fit with reality. In fact, you'll begin to question a lot of your childhood memories. You'll do what every grown-up does; you'll reinvent your past, based on the logic of your present. You'll say, "No, I didn't really see that. I must have dreamed it." '

'Dreamed it?' said I. 'Like I feel that I'm dreaming this now, in a way.'

'You'll never know what's real and what isn't,' said Mother Demdike. 'Because no one has the time to find out. Life is too short. We all see a little bit of the whole picture. We all take in a little snatch of history, the bit we're born into. Then after we're gone, some-one writes it down inaccurately. What *really* happened in history there is no one alive to know for sure.'

'Golly,' I said, as I couldn't think of anything else to say.

'You,' said Mother Demdike, 'may be poised upon the brink of something big. Tell me that list of herbs once again. In fact, show me the book you got the list from. It's there in your pocket, I believe.'

I took out my copy of *Voodoo in Theory and Practice* and handed it to her.

'You stole that from the library,' said Mother Demdike.

'I did,' I said. 'I see you've nicked a few yourself.'

Mother Demdike chuckled. 'All in a good cause,' she said.

'Of course,' said I.

'Then read me the list.'

She returned the book to me. I thumbed through the pages and read her the list.

Mother Demdike busied herself about the place. She delved into jars and drawers and when she had found everything that I sought she packaged all in a brown paper bag and handed it to me.

'Thank you,' I said.

'Your hand,' said Mother Demdike. 'Your part of the bargain. You must let me read your hand.'

'Certainly,' said I. 'That's fair.' I stuck my hand out and she took it between her own.

'Oh yes,' she said. 'Oh yes.'

'Oh yes?' I asked.

'Oh yes. It's all here, written right through you. You will perform great deeds. You will do special things. But society will hate you for the special things you will do. You will become a hated person. A social pariah.

But you will advance humankind, you will be remembered, as I will be forgotten.'

'I'll remember you,' I said.

'No, you won't.'

'I will.'

'You won't.'

'Check my palm again.'

Mother Demdike checked my palm again. 'Oh yes,' she said. 'I will be remembered. That's nice, although I take exception to being called "the rankest hag that ever troubled daylight".'

'But at least you get a mention.'

'Do me one favour, Gary,' said Mother Demdike.

'I'll try,' I said. 'What is it?'

'Put a blue plaque up. On the site of my hut. If you can. If you have the power.'

'And will I have the power? Check my hand again and tell me.'

Mother Demdike checked my hand again. 'Yes,' she said and she smiled at me. 'You *will* have the power. You *will*.'

'Then I'll make sure the blue plaque goes up.'

'Thank you,' said the old one and she kissed the palm of my hand.

I took my leave of Mother Demdike. She'd given me not only the herbs I required, but also a whole lot more. I don't know how to explain it, but when I left her little hut I felt real. As if I could do things that mattered, really do them. That I would make my mark upon mankind. Do something big.

I have a lot to thank that old woman for. She

didn't say much to me, but she said the right things.

And the day eventually came when I did have the power to get that blue plaque up. Her little hut had gone by then, she had gone and the memories of her were fading. A new block of flats was up and new thoughts and ways were on the go.

I didn't bother to get the blue plaque put up, though. I mean, ugly old cow. I could never see the point of ugly people.

5

Dave was already at the launderette. He loved that launderette, did Dave.

He'd been introduced to the joys of launderettes by a friend of his called Chico, who lived in Brentford's Puerto Rican quarter. Chico had explained to Dave about the pleasures of watching the washing go round and round in the big new washers. These pleasures are really subtle; they have to be explained. They have to be understood and they have to be mastered.

That doesn't sound altogether right, does it? Mastering pleasure. But it's true. To appreciate anything fully and completely, you have to be its master. You can have moments of exquisite pleasure, drinking, drugging or sexing it away. But if you are not the master of the pleasure, you will eventually be its slave.

I never mastered the pleasures of watching the washing go round and round in the washers. But I never felt slave to them, either. I just thought the whole thing was stupid. I just didn't get it.

Dave was seated on the bench, his eyes fixed upon a white wash. A look of ecstasy upon his face, his knees held tightly together. He was entranced.

'Oh, wow,' went Dave. 'Oh, bliss.'

'Enjoying yourself?' I asked, as I sat down beside him.

'Immensely,' said Dave. 'Do you know, I foresee a time when almost every household in the country will own a washing machine.'

'*Own* a washing machine?' I laughed out loud. 'What? People will have washing machines in their homes? Instead of here in launderettes?'

'Mark my words,' said Dave. 'And televisions too.'

'What is a television?' I asked.

'It's a wireless with pictures.'

'What? Pictures of a wireless?'

'Moving pictures, like in a cinema. It's a sort of miniature cinema for the home. There's one on display in the window of Kay's Electrical in the High Street.'

'I'm not allowed to go near the High Street,' I told Dave. 'My dad says that homos hang around the High Street.'

'Do you *actually* know what a homo is?' Dave asked, although his eyes never left the washing white wash.

'Of course,' I said, though I didn't. 'But you're mad, Dave. A washing machine in your house. Where would you put it?'

'I'd put mine in my bedroom,' said Dave. 'And I'd have it on while I was having it off with Betty Page.'

I stared hard at the washing machine. I could see the white wash going on behind the glass door panel. It reminded me a bit of the octopus in the movie *20,000 Leagues Under the Sea*, being viewed through a porthole in Captain Nemo's *Nautilus*. But without the tentacles or the suckers. Or even the octopus. Or even, now I come to think of it, the movie, for that was made several years later. But pleasure, eh? It's a funny old game.

'Mad,' I said. 'Quite mad.'

'Hold on,' said Dave. 'Don't speak. There's a good bit coming up.'

I held my counsel and also held my breath.

'Wow,' went Dave once again. 'Brilliant.'

'It's completely lost on me.'

'Speak English,' said Dave.

'I don't understand it. But, listen, you know I told you that I had a big idea?'

Dave nodded, but he wasn't really listening.

'I went down to the library,' I continued, speaking clearly and loudly, in the hope that some of it might get through. 'I went to the library and while I was there I heard two men talking about something really strange. But I'll tell you about that later. I got the book I needed and I also got some other stuff I needed, which I've hidden away in a secret place. You're going to love this.'

'I *am* loving this.' Dave was all misty-eyed.

'I've got a big idea,' I told Dave.

'I've got a big bulge in my trousers.'

'*What?*'

'What?' said Dave. 'What are you talking about? Can't this wait till later?'

'All right,' I said. 'I'll be having a fag. Come and talk to me when you're finished.'

'I can't finish properly. I haven't reached puberty yet.'

'Completely lost on me.'

61

I went outside and had a fag.

Naturally I smoked Woodbine. Well, I would, wouldn't I? I mean, Lazlo *Woodbine*? What else was I likely to smoke? All children smoked in those days. But then in those days cigarettes were good for you. Like nuclear radiation and lead soldiers. In fact, almost everything was good for you in those days: a good smacked-bottom; a good dose of castor oil; a good helping of National Service; a good stretch behind bars. They were good times all round, really.

I was finishing off my fag when Dave came out of the launderette. 'Give us a puff,' said Dave.

And I gave Dave a puff.

'My big idea,' I said to Dave. 'It's about P. P. Penrose.'

'Go on, then,' said Dave, taking another puff at my fag.

'You know what you said about taking relics? I think we can go one better than that. Take his whole body and bring him back to life.'

Dave took a final puff from my fag and stamped the tiny butt end out upon the pavement. 'You're having a laugh, aren't you?' he said.

'No. I'm serious. I've got this book about how to make zombies. And it needs special herbs and I've got the herbs and everything. Including a human skull to mix them up in. I can do all that part in my sleeping cupboard.'

'Cool,' said Dave. 'Will it really work, do you think?'

'If it's done properly, I think it will.'

'And do you know how to do it properly?'

'I think so. It's all in my book. You do a ritual with the herbs, then you feed the herbs to the dead corpse and it comes back to life.'

'It's got to be a load of twonk, hasn't it?' said Dave, which surprised me somewhat. 'I mean, well, if it did work, then everyone would be doing it and people wouldn't die any more.'

Dave had a good point there.

'You have a good point there,' I said to Dave. 'But the reason everyone doesn't do it is because it's a secret. This book is a secret book; the formula for the herbs is a secret formula. Only very few people know the secret, so only a very few people ever get brought back to life. Probably very rich people like the royal family. I'll bet the Queen Mum will live to be at least a hundred years old. Because each time she dies, they'll bring her back to life with voodoo magic.'*

'You've won me over,' said Dave. 'So when do we do it?'

'I thought we'd follow the funeral and see where they bury Mr Penrose. Then come back at night and dig him up.'

'Too much trouble,' said Dave. 'All that digging. Why not do it at his wake? When all his friends are there. They'll be dead pleased to see him up and about again.' Dave tittered.

'Why do you titter?' I asked.

'*Dead* pleased,' said Dave.

---

*I might not have been able to foresee a washing machine in almost every home in the country. But at least I was right about that one.

63

'That isn't very funny,' I said.

'No,' said Dave. 'You're right. But I heard this really funny joke. Would you care to hear it?'

'I would,' I said.

'OK,' said Dave. 'It's the one about the man with the huge green head. Have you heard it?'*

'No,' I said.

'OK,' said Dave again. 'So this bloke is standing at a bus stop and he's got this huge green head, and I mean *huge*. It's enormous. And this other bloke comes up and keeps looking at it; he's fascinated, he can't take his eyes of this first bloke's huge green head. Finally the bloke with the huge green head says, "OK, go on, ask me." And the other bloke says, "What?" And the bloke with the green head says, "Ask me how I got this huge green head. You want to, I know." So the other bloke says, "How did you get that huge green head?" So the bloke with the huge green head says, "Well, it's a really funny story. I was walking along Brighton beach and I found this old brass lamp and I rubbed it and this genie came out and said, 'You've freed me from the lamp and so you can have three wishes.' So I said, 'All right! Then for my first wish I want to be incredibly wealthy with this huge mansion with secret rooms with soldiers in and kitchens full of cakes and sweets and suitcases with diamonds and emeralds in them.' And there's a big puff of smoke and I'm in this huge mansion with all the things I'd asked for. And the genie says, 'What do you want for your second wish?' And I say, 'Right, I want the most beautiful woman in

*If you have heard it, just flick on. If not, enjoy.

the world to be my wife and she has to want to sex me all the time, with brief breaks while she cooks me sausages and cuts me pieces of cake and pours me Tizer and stuff like that.' And there's another puff and she appears. Just like how I wanted. Incredible."

'And the bloke with the huge green head pauses and the other bloke looks at him and says, "OK, go on. What did you wish for with your last wish?"

'And the bloke with the huge green head says—'

'"I wished for a huge green head, of course,"' said I. 'I have heard it.'

'And isn't it a blinder?'

'I think it's probably the funniest joke in the whole wide world,' I said. 'I can't imagine there being a funnier one.'

'I only wish I understood it,' said Dave.

'Don't worry,' I said. 'You understand the pleasures of the launderette. That's something in itself. So, are you up for this? We go to Mr Penrose's wake and bring him back to life. This is a good plan, yes?'

'It's a great plan,' said Dave. 'We'll probably get a medal from the Pope and a special certificate from Her Majesty the Queen for this. If it works.'

'It will work,' I said. 'Trust me. It will work.'

Over the next few days I kept pressing the Daddy regarding the matter of Mr Penrose's wake and how it would be such a good idea for me to come to it too. How it would be so educational for me and everything. But the Daddy wasn't having any of that. He was adamant. I was not going. It was by invitation only and it wasn't for children.

I kept an eye on the doormat for incoming invitations. I was up every day in time for the postman. No invitations slipped by me and the days were slipping away.

The next Wednesday came round and I feigned a cold so I could stay off school. I'd arranged with Dave that he should feign a cold also. But Dave felt that feigning a cold was for homos and so he feigned the Black Death, was given a good smacked-bottom by his mum and sent to school.

Dave bunked off school at lunchtime and came round to my house. I slipped quietly out of my bed of feigned pain and joined him across the street.

'The Daddy is getting all dressed up,' I said to Dave. 'He's getting ready for the wake.'

'Then we'll follow him, commando-fashion.'

'What is commando-fashion?' I asked.

'Mostly camouflage,' said Dave. 'Green is the new black this year.'

We hid behind a dustbin.

At a little after two, the Daddy left our house and swaggered up the street wearing his Sunday suit. My mother wasn't with him. 'Wakes are men's business,' my father had said.

The Daddy swaggered up our street, turned left into Albany Road, right into Moby Dick Terrace, swaggered past the hut of Mother Demdike, then past the Memorial Park, turned right at the Memorial Library and eventually swaggered into the Butts Estate, where all the posh people of Brentford lived. Dave and I occasionally went into the Butts to throw stones at rich people's windows and get chased away by their manservants, but we didn't really know much about the place.

It had been built in Regency times with the money earned from the slave trade and the importation of tea and carpets and strange drugs. The houses were big and well dug in. There was that feeling of permanence that only comes with wealth. The poor might appear to be settled right where they are. But they're only waiting to be moved on.

The Daddy swaggered up to a particularly fine-looking house, one with a Grimshaw-style front door and Fotheringay window staunchions, and knocked heartily upon the Basilicanesque knocker.

I was very impressed when the door was opened and he was actually let inside. It confirmed, I suppose, that he actually *had* known Mr Penrose.

'What now, then?' I asked Dave.

'Why are you asking me?'

'How do you think we're going to get in?'

'We're not,' said Dave. 'Well, not yet at least.'

'Not yet?'

Dave shook his head. 'It's a wake. Which is to say, as you know, a party. For a dead man. But a party. People will drink lots of booze. And then they'll get drunk and then they'll come and go. And they'll leave the front door open and we can sneak in.'

'You are wise,' I said to Dave. 'We'll wait, then.'

So we waited.

And we waited.

And then we waited some more.

'I'm getting fed up with all this waiting,' said Dave. 'Hang on, someone's coming out.'

But they weren't.

So we waited some more, some more.

'Do you think they're drunk by now?' I asked.

'Must be,' said Dave.

'Then let's just knock. They'll let us in.'

'Yes, of course they will.'

We knocked.

A pinch-faced woman opened the door. 'What do you want?' she asked.

'My daddy's inside,' said Dave. 'At the wake. I've a message for him from my mummy.'

'Tell it to me,' said the pinch-faced woman. 'I'll pass it on.'

'It's in Dutch,' said Dave. 'You wouldn't be able to pronounce it properly.'

'Wah!' went the pinch-faced woman.

'Not even close,' said Dave.

'No! Wah!' The pinch-faced woman turned away and the distinctive sound of a hand smacking a face was to be heard.

'That's a bit harsh,' said a man's voice. 'I didn't mean to touch your bum – I tripped on the door mat.'

'Rapist!' screamed the pinch-faced woman, leaving the door ajar.

'Let's slip in,' said Dave.

And so the two of us slipped in.

It was a very big house. Much bigger on the inside than on the outside. But so many houses are. The big ones anyway. Estate agents refer to the phenomenon as 'deceptively spacious'. But I don't think that it's fully scientifically understood.

'This is a very big hall,' said Dave. 'It stretches away right into the distance.'

'Well, at least as far as that door at the end,' I said. 'Which is the door where all the noise is coming from.'

'There's quite a lot of noise here,' Dave obsessed. 'And quite a lot of violence too.' The pinch-faced woman struggled on the floor, punching at a fat man who lay on his back. He wasn't putting up much of a fight. In fact, he seemed to be smiling.

'Come on,' said Dave. 'Follow me.'

We went along the hall, then stuck our heads round the door at the end of it. And then we viewed the wake that was going on beyond.

Having never seen a wake before I didn't know what to expect, so I suppose that I was neither surprised nor disappointed. Nor even bewildered nor bemused. Nor was I amazed.

But I was *interested*.

The room that lay beyond the door was a withdrawing room. The room to which rich men of yesteryear withdrew after the completion of their feasting at the dining table, where they left the womenfolk to chat about things that womenfolk love to chat about. Particularly fashion. Such as, what particular colour commandos would be wearing that year.

The rich men withdrew to the drawing room and talked about manly things. Like port and cigars and football and shagging servant women and stuff like that. They probably talked about commandos too, but only about what colour their guns would be. It seemed pretty clear to me that if we were having good times now, and we were, those rich men of yesteryear had had better.

The room was tall and square with frescoed walls in the Copulanion style. There were over-stuffed sofas all around and about and these were crowded with red-faced men who held glasses, and all, it seemed, talked together. They talked, as far as I could hear them, mostly of P. P. Penrose. Of what a great sportsman he'd been. And of his love of sportsmanship. And of his skills as a writer. And of how amazing his Lazlo Woodbine thrillers were. And of what rubbish the Adam Earth science-fiction series was.

Although I understood their words, the manner in which they spoke them was queer to my ears. They all talked in up-and-down ways. Beginning a sentence softly, then getting louder, then all fading away once more.

'They're all drunk,' said Dave. 'They'll all be singing shortly.'

'How does "shortly" go?' I asked. Which I thought was funny, but Dave did not.

'Look there,' Dave said and he pointed.

I followed the direction of Dave's pointing. 'The coffin,' I said.

In the middle of the room, with the over-stuffed sofas and the men sat upon them with the glasses in their hands, talking queerly and on the verge of singing, lay the coffin.

Up upon a pair of wooden trestles, it was a hand-some casket affair, constructed of Abarti pine in the Margrave design with Humbilian brass coffin furniture and rilled mouldings of the Hampton-Stanbrick persuasion. And it was open and from where we were standing we could see the nose of the dead Mr Penrose rising from it like a pink shark's fin or an isosceles triangle of flesh, or in fact numerous other things of approximately the same shape.

But it was definitely a nose.

'Cool,' went Dave. 'I can see his dead hooter.'

'Here's the plan,' I said to Dave. 'You create a diversion, while I perform the complicated ritual and feed him the magic herbs.'

Dave turned towards me and the expression on his face was one that I still feel unable adequately to describe. Expressing, as it did, so many mixed emotions.

I smiled encouragingly at Dave.

Dave didn't smile back at all.

'Not a happening thing, then?' I asked.

'Speak English,' said Dave.

'I mean, you don't think you can do it?'

'No,' said Dave. 'I don't. Why don't we just try to mingle amongst the drunken men — bide our time, as they say, await the moment.'

'Well put,' said I. 'You go first, then.'

'Not me,' said Dave. 'This is *your* big idea.'

'No, it's not. My big idea was to dig him up later.'

'All right,' said Dave, pushing open the door. 'Let's risk it. Let's mingle.' And he strode right into the withdrawing room.

I followed cautiously, trying to avoid the eyes of my father. They were rather red-rimmed and starey eyes, but they *were* his none the less. I could see my Uncle Jonny sitting over by one of the windows and I didn't want to look at his horrible eyes.

71

''Afternoon,' said Dave, to no one in particular. 'Hello there, hi.'

We made our way across the richly carpeted floor towards the coffin. It's funny how certain things stick in your mind and even now, all these many years later, I can remember that moment so very, very clearly. What happened next. And what was said. And what it meant.

I can recall the way my feet felt, inside my shoes, as they trod over the thick pile of that carpet. And the smell of the cigarette smoke and the way it coloured the light that fell in long shafts through the tall Georgian casement windows. And the dreamlike quality of it all. We weren't supposed to be in this room, Dave and I: it was wrong, all wrong. But we *were* there. And it *was* real.

'Stop,' said a voice and a big hand fell on my shoulder. I turned my head round and up and found myself staring into the long, thin face of Caradoc Timms, Brentford's leading funeral director.

Caradoc Timms leaned low his long, thin face and gave me a penetrating stare with his dark and hooded eyes. 'You, boy,' he said in a nasal tone. 'Can't stay away from the dead, can you?'

I made sickly laughing sounds of the nervous variety. 'I've just come to pay my respects,' I said. 'Mr Penrose is my favourite author.'

Mr Timms shook his head. 'And all those times you've come round to my funeral parlour, asking to be taken on as an apprentice?'

'I just wanted an after-school job, to earn money for sweeties,' I whispered.

72

'And all the funerals you follow, when you duck down behind the tombstones and watch?'

'Research?' I suggested. 'I'd still like a job, if you have one going.'

'Unhealthy boy,' said Mr Timms. 'Unspeakable boy.'

'Is that *my* boy?' I heard the Daddy's voice. 'Is that my Gary you have there?'

'Dave,' I said. 'Let's run.'

But Dave was suddenly nowhere to be seen.

'Gary?' My father rose unsteadily from his seat upon an over-stuffed sofa. 'It *is* my Gary. Smite him for me, Timms.' And my daddy sat down again, rather heavily, and took out his pipe.

'Shall I smite you?' Mr Timms asked.

'I'd rather you didn't.' I prepared myself to run.

'So what should I do, then? Throw you out on your ear?'

'I'd rather you just let me stay, sir. I won't be any trouble to anyone. I'll just sit quietly in a corner.'

Mr Timms nodded his long, thin head. 'I hope I live long enough to see it,' he said.

'What, me sitting quietly? I'm sure you will.'

'Not that,' said Mr Timms. 'But you at the end of a hangman's rope.'

'*What?*' said I, rather startled by this statement.

'You're a bad'n,' said Mr Timms. 'A bad'n from birth. I see'm come and I see'm go. The good'ns and the bad. I'll tuck you into your coffin when your time comes, you see if I don't.'

'I've done nothing wrong,' I said, in the voice of one who felt he truly hadn't.

'If you haven't yet, then you will.' Mr Timms stared deeper still into my eyes. Right through my eyes, it seemed, and into my very brain.

I got the uncanny feeling that this man could somehow, not read, but *see* my thoughts. And not just my thoughts at this moment, but the thoughts that I would have at some time in the future. See things that I would do in the future. But how could anybody do that? It was impossible, surely? But it seemed to me that this man was doing it. That he really *did* know. Well, that's how if felt. It was not just an uncanny feeling, it was a terrible feeling. A feeling of inner violation. It put the wind up me something terrible. And I *was* a *very* brave boy.

'You'll hang,' said Mr Timms. 'I know it.'

'No, I won't,' I said. 'I won't.'

Mr Timms gazed down at me with his penetrating eyes. His long head went nod, nod, nod, and his voice said, 'Yes, you will.'

I held my ground and stared right back at him and then, because I felt so absolutely sure that he could see my thoughts through my eyeballs, I turned those eyeballs down to the floor and studied the pattern on the carpet.

A number of options lay open to me and I pondered on which one to take.

I could run straight out of the door. That one was obvious, but that one would be to accept defeat.

I could burst into tears and tell my daddy what Mr Timms had said to me, in the hope that my daddy would smite him on the nose. But my daddy might well take Mr Timms's side and smite me instead.

Or I could burst into tears and shout, 'Get off me, you homo.' I'd seen Dave do this once to the owner of the sweetie shop who had caught him nicking Black Jacks. A crowd of young men had closed in about the shopkeeper and Dave had managed to make good his escape, taking the Black Jacks and a Mars Bar as well.

So I burst into tears, kicked Mr Timms in the ankle, shouted, 'Get your hands off me, you homo. Help me, Daddy, please,' and ran straight out of the door.

6

Dave was in hiding across the street, behind a hedge in someone's front garden. As I ran out of the front door he called me over and I joined him there.

'You're crying,' said Dave.

So I told him what happened.

Dave put his arm around my shoulder. 'You did brilliantly,' he said. 'I'm sorry I wasn't there to see it.'

'You ran off and left me behind, you coward.'

'I wasn't scared,' said Dave. 'But I have a gyppy tummy and had to come outside to use the toilet. It's this touch of Black Death I've got.'

'Don't breathe on me, then,' I said. 'I don't want to catch it.'

Dave slid his arm from my shoulder and took to picking his nose.

'I suppose we might as well go home,' I said. 'We're not going to get back inside now, are we? This has all been a waste of time.'

'Seems a shame,' said Dave. 'It would be so much easier to bring Mr Penrose back to life now, rather than go to all the trouble of digging him up later.'

I shrugged. 'So you think we should wait some more?' I asked.

'It would be good practice,' said Dave.

'Practice for what?'

'For the future. It seems to me that adults spend most of their time waiting for something or other. A bus or a train or, for those who have a telephone, a telephone call. Or waiting for the postman or the milkman or the man to fix the broken pipe or their girlfriend to arrive. Or . . .'

'Stop it,' I said. 'There must be more to being an adult than that. You can get into pubs and drink beer.'

'Waiting at the bar to get served,' said Dave. 'Waiting for the cubical in the gents to be free so you can be sick in it. Waiting—'

'Stop!' I put my hands over my ears.

'Adults spend most of their time waiting,' said Dave, in a voice that was loud enough for me to hear. 'Because all they're really waiting for is death.'

'You paint a rosy picture of the future.' I took my hands away from my ears and took to picking my own nose. 'According to Mr Timms, my death waits for me at the end of the hangman's rope.'

'I hate adults,' said Dave. 'And adults secretly hate children. Because children have more life left to them than they do. Adults are jealous. And they think they know more about everything than children do.'

'That's because they *do*,' I observed.

'There's some truth in that, I suppose,' said Dave. 'And I get well peeved because there are so many things that I don't understand yet. But I would be able to understand them if adults answered my questions.

But they don't. The reason children don't understand as much as adults is because adults don't tell them everything they know. They keep secrets from children. Adults complicate the world to death, but children see the world as it really is. They see it as simple. For some reason, adults don't like "simple", they like "complicated". So adults screw up the world and children suffer for it.'

'You really *are* wise beyond your years,' said I.

'How dare you,' said Dave. 'I'm wise because I'm wise. Right now, as I am. And you're wise too. You know how to raise the dead. How many adults know that?'

'It was an adult who thought up the formula and the rituals and everything.'

'Only because stuff like that takes years to work out. If you started from scratch now, it might take you twenty years before you got it right. But once you had got it right, you could pass the information straight to your ten-year-old son and he'd know it too. Or you could keep it a secret to yourself. Which is what adults do about practically everything. They're all a lot of homos, adults.'

All? I puzzled over this. I felt that one day I was bound to find out what a homo was, but it probably wouldn't be before I was an adult. And then it might be too late: I might actually *be* a homo myself. The thought didn't bear thinking about, so I didn't think any more about it.

'I have this theory,' said Dave. 'About Life, the Universe and Everything.'

'Sounds like a good title for a book,' I said.

78

'Don't talk silly,' said Dave. 'But I've thought hard about this theory. It's in the form of a parable. Do you know what a parable is?'

'Of course I do,' I said. 'It's a bird that a pirate has on his shoulder.'

Dave shook his head.

'I was only joking,' I said.

'Oh,' said Dave. 'I still haven't worked out the one about the man with the huge green head. But a parable is a moral story, like in the Bible. Would you like to hear mine?'

'Are there any spaceships in it?' I asked, for I greatly loved spaceships. Although not all spaceships. I didn't, for instance, like the spaceships in P. P. Penrose's Adam Earth books. They were rubbish, those spaceships.

'Of course there are spaceships in it. I only know parables that have spaceships in them.'

'Go on, then,' I said.

'All right,' said Dave. 'This parable is called "The Parable of the Spaceships."'

'Good title,' I said. 'I—'

'Shut up,' said Dave. And I shut up.

And this is how it went.

THE PARABLE OF THE SPACESHIPS

Once upon a time there was a planet called Earth. And it was the future and people had cars that flew in the air and telephones that didn't need wires and wore televisions on their wrists and had futuristic haircuts and big wing shoulders on their plastic jackets and lived in huge tower blocks that reached up into the clouds.

And they had spaceships. But the spaceships could only go fast enough for people to commute between the planets in this solar system, which they did all the time, for going to work and stuff like that. Mostly mining emeralds on Saturn.

Everybody was not doing OK in the future. Because there were so many people and all the planets in the solar system were getting completely overcrowded. So the scientists worked really hard on developing this spaceship that could travel at the speed of light and they built a special chamber in it where the pilot could be frozen up and stay in suspended animation until he got to his final destination, which would be the nearest planet capable of sustaining human life. They programmed the computer in the spaceship to search out the nearest planet that would comfortably support human life and then they looked for a volunteer. They wanted someone a bit special, because he would be the first man ever to set foot on this planet, which would mean that his name would go down in history and everyone would remember him for ever more (after his mission had been successful, of course, and later people had gone out to colonize this new world).

Eventually they settled on this chap whose name was Adam. Well, he had the perfect name, didn't he? And he had a nice family with three sons and was an all-round nice fellow. And a very good spaceship pilot who flew flights to Uranus.

And so Adam said that he would be pleased to go, even though it meant that he might never see his family again, but he felt certain that he would, because it was such a good spaceship and the scientists were so clever and everything.

So, there were a lot of broadcasts on everyone's wrist televisions and a big parade and Adam got into the spaceship and waved goodbye and was frozen up and the rocket blasted off into space.

And that was the last that anyone on Earth ever saw of Adam.

He travelled across the universe at the speed of light, covering unimaginable distances, and his spaceship went on and on and on, searching for the perfect planet.

And then one day – it must have been thousands of years later – his spaceship eventually found the perfect planet and landed and Adam unfroze and opened the door and stepped out of the spaceship.

And found that he was back on Earth.

Well, at least it looked just like Earth.

And not just because of the trees and flowers. But because of the buildings and flying cars and all the people who were gathered around looking up at his spaceship.

And then out of the crowd appeared this chap who looked just like Adam. Just like him. And this chap said, 'Hello, Dad,' and another chap said, 'Hello, Granddad,' then another appeared and said, 'Hello, Great-Granddad,' and another who said, 'Hello, Great-Great-Granddad.'

And they all looked like Adam.

And Adam got a little confused.

And so the one who had said, 'Hello, Dad,' explained the situation to him. He said, 'Well, Dad, after you'd gone, time passed and I grew up, and I became a scientist and I looked at the plans for your spaceship and I said, "I can improve on that. I can make a spaceship that will travel twice the speed of light." So I did and I got in it and I got here in half the time it took you to get here. But when I did, I found that my own son was already here, because while I'd been gone he'd grown up and become a scientist and looked at the plans of my spaceship and said, "I can improve on that," and built a spaceship that could go four times the speed of light and he'd got here in half the time it had taken me to get here. But when he'd got here, he'd found that his own son was already here, because he'd grown up and improved the spaceship even more and got here in half the time again. But when he got here, he found that *his* son was already here because—'

'Stop, stop,' said Adam. 'This is driving me insane. How many generations of me are there here?'

'Thousands and thousands and thousands,' said the son, 'and not just here, but on every other habitable planet in the universe. The universe is now all completely overcrowded by generations and generations of you.'

Adam went back into his spaceship, and if he'd had a revolver to hand he would have shot his brains out. But he didn't. Although he might well have done. But he was a very nice man and none of this was really his fault, so he left his spaceship and went down to the crowd and was carried shoulder-high by the crowd, for being such a pioneer and everything, and finally he had a meal out at a nice restaurant that had about three thousand tables in it, so that a few of his descendants could dine with him too.

And it was over the meal that his son put a proposition to him.

'Dad,' said his son. 'As the universe is all full up now, mankind is looking for new places to live in and your great (to the power of 23,000,000)-grandson has come up with this new spaceship drive system that will take a pilot into an alternative universe in another dimension. And we're looking for someone to pilot the ship.'

And Adam, who was frankly pretty much off his rocker by now, said, 'I'll do it. Can I do it now, or at least as soon as I've finished my dinner?'

And his son said, 'Sure thing, Dad. First thing in the morning. The ship's all fuelled up and waiting. We knew you'd want to volunteer.'

So the very next morning there was this big procession and a broadcast on wrist televisions that went out to planets all over the universe and Adam got into the special new interdimensional spaceship and got frozen up in the very modern cryogenic capsule. And his son pressed the launch button and the spaceship vanished into an alternative universe.

And you'll never guess what happened when the spaceship landed on the first habitable planet it came to in the alternative universe in another dimension.

THE END

'What did happen?' I asked Dave, after he had said, 'THE END.'

Dave rolled his eyes. 'Same thing,' he said. 'Except that now it was far more complicated, with more millions of descendants involved. And one of them had invented another spaceship that could travel into an alternative alternative universe. I had to end the parable somewhere, so I ended it there. I did toy with the idea that on his final voyage in an infinitely alternative universe Adam took a woman with him for company. And, as it turned out, when he reached the next habitable planet in a universe so many times alternative from the first one that it didn't have a number to cover it, he finally found himself on a planet that no descendant of his had got to before him. Because the spaceships they'd designed had finally reached the point where they could no longer be improved upon. So there was only him and his woman all alone on this new planet that was just like Earth but no one had ever been to before. The woman's name was Eve, by the way.'

'That's a far better ending,' I said.

'Nah,' said Dave. 'That's a stupid ending. Too far-fetched.'

I removed my finger from my nose and scratched at my head with it. 'I always thought that parables were supposed to have a moral to them,' I said.

'They are,' said Dave.

'So what's the moral to yours?'

'It's obvious,' said Dave. 'Think about it.'

I thought about it. 'Oh yes,' I said. 'I get the moral. I understand it.'

Dave nodded thoughtfully. 'I knew you would,' he said. 'I only wish that I did.'

7

I lay behind the hedge with Dave and thought about his parable. It was a pretty good parable, as parables go, because it did have spaceships in it. But the more I thought about the substance of that parable, the more I realized that it really didn't work at all.

The space pioneer Adam could never have met his own son on that far-away world. He'd have died there thousands of years before. And how could there be all those generations of descendants all still alive? Had they discovered the secret of immortality? But all the same it was a good parable and I thought that if the time ever came to tell it I'd tidy it up somewhat and put my interesting ending at the end.

But the time never came for me to tell it, so I didn't.

'I'm growing impatient with all this lying around in wait,' I said to Dave. 'We should do something to precipitate some action.'

'Do speak English,' said my bestest friend.

'Go and knock on the door, or something.'

'Just be patient,' said Dave to me. 'Pretend you're an adult: wait.'

And so we waited a little while more and finally our patience was rewarded.

'A police car,' said Dave. 'I've been expecting that.'

'You have?'

'I have. When I left the wake house before you, I telephoned the police.'

'Why?' I asked, which seemed a reasonable question.

'So we could have time alone with Mr Penrose.'

'I don't understand,' I said, and I didn't.

'Just watch,' said Dave. 'Just watch and learn.'

And so I watched and I learned.

The police car, all glossy black, an Armstrong Smedley, one-point-five-litre, with running boards and the big bell on the top, slewed to a halt outside the wake house. Four coppers, as we knew them then, before they were known as 'the Filth', jumped out of the car and took to beating upon the front door. And shouting very loudly.

'I'm impressed,' I said to Dave. 'But surely they're beating upon the wrong front door? That's the one next door to the wake house.'

'Just watch,' said Dave, 'and be ready to run inside the wake house, as soon as I give the signal.'

'What will the signal be?' I asked.

'I'll hoot like an owl.'

'It's the wrong time of day for that, surely? Why not moo like a cow?'

'A cow? In Brentford?'

'Bark like a dog, then.'

'I don't do dogs,' said Dave. 'Doing dogs is common.'

'You could whinny, like a horse.'

'That's too posh,' said Dave. 'Only girls who go to posh private schools can do that properly.'

'Is that true?' I asked.

Dave nodded knowingly. 'When the day comes, and it will, that you find yourself in the company of a posh woman who once went to a posh private school, you just ask her whether she and her friends used to whinny like ponies.'

'And?'

'And I bet you she'll say she did.'

'All right, then,' I said to Dave. 'I'll bear that in mind for the future. It is my intention to marry a very posh woman one day. I'll ask her on our wedding night.'

'Ask her earlier,' said Dave. 'Then you'll know for sure whether she's really posh or not. You ask her the first time you take her out. Before you've queued up for the pictures or bought her a portion of chips, or anything. No, on second thoughts, wait until after you've had a bunk-up with her. Until you've had that, it doesn't really matter whether she's posh or not.'

'I'll bear all that in mind,' I said. 'So what *will* the signal be, then?'

'It will be an owl,' said Dave. 'Let's speak no more about it.'

I shrugged beneath the hedge and viewed the doings across the road. The front door of the house next to the wake was now open and a man in pyjamas was remonstrating with the policemen. He was shouting things at them. Things like: 'I'm *not* a homo!'

I glanced at Dave. Dave was grinning wickedly.

'I know that man in the pyjamas,' I whispered.

'Of course you do,' said Dave. 'It's Mr Purslow, the maths teacher. Didn't you know he lived there?'

I shook my head.

'I did,' said Dave. 'He's off sick with diphtheria.'

'He looks very angry.'

'He's always angry. I hate Mr Purslow.'

'Oh, look,' I said. 'He's punched that copper.'

'I knew he would,' said Dave.

And now other front doors were starting to open, as front doors always do at the arrival of a police car. Folk were issuing from them and into the Butts Estate. Posh folk, some of them, folk who looked as if they surely must have daughters who were good at impersonating ponies.

And then the front door of the wake house opened and a number of drunken men, who looked for the most part as if whatever offspring they might have had would all be rubbish at whinnying, came a–blundering out with greatly raised voices of their own.

Amongst these were the Daddy, who, to my surprise, and also my satisfaction, was accompanied by Mr Timms the undertaker, whose head he held firmly underneath his arm.

'It seems that your daddy took your side,' Dave observed. 'They must have been fighting for quite some time. It looks like your daddy is winning.'

A policeman turned upon my father and asked what he thought he was doing with the undertaker's head.

My daddy told him and I heard the word 'homo' once more being used.

I shall get to the bottom of this homo-business, I

told myself. Which might have been funny if it had meant anything to me.

I heard one of the coppers saying something about the Butts Estate being 'a den of vice'. But as the only vice I knew was in the woodwork room at school this didn't mean anything to me either.

'Wooo-eee,' went Dave.

'Yeah, it's good this, isn't it?'

'No, wooo-eee, woo-ee.'

'Eh?' said I.

'I'm hooting.'

'In your pants?'

'Like an owl. It's the signal.'

'Oh,' I said. 'Right.'

'Follow me,' said Dave. And I followed him.

Things were warming up nicely in the road, if you like that sort of thing. Fists were beginning to fly and truncheons to be drawn. Those were the days before riot sticks, CS gas, electric prods, stun-canes and phase-plasma rifles with a forty-watt range. These were the days when villains put their hands up when caught and said things like 'It's a fair cop, guvnor'. There was respect for the law in those days.

A constable struck down Mr Purslow with his truncheon.

My Uncle Jonny, who played darts with Mr Purslow, struck down the copper with his blind-man's cane.

We skirted around the growing chaos and slipped back into the wake house.

Dave shut the front door quietly behind us and put on the security chain. 'Mr Penrose awaits you,' he said to me, as we stood by ourselves in the hall.

I hesitated for just a moment. Well, it *was* a big deal. I was about to reanimate a dead man. I was in uncharted territory, so to speak.

'Are you scared?' asked Dave.

'Of course I'm not.'

'Then, get on and do it.'

'All right, I will.'

I strode down the hall to the wake-room door and pushed it right open. Before me the room lay in silence. Shafts of smoky sunlight still fell through the tall casement windows, onto the coffin of the great author, lighting up his nose.

I hesitated once more.

'Go on,' said Dave. 'Go on.'

But I was now having second thoughts. I don't know why this was. Well, perhaps I do. I think it must have been the silence and the sense of peace. The repose of death, if you like. Death is first of all about stillness. Of everything becoming still. The senses themselves. The organs of the body, the blood, the cells. All the things that were chugging away – the lungs going up and down and the heart going pump, pump, pump, and the bits and bobs in the brain going think, think, think – all have become still. All are silent. Still.

Well, for a brief while at least. Until the putrefaction begins. Then there's lots of activity.

The nose of Mr Penrose looked terribly, terribly still.

'What are you waiting for?' Dave asked. 'Get on with the reanimating.'

'I don't know if it's right,' I said.

'What?' Dave stared at me. 'Are you bottling out?'

'Don't say that. I'm not. It's just . . .'

'Give me the herbs,' said Dave. 'I'll stick them into his gob.'

'You can't just stick them into his gob. You have to do the ritual. Say the words.'

'Go on, then, if you really are as brave as you're always saying.'

I crept slowly forward, reached the coffin and peeped in at the face of Mr Penrose.

And didn't it look peaceful. So at rest. So in repose.

'He looks happy as he is,' I said to Dave.

'I don't believe this,' Dave said to me. 'After all the trouble I've gone to, telephoning the police and everything, and now you're bottling out.'

'I'm not. I don't know. It doesn't seem right.'

'But he's your favourite author. He wrote the Lazlo Woodbine books, the best books in the world. And if you bring him back to life he can write us some more.'

'Yes, but . . .'

'And don't you think he'll thank you? He's bound to be happier being alive again rather than being dead, isn't he? And everyone else will be happy too. And the Queen will give you a special badge. And P. P. Penrose might even make you a character in one of his new books. Maybe a baddie who will be shot dead by Laz with his trusty Smith & Wesson during the final rooftop confrontation.'

I shook my head.

'And there's something else,' said Dave.

'What's that?' I asked.

'If you don't do it, I'll punch your head in.'

'Oh,' I said.

Dave made a fist. 'Sorry,' he said, 'but we've come too far to go back.'

I considered Dave's fist. It was a fierce fist. I'd seen it in action. 'I'm sorry too,' I said. 'I'm just being silly. I came here to bring Mr Penrose back from the dead. And that's just what I'll do.'

'Good man.' Dave hugged my shoulder. 'Then, please hurry up.'

I took out the book I'd borrowed from the library and the special herbs that Mother Demdike had given me.

'Take the herbs,' I said to Dave. 'And when I tell you, and not before, you put them into his mouth.'

Dave looked down at Mr Penrose and I saw a look of doubt appear on his face. 'I'm not doing that,' he said. 'That's your job, putting the herbs in.'

'But you just said—'

'I've changed my mind,' said Dave. 'You should take all the glory.'

'You're scared.'

'No, I'm not.'

'You're afraid to touch his face.'

'You can catch the syph from touching a dead man's face.'

'What's the syph?'

'It's a terrible disease.'

'All right, let's forget the whole thing.'

Dave dithered, but only for a moment. 'All right,' he said. 'I'll prise his mouth open with my penknife.'

I shook my head. I really *did* have my doubts.

'All right,' I said too. 'Let's do this.' And I opened the book and began to read out the ritual.

I knew that there was more that should be done than just reading out the ritual. I knew there was supposed to be beating drums and frenzied dancing about by half-naked brown ladies and even a cockerel getting its head chopped off. But it seemed to me that in theory the words and the herbs should be enough.

In theory.

Now, one thing that I didn't know then was that when you perform a magic ritual you have to do it very loudly. You have to shout the words right out. Magic is a very noisy business, which is why its practitioners have always chosen out-of-the-way places like blasted heaths and distant forest glades to perform their rituals. The line that divides the world of man from the world of spirit is not a thin line, it's a chunky solid affair that takes some breaking through. If you want to be heard on the other side of it, you're going to have to shout very loudly indeed. I pass on this information to you in the interests of science. And because I know that passing on little titbits like this, as I will throughout this book, really gets up the noses of ritual magicians, who love to keep things like this secret.

'Speak up,' said Dave. 'I can't hear you.'

I spoke up a bit, then a bit more.

Dave rocked back and forwards on his heels and clicked his fingers and popped his thumbs. 'Go on, my son,' he said. 'Give it ritual.'

I gave it ritual and shouted the words.

'Go on,' I shouted at Dave. 'Feed Mr Penrose the herbs.'

Dave took out his penknife and I averted my eyes as he prised the author's teeth apart and emptied in the herbs.

I shouted away the rest of the ritual.

And then I was done.

Dave stepped back from the coffin. 'What happens next?' he whispered. 'Will he come alive?'

I shook my head. 'I don't know,' I said. 'I suppose so.'

And we waited.

The sunlight fell in shorter shafts now; the room was becoming darker. Outside, in what seemed now a distant realm, the bell-sounds of other approaching police cars could be heard. Here in this old room, this peaceful room, we stood shoulder to shoulder, Dave and I, wondering what would happen next, each alone inside our heads with thoughts that were personal to us.

I don't know what Dave was thinking, but I knew what was going on in my brain.

It hasn't worked, my brain was saying. *It was all rubbish and you will now be for ever a fool in Dave's eyes.*

'Are you sure you did it right?' Dave asked, and his voice seemed now very loud indeed in that room.

'I'm sure,' I whispered. 'Although the herbs might not be right. Mother Demdike might have given me the wrong stuff.' That seemed a very good excuse to me.

'Gary,' said Dave, and he took out his cigarettes.

'Dave?' said I, and I eyed them eagerly.

'Gary, I just want to say this. We are bestest friends, aren't we?' Dave took out two cigarettes.

'We are bestest friends that there can be,' I said.

Dave handed me a cigarette. 'Whatever we do,' he said, 'in the future – like, when we're grown-up and everything – we'll still be bestest friends, won't we?'

'Yes,' I said. 'We will.'

'I want you to know,' said Dave, 'that I never thought this would work. Not really. I hoped it would, because if it had it would have been really special. Something wonderful that both of us had done together. It would have been incredible. And we could have talked about it one day, when we were very old men, sitting on a park bench or somewhere. We would have said, "Remember the time we raised P. P. Penrose from the dead?" And that would have been something, wouldn't it?'

I nodded. 'It would,' I said.

'But it hasn't worked.'

'No,' I said. 'It hasn't.'

'But what I want to say,' said Dave, 'is that it doesn't matter. In case you're thinking you would look a bit of a fool or something.'

I nodded and then shook my head. 'I wasn't thinking that,' I said.

'You were,' said Dave. 'But it's all right. You went to a lot of trouble. Borrowing the book and getting the herbs and the skull from Mother Demdike. That took bottle. I wouldn't go into her stinking hut. But it's OK. This was a brave thing. We're here in this room with this dead man, this great man, and we did try. That's something.'

'It is,' I said. 'We tried.'

'So, in a way, we'll be able to look back on this.

96

We'll even laugh about it. We'll say, "Remember when we were kids and we tried to raise P. P. Penrose from the dead?" We'll laugh, we'll chuckle. We'll have smoker's cough and tweed suits and we'll smell of wee-wee like old people do and we'll laugh together.'

'I like that idea,' I said. 'That sounds nice. Although I don't fancy smelling of wee-wee.'

'So we must promise,' said Dave, 'you and me, we must promise that no one will ever know about this. It will be our secret. Just the two of us. We tried to do a great thing, and we failed. But the magic, the magic which is our friendship, is in that we *did* try.'

'You are *so* wise,' I said to Dave. 'With a wisdom of your age, of course. But you are wise and I am proud to call you my bestest friend.' I put my arm around Dave's shoulder.

'We did a brave thing,' said Dave. 'We did a noble thing. And now, as I can hear the front door being opened and the security chain being bashed about, I suggest that we climb out of the window and have it away on our toes.'

'I so agree,' I said, and Dave upped the nearest window.

I took a final look at Mr Penrose. He remained in silence. In repose. His eyes were closed and his nose shone in the sunlight. His mouth looked somewhat wonky though. 'Goodbye, Mr Penrose,' I said. 'I'm sorry that I couldn't raise you from the dead. Dave and I tried. Goodbye.'

Mr Penrose had nothing to say and Dave and I took our leave.

★　★　★

The funeral of Mr P. P. Penrose, sporting man, best-selling author of the Lazlo Woodbine thrillers and Brentford's most famous son, was held the very next day.

Dave and I didn't need to bunk off school: a public holiday had been declared by the Brentford Town Council and the school was closed.

We followed the horse-drawn hearse, with its plumed black horses and its wonderful etched-glass windows and polished coach lamps, led by the slow-striding mutes in their veiled top hats and ceremonial coats.

Behind walked figures of renown. The Prime Minister was there and the heads of state from several countries of the British Empire.

Crowds lined every inch of the funeral route, casting roses over the road before the funeral carriage. It was a very moving affair and I was very moved by it all.

Mr Penrose had sportingly written in his will that if his coffin should be preceded to the graveside by twenty proven virgins of the parish, then one thousand pounds would be given to the Mayor of Brentford to be used at his discretion.

As I was young and ignorant and all, I didn't understand at that time the concept of virginity, and therefore I had no idea at all about the lather the Mayor got himself into regarding how he could get his hands on (so to speak) twenty proven virgins.

I learned later that he consulted an aged mystic, a certain Professor Slocombe, resident of Brentford, who was considered by many to be the borough's patriarch.

Professor Slocombe whispered words into the Mayor's ear and Mr Penrose's coffin was preceded to the graveside by twenty five-year-old girls from the infant school.

The Mayor, apparently, took the thousand pounds and absconded with it. A thousand pounds was a lot of money in those days.

Dave and I got ahead of the procession and dug ourselves in beneath another hedge of the borough cemetery. We got a pretty good view of the burying.

'It was a very good do,' said Dave to me. 'Very dignified. And I've heard that there's to be an obelisk put up on his grave and also a special bench with a brass plaque on before the Memorial Library. That's nice. Someone famous might one day sit on that bench and muse about things. It's nice. All nice.'

I agreed that it was nice. Mr Penrose was resting in peace. With the respect of all those many people who had loved his books and thought that he was a great man. It was a good thing that we hadn't managed to raise him from the dead. He was better at rest and at peace.

When the funeral service and the burying was over and the crowds had all gone away, Dave and I lazed upon the marble bed of Mr Doveston, smoked cigarettes and looked up at the sky and all the passing clouds.

'Nice,' said Dave. 'All nice.'

'A pity there won't be any more Lazlo Woodbine books, though,' I said.

'Yes,' said Dave. 'A pity, but all good things must come to an end.'

'You are so wise,' I said to Dave. 'So very, very wise.'

As it happened, there was just one more Lazlo Woodbine book. And a really good one at that. *Death Wears a Grey School Jacket*, it was called. It would never have been published at all if it hadn't been for Mr Penrose's wife.

Apparently the manuscript had been buried with Mr Penrose at his request. Unknown to Dave and me, when we had been trying to raise him from the dead that manuscript had been sitting there in the coffin under his bum. If Dave had known that, he would certainly have nicked it.

Mr Penrose's widow contested her husband's will, had his body exhumed and the manuscript retrieved and published.

It made the papers at the time. But not because of the manuscript.

It was because of something else entirely.

Apparently, when they opened his coffin to take out the manuscript, the cemetery workers got a bit of a shock.

The body was all twisted up. The face was contorted, the hands crooked into claws with broken, bloody fingernails. The underside of the coffin lid was covered in terrible scratches. It appeared that Mr Penrose had awoken in his coffin only hours after he'd been buried and he'd tried to fight his way out. Mr Timms the undertaker gave evidence in court. He swore that Mr Penrose was definitely dead when he was buried, that he had been drained of blood and embalmed and that there was no way on Earth that he could possibly have been buried alive.

Mr Timms said that it must have been post-mortem spasms and gaseous expansion and all kinds of stuff like that which had caused the semblance of reanimation. And he was acquitted of all charges of negligence.

Dave and I never got to sit on that bench in our old age and chat about our past. So we never got to discuss the time when, as children, we had tried to reanimate a dead man, not realizing when we performed the ritual how long it would take to work its terrible magic. In fact, we never spoke about that subject ever again.

Some things are better not spoken of.

Nor even thought about.

8

Everything changes. And the present soon becomes the past and is gone.

I awoke to find that there was silence in our house. It was Thursday, yet there was silence. I was seventeen years of age.

Uncle Jonny came no more to visit. My father had died the previous year. A trapdoor he was standing on gave way beneath his feet. Few men can predict with accuracy the day and the hour of their passing. My father did. He knew the exact minute when he would die.

The judge had told him.

I did not attend the Daddy's trial. There were no spare seats in the public gallery. My mother had reserved them all for herself and her personal friends. They all had banners with them and specially printed badges that they wore. These appealed for justice to be done.

No clemency, they said. And *Hang the blackguard high*.

Whether the Daddy was really guilty of all the charges laid against him, I cannot say. Certainly he murdered the ice-cream man, but that fellow had it coming. The Daddy had warned him on numerous occasions not to park outside our door and ring his damnable bells. He had told him what he could do with his chocolate nut sundaes and where he could stick his Cadbury's Flakes, and what would happen if he didn't move his van to places far away. But the fellow persisted. It was a free country, he said. He had a special licence, he said. He could park wherever he pleased, he said. Move or die, the Daddy said. The ice-cream man stayed put.

In the months leading up to his murderous assault upon the vendor of iced sweeteries, the Daddy had, as they say, lived on his nerves. He was a troubled daddy. He eschewed good food and dined on drink alone. He developed strange compulsions. He would spend hour upon end sniffing swatches of tweed in the gents' out-fitters. He became prone to outbursts of uncontrollable laughter. He bethought himself a Zulu king and dressed in robes befitting. He became obsessed with the idea that an invisible Chinaman called Frank was broadcasting lines from Milton directly into his brain.

His plea of insanity was ignored by the court. And rightly too, in my opinion. I did not consider the Daddy to be mad. Perhaps a tad eccentric – but then, who isn't?

Upon that fateful night, the ice-cream man was simply in the wrong place at the wrong time. This is the story of most of our lives. My daddy had just too many things all preying on his mind. The ice-cream man's bells pushed him over the edge. And if the bells weren't bad enough, the fact that my daddy caught the ice-cream man sexing my mummy was.

The French have a special term for this kind of crime. And the perpetrator often gets off scot-free in their courts. But that's just typical of the French. We're far more civilized here.

So, I suppose, fair do's, the Daddy got what he deserved. And I, for one, was glad to see the back of him. I really enjoyed the street party that was held to celebrate his hanging. But I do feel that the court should have left it at that. Punished him for the crime he had committed, without bringing in all that other stuff, which seemed to me to be done for no good reason other than spite.

The counsel for the prosecution called a special witness: a research scientist who worked for a government department, which didn't have a name, or did, but it was a secret. This special witness gave evidence that my daddy had been directly responsible for all manner of terrible crimes against mankind and the planet in general. Climate changes; the extinction of a breed of rare miniature sheep; Third World famine. He even blamed my daddy for the rise of rock-'n'-roll.

I heard this all from Dave, who, having recently become very close with my mother, had got a good seat in the public gallery.

When I expressed my doubts to Dave regarding the scientist's claims, Dave had shaken his head and no-no-no'd me into silence. The scientist had brought in a blackboard, Dave said. He had drawn equations on it. Dave said he had explained in terms that even the layman could understand how all the equations pointed to my father being the culprit and there was no room for error. So said Dave.

'It's a new science,' Dave said to me. 'Based upon the discovery that we human beings do not actually think with our brains. Our brains are, apparently, receivers and transmitters, which receive information from our surroundings and transmit it to a distant point in the universe; then instructions to proceed in this or that endeavour are transmitted back, or some such, in so much and so on and suchlike. And things of that nature generally.

'And half of the rubbish that's going on in the world is all your daddy's fault,' said Dave.

I pricked up my ears at this, which got a cheap laugh from Dave. But what he said rang a distant bell with me. I thought back to that time when I'd been hiding in the restricted section of the library (a section that had recently been removed to an unknown location) and had overheard those two young men talking about this very thing.

Curiously, there was no mention of this scientist's evidence in the newspaper coverage of my father's trial. The press just stuck with the business of the ice-cream man being run through the backside with my daddy's Zulu *assagi*.

The editor of the *Brentford Mercury* excelled himself.

ICE CREAM, I SCREAM, EYES STREAM

I had that front page stuck up on my bedroom wall for years.

★ ★ ★

So, as I say, it was now very quiet in our house.

I didn't miss the Daddy. I'd loved him, for he was my daddy, but I'd never liked him very much. I blamed him for all the bad traits I now possessed. Whatever you learn in your childhood stays with you for life. It colours your opinions: it structures your thinking. You are programmed when young. You can never alter your basic programming.

I can't blame the Daddy for all the mistakes I've made in my life. That would be absurd and irresponsible. But I blame him for most and that is enough for me.

So, as I say, and I'll say once more: it was now very quiet in our house. And as I'd always loved quietness, I was grateful for it.

And, as I said, everything changes. The present soon becomes the past and is gone.

The borough was changing. The old streets were coming down and new blocks of flats were rising to take their place.

This was now the nineteen sixties. Change was fashionable. And I was fashionable too. I was a mod.

And I was a homo.

That might come as a bit of a surprise to you. It did to me, when I finally found out what the word meant. I was rather disappointed about that, I can tell you. I'd thought that it must mean something really, really bad. I didn't expect it just to mean *that*. I'd been doing *that* for years. I went to an all-boys school and everybody did *that*. We did *that* whenever we got the opportunity. Doing *that* took our minds off the fact that there weren't any girls around for us to do *that* to. And when you did *that* to boys, you couldn't get them pregnant, so you didn't have to marry them. So I quite liked being a homo.

Ultimately I didn't stick with it, though.

You could say that I tried to be a homosexual, but I was only half in Earnest.*

But things were definitely changing.

I wandered down Moby Dick Terrace one day, wearing-in my new Ivy Shop loafers with the gilt bar and low-level Cuban heels, to discover that Mother Demdike's hut had gone. Workmen were laying the foundations for a new three-up, two-down, with an indoor lavvy. I asked one of the workmen what had happened to the witch's hut and indeed to the witch herself. But the workman told me that he knew nothing about any old witch, he was just laying the main drains.

He was a nice-looking workman, with tight jeans that flattered a pert little bum. I asked whether he'd like to come out to the pictures some time. The workman took umbrage at this and called me a poof to my face. And he said that he'd give me a kicking if I didn't clear off pretty sharpish.

I have always found homophobia offensive and I don't take kindly to threats of violence. I took the workman quietly aside and discussed the matter with him. And then I hurried on about my business.

But I wondered over Mother Demdike and her hut. I recalled the hag telling me that one day she and her kind would be gone and forgotten. Gone, as if in a dream that vanishes upon waking.

---

*Humour. Courtesy of Ivor Biggun.

And indeed she was gone.

Dave was also gone for a while. To a young offenders institution. They say that if you want to learn how to be a real criminal, then prison is the place to go. If you're not a crim when you go in, you'll certainly be one by the time they let you out again.

It isn't utterly true. Criminals in prison can't really teach you very much. Because, let's face it, if they were any good at being criminal, they'd not have ended up in prison, would they? Their advice and their criminal knowledge really isn't worth much at all. The only criminals whose advice is worth taking if you wish to pursue a life of crime are those who have never been caught. And those criminals will never give you any advice at all. Because they will deny to their dying breath that they *are* criminals.

Because how *can* they be classified as criminals? They've never been convicted of a crime!

Dave came out of the young offenders institution full of all kinds of rubbish. Theories on how you could commit the perfect crime. I argued with him that there was no such thing as the perfect crime. Silly, I know, but I was a teenager.

Actually, if you'd like to commit the perfect crime just once in your lifetime, I'll tell you how to do it. It's a secret, so you'll have to promise me that you won't pass it on to anyone else. Do you promise?

All right, I'll tell you what to do.

What you need to have is a bank account that's in credit to more than one hundred pounds, a hole-in-the-wall cash card and a sombrero. If you have these, then this is what you do.

108

Put on your sombrero,* go to the hole-in-the-wall when there's no one around, insert your cash card and order up one hundred pounds. When the money appears through the little slot, very carefully ease out the middle twenty-pound note, leaving the rest where they are. Then wait. After a couple of minutes the cash machine will take back the money. It will credit one hundred pounds back to your bank account. Leaving you with twenty pounds in your hand. This is of course illegal, so I would be committing a crime if I encouraged you to do it. Or in fact even told you about it. So I won't.

Instead I'll continue with my tale. The Daddy was dead, I was an uncommitted homo (because now I'd left the all-boys school to seek employment). Mother Demdike was gone and all but forgotten and Dave was back from the young offenders institution.

It was Thursday. And it was seven o'clock.

I met up with Dave at the launderette.

'I can't believe that you still get a feed out of this,' I said to Dave, as I watched him watching the washing going round and around.

'A feed?' said Dave. 'Speak English.'

'You still enjoy this stuff,' I said. 'It still excites you.'

'One day,' said Dave, 'you'll appreciate it for yourself. Oh God, there's a spin cycle coming up. Don't talk to me till it's over.'

---

*Hole-in-the-wall cash dispensers have CCTV cameras, so keep your head well down and you won't be recognized. If there is any trouble, you can always say that your cash card was nicked by a Mexican and it wasn't you that did this.

I kept silent and left him to his pleasure. I went outside and lit up a Passing Cloud.*

They don't have Passing Cloud cigarettes any more. Few folk remember them now. Wills made them. In a flip-top pink packet, in two rows of ten. Oval, untipped cigarettes, with Big Chief Passing Cloud on the front, smoking a clay pipe. I never understood about that. But we had some really classy fags back in those days. Balkan Sobranie, Spanish Shawl, a perfumed cigarette, Three Castles, Capstan Full Strength.

Those were the days.

And, frankly, I miss 'em.

Presently Dave emerged from the launderette with a pale, young face and a bit of a sweat on.

'That was nice,' he said. 'I missed that in the nick.'

'Didn't they have a launderette in there?' I asked.

'No,' said Dave. 'You had to wash out your undies in the slop bucket.'

'Were you "the Daddy" in there?' I asked. 'Did you have "bitches"?'

'I think you're in the wrong decade,' said Dave, shaking his shaven head. 'We had snout and screws and vicars with long hair who taught us how to turn dolly pegs on a lathe.'

'Will you be going back, do you think? Or, having paid your debt to society, will you henceforth be a model citizen?'

---

*I know that I mentioned that I smoked Woodbines, but they did give me a terrible heaving cough, so I switched to Passing Cloud. Just in case you were wondering.

'I liked the food,' said Dave. 'I think I will become a repeat offender.'

'Each to his own,' said I. 'What shall we do tonight?'

'We could break into the sweet shop and steal humbugs.'

'Not keen,' I said. 'There's a dance on at the Blue Triangle Club. Pat Lyons and the Second Thoughts are playing.'

'Is it booga-booga music?'

'It's Blue Beat, I think.'

'Let's go, then. I'll nick some parkas from the cloakroom.'

We went to the Blue Triangle Club.

Every other day of the week, the Blue Triangle Club was a YMCA sports and social hall. But Thursdays were different. On Thursdays there were bands – real bands with guitars and amplifiers. Most of the bands had Jeff Beck in them. You couldn't really have a band back then if Jeff Beck wasn't in it. He was 'paying his dues', which was what you did in those days if you wanted to become famous as a musician. You didn't go along to auditions that were being shown as a TV series, you learned your craft. You paid your dues. And you ultimately became Jeff Beck.

Jeff Beck played lead guitar with Pat Lyons and the Second Thoughts on Thursdays. I don't know what ever happened to Pat Lyons. Obviously he never paid enough dues. Because he never became Jeff Beck. I heard that he became a butcher, as did Reg Presley from the Troggs, before he gained a temporary reprieve when some nineties band took one of his songs to the top of the charts again and he got some royalties in. Spent it researching crop circles, I understand.

But Jeff Beck did become Jeff Beck and he played some blinding guitar that Thursday night at the Blue Triangle Club.

Somewhere, amongst my personal effects, exists my Blue Triangle Club member's card. It's blue and it's got my name on and it's triangular in shape. My membership number was 666, which meant a lot to me at the time.

'Got any pills?' asked the bouncer, barring our way into the club. 'I'll have to search you.' The bouncers were so very big in those days. And they were *bouncers* then, not *door supervisors*. Harry was huge.

'Turn it in, Harry,' I said. 'We don't have any pills.'

'Would you like to buy some, then?' asked Harry.

'Now you're talking,' said Dave. 'Got any purple hearts?'

'Shilling each,' said Harry.

'I'll take a quid's worth,' said Dave.

I sighed a little for my bestest friend. 'You're on probation,' I said. 'You'll be in trouble if you're caught popping purple hearts.'

'Are you going to grass me up?'

'Of course not,' I said.

'Then, a quid's worth for my friend too.'

'Nice,' I said, trying to look like I meant it.

In truth I'd never taken any drugs. When people offered them to me, I accepted gratefully and pretended to pop them into my mouth. But really I pocketed them, took them home, sorted them out, packaged them up and generously handed them around when the time was right. So my friends thought I was pretty 'right on'. But in truth I was afraid of drugs.

I've never cared for being out of control – which is to say, not being in control of myself. I like what thinking I do to be of my own volition. I like to be the master of my own self. I took the quid's worth of purple hearts and appeared to toss them down my throat.

Dave made short work of his.

We paid our entrance fees, had our hands stamped with ultraviolet paint for our pass-outs and entered the Blue Triangle.

The joint was not exactly a-jumping. A few embarrassed-looking girls in droopy dresses half-heartedly slopped about the dance floor, circumnavigating their handbags. A few young blokes in full mod rigout lounged at the bar, too young to get served, too cool to admit that they couldn't.

Dave made for the bar, ordered drinks, was turned away and returned without them.

'In prison,' he said, 'we drank piss and got right out of our faces.'

'What?' said I. 'You drank your own piss?'

'Certainly not,' said Dave. 'Do I look like a pervert?'

I shook my head, for in truth Dave didn't.

'We drank the piss of Goldstein the shaman.'

'Why would you want to do that?'

'Goldstein the shaman grew Peyote cactus in his cell. If you eat Peyote buttons the drug comes out in

113

your piss stronger than when it went in. It's something to do with the acids in the human digestive system.'

'That can't be true,' I said.

'It is,' said Dave.* 'I wonder if it works with lager.'

'Don't even think about it.'

'No,' said Dave. 'You're probably right. So, shall we chat up some girls? What do you think?'

I cast an eye over the womenfolk. There was a particularly pretty blonde girl chatting with a big fat friend.

'There's a couple over there,' I said. 'But I don't like the look of your one much.'

'They all look the same in the dark,' said Dave, wise as ever for his years. 'I think these purple hearts are kicking in. How do my pupils look?'

I stared into his eyes. 'Well,' I said, 'that's interesting.'

'Have they dilated?'

'Not exactly,' I said. 'But it would appear that both of your pupils are now located in your right eye.'

'*No?*' Dave covered his left eye with his hand. 'Damn me,' he said, 'you're right.'

'This might affect your chances of chatting up that big fat girl.'

'No probs,' said Dave, reaching into his pocket and bringing out a pair of sunglasses. 'I was going to put these on anyway. They make me look like Roy Orbison.'

'Who's Roy Orbison?'

'He's the lead singer with a band in Acton. Jeff Beck

*And it is. Although I wouldn't fancy it.

plays bass for them on Tuesdays.' Dave put on his sunglasses. 'How do I look?' he asked.

'A bit of a nelly. Those are women's sunglasses. Does Roy Orbison wear women's sunglasses?'

'I don't know,' said Dave. 'I've never seen him.'

Drinkless, feckless, young, dumb and full of commercial enterprise, Dave and I set out to pull.

Dave, the uncrowned king of the chat-up line, marched straight over to the fat girl and introduced himself. 'Black's the name,' said Dave. 'Count Otto Black, swordsman and adventurer, and you, I believe, I have seen in the movies.'

'Me?' said the fat girl. 'Me in the movies?'

'Come on,' said Dave. 'Don't be shy. I've seen you in a film, haven't I?'

'No,' said the fat girl. 'You haven't.'

'Oh,' said Dave. 'I could have sworn you were Robert Mitchum.'*

The fat girl tittered foolishly, which meant that Dave was 'in there'. The blonde girl, however, maintained a stony silence.

'Don't mind him,' I said to her. 'He's stoned out of his face. We both are. We're wild ones. Live fast, die young, that's us.'

'Then don't let me keep you,' said the blonde girl. 'Feel free to die whenever you want.'

'My name's Gary,' I said. 'What's yours?'

'Mine's a gin and tonic.'

'Are you a Red Indian, then?'

---

*Later in life Dave revised this line to: 'I could have sworn you were Jabba the Hutt.' But I always preferred the original.

'What?' said the blonde girl.

'Well, when they christen Red Indian babies, they baptize them in the river, hold them up and then name them after the first thing the mother sees. Like Standing Bear, or Sitting Bull, or Passing Cloud, or Two Dogs Sexing.'

'What are you blathering about?'

'You said your name was A Gin and Tonic. Perhaps your mum didn't live near a river, so you were christened in a cocktail bar. That would explain it.'

'Fugg off!' said the blonde girl, upon whom the subtle nuances of my sophisticated humour were obviously lost.

'I suppose sex would be out of the question, then?' I said.

'Fugg off or I'll call the bouncer.'

'Harry's a friend of mine,' I said.

'Harry's my brother,' said the blonde girl.

'Look,' I said, because I was rarely put off. Knowing, as most teenage boys have always known, that nine times out of ten persistence will eventually wear down a teenage girl. 'I think we've got off on the wrong foot here.'

'Take both your feet and walk.'

Having a secret weapon in my bird-pulling arsenal, I chose now to employ it. 'I love your perfume,' I said.

'Yeah, right.'

'It's Fragrant Night, by Fabergé, isn't it?'

'It might be.'

'And your lipstick. I love that too. That's Rose Carmethine, by Yardley.'

'It might be.'

116

'And your frock is a Mary Quant. And your shoes . . .'

'You know an awful lot about women's fashion.'

I leaned close to the blonde girl's left ear and whispered the words: 'I'm a homosexual.' Then stepped back to let them take effect.

The blonde girl stared me full in the eyes. 'Oh,' she said. 'I, err . . . do you really like my frock?'

'It's beautiful,' I said. 'The colour really flatters your complexion. You have beautiful skin, if I might say so. Flawless.'

'Thank you. My name's Sandra, by the way.' And she put out her hand for me to shake.

So I shook it.

I know what you're thinking. You're thinking, dirty trickster. Yeah, all right, OK. But I *was* a homo; well, I *had been* a homo. I was all for having a go at hetero-sexuality. But it's actually a great chat-up line. When you confide your homosexuality, the woman no longer feels threatened. She views you differently. And if she finds you attractive, she wonders, just wonders, whether she could 'straighten you out'. Women won't admit to this, of course, but then there are so many things that women won't admit to, particularly when it comes to sex. And as this particular ploy had proved effective on several previous occasions, I had no reason to believe that it would fail upon this one.

Sandra bought me a gin and tonic. Well, *she* looked eighteen. Then she led me to one of the tables at the end of the hall away from the stage and talked to me about fashion and boyfriends. I listened to it all, offer-ing sensitive comment when I felt the need arose, but basically letting her do all the talking. Women, I have learned, like this a lot. They like a man who listens, rather than just rabbits on about himself. So I listened and I waited, waited for the question that I knew would eventually come.

'Have you ever been with a girl?' Sandra asked.

Result!

'No,' I said. 'Never.'

'You must have thought about it, though.'

I shrugged strategically. It was not a direct question – a direct answer could blow the whole thing. 'The band's starting up,' I said. 'Would you like to dance?'

Sandra nodded. And so we danced.

Jeff Beck played a stormer that Thursday night. He was joined on stage by Alan Price, Eric Clapton, Jimmy Page and Bill Wyman, who were all paying their dues.

Sandra got the rounds in all evening, although I did pay for at least half of them. By checking-out time I was rather drunk and she was rather drunk and very stoned.

I know it is an evil thing to slip purple hearts into a young woman's gin and tonic every time she goes off to the toilet, but I was a teenage boy and few teenage boys have a conscience.

We left the Blue Triangle and while Sandra was throwing up in a dustbin around the back I spied Dave in congress with the fat girl up against the fire door. He gave me the thumbs-up and I returned it to him.

Then I took Sandra off to show her Mr Doveston's marble tomb by moonlight. It was a favourite place of mine to bring my lovers. I even had a sleeping bag stashed nearby in one of the above-ground crypts, for those who felt the marble rather cold upon their backs.

I think that Sandra was rather pleased with herself afterwards. She had, after all, 'cured' me of my homosexuality.

I might just have notched her up as one more easy conquest, but there was something about Sandra that I really liked. It wasn't her perfume, or her lipstick, or her frock, or her shoes. I determined that I'd change all of them soon enough. But it was something about *her*. The person that was *her*. She seemed special. I couldn't put my finger on quite how she was special. She certainly wasn't very clever. But she had a certain something. And, as I had always seen myself marrying a posh woman and the whinnying noises she made whilst I was sexing her led me to believe that she was indeed very posh, I decided to see her again.

And again.

And again.

And again.

9

And then I awoke once more. And my teenage years were behind me and I was twenty-two.

And I was married.

To Sandra.

I was sitting in a dingy kitchenette in a ground-floor flat in a road called Mafeking Avenue in Brentford. I looked out of the window towards a dismal little yard and the back wall of a public house and I thought, Whatever am I doing here?

I thought back to my teenage years, but they were all out of focus. A snatch of detail here, a little incident there. This was the real and for now and I was here and it was all rather dull.

In fact, it was very dull indeed.

I stubbed out my cigarette. The ashtray overflowed onto a pink gingham tablecloth of grubby vinyl. From upstairs came the sounds of arguing voices.

'Mike! I hate you, Mike.'

Mike had flown Spitfires in the war. Mike, I knew, was dying of TB.

'Shut up, woman. You're drunk!'

The woman's name was Viv. She drank a bottle of

dry Martini a day and went to Weight Watchers on a Thursday evening. At the YMCA hall that no longer housed the Blue Triangle Club. There weren't any clubs like that any more. The council had tightened up on the licensing laws.

'Go out to work, Mike. Get yourself a job.'

'I'm retired. I have a disability allowance.'

'You're a lazy skiver.'

'I'm dying of TB.'

'Liar! You're a liar.'

But he wasn't and in six months he would be dead. I stared all around and about my dire surroundings. How had I come to this? What was I doing here? Was *this* my life? Was this *my* life?

I took out another cigarette and lit it up. It was a Players Number 10. Cheapest fags that ever there were. I couldn't afford Passing Cloud any more. I didn't even know whether they made Passing Cloud any more.

I was out of work. Again. Work and I didn't get on. My face never fitted and I could not subscribe to the 'company ethic'. I kept on getting sacked. Which was OK in those days. You could draw the dole immediately even if you were sacked. They knew me well enough at the dole office.

'Wotcha, Gary boy,' they would say. 'How did you screw up this time?' And they would tell me to get my hair cut. Get my hair cut? Get real!

But the thing was, these were the early nineteen seventies and there was plenty of work about. Loads of it. There wasn't any unemployment. The blokes at the dole office kept finding me more work. They said that

I was the only officially unemployed person in Brentford and it looked bad on their records and I'd have to start work again on the following Monday. And so here I was, sitting at this table, and Sandra had gone off to work at the new nylons company on the Great West Road and I had an interview at ten-thirty. And it was nearly ten now and I didn't want to go.

I was sure that I'd had some aspirations when I was young. I'm sure that I wanted to be a mortician. Or a coroner, or an embalmer, but I'm sure that I never wanted to be this.

I turned the piece of paper between my fingers. A telecommunications engineer. What was one of those anyway? Telephone man. Rooting amongst wires. I wondered whether they'd let me empty the coin boxes in telephone booths. I knew how to do that anyway. Dave had shown me.

I missed Dave. He was in proper grown-up prison now. For breaking and entering, this time. His brief had asked for over two hundred similar offences to be taken into consideration and Dave was away on a five-year stretch.

The local authorities were never happier than when I was employed and Dave was banged up. It meant that not only was there no official unemployment in the area, but there was no crime either.

I gazed once more at the piece of paper. Telecommunications engineer. What *was* that all about? How dull was that? What could you do? There wasn't much to telephones. You spoke in one end, words went down wires and came out the other. If the wires got broken you joined them up again. Fascinating? Challenging?

I didn't think so.

I won't go, I told myself. I'll make some excuse. I'll be sick.

A shadow fell across the piece of paper. I looked up to see Harry peering in through the window. Harry was now employed by the dole office to escort un-enthusiastic would-be employees to interviews at their new definitely soon-to-be places of employment.

One of the reasons that there was full employment in those days was that by law companies were obliged to employ the first person who arrived for an interview when a vacancy came up.

Actually it was a blinder of a system. How many times have you seen some big fat blackguard on TV who was the head of some huge multinational con-sortium, wining and dining it, living high off the hog, burning the candle at both ends and indulging in numerous other clichés, and said to yourself, 'I could do *that* job!'? But you know that you'd never get the opportunity to do so. Because it's always 'jobs for the boys' or the Masonic handshake, or nepotism, or some such thing.

Well, back in the early nineteen seventies it wasn't like that. If a job as a managing director came up, folk who fancied being a managing director would rush along and apply for it and the first in the queue would get it. You don't believe me, I can tell. But ask your-self this: what has Richard Branson got that you haven't got? A beard, a toothy smile and a jumper? And that's it, right? Richard Branson answered an ad in the early 1970s: 'Young man wanted to run soon-to-be multimillion-pound music empire'. He won't own up to it now, of course. He'll tell you he worked his way up from nothing.

But then, he would, wouldn't he?

No, in truth, that's the way the seventies did business. It was a seventies tradition, or a new charter, or something.

And it worked.

It did.

It really did.

And I'd been offered the job of telecommunications engineer. Not 'Young man wanted to start off multi-million-dollar computer industry. Name of Bill would be a benefit.' Some other specky twonk got that one. I got telecommunications engineer. I didn't want to. But I did.

'Up and at it,' called Harry through the now open window. All now open because he'd put his big elbow through it.

'I'm not well,' I said. 'I've got Bright's disease.'

'Take it up with Bright,' said Harry. 'You're off to an interview. I've a car waiting outside.'

'Is it a Mini Metro?' I asked.

'No,' said Harry. 'They haven't been invented yet.'

'I hate you, Harry,' I said.

'And I respect you for it,' said Harry. 'But up and at it, or – and this is not a personal thing, but merely in the line of duty – I will come in there and smash your face in.'

I got up from the table.

'Put your tie on,' said Harry.

I put my tie on.

'And your trousers.'

I put my trousers on too.

'Put them on the right way round.'

I took them off again and did so.

'There,' said Harry. 'You look very smart. You really should get your hair cut, though.'

'I've tucked it into my trousers, haven't I?'

'You're a weirdo,' said Harry. 'Although, don't get me wrong, weirdo has its place in the overall scheme of things.'

'You have a heart of gold,' I said.

'Let's go,' said Harry.

I had never seen the inside of a telephone exchange. And I can't say that I liked the look of it. I did like the smell, though. A kind of electrical burning smell of the type that you only get now in the carriages of intercity trains. The smell is called ozone, apparently. I'd always thought that ozone was the smell you got at the seaside when you sniffed near the sea. But apparently that's something else entirely. That's sewerage. Ozone is different. It smells ever so nice, though. I was really taken with it. Mr Holland showed me around. He'd been in telecommunications all his life so far. His dad had known Alexander Graham Bell and Faraday.

'Let me tell you something about the history of telecommunications,' said Mr Holland.

'Must you?' I said.

'I must.'

'Go on, then.'

'It all began with Adam and Eve.'

'This would be quite a long history, then. Could we move on a bit?'

'And then the 83102 superseded the 83101 and the coil-exchanger really came into its own.'

'Fascinating,' I said. 'I never knew there was so much to it.'

'You start on Monday, then.'

'But what do I have to do?'

'Ah,' said Mr Holland, and he led me to a tiny booth. It was even smaller than my kitchenette. And it didn't have any windows at all, although it did have a door and a table.

'Sit there,' said Mr Holland.

And a chair.

I sat on the chair.

'Now,' said Mr Holland. 'Do you see this?' He pointed to a bulb that was attached to a Bakelite fitting that was in turn attached to the table.

'I see it,' I said. 'It's a bulb.'

'It's an attached bulb. From the fitting, wires extend through the table and down into the floor.'

I peered beneath the table. 'You're right,' I said. 'They do. Bravo for those wires.'

'And do you see this switch?' He pointed to the switch in question. It was also attached to the table and certain other wires ran from it, through the table (which to me seemed a pretty sad table, what with all these holes cut through it and everything), and similarly vanished into the floor.

'I spy this switch,' I said. 'There it is: I have it.'

'Good,' said Mr Holland. 'I can see that you're a natural for this job.'

'Hm!' said I, thoughtfully.

'The nature of the job is this,' said Mr Holland,

whom I noted wore a bow tie – always a bad sign, in my opinion. 'At certain times the light bulb will come on and it will be your duty to press the switch and turn it off.'

'Why?' I asked.

'Because it has come on.'

'Oh,' I said. 'But why?'

'But why what?'

'Why does it need to be switched off?'

Mr Holland laughed. 'Because it has come on, of course.'

'I see,' I said, but I didn't. 'No,' I continued, 'I don't see. Why does the bulb come on?'

Mr Holland stared at me queerly. And it wasn't *that* kind of queerly at all. 'You have applied for the post of telecommunications engineer, haven't you?' he asked.

'Yes,' I said.

'So I am assuming that you do know how to switch a light bulb off.'

'Of course,' I said. 'Everybody knows how to do that.'

'You'd be surprised,' said Mr Holland. 'You'd be surprised.'

'So this is what a telecommunications engineer does: switch off a light bulb?'

'Switch it off *when it comes on*. And not before. You didn't think it was going to be all glamour, did you? Out joining broken wires together?' Mr Holland laughed again.

'Perish the thought,' I said. 'My constitution would not survive such constant excitement.'

'Are you taking the piddle?' asked Mr Holland.

'Definitely. Yes.'

'Well, it's not a necessary requirement for the job. But it's not prohibited, as long as you do it in your own time. Do you have your own gloves?'

I shook my head.

'You'll need your own gloves.'

'Why?' I asked.

'For when it's winter,' said Mr Holland. 'When you're coming to work, if it's cold you'll want to wear gloves. I can't lend you mine. I only have one pair.'

'I'll get some from Woolworth's,' I said.

'False economy,' said Mr Holland. 'Buy a leather pair from Rowse's in Ealing Broadway. You'll pay the extra, but they'll last you a lifetime.'

'I'll bear that in mind,' I said.

'I think you're the right man for this job,' said Mr Holland. 'Do you want me to run through your duties once again?'

'It's switch off the bulb if it comes on, isn't it?'

'Are you sure?'

'Sure,' said I, nodding my head.

'You're a natural. I think we can say that the job is yours. Any questions?'

'Why does the bulb go on?' I asked.

Mr Holland laughed once again. 'You young blokes,' he said. 'Always trying to run before you can walk. Always wanting to know more, more, more. You tickle me, you really do. Where will it all end, eh?'

'In the heat death of the universe, or so I've read.'

'Well, let's hope that doesn't happen before I go on my holidays. I've booked a caravan at Camber Sands, one of the most beautiful spots in the country. Ever been there?'

'Only in my worst nightmare,' I said.

Mr Holland laughed once again. And then he stopped laughing for ever. 'Enough of humour,' he said. 'Telecommunications is a serious business. You do your job, young Barry, and I'll do mine, and everyone will be happy for it and able to make phone calls as they like.'

'Praise be to that,' I said. 'And it's Gary.'

'I'll just bet it is. See you on Monday morning, then, Barry. Sharp at seven.'

'*Seven?*' I said. 'What, seven in the morning?'

'Telecommunications never sleep. An unmanned bulb station is an accident waiting to happen. Seven till seven. Weekends off. Who could ask for more?'

'Would you like me to make a list?'

'It was a rhetorical question. See you on Monday. Sharp at seven.'

'In your dreams, you will.'

The bulb booth door opened and in came Harry. 'Everything hunky-dory?' he asked.

'No,' said I.

'Yes,' said Mr Holland.

'Good,' said Harry. 'I'll get Gary here sharp at seven on Monday.'

'Whatever,' said Mr Holland. 'I'm so glad that the vacancy is filled. We'll miss old Mr Hurst. Thirty-five years, man and boy, and woman in his later years, he boyed, manned and womanned that bulb switch. Things will never be the same without him, but we live in changing times and I'm sure young Barry will follow the example of his predecessor.'

'In a pig's ear, I will,' I said.

'He certainly will,' said Harry.

'Seven on Monday,' said Mr Holland. 'Look forward to it. Goodbye.'

'Goodbye,' I said. 'For ever.'

'You'll be here,' said Harry.

'I bloody won't,' I said.

But I would.

Oh yes.

I would.

I really would.

10

I was rudely awakened at six of the morning clock. It was the following Monday and my awakening, though rude, was pleasurable.

'I love the way you always wake me up like that,' I said to Sandra.

'As a wife, my duties lie in pleasuring my husband,' replied my loving spouse. 'Such is the way with us women, we are never happier than when we are serving our masters.'

The alarm clock jingle-jangled and I was rudely and *really* awakened.

'Sandra! Make my breakfast!' I said, in my sternest tone.

'Make it yourself,' said Sandra. 'And when you're doing so, make some for me.'

'Let's do some sexing first, then.'

'In your dreams,' said my loveless spouse, and I went off downstairs.

Then, recalling that we lived in a ground-floor flat, I came up from the cellar and dragged my feet into the kitchen. It was still rather dark, but looking on the bright side it would soon be Saturday.

'I wasn't born for the grind of nine to five,' I told the cat. 'I'm not like the rest of these walking dead. I'm made of more superior stuff. I deserve better. I do. I really do.'

The cat yawned then rubbed itself against my legs like a silken pervert.

'You want food, don't you?' I asked it. 'Well, you can damn well wait for it. I'm a working man and I don't have time to pamper pussies.'

I brewed coffee, munched upon cornflakes and prepared myself for the day ahead. 'Now then, what will I need to take with me?' I asked myself. For the cat had left the kitchen in a huff (which was the height of feline fashion at the time).

I wandered into the sitting room and ran my finger all along a bookshelf. 'Let's see. *Death Wears a Hoodless Cagoule*?* *Babe in a Body Bag*?† *Bleed on Me Gently*?‡ *Werewolf in Manhattan*?'§ So many to choose from. Tricky decision.

Well, I mean, what do you want from me? I was supposed to spend my days sitting in a dire little windowless cell, waiting for a light bulb to flash on, so I could switch it off again. I was going to need something to pass the time, wasn't I? And what better than the entire genre detective works of P. P. Penrose? Eighty-five Lazlo Woodbine thrillers?

Yes, well, OK, I know. I'd read them all before.

---

*A Lazlo Woodbine thriller.
†Ditto.
‡Ditto.
§And ditto once again.

Read each of them many times before. But I loved these books and the more you read and reread them, the more you seemed to learn about them. You noticed all these little details, these cross-correspondences, references to other novels, recurring characters, running gags. Not to mention all the trenchcoat humour and the toot that Laz talked in bars with Fangio the fat boy.

'I'll dip for it,' I said. 'Ip, dip, sky blue, who's it? Not you.' And all along the shelf I went, until I was down to one. One book a day would be sufficient. And I could do what I always did when I read one: imagine myself as a Hollywood director making the film version. Cast with stars of my own choosing, even adding a few scenes of my own, which would involve famous Hollywood actresses getting their kit off in the cause of high art.

I had dipped up *The Toytown Murders*, which was handy as it was one of my favourites. It's a bit of a weird one, *The Toytown Murders*. The entire book is a dream that Laz has while he's lying in a coma, having been shot in the back by a murderous dame. In the dream Laz is a teddy bear – Eddie Bear, private eye – and he's called in to solve a series of murders in Toytown, where nursery-rhyme characters, all rich and famous from the royalties on their nursery rhymes, are being bumped off one after another. In case you haven't read it, I won't give away the ingenious trick ending. But it's truly a blinder.

I dressed up for the coming day, being careful to tuck my Fair Isle slipover into my trousers, so I could hide the book in it. Just in case I was body-searched by Harry.

At six forty-five the front-door bell rang and I went off to meet my fate.

'You aren't going to be difficult about this, are you?' Harry asked, as he drove me through the all but empty streets of Brentford. 'I mean, it will save us both an unnecessary amount of fuss and bother and blows to your skull, if you just keep this job for a couple of months.'

'A couple of months!' I shook my head.

'It's eight weeks,' said Harry. 'Long enough for you to read all your stupid Lilo Windborne novels.'

'The name's Woodbine,' I said. 'Lazlo Woodbine. Some call him Laz. And how did you know I was planning to do that anyway?'

'I watched you through your sitting-room window wandering about in your Y-fronts and dipping for a book to read today. And it's all you ever do when you're supposed to be working. How many times have you been sacked for doing it?'

'I've lost count,' I said. 'Who cares?'

'I don't,' said Harry. 'The council employ me to see that you stay employed. If you didn't keep fouling up, I'd be out of a job. And I can't have that. I'm saving up for a motorbike.'

'What do you want a motorbike for?' I asked. 'You've got a car.'

'I want to run the most famous night club in the world,' said Harry, swerving to run over a ginger tom.

'And you need a motorbike for that?'

Harry sighed. 'You're not too bright, are you?' he said. 'If a job comes up to run the most famous night club in the world, it will go to the first applicant for the job, won't it?'

I nodded.

'So the first applicant will be the man who gets to the interview first – which is to say, faster than anyone else – won't it?'

I nodded again.

'You don't even have a pushbike, do you?' Harry asked.

I shook my head.

'Which is why you will be switching a light bulb off all day.'

I mulled over this. And I cast a sidelong glance at Harry. 'It really is as simple as *that*, isn't it?' I said.

'I'd save up for a motorbike too, if I were you,' said Harry. 'But don't even think about racing me to the night club job. I'll run you off the road.'

'I wouldn't dream of it,' I said. 'But I am impressed. Trouble is, I'm in a bit of a Catch 22 situation. I can't be bothered to stay in the duff jobs long enough to earn sufficient money to buy the motorbike so I can be first at the interview for the good jobs.'

'You could just top yourself,' said Harry, helpfully. 'But not before I've bought my motorbike. Or I'll beat the poo-poo out of you.'

'That's more like it,' I said. 'You had me going there for a while. I really *did* think that you were intelligent.'

'April fool,' said Harry.

'It's not April,' I said.

'Had you again,' said Harry. 'Could you just open the door on your side?'

'Why?'

'Just open it, please.'

I opened it and Harry pushed me out. 'See you tomorrow,' he called, as he sped away.

I picked myself up from the road and dusted down my Fair Isle, then I plodded, as the doomed must plod, across the car park and into the telephone exchange.

A receptionist sat at a desk in the reception area. Her desk had a little sign with the word RECEPTION printed on it. The sign matched the badge that she wore upon her breast. And also the one that she wore upon her jaunty-looking cap.

'Are you the receptionist?' I enquired, putting on the face known as brave and smiling out of it bravely.

The receptionist viewed me down the length of her nose. 'Are you the new bulb boy?' she asked, in the tone known as contemptuous.

'Telecommunications engineer,' I corrected her.

The receptionist, visibly unimpressed, leaned forward and produced from beneath her desk a light bulb.

'And what will I need that for?' I asked.

'In case your present light bulb burns out. It's your initial replacement. All subsequent replacement bulbs must be ordered by you with a green requisition docket. I am not authorized to issue you with a green docket. You must request that from Stores Requisition Documentation on the fourth floor.'

I took the bulb from her hand and examined it with more care than it truly deserved. 'Is my present bulb likely to burn out?' I enquired.

The receptionist laughed. Loudly and longly.

'Why are you laughing?' I asked. 'And why so loud and long?'

'Because you are so thick,' she replied.

'I beg your pardon?' I said.

'What does this badge say?' asked the receptionist, pointing to her breast badge. 'Does it say "electrical supervisor"? Well, does it?'

'No,' I said. 'It says "receptionist". Which must be an anagram for stupid tart.'

The receptionist stared me pointy daggers. 'It says "receptionist". Which means that I deal with matters appertaining to reception. If you wish to know the likelihood of your bulb burning out, you must address your enquiry to an electrical supervisor.'

'I see,' I said. 'And where might I find him? Up on the fourth floor?'

'Fourth floor?' The receptionist laughed again. 'You really are thick, aren't you? Fourth floor is Stores Requisition Documentation, Stationery Outgoing and Sales Division. You'll want first floor annexe, Electrical Supervisor Services.'

I shrugged my shoulders. 'I think I'll just mooch up there now, then,' I said. 'Get a crate of bulbs in, in case I have a really high burn-out day.'

'Bulbs have to be requisitioned singly.' The receptionist rolled her eyes heavenward. 'God, you are *so* thick.'

'Then why are you calling me God?'

'You'll have to sign this,' said the receptionist, producing a clipboard with a bright white document clipped to it. And a wee biro dangling down on a string.

'And what is this?' I asked.

'The Official Secrets Act.'

'Whoa!' I said. 'I've never seen one of those before. Let's have a look at it.'

'You can't look at it,' said the receptionist. 'You just have to sign it. At the bottom, where it says "signature".'

'I think I'd like to read it first.'

'Are you an anarchist?' asked the receptionist.

'Why? Is there a job going in the Anarchy department?'

'Just sign the form,' said the receptionist.

'And what will happen if I don't?'

The receptionist laughed once more.

'No, don't tell me,' I said. 'You can't answer that question. If I want an answer to that question, I'll put it in writing, possibly on a pink docket, to your legal division on Floor 32.'

'Correct,' said the receptionist. 'So please sign the form.'

I really should have read that form. I should have, I really should have. Because in a future that was not too far distant, only a few short hours distant, in fact, the fact that I *had* signed the Official Secrets Act was going to cost me very dearly indeed. But you know what it's like. When a form is put in front of you, especially one with lots of small print, you just can't resist signing it, can you? It's a forbidden-fruit kind of thing, isn't it? The temptation to get yourself into all sorts of really big trouble just by flourishing a single signature. I didn't really want to read it anyway. It looked very boring. Although it would have wasted a bit of time, which wouldn't have been all that bad. But I *did* have a bulb to switch off. Especially if I was going to earn enough money to save some up and buy a motorbike. Which I had now definitely decided to do.

'There you go,' I said, signing the document with the wee biro on the string and handing the clipboard back. 'In for a penny, eh?'

The receptionist peered at my signature. 'Cheese,' she said. 'Gary Cheese. That's a pretty stupid name, isn't it?'

'You've really blown any chance you had of having sex with me,' I told her.

Mr Holland came out of his office to welcome me. He escorted me to my little booth the next door along, reacquainted me with my duties, in case I had forgotten some of them, patted me upon my shoulder as I sat down upon my chair, wished me well and departed, shutting the door behind him.

I looked at my wristwatch. It was now seven-thirty of the early-day clock. I really should have been home in my cosy bed. But here I was. Here in this – I sniffed – *smelly* little room. It smelled of wee-wee, not ozone. Waiting for a light bulb to go on. Oh well, it was a living.

I leaned back, put my feet up on the table, took out my book and settled down to chapter one.

At eight forty-five my light bulb went on. So I switched it off again.

It came on once more at eleven-fifteen. Again at twelve-twenty, and at one o'clock I went for lunch.

At one-o-five I was back at my table.

'Have you gone insane?' cried Mr Holland, who

had collared me in the corridor. 'Leaving the bulb booth unattended!' Veins stood out on his neck. His face had an unhealthy glow.

'I was going off for my lunch,' I told him. 'One o'clock is lunchtime. Everyone knows that.'

'You brought sandwiches, surely?'

'Do you mean to say that I don't get a proper lunch hour?'

'Aaagh!' went Mr Holland. 'The bulb's gone on. Switch it off! Switch it off!'

I reached out a languid hand and slowly switched it off.

'Phew,' said Mr Holland. 'That was a close thing. Now, do *not* leave this booth again until it's time for you to clock off.'

'I never clocked on,' I said. 'No one told me about clocking on.'

Mr Holland shook his head sadly. 'Then, that's cost you half a day's pay, hasn't it? As this is your first day, I will break protocol and clock you on now myself. Although it's more than my job's worth to do it.'

'I'll be for ever in your debt,' I said bitterly. 'But actually I need the toilet, so I'll have to pop out anyway.'

'Didn't you bring a bag?' asked Mr Holland.

'A bag? What are you talking about?'

'Your predecessor, Mr Hurst, was so dedicated to his profession that he had a colostomy bag fitted. Paid for the operation out of his own money. Or *her* money at the end. It was confusing. But you should think about doing the same. It can be agony holding it in until home time.'

'I have no intention of "holding it in" until home time,' I said. 'I need a pee and I need it now.'

'But you can't leave the bulb booth unattended.'

'Then you sit in until I come back.'

'I can't do that. It's not *my* job.'

'Well, I'm going to the bog, whether you like it or not.'

'You'd risk five years for a pee. Good God!' Mr Holland threw up his hands.

'Five years for a pee? What are you talking about?' I crossed my legs. I was getting desperate.

'You signed the Official Secrets Act, didn't you?'

'With a flourish,' said I. 'Why do you ask?'

'Because it states quite clearly in the "Terms of Employment" section that, should you leave the bulb booth unattended during your duty period, you will have committed a crime against the state. The punishment is a minimum of five years' imprisonment. Although upon all previous occasions the court has dealt out far sterner sentences than that. Mr Trubshaw got forty years in solitary. That was during the war, of course. I think he served as a good example, which is probably why Mr Hurst had the bag fitted.'

'What?' I said. '*What?*'

'Hold it in, boy, if you value your freedom.'

'No,' I said. 'Hang about, this can't be right.'

'Who's to say what's right? I'm not a philosopher, I'm a technical manager.'

'No,' I said. 'This is ridiculous. Absurd. And what about when I need a replacement bulb? I'd have to leave the booth then.'

'You'd call out to me. I would then initiate a temporary override procedure.'

'Well, initiate one now, while I go and have a pee.'

'Good God,' cried Mr Holland. 'You'd take me down with you. Have you no morals at all? Are you a total degenerate?'

'In a word, yes. I quit this stupid job.'

'You can't quit.'

'Then, fire me.'

'You can't be fired. You signed the Official Secrets Act. And you can't take any days off sick, either. You've taken the job for life.'

'I've what? I've *what*?'

'Don't shout,' shouted Mr Holland. 'I have very sensitive hearing. Had my aural cavities surgically enhanced so that I could hear a request for replacement bulbs being made through the partition wall. You only have to whisper, really.'

'I'm not whispering. And I'm going to wet myself in a minute.'

'I'm very sorry about that. I'm sure it will be very uncomfortable for you. But there's nothing I can do about it.'

'Bring me a bucket, or something.'

'Sorry,' said Mr Holland. 'A bucket is out of the question. There is no procedure for buckets. You can't get a docket for a bucket. It's unheard of.'

'So I have to wet my pants and go without lunch and if I leave this booth for even a couple of minutes or dare to take the day off, I can be dragged away to prison? Is that what you're saying?'

'In a word. And to save us all a lot of time and heart-break, yes.'

'Aaaaaaaaagh!' I went.

And not without good cause.

And then I wet myself.

11

There was something in the way that Sandra laughed that really got on my nerves. It had taken me nearly an hour to walk home, ducking in and out of alleyways to avoid being seen. What with the big wet patch down my trouser front and everything. And I was ravenously hungry and she said that it was my turn to make dinner.

And everything.

'Stop laughing!' I shouted. 'This isn't funny. This is dire. Terrible. Catastrophic. I'm in big trouble here.'

'It will teach you to read documents before you sign them in future.'

'I don't have a future!' I stormed up and down the sitting room.

'You're dripping on the carpet.' Sandra laughed some more.

'I'll write to my MP,' I said. 'This is inhuman. It's nothing short of slavery. This is the nineteen seventies. Is this what all our student protests have brought us to?'

'What student protests? You never were a student and you never protested against anything.'

'I marched for Gay Rights,' I told her, as I plucked at my damp trouser legs.

'You just went along hoping to get shagged.'

'Yeah, well, all right. That's why most of us went. But that's not the point. I can't be treated like this.'

'So what do you propose to do?'

'Have a bath,' I said. 'And have something to eat. And go down the pub and think about what to do.'

'Still, look on the bright side,' said Sandra: 'at least you'll be on a regular wage now. Do you get paid holidays? We could go somewhere nice.'

'Holidays? I never asked about holidays. Perhaps I don't even get any holidays.'

'I don't know what you're complaining about,' Sandra said. She gave me an encouraging smile. 'You have a job for life and it's not exactly taxing, is it? You can read your silly detective books, do an Open University course, learn a second language. Your days are pretty much your own to do with as you please. As long as you don't leave your bulb booth, of course.' And then Sandra sniggered a bit and then she laughed a lot more.

'I'm going for a bath,' I told her.

'You do that,' said Sandra. 'And, darling . . .'

'Yes?'

'It's a bit dark in the bathroom. You can switch the bulb *on*, if you like. A change is as good as a rest, eh?'

And then she laughed a lot more.

I bathed and I dried and I dressed in clean clothes and I stuffed my face with food. And then I went to the pub alone in a very bad mood indeed.

I went to the Shrunken Head. They have music there on a Monday, and every other night too. The Graham Bond Organization were playing that evening. Jeff Beck was on lead guitar.*

Harry was on the door, wearing a smart tuxedo.

'You dirty rotten swine!' I greeted him. 'You got me into this mess.'

'No, I didn't,' said Harry. 'And what mess are you talking about?'

'Forget it,' I said, making my way inside.

The Shrunken Head was a horrible dump. But then, all music pubs are. It's a tradition, or an old charter, or something. The furnishings are always rubbish, the beer is always rubbish *and* overpriced. And there's always trouble and people shooting up in the toilets and an overall sordidness of a type that you just don't get anywhere else.

I loved the place.

I elbowed my way through the crowd of youths and edged towards the bar. These were the days before black T-shirts had become an acceptable form of gig wear. These were still the days of the cheesecloth shirt. You don't see cheesecloth shirts any more – which is a shame, because I really liked them. No shirt fits like a cheesecloth shirt. Really tight across the shoulders and under the armpits, where they soon get a big stain going. And the way they pulled at the buttons, leaving those vertical eye-shaped slits so your chest and

*It was a reunion gig. Jeff had paid his dues by now, earned the nation's love with 'Hi Ho Silver Lining' and done a couple of solo albums that no one remembers now.

146

belly showed through. And those huge floppy collars. And everything.

I'll say this for the seventies. People really knew how to dress back then. I'd looked hot as a mod. And later as a hippie, but I looked my best as a seventies groover. My platform soles were three layers high. And would have made me the tallest bloke in the pub if everyone else hadn't been wearing platforms too.

The landlord in those days was Kimberlin Malkuth the Fourth, Lord of a Thousand Suns. His given name was Eric Blaine, but Eric Blaine possessed a certain gift. It was a gift that was his own. The gift of the True Name Knower.

According to Eric, the names we are given at birth – the surnames we inherit from our parents and the Christian names they choose for us – are not our *real* names. Our *true* names. The names that we should be called.

It didn't make a lot of sense to me at the time, but it did to Eric, or, rather, to Kimberlin Malkuth, Lord of a Thousand Suns, as he was known, having changed his name by deed poll. Because Eric had had a revelation (possibly involving the use of hallucinogenic drugs back in the sixties) whereby he became aware of his *true* name and the fact that he had the ability to recognize the *true* names of others, just by looking at them. It could be argued that, as the landlord of a pub, this might have put him in a certain peril with more truculent patrons, who might well have taken exception to him renaming them. But it didn't.

This was, and is, after all, Brentford. Where

tolerance is legendary and minds are as open as a supermarket on a Sunday.

And also, and this may well have been the *big* also, the names the enlightened landlord bestowed upon his oft-times bewildered patrons were so noble and exotic that few were ever heard to complain and most, indeed, revelled in their new and worthy nomenclatures.

'Lord Kimberlin,' I hailed him. 'Pint of fizzy rubbish over here, when you have a moment free.'

' 'Pon my word,' said the landlord, casting an eye in my direction. 'If it isn't the Honourable Valdec Firesword, Archduke of Alpha Centuri.'

'That's me,' I said. 'Any chance of a pint, all-knowing one?'

'Coming right up.' Lord Kimberlin did the business and presented me with my pint. 'Haven't seen you for a while, Archduke,' he said to me. 'But you've come on a good night. Not only is Quilten Balthazar, Viceroy to the High Grandee of Neptune, playing here tonight but Zagger To Mega Therion, the master bladesman of Alphanor in the Rigel Concourse is on lead guitar.'

'Should be a show worth watching, then,' said I, accepting my pint and paying up promptly.

'You're not kidding there,' said the landlord. 'And what a crowd in to watch, eh? See there the Baron Fidelius, slayer of Krang the Cruel?'

I followed the direction of the landlord's pointing and spied Nigel Keating the postman.

'And with him the Great Mazurka.'

I spied Norman from the corner shop.

'And there is the legendary Count Otto Black.'

I glanced over my shoulder and there was Count Otto Black.

'But . . .' I said.

'The exception that proves the rule,' explained the barlord.

I took up my pint and pushed my way back through the crowd to chat with Count Otto, whom I'd known since a lad.

The count's family had been émigrés during the Second World War. They came from some place or other in the wilds of Europe that had 'vania' on the end of it, but I could never pronounce it properly, having been poorly educated and always having a note that excused me from geography on religious grounds. The count's father had been the other Count Otto Black – the one who ran the Circus Fantastique, with which my Uncle Jon used to perform.

The count worked as a packer at Brentford Nylons. In fact, it was he who'd alerted Sandra that there was a vacancy coming up there. She'd been first in the queue and now was the employment officer at the factory. In charge of future hirings. A sudden thought regarding my present circumstances entered my head. But the bar was noisy and the thought left as quickly as it had entered.

'Count Otto,' said I. 'Hello.'

The count stared down upon me. He was very tall, the count. Always had been. Even when he was small, he was tall. Tall people so often are.

'Gary,' said Count Otto. 'I hear that you've taken employment once more. Tough luck, old fellow. You have my sympathy.'

'I need it more than you know,' I said.

'I think not,' said Count Otto. 'I've heard that you've taken the bulb man's job at the telephone exchange. You really need all the sympathy I have. It's yours; take it with my blessings.'

'I'm in the dog muck,' I said. 'I don't know what to do.'

'You should look on the bright side,' said the count. 'It will soon be Saturday.'

'I think I need a bit more than that. How am I going to get out of this?'

Count Otto shrugged. 'I've no idea at all,' said he. 'If you paid a little more attention to what goes on around you, you'd have noticed that you were the only applicant for that job.'

'The dole office sent me,' I said.

'But you should have *known*. Everyone in Brentford knows about *that* job. You don't inhabit the real world, do you, Gary? You dream your way through life. It's not quite real to you, is it?'

'It suddenly seems very real,' I said. And suddenly it did.

'That's the way with life. It has a habit of catching up with you.'

'So, tell me, what should I do?'

'Learn,' said the count. 'That would be my advice. Knowledge is power, as the old cliché goes. The more you learn, the more you know. The more you know, the more options will open up for you.'

'So I should take an Open University course, or something?'

'Or learn a second language.'

'Sandra said that.'

'Well, she would. We were talking about you today at the factory. I was saying what tough luck it was that you'd taken the job. She just kept laughing.'

'I think I'll smack her when I get home.'

'Can I come and watch? I love that sort of thing. Back in the old country, you could smack servants whenever you wanted. And torture them, of course, and pull all their clothes off and put them out in the snow.'

'Why?' I asked.

'Because you *could*,' said the count. 'And if you *can*, then you *will*. That's also the way with life. But only with the life of the very privileged.'

'Buy me a drink,' I said. 'I've finished mine and I'm really short of money. I'll pay you back at the weekend.'

'Certainly,' said the count and he went up and bought me a drink.

'I'll tell you this,' he said, on his return. 'You want to have a good old think about this job of yours. What it's all about and things like that.'

'I don't understand what you mean,' I said.

'Well,' said the count, 'it seems like a very strange job to me. Switching a bulb off whenever it comes on.'

'It's a stupid job,' I said.

'Oh yes,' said the count, nodding. 'But most jobs are ultimately stupid. There are certain jobs — say, butcher, or baker — that make sense. They're necessary jobs. People need butchers and bakers. But what about all those other jobs, like quantity surveyors, say. Does the world really need quantity surveyors? What does a quantity surveyor do anyway? Does he look at things and say, "Oh, there's a lot of *that*. But there's not too much of *that*."'

I shrugged my shoulders.

'There's thousands of jobs like that,' said the count. 'They have titles but they don't really have meaning. If they didn't exist, the world wouldn't be any different, except that the people who did those jobs would now be out of work. All these jobs just exist to keep people employed. They're not real jobs. Your job isn't a real job.'

I looked up at Count Otto. 'Thanks a lot,' I said.

'My pleasure,' said the count.

'No,' said I. 'I was being sarcastic. Do you think that I don't know that? Do you think that everyone on Earth doesn't know that? People are given jobs so that they can earn money, which they then *spend*. That is the point of giving people jobs, so they can earn money that they can then *spend* . . . on *things* . . . on things that have to be manufactured. Thereby giving work to people in manufacturing industries. I could go on and on about this. But we both know how it works. Everyone really knows how it works, although they won't own up to it.'

'So your job is a stupid job, but it has to be done. Therefore accept it and make the best of it and stop complaining.'

'No,' said I. 'No.'

'Well, there's nothing you can do about it.'

'Do you want a bet?'

'I'm a count,' said the count. 'Counts never bet. We just win by default.'

'Well, I *am* going to do something about this,' I said. 'All right, I *do* know what I'm like. Well, I think I do. I *do* dream my way through life and never really pay much attention to reality. But OK, I'm stuck in this one, but I mean to get out. *And* I mean to change things. I don't know how I'll do it, but I will. This has been a special day for me. I didn't know that it was going to be special. But it is. It has determined me upon a mission. Yes, it has. By golly, yes.'

'And what exactly is this mission?' asked the count.

'To change things,' I said. 'To change everything.'

'Oh dear,' said Count Otto. 'And you having drunk but a pint and a half. Chaps are usually at least seven pints in before they start talking nonsense like this. Back in the old country, talk like this would go on into the night. And they'd always end up with someone saying, "I'm going to change everything. I've had enough of all this."'

'And did anyone?' I asked. 'Change things?'

'No,' said the count. 'Of course not. They'd end up sitting in the courtyard outside the alehouse waiting for the sun to come up and we'd all be hiding inside in the shadows. And up would come the sun and *whoosh-woof-zap* and flash: another vampire gone.'

'Eh?' I said. 'What?'

'Only joking,' said the count. 'Or *am* I?'

I chewed upon my upper lip. '*I'll* change things,' I said. 'You wait and see.'

'I'll wait,' said the count. 'But indoors in the shadows, if you don't mind.'

I let the count buy me further drinks and I enjoyed the band. Quilten Balthazar was great. And what can you say about Zagger To Mega Therion? That master bladesman had paid his dues. But I was thinking. Thinking and plotting and planning.

All right. I know how this works. You don't have to tell me. People only struggle against oppression when they actually *are* oppressed. If they're not actually oppressed themselves, then they only pay lip service to the struggle against other people's oppression. They like to think of themselves as caring individuals. But they don't actually really *do* anything. They might contribute a little money to some worthy cause or other, but they don't actually *do*.

Funny thing is, now I'm looking back at all this and telling this tale, what I didn't know was that my struggle against oppression was actually going to further the cause of My Struggle, *Mein Kampf*, as it were. I suppose that, somewhere down the line, I had actually lost myself. I'd been fascinated by death and the whole idea of death and what might be beyond it. And I had tried to reanimate Mr Penrose, my all-time, then and now, favourite writer, but where had my youthful ideas and interests gone? Into nothing and nowhere. I'd lost my *true* self. But this business at the telephone exchange had actually woken me up from my slumber. Life had hit me right in the face. And life and death being brothers and all that, it all fell together.

But I didn't know that then. I didn't know that this was synchronicity. That I was in the right place at the right time and that my struggle against oppression was going to bucket me into the position that it did. In fact, that it would prove that my life had a specific purpose. And that the purpose it had was linked to what I was as a child, which had led – the child being the father of the man, and all that kind of guff – into what I would become as an adult.

Phew! Are you getting any of this?

Perhaps I have become drunk. I was certainly drunk when I left the Shrunken Head and stumbled home with only the prospect of the good hiding I meant to give Sandra as a distant light to steer my stumblings towards.

But I had really, truly, actually, if drunkenly, found a purpose in life for myself. And I would begin on my quest the very next day.

And I would triumph.

And not just for myself.

But for the good of all.

I'd change things for ever.

I would.

I really would.

12

I suppose I must have dozed off.

Although not on the job.

I never once dozed off on the job.

It would have been more than my job was worth to ever doze off on the job. An unmanned bulb is an accident waiting to happen, as Mr Holland used to say. And he knew what he was talking about. That man knew his business when it came to bulbs.

But perhaps I had dozed off at some time or other. Because the next time I was truly, fully aware, I was drinking again with Count Otto, and he was asking me how things were going at the telephone exchange.

'How are things going at the telephone exchange?' he asked.

'So, so,' I said. 'I had fourteen flash-ups today. I have my reaction time down to point-three of a second. Point-two-two is my fastest ever, but that was in the first summer when there was a double flash. That's quite a rarity, two flash-ups in less than an hour. I kind of sensed it that time: I knew the second one was coming. A good bulbsman has a sixth sense. You develop it. Only last week I—'

'Excuse me,' said Count Otto. 'I need to go and count some tiles in the men's room.' And then he departed and was gone.

'He's a weirdo,' I said to Sandra, because she had come out with me for a drink. For some specific reason that quite escaped me at the time. 'He's always going off to the bog when I'm having a chat.'

'Perhaps it's because you're so boring nowadays,' said Sandra.

'Yeah, right,' I replied.

'I am,' said Sandra. 'Your job is all you ever talk about. That exciting double flash in the summer of 'seventy-one. How you've installed your own bulb tester and how through yoga you can hold your bladder for a twelve-hour stretch without even a dribble coming out of your winkie.'

'Don't be crude,' I said to Sandra.

'You've lost your edge,' said my spouse. 'You're no fun any more.'

'*I'm* no fun? How dare you! If you took a little more interest in my work . . .'

'Ha,' went Sandra. 'Ha ha ha. Switching a fugging bulb off all day long! How interesting can that be?'

'See what I mean?' I said to her. 'That's all *you* know about the job. I don't switch it off *all day long*. Only at the specific moment when it flashes. Not before and not afterwards. Well, obviously afterwards, but you can hardly tell, my timing is so precise.'

'Just listen to yourself.' Sandra was drinking a Cuba Library, which was the popular drink of the day. It was a cocktail — something to do with cigars and library books. Or it might have been gazelles and bicycle pumps, for all I cared. Sandra supped at it and went right on talking at me. 'When you came home after that first day at the exchange you were dripping with piss and ranting like a loon. Then you went off for a drink and came back pissed and ranting like a drunken loon, saying how you were going to strike a blow for the workers and change everything. Do you remember that?'

'Of course I remember that,' I said, for I vaguely remembered that.

'Now it's five years later,' Sandra emptied her drink down her throat and handed me the glass, 'and have you struck a blow for the workers?'

'Well,' I said.

'No,' said Sandra. 'You haven't. The second day in, you took sandwiches and a bucket and another book to read.'

'God,' I said. 'Don't tell me about it.'

'Why?' asked Sandra.

'It's so embarrassing,' I said. 'How could I have been so irresponsible? Taking a book into the bulb booth? I could have been so engrossed in the book that I mightn't have noticed the bulb go on. Imagine that! It doesn't bear thinking about.'

'It certainly doesn't,' said Sandra, pointing pointedly towards her empty glass. 'So I shan't think about it at all.'

'Good,' I told her. 'Don't.'

'Drink,' said Sandra.

So I drank.

'No,' said Sandra. 'I meant drink for me.'

'To *you*, then,' I said, raising my glass and drinking again.

'*No!*' said Sandra. 'Not drink *to* me. Buy me another fugging drink, you stupid twonk!'

'Language!' I told her. 'Language, please.'

'Five years,' said Sandra, spitting somewhat as she spoke. 'Five fugging years. What happened to you? Where did your spirit go?'

'I would have thought you'd have been pleased that I was now in full-time regular employment. A job for life. You wanted security, didn't you? Wasn't that why your brother so diligently made sure that I got there in the first place?'

'Oh yes,' said Sandra. 'I wanted security. There's nothing wrong with security. But I'd also like a holiday once in a while. You know, a week away at a caravan park in Camber Sands. That's not much to ask, is it?'

'A bulbsman is always on the job,' I said to Sandra. 'A bulbsman has no time for holidays.'

'Unbelievable,' said Sandra, shaking her head in what looked for all the world to be dismay. 'You are unbelievable.'

'Thank you very much,' I said and I made my way to the bar.

There wasn't any pushing and shoving to get served in this bar. But then, this wasn't the Shrunken Head. Eric had sold the Shrunken Head to an entrepreneur called Sandy and had moved himself away to a quieter bar.

This quieter bar. The Golden Dawn, on the corner of Abbadon Street. It was mostly a fogeys' hangout. Old boys who played in the bowls league. Regular, dependable fellows, many of whom had worked in the telephone exchange. And put in years of sterling service. Although none of them appeared to be ex-bulbsmen.

I liked the Golden Dawn. It was a good place to come and relax after a stressful day in the booth. Like the one I'd had the Thursday before last when there were twenty-two flashes. Four within a single hour, which was almost an all-time record. The record being six, back in the autumn of 'seventy-four, on the tenth of September, a Tuesday. Three-fifteen to four-fifteen. I keep a record, you see. Study it in the evenings, actually, just to check the patterns. They crop up at occasional intervals. You can be right on the alert then. Not that I could really be much more on the alert than I am now. That would be impossible.

'Well, well, well, well, well,' said Eric Blaine a.k.a. Kimberlin Malkuth, Lord of a Thousand Suns. 'If it isn't my old comrade the Honourable Valdec Firesword of Alpha Centuri.'

'Yes,' I said to him. 'As it was ten minutes ago, when I came up for the last round.'

'Exactly,' said Eric. 'Which means that this time it's Count Otto's round. But he's hiding out in the toilets again, isn't he?'

'He's counting tiles,' I said. 'That's what counts do, I suppose: count things.'

The landlord rolled his eyes. Which I found most unappealing. And then he shook his head from side to side. 'I see the Lady Fairflower of the Rainbow Mountains is looking particularly radiant tonight,' he observed, casting one of his rolling eyes in his shaking head towards my Sandra.

'Nifty eye-work,' I said, for I appreciate talent. 'But,

160

frankly, the Lady Fairflower has been getting right up my nose of late. I labour away at my place of employment, drag my weary body home and what do I get?'

'A blowjob?' asked the landlord.

'No,' I said. 'Not even a blow-dry. Not that I have long hair any more. I keep mine well trimmed behind the ears and especially across the forehead. A flopping fringe is a bulbsman's enemy. I tried keeping it long and wearing a cap, but I felt that it detracted from the dignity of the job. Hey, by the way, what do you think of these?' I raised my arms to the landlord.

The landlord stared hard and then he said. 'You appear to have tiny roller skates strapped onto your elbows.'

'Yes,' I said. 'But they're not tiny roller skates, they're elbow trolleys. I designed them myself.'

'Very nice,' said the landlord, in a tone that I felt lacked for sincerity. 'What exactly do they do?'

'Give me added speed, of course.' I placed my elbows on the bar counter. 'Take that empty cocktail glass.'

'This one?' said the landlord.

'That one. Hold it up.'

The landlord held it up.

'Now drop it.'

'No,' said the landlord. 'It will break on the counter.'

'No, it won't. Go on, do it. Whenever you want. Don't give me any warning.'

'You pay if it breaks, then.'

'No problem. I—'

But the sneaky barman dropped it as I spoke.

And *Snatch*!

'Impressed?' I asked.

And the landlord clearly was. 'You snatched it right out of the air almost before it had left my hand,' he said.

'I'm a bulbsman,' I said. 'Speed is my middle name.'

The landlord pulled me a pint of Large and knocked up another cocktail for Sandra.

'What is this one called?' I asked.

'In your posh bars up west, this would be called a "Horse's Neck",' said the landlord. 'But as this is a poor neighbourhood, I call it a half of lager-top.'

'Wow,' I said. 'Very exotic.'

'And expensive too. That will be four pounds, seventeen and six.'

I parted with a five-pound note.

The landlord parted with the change.

'I'm sixpence short,' I said to him.

And then he parted with the missing sixpence.

'We live in strange days, Gary,' the landlord said to me.

'Gary?' I said. 'Why are you calling me that?'

'I think I might be losing my powers.'

'What, your powers of True-Naming? Never, surely.'

'I don't know. But once or twice, lately, a new customer has come in and I haven't been able to perceive their true name.'

'More exceptions to the rule, perhaps? Like Count Otto.'

'No, Count Otto is a one-off. But it has been odd and I don't understand it.'

162

'Perhaps they don't have any true names.'

'Everyone has a true name. It's just that most people aren't aware of theirs.'

I shrugged. 'I've never truly understood the concept,' I said. 'In fact, I think you'll find that you are possibly the only man on Earth who really understands the concept.'

'Hardly,' said the landlord. And he laughed. Not in the way that Sandra laughed. He laughed in a lower key. 'There was a travelling man in here last week. A tinker looking for old chairs to mend. And I hailed him as Galaxion Zimmer of the Emerald Light. And he said, "Well met, Kimberlin Malkuth, Lord of a Thousand Suns."'

'He knew *your* True Name?'

'He'd had a revelation, like me, back in the sixties.'

'There was a lot of it about,' I said. 'Although I didn't take any of it. Sold a bit, but didn't use. If you know what I mean and I'm sure that you do.'

'Well, he knew and I knew that he knew. He identified all my regulars correctly. But, as I say, there's been one or two. In fact there's one over there.'

'Over where?' I asked.

'Over there. Fat bloke. I can't perceive his True Name.'

I followed the direction of the landlord's pointing. 'That's Neil,' I said. 'That's Neil Collins. He's in Developmental Services.'

'What the fugg is Developmental Services?'

'At the exchange. Seventeenth floor, office twenty-three. Developmental Services.'

'And how would you know that, penned up in your little booth all day?'

I tapped my nose in the manner known as 'conspiratorial'.

'Sinus problems?' asked the landlord.

'No,' I said. 'Interdepartmental memorandums, files, technical specifications.'

'What about them?' asked the landlord.

'They all go through me,' I said.

'You *eat* them?'

'They go through my office. They're not meant to, but they do. After I'd been at the exchange for about six months, this new bob poked his head round the door of my booth.'

'New bob?' asked the landlord.

'Stop asking all these questions,' I said. 'New bob, new boy . . . He said he was lost and he had confidential files for Mr Holland and where was his office. And I don't know what got into me – high spirits I suppose – but I said, "All confidential files come through me." And they have ever since.'

'And you read this stuff in the firm's time?'

I looked aghast at the landlord. 'Certainly not!' I said. 'I would never be that irresponsible.'

'Oh,' said the landlord. 'Sorry.'

'I take them home and read them,' I said. 'Then I pop them into Mr Holland's in-tray next morning, before he gets in. I'm always early. A good bulbsman is always ready and eager and in his booth on time.'

'Unbelievable,' said the landlord.

'Thank you very much,' I said.

'So this Neil Collins is in Developmental Services. And what do they do, then?'

I shook my head towards the landlord. 'You're expecting me to divulge confidential material to a Humburg?'

'I never wear a Homburg,' said the landlord, feeling at his hatless head.

'Not Homburg: Humburg. It's a term we use for plebs, non-company people, folk who don't work in the exchange.'

'Twonk!' said the landlord.

'No, Humburg!' I corrected him. 'So I'm not likely to divulge that kind of information to a Humburg, am I?'

The landlord grinned at me. Well, he didn't so much grin as leer. 'You signed the Official Secrets Act, didn't you?' he said.

'Yes, I did, and I'm proud of it.' And I *was*. *Now*.

'Yet you've already given me classified information by identifying Neil Collins as being in Developmental Services. If I grassed you up, you'd go to prison.'

A terrible sweat broke out on my brow. 'You wouldn't do that, would you?'

'No,' said the landlord. 'Of course I wouldn't.'

'Phew,' I said. And I meant it.

'Not as long as you tell me *all* about Developmental Services.'

'But that's more than my job's worth.'

'It's exactly what your job's worth. You bought into the company ethic, *Gary*. I don't know why. Because you didn't really have the stuff in you to rebel against it, would be my bet. But you're a company man now,

165

and if I grassed you up you'd lose your job and be off to prison.'

'No,' I said. 'Don't do it. If I lost my job, anyone could get it. The first man in the queue. Harry maybe.'

'I don't think Harry would fall for *that*. And, anyway, Harry runs a world-famous night club now.'

'Really?' I said. 'I didn't know that. Perhaps he told Sandra, but she didn't mention it. He got his motorbike and he got the job. Incredible.'

'He had to lie about his name, though.'

'Why?'

'They only wanted applicants called Peter. So he said his name was Peter. So he got the job and now he runs the world-famous night club.'

'What's it called?' I asked.

'——————'* said the landlord.

'Never heard of it,' I said. 'But listen, don't turn me in. I'll tell you everything you want to know.'

'Fine,' said the landlord. 'So, Developmental Services, what do they do?'

'They develop services,' I said.

'I'm reaching for the phone,' said the landlord.

'No, that's what they do. They work on new projects to improve facilities.'

'So what are they working on now? What is this Neil Collins, who has no True Name, working on?'

---

*Obviously the answer is Stringfellows. But the essence of really good comedy is never to say the obvious; instead rely on the reader sharing the same cultural references. There's an art to this kind of thing. So I'm not going to mention the name.

I shrugged. 'I don't know for sure,' I said. 'It's something called FLATLINE.'

'In capital letters,' said the landlord. 'It must be something important, then.'

'I don't know exactly what it is, but it's something pretty big.'

'So how much do you know about it?'

I scratched at *my* head, which, like the landlord's, was also hatless. I've never taken to a hat myself – you get hat-hair, which is frankly embarrassing. Hats are for fogeys, in my opinion. Most of the patrons of the Golden Dawn were hat-wearers. You only really wear a hat if you're a fogey. Or, of course, if you have a problem about your baldness. Of course Lazlo Woodbine wasn't bald, and he never had hat-hair. He wore a fedora, probably with a raised crown, although that was never mentioned in any of the novels. So, where was I?

'It's something pretty big,' I said once more, to get my bearings.

'So how much do you know about it?'

I shook my hatless head. 'I know it's called FLATLINE,' I said.

'Twonk!' said the landlord. 'But I'll say this to you. I'm suspicious, me, and when things don't smell right I don't like the smell of them. You find out about this FLATLINE and you tell me about it, or I *will* grass you up, understand?'

I nodded now with my hatless head. 'I understand,' I said.

'Right,' said the landlord. 'Now take your drinks and go back to your woman. You're supposed to be celebrating your wedding anniversary.'

'Oh yeah,' I said. '*That's* what I came out with Sandra for.'

I took the drinks back to the table.

'Didn't you get one for Otto?' asked Sandra.

'No. Stuff him,' I said.

'Strong words,' said Sandra, laughing.

'Shut up,' I told her, 'and drink your cocktail.'

Sandra took a sip. 'What is this one called?' she asked.

'It's Ruby Tuesday.'

'Very nice too. Very fruity.'

I sighed and rolled my own eyes a bit. 'I get tired,' I said. 'You know that? I get tired.'

'It's all that finger-work.' Sandra mimed switch-flicking. And mimed it very badly too. There's an art to switch-flicking: you don't just flick a switch and you certainly don't do it the way Sandra did it, with thumb and forefinger making an O and the hand going up and down in a sort of stabbing motion. 'You've got Repetitive Strain Injury!' And she laughed again. 'An injury that if caused in the workplace, can enable you to sue the company and get lots of money.'

'Ridiculous,' I said. 'Industrial injuries go with the job. If you can't stand the heat don't go so near the hairdryer.'

'You can sneer,' said Sandra, 'but in *my* new job—'

'New job?' I said. '*New job?* What new job?'

'*My* new job. Count Otto got it for me. He's a solicitor now. And I'm a barrister.'

'I never knew that. You never told me.'

'We don't talk any more,' said Sandra.

'We do. We talk all the time.'

'No,' said Sandra. '*You* talk. I am expected to listen.'

'That's how heterosexual relationships work,' I explained. 'Men talk, women listen. When it's the other way round it ends in divorce.'

'And that's your take on marriage, is it?'

I shrugged. 'Our marriage doesn't work very well, does it?' I said.

'No,' said Sandra. 'It doesn't.'

'And that's because you don't listen when I talk. You should try harder. It would work far better then.'

'I'm going on holiday with Otto next week,' said Sandra.

'What?' I said. '*What?*'

'To Camber Sands. We've booked a caravan.'

'But that's outrageous. You can't do *that*!'

'And why not?'

'Because who's going to make my sandwiches?'

'I'll leave you a week's supply in the freezer.'

'Well, that's all right, then. Will you send me a postcard?'

'I shouldn't think so,' said Sandra.

'Thank God for that,' I said.

'What?'

'Well, I wouldn't have time to read it. This is my golden opportunity to put in some overtime. I'm certain that Barry who does the seven p.m. to seven a.m. shift isn't as quick on the switch as he might be. I can sit with him and give him some pointers.'

'Yes,' said Sandra. 'Why don't you do that?'

'I will,' I said, 'I will.'

Count Otto returned from the toilet.

'Finished counting?' I asked. 'How many were there this time?'

'Same as last time,' said Otto. 'Which is comforting, when you think about it.'

'That is *so* true,' I said. 'So very, very true.'

Otto took up what was left of his pint and supped upon it.

'I was just telling Gary that you and I are going off on holiday next week,' said Sandra.

Otto choked upon his pint.

'Easy,' I said, patting him on the back. 'Are you all right? Did it go down the wrong way?'

'Just a bit,' said the count.

'I was saying to Sandra,' said I, 'not to send me a postcard. I wouldn't have time to read it.'

'Oh,' said Count Otto, glancing over at Sandra, who seemed, if I wasn't mistaken, to be winking in his direction. 'Well, OK, then. I'll keep her entertained. Try and find her something to fill the moments when she would otherwise have been writing you postcards.' And the count squeezed at his groin region.

'Thanks a lot,' I said to the count. 'Would you care for another pint? Seeing as how you're being so kind as to take Sandra on holiday while I'll be busy at work.'

'Yes, please,' said Count Otto. 'A whisky chaser would be nice too.'

'Done,' said I. 'No problem.'

I returned to the bar. 'Same again,' said I. 'Although different for Sandra and one for the count.'

'Phew,' said the landlord. 'You do have money to splash about. I've got fillings from the drip trays here that will pass for a Tequila Sunrise and set you back nearly three quid.'

'In for a penny,' said I.

'Quite so,' said the landlord, emptying the drip tray into a used glass. 'Oh and, Gary . . .'

'Yes,' I said.

'I need to know. It matters to me.'

'Need to know what?' I asked. For I didn't know what he wanted to know.

'About FLATLINE in the capital letters. I need to know what it's all about.'

'Well,' I said, as I accepted the drinks I was given and paid the price that I had to pay for them, 'I'll do what I can. But I do have a lot on my mind at present. I'm going to be doing some overtime. I'll be busy.'

'I need to know,' said the landlord. 'I'm not wrong about the True Names. Even though I thought I was wrong, that travelling man proved to me that I wasn't. This is important, if only to me. Whatever you find out will be between the two of us. You know the old saying, "you scratch my back, I don't stab yours". OK?' And the landlord made a very vicious face.

'OK,' I said. 'It's a done deal. I'll find out, I promise. But I *do* have a lot on my mind.'

I did.

And as I took the drinks back to the table I did a lot of thinking. And I do mean *a lot*. I thought about myself. And what I'd become. And who was the *real* me who was me now. And I thought about Barry who did the night shift and whether I should make him a pair of elbow trolleys.

And I thought about the landlord and his True

Names and how he couldn't divine the True Name of Neil Collins and I thought about FLATLINE and whatever FLATLINE might actually be, it being in capital letters and everything.

And I thought about the landlord grassing me up and me being dragged away to prison.

And I thought about Sandra and regretted that *I* hadn't been able to take her on holiday because holidays weren't written into the Official Secrets Act.

And I thought about Count Otto. And what a good friend to Sandra and me he had been for years.

And I thought about what a shame it was that I would be forced to swoop upon him one night as he lay asleep in his bed. Bind him, gag him and slowly torture him to death.

Because, after all, he was sexing my wife!

And company man and sell-out boy and wimp and twonk that Sandra might have thought I was.

I certainly wasn't having *that*!

13

It's funny how things work out, isn't it?

If Sandra hadn't gone off on that caravan holiday with Count Otto Black, I would never have put in that bit of overtime and found out just how useless Barry was at the bulb.

It was honestly as if he didn't care.

Can you believe *that*?

I was standing there, talking to him about switch technique and what I called 'alert-finger' and the bulb flashed. And Barry just reached out across the table, slow as you please, as if he was answering a telephone, and flapped his hand down on the switch.

I was flabbergasted.

I was stunned.

Stunned, appalled, *and* flabbergasted.

All at once.

'That is *so* bad,' I said to Barry. 'That is *so* bad. I can't believe how so, so, so, so, so, so bad that is.'

'It's just a bulb,' said Barry. 'Just a fugging bulb.'

'Curb that language in this booth,' I said to Barry. 'This is not *just a bulb*.'

'So, what is it, then, *a way of life*?'

'It's a job for life. And I've worked at it for five long years of mine. And it's a responsibility. A *big* responsibility. It's *your* responsibility when you're on your shift.'

'Get a life,' said Barry. 'Get real.'

'Oh dear, oh dear, oh dear,' I said. 'I spy anarchism here. I spy subversion. I smell recidivism.'

'You smell wee-wee,' said Barry. 'And it's yours.'

'No wee-wee on me,' I said. 'Sniff my groin if you have any doubts.'

'Smells of teen spirit,' said Barry. Whatever *that* meant.

'You'll have to apply yourself more to the job,' I told him.

'Barking,' said Barry. 'Barking mad.'

'I've never been to Barking,' I told him. 'I can get mad about Penge, perhaps. But never Barking.'

'Fugg off home,' said Barry. 'I want to read my book.'

'You can't read a book here. You have to be ever alert.'

'I have to switch a stupid bulb off when it comes on. I'll read my book until it does.'

I opened my mouth very wide but no words at all came out of it.

'I'm reading *Passport to Peril*,' said Barry. 'It's a Lazlo Woodbine thriller. Not that you'd know about *that*, I'm sure.'

'On the contrary, young man,' I said. 'I've read every Lazlo Woodbine thriller at least a dozen times. I know the lot. By heart, most, if not all, of them.'

'Yeah, right,' said Barry.

'Yeah, right indeed.'

'Oh, so if I was to ask you a question about Lazlo Woodbine, you'd know the answer, would you?'

'I applied to go on *Mastermind* answering questions on the detective novels of P. P. Penrose as my specialist subject. I didn't get picked, though.'

'All right, I'll ask you questions.'

'Not here,' I said. 'The bulb might flash.'

'Fugg the bulb,' said Barry. 'If it flashes, I'll switch it off.'

'*I'll* switch it off,' I said. 'You're useless at it. I'm going to see if there are drugs I can take that will allow me to stay awake twenty-four hours a day so I can do your shift too.'

'What drug did Lazlo Woodbine take in *Waiting for Godalming* that allowed him to stay awake for twenty-four hours a day for a whole week?'

'Trick question,' I said. 'No drug at all: he did it by willpower. He had to stay awake because if he fell asleep the Holy Guardian Sprout inside his head would have read his mind and given away the trick ending of the book to the readers. *Waiting for Godalming* was a Post-Modernist Lazlo Woodbine thriller – one of the weakest in my opinion.'

'Good answer,' said Barry. 'But it might have been a lucky one. All right, I'll ask you another. In *Death Carries a Pink Umbrella*—'

'Set in Berlin,' I said.

'East or West?'

'Both,' I said. 'And also Antwerp, where Laz identifies Molly Behemoth by her "distinctive birthmark and Egyptian walk" . . .'

'Yes, OK. But who "ate his way to freedom" and never used the word "nigger" when "Frenchman" would do?'

'Callbeck the miner's son, who sold his soul to Harrods in a bet with a Rasputin Impersonator who turned out to be one of the Beverley Sisters.'

'Burger me backwards over my aunty's handbag,' said Barry. 'You sure know your Lazlo Woodbine thrillers.'

'Buddy,' I said, 'in my business, knowing your Lazlo Woodbine thrillers can mean the difference between painting the town red and wearing a pair of red pants, if you know what I mean and I'm sure that you do.'*

'I know where you're coming from,' said Barry. 'Although that was a pretty poor imitation.'

'No one can do it like Penrose could,' I said.

'Too true, brother,' said Barry. 'Although I never had time for his Adam Earth science-fiction books. They were rubbish, in my opinion.'

'True,' I said. And I sighed. 'Listen,' I said, continuing. 'It's really wonderful to meet another fan of the great man, but you really are useless at this job. Perhaps you should just quit and let a more committed individual take over.'

'There's no quitting, is there?' said Barry. 'It's off to prison for the quitter. I foolishly signed the Official Secrets Act.'

'Ah, yes,' I said. 'I signed that too.'

'Which is why you're such a twonk, I suppose. You gave up, sold out and gave in.'

---

*This will mean absolutely nothing to anyone who has never read a Lazlo Woodbine thriller. But who are these people? Anyone?

I didn't like to talk about this stuff. It was personal. 'All right,' I said. 'I thought about rebelling. I really did. I came here on my second day with every intention of smashing the bulb or pulling it out and sitting here with my arms folded to see what would happen.'

'And so why didn't you?'

'I don't know,' I said. 'I was going to do it. I got drunk the night before and determined utterly that I'd do it. Then I got up all hung-overed and came in here and sat down in that chair. Which now has my special sprung cushion on it, you'll notice, and I *was* going to rebel. But I had such a hangover and I thought I'd rebel later and the light flashed and I switched it off. And I thought, "Stuff it. I'll just not switch it off next time." But then it flashed on again and I was all on my own and I thought, "OK, I'll just switch it off the one time more. But this will be the last time."

'And then I thought about my wife Sandra and how she was really ticked off about how I was always out of work. And Harry, her brother, who said about saving up for a motorbike so you could be first at interviews for really good jobs, and I thought, "OK, I'll just stick it out for a week. Or maybe two. Then find some way of getting out." But then it sort of grew on me and I started taking pride in my job. Because I was in it and Mr Holland kept impressing upon me how important it was. Although I've never been able to find out why. But he said it was. And, OK, there was the threat — that was always there in the back of my mind — foul up and you're off to prison.

'But somehow it was more than that, so I kept doing

177

it and now, OK, it's *me*. It's what I am; it's all I've got. There's some bloke sexing my wife. This is all I've got.'

Barry looked up at me. 'I'm sorry, man,' he said. 'You're OK. You know that. You're OK.'

'I'm not OK,' I said. 'I'm all messed up. Once upon a time I was OK. I knew who I was. But I don't know any more. I'm an adult. Adults don't know who they really are. Only children know who they really are. And nobody listens to children.'

'You're so right,' said Barry, 'you're so right.'

Then the bulb flashed on and, without even thinking, I switched it off again.

'I hate this,' said Barry. 'I want to be a musician, like Jeff Beck. But I'm stuck here and I'm really screwed up by it.'

'I'd be prepared to put in a couple of extra hours if it would help you out,' I said. 'I could work up to eight or eight-thirty.'

'Thanks, man,' said Barry. 'But it really isn't the point, is it? This isn't right, is it? We're stuck in something we don't understand. I mean, why does the fugging bulb flash on in the first place?'

I laughed.

'You're laughing,' said Barry. 'Why are you laughing?'

'Because it's a joke. You're asking *me* why the bulb flashes on. Do I look like a technical engineer?'

'And that's funny, is it?'

'No,' I said. 'I suppose it isn't.'

'So why *does* the bulb flash on?'

I shrugged. 'Because it *can*, I suppose.'

178

'And why must we switch it off when it does?'

'Because it's what we do, I suppose.'

'It's a sad indictment on society, man.'

I nodded thoughtfully. 'A bloke from Transylvania is sexing my wife.'

'Count Otto Black,' said Barry.

'You know him?'

'Well, he's the only bloke from Transylvania who lives around here.'

'I'm going to kill him,' I said. 'That's off the record, by the way. Just between the two of us.'

'Big kudos to you, then.'

'Thanks. I also have to find out about FLATLINE. Ever heard of that?'

'Bits and pieces,' said Barry. 'Blokes from Developmental Services come off shift at eleven. They often hang about outside the booth, having a fag. I hear them talking.'

'And what do you hear them talking about?'

'Usual stuff: football, women, cars.'

'FLATLINE?' I said.

'Yeah, they talk about it, but it all sounds like a load of old bollards to me.'

'Go on,' I said. 'Tell me what they say.'

Barry eyed me queerly. But as I was mostly straight nowadays and didn't fancy him anyway, I said, 'I think they're up to something dodgy up there on the seventeenth floor.'

'Something stone bonkers,' said Barry. 'I mean, communicating with beings from outer space. What's that all about, eh?'

'Eh?' I said in an 'eh' that was louder than his.

'Something to do with us not doing the thinking with our brains, but our brains being receivers and transmitters. Or some such rubbish. They've supposedly got some kind of direct communications computer, or something, up there that lets them talk to aliens.'

'That's incredible,' I said, and a distant bell began to ring in my head. Something from long, long ago. And then I remembered: that afternoon in the restricted section of the Memorial Library, the conversation between the two men from the Ministry that had no name, or, rather, did have but it was a secret.

'Are you OK?' asked Barry. 'You look as if a distant bell is ringing in your head.'

'I'm OK,' I said. 'But you *are* sure about this?'

'My ear goes right against the door when they're out there,' said Barry. 'It passes a bit of time and I'm nothing if not nosy. But none of them seem to agree about what's really going on up there and why it is.'

'I wonder,' I said and I glanced towards the ceiling.

'What do you wonder?' Barry asked. 'Do you wonder whether the ceiling could do with a lick of paint? Well, it could, and I might even do it myself.'

'Don't you even think about it. What if the bulb was to flash?'

'It wouldn't,' said Barry.

'It might. You don't know.'

'I do know. It wouldn't.'

'And how could you know?'

'Because I'd take it out,' said Barry. 'Like I do when I slip off to the toilet.'

I clutched at my heart. Well, you would! *I* would. And I did.

'You take the bulb *out*?' My voice was a choking whisper.

'Sometimes,' said Barry. 'I leave it out if I'm having a bit of a kip, or something.'

'You . . . you . . .' My voice kind of trailed off.

'Nothing ever happens,' said Barry. 'No alarms ever go off. There aren't any explosions. No men in riot gear rush in. Here, I'll show you, I'll take it out now. I was going to take it out anyway, so I could pop upstairs to the refectory and phone my girlfriend.'

I began to sway back and forwards and the world began to go dark at the edges.

'Easy,' said Barry. 'Are you all right? Do you want to sit down?'

'Yes, please.' And he guided me onto the chair.

'Do you want a glass of water? I can get you one from the refectory.'

'No!' I said. 'No. You can't leave the booth.'

'I'll take the bulb – no problem.'

'Oh my God!' And I buried my head in my hands.

'You've got it bad, man,' said Barry, patting my shoulder to comfort me. 'You've let the bustards grind you down. I signed the Official Secrets Act, so the bustards have me by the bollards too. But just because they have my bollards, it doesn't mean that I have to let them squeeze them. If you know what I mean, and I'm sure that you do.'

'You take the bulb out.' I whispered the words. 'You actually take the bulb out.'

'Don't tell me you've never done it?'

'Never,' I said, frantically shaking my head.

'Well, you should. It gives you a sense of power.

181

Try it now. Go on, take it out. See what it feels like.'

'No,' I said, shaking my head even more frantically. 'I'd never do such a dreadful thing.'

I looked up at Barry and he grinned down at me. His hand reached out towards the bulb.

'Don't,' I told him. 'Don't.'

'OK,' said Barry. 'I won't if it upsets you so much and clearly it does. But I'll tell you something about this bulb that I'll bet you don't know.'

'That shouldn't be hard,' I said. 'As I don't know anything at all about it, except that it has to be switched off.'

'And you've sat in this booth for five years and you've never wondered?'

'Of course I've wondered. And I've asked, but no one will tell me.'

'And you've never thought of finding out for yourself?'

I sighed. 'Of course I have. But how could I?'

'You could follow the wire and see where it goes.'

'Don't be funny,' I said. 'It goes down into the floor. It could go anywhere from there.'

'Oh, it does,' said Barry. 'And yes, I understand, really, I suppose: you do the day shift, so you couldn't up the floorboards and take a look, then trace the wire up the corridor and into the lift shaft and—'

'What?' I said. 'What?'

'It's taken me months,' said Barry. 'But *I've* traced it, a yard at a time. I know where the wire goes.'

Now I have to confess that I was shaking all over by now, not just my head. I really was. Whether it was anticipation, I don't know. Perhaps it was something more than that. Remember I mentioned in a previous chapter what it might be like for a believer in Christianity if he or she was offered absolute proof that there was no afterlife? Well, it was something like that. I *did* want to know where the wire went, but also I *didn't*! Life can be such a complicated business at times. Can't it?

'It goes up . . .'

'No!' I said to Barry. 'I don't want to know.'

'You do, you know, although you don't know it yet.'

'I don't think that makes sense, but I really don't want to know.'

'Well,' said Barry, 'I can understand that too. If the bulb was simply connected to some random number indicator computer thing and the whole job really is a complete waste of time simply to keep employment figures stable, you've wasted five years of your life. Haven't you?'

I didn't want to nod, so I didn't.

'Well, it isn't *that*,' said Barry. 'The wire goes to a definite place.'

I wiped my hands across my brow, which had a fine sweat on. And slowly, very slowly, I said, 'All right, then, where does it go?'

'Upstairs,' said Barry. 'It goes upstairs. Upstairs to the seventeenth floor.'

'The seventeenth floor?' I said that slowly too.

'The seventeenth floor,' said Barry. 'To Developmental Services.'

14

The evening after I'd had that conversation with Barry, I was wide awake and ready for action. And I was wearing a pretty nifty disguise.

Lazlo Woodbine was a master of disguise. He possessed, amongst other things, a tweed jacket, which when worn without his trademark fedora and trenchcoat literally transformed him into the very personification of a newspaper reporter. I did not think that particular disguise would be suitable for what I had to do, which was to infiltrate Developmental Services, so I chose another, which was.

I wore a white coat.

I confess that the white coat idea wasn't mine. The idea came originally from a friend whom I'd known in my teenage years. A chap called Mick Strange. Mick came up with this brilliant scam for getting into anywhere. By getting in, I mean getting into events, or into virtually anywhere that you would otherwise have to queue up and pay to get into.

The scam was simplicity itself and although nowadays it is attempted (with minimal results) by many, he thought of it first. In order to get in, to virtually anywhere and everything, all you had to do was put on a white coat and carry a large light bulb.

I saw him do it at Battersea funfair and also at Olympia when Pink Floyd played there. He simply walked in, wearing his white coat and carrying his big light bulb. He looked official. He looked like an electrician. He got in. QED. End of story.

I arrived back at the telephone exchange at nine of that evening and clocked on for my overtime. I went into the bulb booth, woke up Barry, who was already having a kip, told him to remain alert, changed into my white coat, which I had brought in stuffed down my trouser leg, and took up my light bulb, which I had secreted in my underpants, and which had got me several admiring glances from young women on the bus. Barry didn't ask me what I was doing. Barry didn't care. I asked him to wish me luck, though, and, very kindly, he did.

'Good luck,' said Barry.

'Thank you,' I said. 'Very kind.'

And then I went off down the corridor and got into the lift.

Now, OK, I confess, I had a sweat on. I had to keep wiping my forehead. And I was upset by this. As a child I had been brave. A very brave boy indeed. But it seemed that over the years, as Sandra had said, I'd lost it. Lost myself. But I was now determined to get myself back. And definitely do it this time. Not like when I'd made that drunken promise to change the world and liberate the slaves of the system.

And I'll tell you this, when that little bell rang and

the light flashed in the number 17 button and the lift doors opened, I was *almost* brave again.

Almost.

Nearly almost.

I straightened the lapels on my white coat and I held my light bulb high and I marched along the corridor, noting that this was a somewhat swisher and better-appointed corridor than the one seventeen floors beneath that led to my bulb booth. But I walked tall and true and I marched, I fairly marched, towards room 23.

And when I got to it, I didn't knock. I opened the door and I walked right in. And I didn't half get a surprise.

Room 23 was a *very* big room. And when I say *big* I mean *big*. It wasn't so much a room as an entire operations centre. It was vast. And it was high, too. I figured that they must have knocked out the ceilings and floors of the eighteenth and nineteenth floors too to accommodate all this equipment and all these walkways and gantries and stairways that all these men in white coats who were carrying light bulbs were walking along and up and down and all around and about.

I fairly smiled.

And then I joined them.

And then a man with a white coat who didn't carry a light bulb but instead carried a clipboard (which singled him out as a 'technician') stopped me.

'And where do you think you're going?' he asked.

'I'm not quite sure,' I said.

'I thought so,' said the technician. 'Let's have a look at that bulb.'

I held up my bulb for his inspection.

'That's an XP103,' he said. 'North end of the Mother Board, gantry five, level four, row ten.'

I looked at him.

'Hurry, then,' he said. 'A missing bulb is an accident waiting to happen.'

'Indeed,' I said. 'North end, you said.'

'Gantry five, level four, row ten. Hurry along.'

So I hurried along. And it did have to be said that when it came to bulbs, the lads in Developmental Services had the market cornered. I had never seen so many bulbs all in one place at one time ever before in my life.* One entire wall of this vast department was all bulbs, so it seemed. Thousands and thousands of them, all flashing on and off and some just flickering in between.

I felt almost sick at the sight of them. Having had only the one to deal with myself, this was all very much too much. A bulbsman's nightmare. I'd had dreams like this myself.

'Hurry,' said the technician once more, for I had paused in my hurrying.

I hurried along gantries and up stairways until I was out of the sight of that technician and then I stopped and took stock. What the fugging Hull was all this? What was a Mother Board? What did all these bulbs do? I almost asked a fellow white-coater. Almost. But not quite. I knew what the answer would be: 'Don't ask me. Do I look like a Grade A bulb supervisor first class?' or something similar. So I didn't ask. I

*Except once, when I went to the Blackpool Illuminations.

milled about, looking as if I was busy, and I listened.

I couldn't understand much of what was being said. It all sounded terribly complicated and technical, but then I suppose that it would. Being so complicated and technical.

And everything.

I overheard the word 'interface' being used a lot. And a lot about 'frequencies', getting the frequencies right. And the dialling codes. 'Exactitudes' regarding the dialling codes. It was all a mystery to me.

And then some oik in a white coat accosted me and asked whether I was 'the new bob who wanted to speak to his granny'.

'Yes, that's right,' I said. 'Is she here, then?'

The oik rolled his eyes. In the way that folks often did when talking to me. 'Well, obviously she's here,' he said. 'Do you have your dialling code worked out yet?'

'Not as such,' I said.

'Which means "no", because you can't do the calculations, am I right?'

'You are,' I said.

'Good grief,' said the oik. 'Didn't they teach you anything at the Ministry?'

I shrugged.

'Come on,' he said. 'I'll take you to the supervisor.'

'I'm fine here,' I said. 'I've got to get this XP103 to the North gantry.'

'So why are you on the East gantry?'

'I was heading north,' I said.

'No, you weren't. Come with me.' And he rolled his eyes again. And I followed him.

'Mr Baker,' said the oik, tapping a white-coated man upon the shoulder. 'Mr Baker, the new bob here, who wanted to speak to his granny, he hasn't worked out his dialling code yet. Is it OK if I show him how to do it?'

Mr Baker turned and stared at me. He was a man of middle years, perhaps in his middle thirties, and he looked strangely familiar to me. I was certain that I'd seen him before somewhere.

And, oh yes, I *had*.

He was one of those young blokes I'd seen in the restricted section of the Memorial Library so long ago. I *did* have a good memory. Sometimes.

'Go ahead,' said Mr Baker. 'But make it quick. He only has a three-minute window. No longer, do you understand that?'

'Absolutely,' said the oik.

'Absolutely,' I said too.

'Follow me,' said the oik, and I followed him. He led me down a couple of stairways and along as many gantries. 'This will really freak you out,' he said as he did so.

'I'm not easily freaked out,' I said.

'Yeah, right,' said the oik. 'Everybody gets freaked out the first time.'

'Why?' I asked.

'*Why?*' The oik turned and looked me in the eyes. 'You're either very brave or very stupid,' he said.

'I'm very brave,' I said. 'Why?'

'Why? Because most people *do* freak out when they speak to a dead relative the first time.'

'A *dead* relative,' I said, stopping all short in my tracks.

The oik stared at me. And then began to laugh. People seem to do a lot of *that* too when they talk to me. 'Oh, very good,' he said. 'Very good indeed.'

'I'm sorry?' I said.

'No,' said the oik. 'That *was* funny. Pretending that you didn't know what FLATLINE was all about. You almost had me going there. Very funny indeed. Good gag.'

'I'm so glad you liked it,' I said, as my brain did cartwheels. Speak to a dead relative? That's what he'd said and he'd said it with a straight face. And FLATLINE, that *was* out of hospitals, wasn't it? When people flatline, they die. The line on the electrocardiograph goes flat. FLATLINE, phoneline? Phoneline to the dead? It made some sort of sense.

'I hope she coughs up whatever it is,' said the oik. 'What do you want to know — where she hid her savings? It's usually that. Mind you, I can't sneer because it's unoriginal. I did just the same when I had my turn. I asked my mum whether she really told my sister that she could have the radiogram. I really wasted my turn and I won't get another one for five years. So I'm not going to be stupid next time. I'm going to ask my mum whether she had any pirate's gold hidden anywhere. I hope you've come up with something good for your first go. Don't mess up like I did.'

I didn't know what to say, so I said: 'Do you think that's fair? Just the one go, every five years?'

The oik drew me near and he whispered. 'No, I don't,' he said. 'But when the service goes on line to everyone, we'll be able to make as many calls as we want. So I suppose we'll just have to be patient for now, won't we?'

'I suppose so,' I said.

'Come on, then. Let's get it done.'

'Right,' I said and I followed him some more.

He led me to a rather extraordinary thing. Not the sort of thing I was expecting at all. I was expecting some kind of Frankenstein's Laboratory sort of thing. Lots of electrical lightning flashes and big wheels turning.

The oik led me to a telephone box.

A classic English big red telephone box. 'Go on,' he said. 'Go inside.'

'This is *it*?' I said.

'Of course,' he said. 'What were you expecting, Frankenstein's Lab?' And he laughed again.

'Of course not,' I said. 'But about the dialling code?'

'I can't see how you can forget something so simple. You dial in the full name of the deceased and the date of their departure. Then times the figure that comes up on the screen by the age of the person when they died and take away the year they were born and, wallah, you have your dialling code. Do you really need me to do that for you or can you figure it out for yourself? How hard can that really be?'

'Not hard at all,' I said. 'I don't know how it slipped my mind.'

'Probably because you're a twonk,' said the oik. 'Now go in, do it. Three minutes is all you get, understand?'

'Of course,' I said.

'And don't think you can go on for longer. You

can't go over three minutes. When you reach three minutes a signal goes to the bulb booth on the ground floor and the bulb-monkey will switch you off.'

'The bulb-monkey?' I said, and I said it very slowly.

'The retard who mans the bulb booth.'

'Right,' I said and I said it through gritted teeth. 'The retard, yes.'

'So, do your stuff, have your go and speak to your gran.'

'Right,' I said. 'I will. Thanks.'

'Then get that XP103 in place.'

'I certainly will.' I entered the telephone box and the door swung shut behind me.

It was strangely quiet in there. Not that it was all that noisy outside. But in here it was quiet. It had a kind of peace. But there always is a kind of peace inside a telephone box. It's probably all to do with 'shape power', all that 'power of the pyramids' stuff. Certain environments *are* special and that's due to their shape. I read about that once. About underground burial chambers that resonate certain notes, like chanting voices and suchlike. The ancients apparently knew all about this sort of stuff, but we in our educated wisdom have lost the knowledge.

But certain people, it appears, seem to know intuitively all about it – certain designers, like the man who designed the telephone box, Sir Giles Gilbert Scott. He also designed Battersea Power Station and Bankside Power Station, which is now the home of Tate Modern.

He was a bit of a genius really.

My hand hovered above the telephone.

Dial up my granny?

Now, why would I want to dial up my granny?

I'd never even met my granny – she'd died before I was born – and I didn't know the date of her 'departure'.

So, really, I couldn't call up my dead granny, could I? So who could I call? Who did I know who was dead and I could call?

Stupid kind of question really. Ridiculous question. The whole thing was pretty ridiculous. Ludicrous, in fact. Although . . . Well, although the oik wasn't taking it as a joke. This *wasn't* a joke. This was FLATLINE and this was what FLATLINE was.

My hand continued to hover.

And then slowly, so slowly, I took up the telephone handset and put it to my ear.

And then slowly, so slowly, and somewhat falteringly, I dialled the letters of my father's name and the date of his 'departure'. Then I multiplied the figure that came up on the screen by the age of my father when he died and took away the year he was born.

And then, all a-tremble and right on the cusp of a freak-out, I listened.

15

It was engaged! Can you believe that?

Engaged?

I slammed down the phone and I fumed not a little.

Stupid, I said to myself. Stupid. Stupid. Stupid. I've been had. They think I'm a new bob. They're winding me up. They'll be out there laughing. I peered out through the glass windows of the phone box.

But no one was out there laughing.

No one.

They were all out there going about their business, carrying bulbs or clipboards, moving up and down stairways and along gantries. They weren't looking in my direction.

I took the telephone handset and I dialled again. And this time a distant bell began to ring.

Ring-ring. Ring-ring. Ring-ring. Like old-fashioned phones used to do.

And then there was a click and a voice said, 'Hello. Who's that?'

And it was the voice of my daddy.

My dead daddy.

It was really his voice.

My throat was suddenly very dry indeed and my heart began to pound like crazy in my chest.

'Hello,' said my daddy's voice again. 'Who's there? Is there anybody there?'

I gagged and swallowed and I said, 'Daddy, is that you?'

'Who's that?' said the voice of my father. 'Gary, is that you?'

'It's me,' I said. 'Is that really you?'

'Of course it's me. Who did you think it was?'

'But you're, well . . . you're . . .'

'I'm *dead*,' said my father. 'We do use the "D" word here. What are you doing up at this time of night? You should have been in bed by eight.'

'I'm all grown up,' I said. 'I'm not a little boy any more.'

'Yes, well, I knew that. I'm not stupid. How old are you now? thirteen, fourteen?'

'I'm twenty-seven.'

'As old as that. Time's different here. Because there isn't any, I suppose.'

'Is that really, really you?'

'Have you been drinking?' asked my daddy.

'No,' I said. 'No. But I can't believe that I'm really talking to you. You being, you know, *dead* and everything.'

'Yeah, well, I'm sure you're thrilled. So what do you want?'

'I don't want anything.'

'So why are you bloody bothering me? Can't you let me rest in peace?'

'I'm speaking to you,' I said. 'I'm alive and

you're dead and I'm actually speaking to you.'

'Well, that's no big deal. Spiritualists do it all the time. Although mostly we just ignore them. Lot of fat ugly women or nancy-boy men, most of them. Who'd want to speak to that bunch of losers, eh?'

'Quite so,' I said. 'But, Daddy, this really is you and I'm speaking to you. This is incredible. Incredible. This is wonderful. This is amazing.'

'I'm not impressed,' said my daddy.

'I am,' I said.

'Then you're easily impressed, son. But I'll tell you something. If you want to be *really* impressed, I know something absolutely fantastic. Would you like to hear it?'

'Yes, I would,' I said. 'I would.'

'All right,' said the Daddy. 'Then listen up good, because—'

Then he got cut off.

And then the line went dead.

16

'You bollard!' I shouted. 'You gimping no-nads!'

But I wasn't shouting at my daddy. I was shouting at Barry.

I was back in the bulb booth now and I was shouting at Barry.

Loudly.

And I was waving my arms about and making fists with my fingers.

Violently.

'You switched me off! You fugging switched me off!'

I shouted loudly as I waved my arms and made my fists. 'You brusting swabster!'

'I've never heard such language,' said Barry, 'and I did nothing of the kind. What are you talking about?'

'The bulb flashed on and you switched it off.'

'And *you're* complaining about *that*?'

'Of course I'm complaining. You stupid bulb-monkey. You switched me off.'

'I do wish you'd calm down, man,' said Barry. 'All this shouting is giving me a headache.'

I took Barry by the throat and shook him all about.

'Gggmmmuurgh . . .' went Barry, eyes popping out and face turning red.

'Upstairs,' I shouted. 'Upstairs on the seventeenth floor. There's this huge computer room thing and it's all to do with frequencies and stuff. And there's a telephone box and . . .'

'Mmphgrmm . . .' went Barry, face rather purple now.

'And you can dial up the dead. That's what FLATLINE is. A hot line to the dead. And I was talking to my daddy and you switched off the bulb, you stupid . . . Barry, are you listening to me?'

But Barry's face had gone rather blue.

I let him sink to the floor and I nudged him a bit in the ribs with the toe of my boot.

Barry took to coughing and gagging and curling into the foetal position.

'Are you listening to me?' I asked him once again.

'Yes, yes.' And Barry waved a limp-looking hand. 'Don't kick me any more.'

'I wasn't kicking, I was nudging.'

'Then don't nudge, please.' And Barry was sick on the floor.

Of *my* bulb booth.

My . . . I prepared to put the boot in some more, but halted my boot in mid swing. *My* bulb booth. Where the *bulb-monkey* sat. Of course it wasn't Barry's fault. What did he and I know? We knew nothing. We just switched the bulb off. But at least I now knew why.

'I'm sorry,' I said and I dragged Barry up and

198

deposited him in the chair. 'I'm sorry. I got a bit stressed there. Are you OK?'

'No,' spluttered Barry, feeling at his crumpled windpipe.

'Well, I'm sorry. But how would you feel? Talking to your dead father on the phone and someone cuts you off.'

'And I did *that*?' Barry looked up at me with eyes all red and tearful.

'That's what the bulb does. Operatives up there are given three minutes to speak to a dead person of their choice. Then the bulb flashes here and we switch them off.'

'Why?' Barry managed to say.

'I don't know,' I said. 'But I actually talked to my dead father.'

'Why?' went Barry once more.

'I just said that I don't know.'

Barry coughed a bit more and wiped away some flecks of vomit from his mouth. 'The second why meant: why did you talk to your father?'

'That's a pretty stupid question, isn't it?'

'Are you kidding?' said Barry, which had me rather confused.

'What are you talking about?' I asked.

'What I'm talking about' – Barry coughed a bit more – 'what I'm talking about is: you had the chance to speak to the dead person of your choice and you chose to speak to your father. Why?'

'Eh?' I said.

'I mean, it didn't cross your mind to speak to someone really special instead, such as . . .'

'Aaaagh!' I went, clapping my hands to my face.

'Such as P. P. Penrose,' said Barry. 'That's who I would have spoken to.'

'Aaaagh!' I went once more and I punched myself right in the face.

'Now *that* must have really hurt,' said Barry, as I struggled to pick myself up from the floor.

'You fell down in the vomit,' Barry continued and he laughed. Or tried to. Then he vomited some more.

'My God,' I said. I was up on my knees and rocking somewhat on them. 'I could have spoken to Mr Penrose, but I chose to speak to my wretched father. What was I thinking of?'

'Perhaps you miss your dad,' was Barry's suggestion.

'No, I fugging don't.'

Barry shook his head painfully. 'But this is *really* true?' he said. 'That's what they're doing up there? Talking to the dead? I thought it was something to do with extraterrestrial life or some such toot. But it's really the dead? This is incredible. This is unlike anything. This is really truly far-out, man. I mean, the dead. At the end of a phone line, the dead.'

'It's the dead,' I said. 'It's really the dead.'

'Then I want a go. Lend me your white coat and your light bulb.'

'Stuff that,' I said. 'You're on duty. You do it in your own time.'

'What? And have *you* switch *me* off?'

I looked at the bulb and Barry looked at the bulb and then on some metaphysical level certain thoughts were exchanged.

'Are you thinking what I'm thinking?' asked Barry.

'If it's what I'm thinking, then yes,' I said.

'I'm thinking chats with the dead,' said Barry. 'Lots of chats with the dead and all a lot longer than three measly minutes.'

'Yes,' I said, nodding my head. 'I'm up for that. But how and when?'

'Both easy,' said Barry. 'After eleven, when they all go home.'

'Hold on,' I said. 'They *all* go home after eleven? Does that mean that the bulb never flashes after eleven?'

'Not as far as I know,' said Barry. 'I usually get my head down for some sleep after eleven. I have to be up bright and early in the morning. I have another job as a milkman. I'm saving up to be a millionaire.'

I made a fist, but I didn't use it. 'So Developmental Services closes at eleven?'

'It has as long as I've been working here. The bulb never flashes after eleven. In fact, there's hardly anyone left in the building. That's how I traced where the wire went. There's only the night watchman and he just sits at the front desk reading nudie books.'

'All right,' I said. 'After eleven it is.'

And so we waited until after eleven. We listened at the bulb-booth door as the technicians chatted and smoked before clocking off for the night. And then when all was still and quiet we left the bulb booth and took the lift to the seventeenth floor.

'It will all be locked up, won't it?' I asked as we sidled up the corridor towards room 23.

Barry shrugged as he sidled. 'Dunno,' he said. 'I traced the wire up to this floor, but I never tried any of the doors. I was going to, but then' – he shrugged again – 'I couldn't be arsed. I was just so sure that it would be a terrible disappointment, so I didn't bother.'

'Fair enough,' I said, although I wasn't altogether convinced. We had reached the door to room 23, so I put my ear against it.

'Hear anything?' Barry asked.

I withdrew my ear and shook my head. And then I tried the handle. And the door was locked.

'Let's kick it open,' said Barry. 'Stuff it, who cares?'

'I do,' I said. 'If we can get away with this without anyone knowing, we can do it every night.'

'Good point. Which leaves us stuffed. Unless you happen to know how to pick locks.'

I grinned at Barry. 'Of course I do,' I said. 'My friend Dave, who is a criminal by profession, taught me. All I need is a couple of paperclips.'

'No problem,' said Barry, producing them out of thin air.

'How did you do that?' I asked.

'My friend the Great Gandini taught me. He's a magician by profession. Used to do an act in Count Otto's dad's circus.'

'Yeah, right,' I said.

'Well, it's as believable as your mate Dave teaching you how to pick locks.'

I took the paperclips and picked the lock.

'Coincidence is a wonderful thing,' said Barry. 'Let's go and talk to the dead.'

The lights were still on in room 23. All the lights. All the bulbs, flashing and flickering, going on and off.

'It's a Mother Board,' said Barry, staring up in awe.

'What is a Mother Board?' I asked him.

'It's the central framework of a computer.'

'Oh,' I said. 'Well, that would explain it. It's a *very* big computer. Come on, I'll take you to the phone box.'

And I took Barry to the phone box.

'Right,' said Barry, rubbing his hands together. 'So what do I have to dial?'

'You dial in the full name of the deceased person and the date of their death. Then multiply the figure that comes up on the screen by the age of the person when they died and take away the year they were born in and, wallah, you have your dialling code.'

'And it's as simple as *that*?'

'I suppose the big computer does all the calculations and works out the frequencies and stuff.'

'Fair enough.' Barry opened the phone-box door. 'Let's go and speak to Mr Penrose.'

'Now, hold on,' I said. 'If anyone's going to speak to him, I think that someone should be me.'

'Why?' Barry asked. 'It was my idea. You wanted to speak to your dad. I suggested Mr Penrose.'

'It should be me,' I said.

'No, it shouldn't,' said Barry.

'Should,' I said.

'Shouldn't.'

And so I hit Barry right in the face.

'That is so unfair,' said Barry, dabbing at his bloody nostrils. 'You wouldn't be up here if it wasn't for me.'

'That is so a lie,' I told him. 'But stuff it, I don't care, you go first, if you want.'

'Thanks,' said Barry and he went into the phone box, took up the receiver and dialled the name and the numbers. Then he waited for a bit and then he slammed down the receiver and came out and scowled at me.

'It didn't work,' he said. 'It did nothing. This is all a wind-up, isn't it?'

'No, it's not,' I said. 'I spoke to my dead dad.'

'Are you sure they weren't just pulling some trick on you up here?'

'No, I thought of that. It worked. It was real.'

'Well, it doesn't work. I dialled him up. It didn't work.'

'It must work. What did you dial?'

'I dialled up P. P. Penrose and the date he died and all that other stuff.'

'Yeah, well, that's because you're a twonk. His real name wasn't P. P. Penrose. It was *Charles* Penrose. My daddy knew him. I was at his wake, you know.'

'You never were?'

'I was, and at his funeral.'

'And were you at the exhumation, when they found him all mashed up in the coffin because he'd been buried alive?'

A terrible shiver went down my spine. 'No,' I said. 'I wasn't at that. Terrible, that was. Horrible.'

'Yeah,' said Barry. 'So go on, then, if his name was Charles. Dial him up.'

My hand was on the door, but suddenly I felt rather sick. I was the one who'd done that to Mr Penrose. Brought him back to life in his coffin with voodoo. Put him through hideous torment until death had taken him again. I wasn't so sure that I really wanted to speak to him. What if he knew it was me? There was no telling what the dead might know about the living. What they could see. Where, exactly, they *were*. He *might* know I'd done it. He wouldn't be too pleased to speak to me.

'You do it,' I said. 'You dial him up again.'

'Why not you?'

'Do you want to speak to him or *not*?'

'I do,' said Barry and he waited outside, while I did the dialling this time. And it took me a couple of goes to get it right. Because the real date of Mr Penrose's real departure was the day that he died, for the second time, in his coffin.

At the other end of the line a distant bell began to ring. I opened the door, handed the phone to Barry, went outside and listened.

'Hello,' I heard Barry say. 'Hello. Mr Penrose, is that you?'

And something must have been said in reply, because Barry turned to me and gave a thumbs-up. I gave a thumbs-up back to him and he turned away once more and went on speaking.

And speaking.

And listening.

And speaking some more . . .

And some more . . .

I looked at my wristwatch. It was now twelve-thirty. I bashed my fist on the glass of the door. Barry turned and made sssh-ing noises.

I dragged open the door.

Barry put his hand over the mouthpiece of the phone. 'Go away,' he said. 'I'm talking to Mr Penrose.'

'Well, I want a go.'

'Do you want to speak to him?'

'Er, no,' I said. 'Not at this moment.'

'Then, go away. Come back in half an hour.'

'No,' I said. 'I won't.'

'Well, who do *you* want to speak to, then?'

'I don't know,' I said.

'Then, go away and think of someone.'

I let the telephone-box door swing shut. I so, so, so wanted to talk to Mr Penrose. Tell him I was sorry. Ask him to forgive me. Just to talk to him. But I confess I was scared. I know I should have been scared anyway. After all, he *was* dead. This was a pretty big number. But it was more than the business of awakening his corpse in his coffin. It was the matter of speaking to *him*. To P. P. Penrose, the greatest writer of the twentieth century. The creator of Lazlo Woodbine. Penrose was my hero. I was a fan.

I was totally stuffed.

And so I just stood there, outside the phone box, while Barry rabbited on and on, then listened, then rabbited on some more.

And then, at four-fifteen in the morning, Barry came out of the phone box.

'Finished, have you?' I asked in a tone that was far from friendly.

'I have to go,' said Barry. 'To the toilet. I'm bursting for a piss.'

I glanced towards the phone. The receiver was down. 'He's gone, then, has he?'

'Yeah, he had to go for his lunch. Time is different there. Everything is different there. Well, not everything. Actually, it's mostly— No, listen, I really do have to go to the toilet. Use the phone now. Call someone.'

'I don't know,' I said.

'You're acting really weird,' said Barry. 'Go on, call someone. It's no problem – they're really anxious to say hello. They're dying to talk. Hey, that's a good'n, isn't it, *dying* to talk.'

'Go to the toilet,' I said.

Barry went off to the toilet.

And I just dithered. If Mr Penrose had gone off for his lunch, then I couldn't speak to him. So who could I speak to? What famous dead person would I really like to speak to? I thought hard about this, even harder than I had been thinking for the last couple of hours, and my conclusion was the same: quite a few of them. But I didn't know the exact dates of their deaths. I was going to have to come back tomorrow night.

But then I thought of my daddy. I could phone him. And he had said that he had something fantastic that he wanted to tell me. I could phone my daddy.

Barry returned with a smile on his face.

'That was quick,' I said. 'Where is the toilet?'

'I've no idea,' said Barry. 'I just pissed in someone's desk drawer.'

'You stupid sod.'

'Calm down,' said Barry. 'It will be dry in the morning. Just a bit smelly. No one will suspect anything.'

'Let's go,' I said.

'What? Aren't you going to phone anyone? Mr Penrose will probably have finished his lunch by now. Time *is* different there.'

'I have to think,' I said. 'I don't want to waste this. I want to do it properly. To some purpose.'

'Please yourself, man. But if you're not having a go, then I'm going to speak to Mr Penrose again.'

'What did he say?' I asked. 'What is he like?'

'He's OK,' said Barry. 'A really nice bloke. Very forthcoming, very open. Talks a lot about sportsmanship. He's very big on that. But he's so angry. Someone did something to him. Did voodoo on him or something after he died and—'

'I don't want to know,' I said. 'I'm going home. Close the door on your way out. I'll see you tomorrow evening.'

'I'm going to bring a tape recorder,' said Barry. 'Get this on tape. This is big news. The world should know about this.'

'No,' I said. 'Hold on. You can't tell anyone about this.'

'Are you kidding?'

'No, I'm not kidding. This is beyond big. This is beyond anything. And it's a secret. A government secret. If anyone found out that we're doing this, that we're unauthorized and doing this, we'd be in really big trouble. This is our secret. We can't tell anyone. No one must know.'

'OK,' said Barry. 'It's our secret.'

'Let's shake on this.' I put my hand out and Barry shook it. 'Fair enough,' I said. 'Now, I'm off. Some of us have to work in the morning.'

'Both of us have. Stuff it, I'll call it a night in half an hour. See you tomorrow evening.'

'See you.' And so I left Barry and wandered off home.

I slept all alone in my bed, but I didn't sleep very well. There were far too many bits and bobs whirling about in my head. FLATLINE was something so big that the implications of it all were beyond imagining. The very concept of definite contact with the dead. That changed everything, didn't it? All theories of God and the hereafter. All of recorded history. It would now be possible to know literally everything. About exactly what happened in the past and exactly what happened after you died. Everything would be known. It was too much to think about. Too much for me, anyway.

The more I thought about it all, the more messed up I became. There was power here. Those who could speak with the dead could learn a lot. A whole lot. Einstein had probably thought up loads more important equations since he'd snuffed it. And all those other scientists and composers and geniuses. And all the murdered could identify their murderers – well, the ones who'd seen them, anyway. And, oh, the more I thought, the more messed up I became. This was such a *big* secret. The *biggest* secret.

And Barry and I were on the inside of it. We were an even bigger secret, because the men who held this secret didn't know that we knew about it.

Eventually I did fall asleep, but, as I say, I did not sleep very well and when the alarm rang and I crawled off to the telephone exchange I was feeling very sick indeed.

And when I went into the bulb booth to relieve Barry, I was not altogether thrilled to find that Barry was fast asleep.

I awoke him with a kick in the ribs.

'Whoa!' went Barry, lurching into consciousness.

'Time to go home,' I told him.

'Oh yeah, man.' Barry yawned and stretched.

'Have a good night?' I asked him. 'Chatting with Mr Penrose?'

'You're not kidding. What a man. He told me all about the people he'd met and the things he'd done. I'm going to write his biography.'

'What?'

'Straight from the hearse's mouth,' said Barry, grinning foolishly. 'He'll dictate it to me down the phone. It's a secret, though; you can't tell anyone.'

I made fists once again. 'I'm not going to tell anyone, am I? But you can't do this.'

'Why not? Give me one good reason.'

I couldn't. 'This is ridiculous,' I said.

'I think it's brilliant. And when I've done Mr Penrose I'll do some others. Mr Penrose says that the famous dead are crying out to the living, but the living can't hear them. But we can hear them down the FLATLINE phone and they all want to dictate their life stories. You can do some too. We'll be rich authors – there's millions to be had in this.'

I gave my chin a stroke. Barry was right of course.

'I'm going to buy a tape recorder today,' said Barry. 'We can just set it up at the phone and let Mr Penrose talk for as long as he likes each night. This is *so* brilliant.'

I gave my chin another stroke. This *was* brilliant, there was no doubt about that. 'We will have to be *so* careful.'

'I'm going to call myself Macgillicudy Val Der Mar.'

'Eh?' said I.

'My pen name. My *nom de plume*. Mr Penrose gave it to me. I'll keep working here until I've made a couple of million, then I'll just vanish. Of course, by then I'll have about a dozen other "biographies" on the tape. So more millions, but far away from here and the Official Secrets Act. Somewhere that has no extradition treaties with the UK.'

'You've got all this worked out very quickly,' I observed.

'It's all down to Mr Penrose.'

'This is dangerous,' I said. 'Very dangerous.'

'You're not kidding. But we can both get very rich on this. And we can get out of here. Do you want to spend the rest of your life flicking this switch, or do you want riches and out?'

I gave the matter a bit of thought.

'I want riches and out,' I said.

17

Life eh?

What's it all about, then?

How many times have we heard that question asked? And how many answers are there to that question? Hundreds? Thousands? Of all the questions man has ever asked, that one seems to have the most answers. And the thing about those answers, which in fact unites those answers, no matter how diverse and contradictory those answers might be, is that they all come from people who think they know; are sure they know; but don't really know at all.

No one knows.

No one living, anyway.

The dead know. But the dead know everything. The dead know so much stuff that if the living were to find it all out from the dead, the living would be scared to death. And then they'd know it all for themselves anyway.

The trouble is, and it is a *big* trouble, that although the dead know everything, they are not always entirely honest and forthcoming when they pass their knowledge on to the living.

Take the Virgin Mary, for instance. She's dead and she knows everything. But when she chooses to manifest in front of some peasant boys and girls on some hillside somewhere, does she ever have anything interesting to say? Anything profound and earth-shattering? Not a bit of it. And this woman was the mother of God.

Mind you, I don't blame her for not having much to say. She must still be a very confused woman. Unless someone has got around to explaining to her exactly what her relationship with her son really is. I mean, as far as I've heard it, there is God the Father, God the Son and God the Holy Ghost. The Holy Ghost inseminated Mary and she gave birth to God the Son. But the Holy Ghost and God the Son are both aspects of God the Father; they are ultimately one and the same. Which means that Jesus was his own father and Mary was inseminated by her own, as yet unborn, son. Which might mean that Jesus sends himself a card on Father's Day, but can't send Mary a card on Mother's Day, because being also God the Father he was around long before Mary was even born.

Christmas dinners must be a laugh at God's house. And although Jesus, God the Son, has a birthday to celebrate, His dad, who is also Himself, doesn't, because He was never born.

So, yeah, Mary manifests and she doesn't have much to say. But the rest of the dead, and there's a lot of 'em, they've all got something or other they'd just love to say to the living, but they can't. They can't get through because it just doesn't work like that.

But then, once in a very long while, one of them

does manage to get through and, having made this momentous move, do they say something incredible? Do they pass on their profound cosmic wisdom? Do they heck! They all screw up. They do, they really do. They lie, they deceive, they are frankly dishonest. Why? Won't someone tell me why? Does anybody know?

A century or more of hard grind on the part of the Society of Psychical Research has turned up positively nothing. Nothing that will hold up in court as definite irrefutable contact with the dead. And why? Not because the dead did not contact the living, but because when they did they came out with a lot of old toot and confused the issue further.

My heart truly bleeds for all those mediums sitting at tables trying to contact 'the other side'. And those psychic questers like Danbury Collins constantly being led up blind alleys by spirit guides. And the channellers, channelling away and the Spiritualist Church and all those who receive information from 'Higher Sources'.

I'm sorry, it's not my fault, but the dead cannot be trusted.

So, yeah, right. *Now* I'm asking. Now, at the point in my life that I've reached. The point that I'm writing about now. Because at this point I didn't know. But then at this point I wasn't aware that the dead did lie to the living. I wasn't really sure that the dead could talk to the living. Although I had had that brief conversation with my father. Or thought I had. Or believed I had. Because I had a real problem convincing myself that what was going on with the FLATLINE programme was actually real.

I wanted it to be real and I really, really wanted to talk to Mr Penrose. If just to say that I was sorry for reawakening him in his coffin. But I was having difficulties with the concept of the thing.

Because, I suppose, I was having difficulties with the concept of life. My life. Everything that happened to me seemed to happen so fast. It just came out of nowhere and hit me. It woke me up out of my dreams. Or it *was* my dreams and I didn't remember the times when I was awake.

Or something.

But I couldn't seem to keep up. And I certainly couldn't sleep. If sleeping *was* sleeping and being awake *was* being awake.

I remember that I did a lot of late-night pacing. Up and down in the bedroom. *All alone* in the bedroom.

I was certain that Sandra had said that she was only going away for a week. But it was nearly two weeks now and she still wasn't back. And I actually missed her. I know that we didn't have much of a marriage. Well, anything of a marriage, really. We didn't have sex any more and when she wasn't laughing at me, or criticizing me, she was away at work and I wasn't seeing her anyway. And now she was away on holiday with Count Otto and I was missing her like crazy.

Why? Well, I don't know why. Because I loved her, I suppose. I know that there wasn't much to love about her any more. But I could think back to our honeymoon in Tenerife, when I loved her and she loved me in return and that was a happy time. We would make love in the banana plantations and she would run around afterwards with her clothes off, impersonating ponies. Those were the days. They were. They really were.

And I felt certain that those days would return. Because I had the power to make them return. Barry and I would become millionaires, and Sandra would like being married to a millionaire. Even if that millionaire had to flee the British Isles. Perhaps we'd move to Tenerife. She would love me again, I knew that she would, and all would be well and happy again.

The matter seemed simple to me. My wife no longer loved me because she no longer respected me. So I would regain her respect and she would love me again.

Sorted. She would respect me if I became a millionaire, I was certain about that. Which left only the matter of the opposition, the fly in the marmalade, the sand in the suntan lotion, the boil on the marital backside, Count Otto Black.

He'd have to go. And go for good.

The count would have to die.

Now, don't get me wrong here. I didn't come to this decision without a great crisis of conscience. In fact, it was the greatest crisis of conscience that I had experienced in nearly ten years.

The last time I had such a crisis of conscience was at the trial of the Daddy.

When I had given evidence in the witness box.

I know I said earlier that I didn't attend the trial, and I didn't, *not as a spectator*. And I was only there for half an hour anyway. And the trial did drag on for weeks. I think it would have dragged on for weeks and weeks more, and all at the taxpayers' expense, if I hadn't given my evidence. If I hadn't got up in the witness box and had my say.

You see, it all hinged on the mother's evidence. She'd been there when the butchery took place. But the counsel for the defence said that she was an unreliable witness.

So I got up and said my piece. And it did involve a crisis of conscience. Because I had to swear on oath and tell the truth and everything. So I explained how I knew that Mum was being sexed by the ice-cream man on Wednesday evenings when Dad was out playing darts at the Legion. And how I saw everything happen on that terrible evening.

It was my evidence that hanged him.

Crisis of conscience, you see. You can understand that. Should I own up and be honest and tell the truth, or should I lie? I chose to tell the truth, which hanged my daddy. I could have kept quiet, I could have lied, but I didn't.

Well, I wouldn't have, would I?

I'm an honest fellow.

And I'd gone to a lot of trouble anyway.

A lot of trouble. But then, it takes a lot of trouble to commit the perfect crime. Which I had done.

You see, I really hated that ice-cream man for sexing my mother. I wanted him dead. But I didn't have the nerve to kill him myself and I was sure that, even if I'd had the nerve, I'd have been caught. So I needed someone to do it for me. Which was why on that fateful night I phoned the Legion and tipped off my father, in a disguised voice, of course, that the ice-cream man was on his way over to sex his wife. I phoned a little early, you see, because I needed time to go and hide myself in the wardrobe. So I could watch the murdering. So I could give evidence. Because I wanted the Daddy dead too, horrible swine that he was.

It was two perfect crimes in one, really. Which is pretty damn good, in my opinion.

So one more perfect crime wasn't going to hurt.

And I had, during the course of all my pacing and heart-breaking, come up with a really good one to rid myself of Count Otto. It was such a good one, in fact, that I felt certain that even if Sherlock Holmes teamed up with Miss Marple, Ironside, Lazlo Woodbine and Inspector Clouseau, my name would never come up once during the course of the investigation.

It would be the perfect crime.

And it sort of was. Or would have been. I'm not quite sure, really. Things certainly didn't turn out the way I'd planned. But that's life for you, isn't it? Full of surprises, and none of them, in my opinion, pleasant.

So let me tell you the story of what happened. I'm sorry if I bored you for a bit with all the talk about life and death and the dead not telling the truth and me not knowing why and suchlike. But it's all relevant and it did provide the opportunity for me to own up about my dad and the ice-cream man, because I'm being honest here: I'm telling you all of the truth, the whole truth, as it happened.

I had come up with a three-phase plan to win Sandra back and I was certain it would work.

Now, I must have been asleep. My face was in the

ravioli. I'd cooked it myself in the new macrowave oven the night before last. You probably don't remember macrowave ovens. They were the Betamax of the microwave revolution. They never really caught on. I suppose it was their size. Ours, which was about the size of a Mini Metro, took up most of the kitchen area. But it *was* fast. It could reduce an entire Friesian cow to ashes in about 0.3 seconds. I think the macrowave oven accounted for a lot of people who supposedly went 'missing' back in the early seventies. You could definitely commit the perfect crime with a macrowave oven.

They were soon withdrawn. The macrowaves leaked out, apparently. I know that all my checked suits became plain suits and the wardrobe was two rooms away. And all the fur fell out of our cat. And it used to cast my shadow up the kitchen wall when it was on. And years later the shadow was still there and couldn't be washed off.

It was red hot with ravioli though. It cooked up ravioli so fast that it was done before you even put it in.

So there I was, asleep or something, face down in my plate of ravioli, when suddenly I'm being struck around the back of the head by something hard, which I later identify as being the piece of breezeblock that I was carving into a facsimile of Noddy Holder,★ by Sandra, who had made an unexpected return to the marital home.

★I liked the Slade in those days. But then, didn't everyone? I believe Jeff Beck played with them on their first album.

'Wake up, you piece of scum,' Sandra shouted, loud enough for me to hear but not appreciate. 'Wake up and look at this mess.'

I woke up and looked at the mess.

And when I'd got over the shock of being woken, I showed no surprise at the mess whatsoever.

'I recognize this mess,' I told Sandra. 'It was here yesterday and also the day before. Why are you striking me on the head to draw my attention to it?'

'It's *your* mess!' shouted Sandra, and she surely shrieked.

'Cease the shrieking!' I said to her. 'There's a man upstairs who flew Spitfires. You'll frighten him.'

'He died years ago. You lazy bastard. I go away for a few days of well-earned rest . . .'

'Did you have a nice time?' I asked, from beneath the table where I cowered, still ducking from the blows.

'No,' said Sandra. 'I got thrush.'

'Give it to the cat,' I said. 'It will be grateful for a bit of fresh meat. I haven't fed it for a week.'

Sandra struck me with renewed vigour.

I crawled out from under the table and now, being fully awake, clopped her one across the nose, which sent her reeling and caused her to relinquish her hold upon the breezeblock, which she dropped, breaking Noddy Holder's nose.

'Now look what you've done,' I said.

'What *I've* done,' said Sandra, clutching at her bloodied nose. 'You hit me! You hit me!'

'You started it,' I said.

'I'll have you for this. I'll sue you. You're finished.'

I sighed sadly. 'Welcome home,' I said.

'You call this home?'

'Let me make you a cup of tea,' I said. 'Did you bring me back a stick of rock?'

'I'm leaving you,' said Sandra. 'I can't take any more.'

I sat myself back down in the chair I had so recently been knocked from. 'We've got off to a bit of a bad start here,' I said. 'So let's let bygones be bygones and start again. I've been doing a lot of thinking about our relationship and I think I've come up with a solution. Firstly—'

'Shut up!' shouted Sandra. 'Shut up!'

'Firstly, I think we should go out together more. No, not now, because I have a lot on in the evenings, but soon, then—'

'Shut up!'

'And I've bought this book, *Bring the Bounce Back into Your Marital Sex Life Through Bestiality*. We'll have your pussy earn its thrush, eh?'

'Shut up!' Sandra took up dirty plates and threw them in my direction.

'And counselling,' I said. 'Marriage counselling. I found this ad in the *Brentford Mercury*. We can go and see this marriage counsellor. She's a young woman and she'll help us sort things out. It costs quite a bit, but it will be worth it. We'll be all right for a threesome and if you're not too keen to do it with me at first, I don't mind, I'll just watch.'

Sandra tried to throw the macrowave at me. But, come on, it had taken six strong lads to get that thing in here.

'I hate you!' shouted Sandra.

'Hate is healthy,' I told her. 'Hate is just love trapped inside and trying to get out. You can beat me if you want. And I'll beat you. We can hurt each other until we both cry for mercy. Come on, let's do it now.'

I'll swear Sandra had that macrowave oven up off the floor by a couple of inches, but then her strength failed her and she dropped it again. And then she stormed out of the kitchen. And I listened as she broke things in the sitting room, then went into the bedroom and threw her most precious belongings into *my* suitcase, then returned to the kitchen and called me names that were not mine, then marched up the hall and stormed out of the front door and was gone.

This meant that phase one of my three-phase plan had gone even better than I could have hoped it would.

Which just left the other two and then she would be putty in my hands.

Oh yes.

She would.

She really would.

18

I didn't make it to bed that night. I'd meant to go down to the telephone exchange and take some dictation from Vlad the Impaler. But, frankly, I was sick of listening to him going on and on about the battles he'd won by superior strategies and how the world had him all wrong about being such a bad-bottomed blackguard and everything. And so much of what he was telling me didn't tie up with my own researches into his life that I'd been doing at the Memorial Library.

Vlad wasn't telling me all of the truth, and I could see some scholarly script editor going through my manuscript and rubbishing it as grossly inaccurate. I began to pray very hard at night that someone really famous and loved by everyone would die soon and then I could get straight onto them and come up with a big fresh biography that everybody would like to read. Marc Bolan, perhaps, or Groucho Marx, or even Elvis.

But I couldn't see any of them dying in the nineteen seventies. And I began to worry that I might not make the millions I had been hoping for.

Barry's hopes, however, were high. For in the fullness of time, which in his case filled to the brim within six months, I found myself attending the launch party for his 'biography' of P. P. Penrose: *P. P. Penrose: The Man Who Was Lazlo Woodbine.*

The launch was to be held at Mr Penrose's favourite London night club. Which he had written into many of his books as Fangio's bar, Lazlo Woodbine's favourite hangout. Where he ate hot pastrami on rye, drank bottles of Bud and talked toot with Fangio, the fat boy barman. The club had changed its name now, as it was under new management. But I was still thrilled at the prospect of treading in the footsteps of the legend. Maybe going up to the bar and ordering a hot pastrami on rye and a bottle of Bud, as Laz would have done. And talking a lot of old toot, as Laz did on so many memorable occasions.

I had been meaning to go to the night club for ages. Not just because of its associations with P. P. Penrose, but because the new management it was under was none other than that of Harry, my brother-in-law, who now answered to the name of Peter. And most successfully too.

Sandra took an age to get changed and made up. She still dressed in black. Even though it was nearly five months since Count Otto had met with his tragic demise. I felt it right that she should continue to wear black, black being the colour of mourning as well as the name of the one being mourned. It was a constant reminder. I felt it was fitting.

I waited patiently while Sandra did all the things that she had to do. I wanted her to look her best for the book launch. And I knew that getting her to look her best took a bit of time.

Sandra required considerable care and attention nowadays.

Considerable maintenance, in fact.

She was no longer the same fiery, feisty, sassy Sandra who had returned from that holiday in Camber Sands. This was a far more subdued Sandra. A well-behaved Sandra. A Sandra who didn't answer back any more. A Sandra who did what she was told. A Sandra who never left the house without me and only then by the back door and at night. She had been severely traumatized by the sudden death of Count Otto, and although she was now in my care I knew that she would never again be the same person that she had once been.

I myself was bearing up well. It's a tragic thing when someone you care deeply about dies. It can really mess you up. But you have to muddle through and get on with life, don't you? Life being so full of surprises and everything.

Not that I missed Otto, you understand.

I didn't grieve for Count Otto.

Oh no, Otto had got what was coming to him. He had messed about with what was mine and he had paid the price. According to the note he left behind, it was suicide. And the note was genuine. It was written in his own hand and handwriting experts attested to this. The long and rambling account he had written confirmed that a madness had come upon him during the final month of his life. He became a creature obsessed. He eschewed good food and dined on drink alone. He developed strange compulsions. He would spend hour upon end sniffing swatches of tweed in the gents' out-fitters. He became prone to outbursts of uncontrollable laughter. He bethought himself a Zulu king and dressed in robes befitting. He became obsessed with the idea that an invisible Chinaman called Frank was broadcasting lines of Milton directly into his brain.

And so Count Otto had taken out his father's Luger and blown off the top of his head with it.

Tragic.

But more tragic was the fact that the count had not died alone. The voices in his head had apparently decreed that he should make a human sacrifice before he took his own life.

And this is where, in the previous chapter, I mentioned that things didn't work out exactly as I had planned. The voice of Frank definitely ordered the count to sacrifice Eric, the landlord of the Golden Dawn. I know this for a fact, because I was the voice of Frank. As I had been to my daddy all those years before. And I know what, through voodoo magic, I said to Count Otto. But obviously in his confused state of mind he misheard what I said and sacrificed some-one else entirely.

Which was why I had to do some grieving. Which is why I said that it's a tragic thing when someone you care deeply about dies. Because the person that Count Otto sacrificed meant a lot to me.

After all, that someone was my wife, Sandra.

Which was why she required so much maintenance nowadays.

Because using the spell I had used upon P. P. Penrose I had raised Sandra from the dead. Being careful that I didn't make the same mistake as I had with Mr Penrose. I'd dug Sandra out of her grave and brought her home before she'd returned to life.

Or at least to a state of reanimation.

Because, in all honesty, you could hardly say that Sandra was alive any more. She was 'undead', that's about the best you could say. And, frankly, that was flattering her. When I say that she required a lot of maintenance, I'm not kidding you at all. Bits of Sandra kept falling off and she didn't smell like a breath of spring. But she did what she was told, or commanded, because he who raises the zombie has total command of it, and there were no more problems with our sex life. Other than for the occasional maggot, but I kept her dusted down with Keating's Powder.

I was happy with Sandra now. And I know that had she been able to form entire sentences, she would certainly have said that she was happy with me.

I'm sure.

'How are you doing, darling?' I called through the bedroom door. 'Do you need any help with your legs?'

I heard grunting, and a dull and uninspired thump.

'Leg fall off again,' called Sandra, whose husky tones reminded me of the now legendary Tor Johnson. 'Need glue.'

'Coming, dearest.' And I went to her assistance. 'We really must hurry a little – a cab is picking us up.'

'Lion cub?' said Sandra, as I helped her with her leg.

'Cab, not *cub*,' I said. 'Remind me to poke a pencil in your ears. I think they're clogged up with pus again.'

'Thank you, Masser Gary,' said Sandra, as I got her looking presentable. 'Sandra love Masser Gary. Masser Gary love Sandra?'

'Masser Gary love Sandra very much,' I said. 'Now get a shift on, or I'll confiscate your head again.'

I do say that by the time we'd finished, Sandra looked pretty good. She'd have passed for living any day of the week. Except, of course, Tuesdays. And when the cab came to pick us up and whip us off to the world-famous night club, I knew that it was going to be a night to remember.

Which, of course, it was.

I don't know about you, but I love dressing up. I've always been something of a dandy and I see nothing wrong in that. If you've got it, flaunt it. And if you haven't got it, then at least you can make the effort, so the fact that you haven't got it isn't so glaringly obvious.

Clothes maketh the man, so said the Bard of Brentford. And I'll tell you this, I looked pretty damn fab dressed in the height of seventies fashion. High stacked shoes with double snood gambol-bars and trussed tiebacks of the purple persuasion. A triple-breasted suit cut from Boleskine tweed (as favoured by Mr Penrose, though of course the style was different when he cut a dash as the Best Dressed Man of nineteen thirty-three). A kipper tie, made from a real kipper, dipped in aspic and with flounced modulations on the soft underbelly that glittered against my shirt of quilted fablon. I looked the business and I did feel sure that one day soon I would actually *be* the business.

If only someone really famous would hurry up and die.

Over my dazzling ensemble I wore a trenchcoat and fedora, in homage to Lazlo Woodbine. Sandra wore a trenchcoat and a fedora too. All invited guests were required to do so. And of course we wore our masks.

The masks were Barry's idea. He had to maintain anonymity. The book was published under the name that Mr Penrose had given to him, Macgillicudy Val Der Mar. But Barry didn't dare to be seen. So he'd come up with the idea that everyone should wear masks. Which suited me fine, as I didn't want *my* picture in the paper. Nor Sandra's: questions might be asked if Sandra was seen again in the flesh. They might well be asked by Harry, who was Peter now. So Sandra and I and Barry were all better off in our masks.

I wore an elegant domino in black-and-white check. Sandra wore a rather fetching facsimile of Roy Rogers' Trigger.

Well, she wasn't really up to impersonating ponies any more and I thought she looked good in it. Both masks had nice big mouth holes, so that we could talk and drink and stuff our faces with expensive food, which was what you did at such functions.

At a little after nine of the summery evening clock the cabbie drew us to a halt outside 'Peter's' night club.

Now, I don't know what gets into cabbies. They seem to live in a world of their own. They take you (eventually) to where you want to go, by a route picturesque and circuitous, and then they charge you some fabulous sum and expect you to pay up without a fuss. And then if you *do* make a fuss they become surly and make threats about calling the police.

When our cabbie disclosed to me the extent of his

charges, I counselled him that he should drive us on a little bit and park up a quiet side road, so I could 'deal with the matter'.

Which I did.

Peter's night club looked simply splendid. It was very posh, with lots of flashing light bulbs on the front. They were very nice flashing light bulbs. Mostly PR177s, although I noted several XP701s and a couple of DD109s. I really knew my bulbs by then. I took a pride in it. Knowledge being power and all that.

The bouncer looked like a right sissy boy to me. He was tall and thin and certainly didn't look as if he knew how to handle himself. I showed him our gilt-edged invitations.

'Got any drugs?' he asked, as he frisked me.

'No,' I said.

'Good,' he replied. 'Pass on, sir.'

' "Pass on, sir"?' I said. 'Do you mean to tell me that you're not going to try and sell me any drugs?'

'Certainly not, sir,' said the skinny boy bouncer. 'This is *not* that kind of night club. Now, pass on, sir, while I frisk this spastic with the horse's-head mask.'

'Spastic?' I said. 'That's no spastic, that's my, er, sister.'

'So sorry, sir,' said the skinny boy. 'But her left leg is – how shall I put this? – a bit funny. The foot facing backwards and everything.'

'Ah,' said I. And I corrected Sandra's foot.

The sissy boy reached out his hands to frisk Sandra, then thought better of it and waved her on. And so we entered the night club.

And we were greeted at once by Harry/Peter. 'Greetings,' he said. 'And welcome.'

'Good grief,' I said. 'Harry, you've changed.'

'Who's saying that to me?' asked Harry/Peter.

I lifted the chin of my mask.

'Gary,' said Harry/Peter. 'Good to see you. I haven't seen you since Sandra's funeral. Are you doing OK?'

'I'm fine,' I said. 'You know, bearing up. But look at you. You're all slim and stylishly dressed and what about that haircut.'

'It's a mullet,' said Harry/Peter. 'The very acme of style. And as style never dates I shall be keeping it for the rest of my life.'

'And all power to your elbow,' I said.

'And are you still working at the telephone exchange?'

'Job for life,' I said. 'And still loving every minute of it.'

'Well, good for you. Go in and mingle. I have to greet guests. Here comes the Sultan of Brunei. See you later.'

I led Sandra into the glittering bowels of the world-famous night club.

Barry sat at a table signing copies of his book. He wore upon his head a paper bag with two eye-holes and a mouth cut out. The ironic wit of this disguise wasn't lost upon me.

I jumped the queue and tipped him the wink. 'How's it going?' I asked.

'Who are you?' asked Barry.

I lifted the chin of my mask. 'And who are *you*?' I asked.

Oh, how we laughed.

Barry signed me a freebee.

'I shall treasure this,' I said. And then a thought suddenly crossed my mind and I leaned towards Barry.

'Barry,' I said, 'a thought has just crossed my mind. If you're here, who's manning the bulb booth?'

'My brother Larry. He's my twin brother, so no one will know the difference.'

'Fair enough,' I said. 'Drinks later?'

'Sure thing,' said Barry. 'By the way, who's the spastic? Is she with you?'

'See you later at the bar,' I said.

Now, I don't know whether you've ever been in Harry's/Peter's world-famous night club. Probably not, if you're poor, or just working class, which accounts for most of us, but I do have to tell you that it's rather swish.

There's lots of chrome and marble and black shiny stuff and lots and lots of women. Beautiful women, and most of those women have hardly any clothes on.

I looked all around and about, at the place and at the women, and I thought to myself, this is for me. This is the life-style that is for me. The life-style I was born to. Oscar Wilde once said that every man reaches his true station in life, whether it is above or below the one he was originally born into. And old Oscar knew what he was talking about. And not just because he was a homo.

I knew instinctively that this was for me. This was where I belonged.

'Masser Gary buy Sandra drink?' asked my lady wife, the late Mrs Cheese.

'Indeed,' I said to her. 'I'll get you a cocktail.'

I ordered Sandra a Horse's Neck – well, it went with her horse's head. I was impressed that this time it didn't come out of the drip tray and it had a cherry and a sunshade and a sparkler on the top.

The barman told me the price of it and I laughed politely in his face. 'I'm with Mr Val Der Mar,' I told him. 'A close personal friend. The drinks are on his publisher tonight.'

'Fair enough,' said the barman. 'I was only trying it on. I'm saving up for a motorbike.'

'Stick to fiddling the till,' I told him. 'A bottle of Bud for me and a hot pastrami on rye.'

The barman served me with a bottle of Bud. 'The hot pastrami is off,' he said. 'Irani terrorists broke into the fridge and liberated the last jar we had.'

'I hate it when that happens,' I said. 'I once had a pot of fish paste liberated from my kitchen cupboard by members of Black September.'

'Horrid,' said the barman. 'My mum was shopping in Asda and had her pension book nicked out of her handbag by Islamic Jihad.'

'Bad luck,' I said. 'Weathermen ate my hamster.'

'Isn't it always the way?' said the barman. 'But you'll have to pardon me, sir, because much as I'd love to go on talking toot with you regarding the crimes committed upon you and yours and me and mine by extreme fundamentalist groups and terrorist organizations and the distress that these crimes have wrought upon you and yours and me and mine, frankly, I can't be arsed. And as I see Mr Jeff Beck up at the end of the bar calling out to get served, I think I'll go and do the business. If you know what I mean, and I'm sure that you do.'

'Fair enough,' I said to him. 'I hope you die of cancer.'

'Thank you, sir. And if I might be so bold as to mention it, your girlfriend's left hand is weeping into the stuffed olives. Kindly tell her to remove it, or I'll be forced to call the sissy boy bouncer, who will politely eject you from the premises.'

'I hope it really hurts when you're dying,' I said.

'Thank you, sir. Coming, Mr Beck.'

I lifted Sandra's hand from the olive bowl and folded its fingers around her Horse's Neck. 'Enjoy,' I told her.

'Thank you, Masser Gary,' said Sandra.

'Just call me "master",' I said. 'Master Gary makes me sound like a schoolboy.'

'Cheers, masser,' said Sandra, pouring her drink into the vicinity of her mouth.

'I think we should mingle,' I said to her. 'There's lots of famous people here and as I mean to be very rich very soon I want to get used to mingling with rich and famous people. I can get in a bit of practice tonight.'

'Masser,' said Sandra.

'Sandra?' said I.

'Masser, everyone wear mask tonight, yes?'

'Yes,' I told her. 'Everyone wear mask, yes.'

'So how come barman recognize Mr Jeff Beck and Harry recognize Sultan of Brunei?'

'Ah,' I said.

'And how come you *know* lots of rich and famous people be here, if all wear masks?'

'I'll confiscate your head again if you try to get too smarty-pantsed,' I said to Sandra. 'Rich and famous people are still recognizable no matter whether they're wearing masks or not. It's only in stupid films like *Superman* where Clark Kent can put on a pair of glasses and comb his hair differently and not be recognized.'

'Clark Kent is Superman?' said Sandra.

'Shut up and drink your drink,' I said to Sandra.

'Drink all finished. Most of it go down cleavage.'

'Go and speak to Olivia Newton John,' I said, pointing towards the instantly recognizable pint-sized diva. 'I'll mingle on my own.'

And so I mingled. I mingled with the rich and famous. They'd all turned out for the occasion. Because that's what they do, turn out for occasions. First nights, film premières, fashion shows, 'audience with' evenings. All those events are peopled with the rich and famous. Nonentities need not apply. Because, let's face it, the rich and famous have to have somewhere to go. Something to do. If they didn't, then they'd just have to stay at home watching the TV like the rest of us. So the rich and famous go to 'dos' where they're on the guest list. It's a very small world and the same rich and famous meet the other same rich and famous again and again. In fact, that's all they ever meet. Which is why they have affairs and intermarry and divorce and do it all again. In the same little circle. And it's a tiny little circle. There are two hundred and twenty-three of them. You can look them up and count them if you don't believe me. There will always be, at any one time in history, exactly two hundred and twenty-three rich and famous people

235

alive and all going to the same places at the same time in the world. Why? I just don't know, but there it is.

Most of them turned up for Barry's book launch that night. And I mingled with as many as I possibly could.

But I didn't have any idea at the time where this mingling was going to lead me and I certainly wasn't expecting the evening to end in the way that it did.

Which was not a pleasing way.

Although it was certainly different.

19

I really like the rich and famous. In my opinion, the rich and famous prove Darwin's theory of evolution. It took millions of years for man to evolve into man. The state of manness that we are today. And no one has ever found the missing link, or the many missing links, that join the chain of human evolution together. But if you want to see the entire process played at fast forward as if on a video machine, then view the life of a self-made rich and famous personality. They start out as nothing – just another part of the great homogeneous mass of mankind, that great seething organism. But they evolve, they take on an identity of their own, an individuality; they rise from the collective primordial mire, they raise their heads, they *become*. It's a complete evolutionary cycle. They demonstrate the potential of mankind. They are an example to us all of what is possible.

Not that most of them deserve their fame and fortune. Do me a favour!

Most of them are talentless cretins who just happened to be in the right place at the right time and *made* it.

Do I sound bitter about this? Do I?

Well, I'm not. I know that it's true. But I do like them. And what I really like most about them is their excess. The way they waste away millions. I was brought up in a poor household and I was conditioned to be careful with my money. I spend a bit on clothes, but not a lot, and I never *waste* money. I was taught to understand the value of money. My daddy was really hot on the *value* of money, which was probably why he never gave me any. 'Money must be earned and then looked after,' he used to say, which was another reason that I hated him. It's hard to break away from that kind of early programming. The rich and famous are able to do that. They can squander, big time. They have it, so they spend it and they enjoy spending it. They don't turn off lights after them, they don't have to sniff the milk from the fridge to see if it's fresh (it always *is* if you're rich). They can buy the fluffy toilet rolls that cost that bit too much. They don't give a damn for a 'two for one' offer. They don't say, 'A watch is a watch. I'll have this cheap one.' They say, 'That's a *really* nice watch. I don't give a damn how much it costs, I'll have it. And the car too, and the house – no, make that two houses. And a yacht.'

I sort of yearned to be like that. But it was different for me. I was programmed. I'd been conditioned. I had been taught to be frugal. So I didn't know whether I had in me that special something that would allow me to squander money if I ever got to be rich and famous.

I thought I'd go and have a word with Jeff Beck. I'd heard that he'd bought himself some really expensive guitars. Had them handmade to his own specifications. Paid a fortune for them. I thought I'd like to shake the hand that played those exclusive guitars.

But although I hung around on the periphery of Jeff's group of chatting chums, I didn't get the opportunity to say hello and tell him about how I'd seen him back in the days when he was paying his dues at the Blue Triangle Club. So I thought, stuff it, and went off to mingle elsewhere.

And while I was trying to find someone to mingle with, I found myself in the vicinity of the food table. And what a lot of food was on it, and all expensive too. It was quite a trouble getting into the *near* vicinity of the food table, there were so many rich and famous crowded around and filling their porcelain plates.* They do like to trencher down free grub, the rich and famous, which is another thing I admire them for.

I had to make my presence felt in order to get near that table. I had to tread on David Bowie's toe and elbow Cat Stevens in the ribs, but when I did get myself right up close to the extravagant nosh I spied a most curious thing. I spied someone slipping silver spoons into their pocket.

Now I know that the rich and famous are not averse to this kind of behaviour. And I know that their status makes them immune from prosecutions. Like that secret law that allows people with expensive four-wheel-drives to park on double yellow lines, when the rest of us would get nicked for it. But I was strangely shocked to see it happening right before my eyes. And

*Not paper plates, you note, but porcelain. There's posh for you.

239

as this was Barry's bash and those were Harry's/Peter's spoons, I was doubly offended by it.

I leaned over and grasped the wrist of the offender. 'Excuse me, sir,' I said, for he was a he, 'but I think you've inadvertently slipped a load of silver spoons into your pocket. I think we should perhaps go and discuss this matter outside.'

The offender turned to face me. He wore one of those burglar eye masks, the sort that the Lone Ranger used to wear. He also wore what appeared to be a prison uniform of the comic-book persuasion that have the arrowhead (or is it crow's-foot?) motifs all over them.

'Blimey,' said the malcontent. 'Blimey, Gary, it's you.'

I stared once and then I stared again.

'Dave,' I said. 'Dave Rodway, it's you.'

'It was, the last time I looked,' said Dave. 'But I don't look often, in case I'm up to something. If you know what I mean, and I'm sure that you do.'

'I certainly do,' I said. 'But what are you doing here? I thought you were doing a five stretch in Strangeways.'

'I absconded,' said Dave. 'Stole the governor's keys and his motorcar and absconded. It was dull in there and they wouldn't let me work in the laundry room.'

'Well, bravo, Dave,' I said. 'Let me get you a drink.'

'Nice,' said Dave. 'But let me nick you one instead.'

'I can get the drinks for free,' I said.

'Where's the sport in that?'

I let Dave nick us a bottle of bubbly, then we ejected a couple of Miracles* from a comfy-looking

---

*Naturally we wouldn't have dared to do this if Smokey Robinson had been about, for we knew his reputation as a bad man to mess with.

sofa and sat down.

'Cheers,' said Dave, pouring drinks, and we drank.

'This is brilliant,' I said. 'Seeing you again. I've missed you, Dave.'

'No, you haven't,' said Dave.

'I have, *a bit*.'

'I heard about Sandra. I'm sorry about that.'

'She's over there, chatting with Olivia Newton John,' I said.

'She's *what*?' said Dave. 'But she's *dead*.'

'*Was* dead,' I said. 'I reanimated her, like with Mr Penrose. I dug her up first, though.'

'Well done,' said Dave. 'You're still into all that death and magic stuff, then? You're still a weirdo. I'm glad. I thought you'd sold out to the system.'

'*Me?* Never.'

'So what are you doing? Up to no good? Wheeling and dealing? Being your own man?'

'Absolutely,' I lied. 'The nine-to-five will never be me, as Sid Barrett used to sing.'

'Cool,' said Dave. 'And what about Harry? Fell on his feet with this job, eh?'

'Bought a motorbike,' I said, draining my glass. 'But what are you doing here?'

'I happened to be passing by – well, *running* by. I'd been perusing a civilian suit in a West End tailor's and the alarm went off. The sissy boy bouncer saw my mask and thought I was a guest.'

'And so we meet up again. What a happy coincidence.'

'Yeah,' said Dave. 'What about that, eh?'

We got stuck into the bottle of champagne.

'So,' said Dave, by way of conversation. 'How is Sandra holding up? Is she – how shall I put this delicately? – is she, well, decomposing?'

'Sadly, yes,' I said. 'I have to keep gluing bits back on. But they're making all kinds of advances in the field of medicine nowadays, grafting and suchlike. I have high hopes for the future.'

Dave nodded thoughtfully and the eyes behind the mask followed a particularly delicious-looking young woman in next to no clothing, who was clicking her high-heeled way towards the ladies. 'Look at the body on that,' said Dave.

'Yes,' I said, and I sighed.

'Sandra had a good body,' said Dave.

'Very good,' I agreed.

'Very curvy in all the right places.'

'Very curvy, yes.'

'And that little mole on her bum. And the way she whinnied like a pony when she—'

'Eh?' I said. 'What?'

'Oh, nothing,' said Dave. 'All women have moles on their bums. And the posh ones always whinny when they, you know . . .'

'Do they?' I asked.

'So I am reliably informed.'

'I quite miss the mole,' I said. 'It came off last week.'

'Shame,' said Dave. 'You should get Sandra a new one.'

'A new mole? Where do you buy new moles?'

'I wasn't suggesting that you buy one. I was thinking more that you *acquire* one.'

'*Acquire* one? What are you talking about?'

242

Dave set his glass aside and put the champagne bottle to his lips. He took a big swig and then wiped his mouth on his sleeve. 'She needs spare parts,' said Dave. 'She's your wife; you care about her. Her welfare should come first.'

'It does,' I said.

'Then get her some spare parts. If a leg gets ropy, get her a new one. Get her two. And a bum.'

'Her navel's caved in,' I said.

'Then get her a new stomach, and tits.'

'She could certainly do with new tits,' I said.

'Then go the full Monty: get her an entire new ensemble. A whole new body. It would be great for her, like having a new dress. And it would be great for you. A new body. A *fresh* new body.'

'It's a thought,' I said. 'And a good one. I could dig one up for her, I suppose.'

'Use your brain,' said Dave. 'Why dig up a dead one? It would already be going mouldy. Get her a new fresh body. Get her a live one.' He nodded towards the delicious young woman who was now coming out of the Ladies. 'Get her *that* one.' And he turned and winked through his eye mask. 'Sandra would really appreciate *that* one.'

'What are you saying?' I asked, but I knew exactly what he was saying.

'You know exactly what I'm saying,' said Dave. 'How long have we been bestest friends, Gary?'

'For ever,' I said. 'As long as I can remember.'

'And we trust each other, yes?'

'No,' I said. 'I wouldn't trust you as far as I could poke you with a stick.'

'That's not what I mean. I mean that we can trust each other in that what we say to each other will never go any further. We can trust *in* each other.'

'Absolutely,' I said. 'How could it be any other way?'

'Exactly,' said Dave. 'So we are honest with each other.'

'Absolutely,' I said.

'So let's be honest,' said Dave. 'Where are you working, Gary?'

'At the telephone exchange,' I said. 'I've been there for five years.'

'There,' said Dave. 'That wasn't difficult, was it?'

'No,' I said. 'I didn't like lying to you.'

'Good,' said Dave. 'So, I'll ask you another question and you'll give me an honest answer, yes?'

'Yes,' I said.

'OK,' said Dave, in a lowered tone. 'To your knowledge, how many deaths have you been responsible for, Gary?'

I scratched my head. What kind of question was *that*? I mean, what kind of questions *was* that?

'I'm waiting,' said Dave.

I stared at Dave.

'How many?' said Dave.

'A few,' I said. 'Maybe.'

'A few,' said Dave. 'Maybe. And that would account for your daddy, the ice-cream man, and Count Otto Black and Sandra, by proxy. I might have been in the nick when Count Otto copped it, but I knew what he was up to with Sandra. And I recognized your hand in his tragic demise.'

I shrugged and made an innocent face, but as I was wearing a domino mask Dave couldn't see me making it.

'So, that would be four,' said Dave. 'You never actually laid a hand on them, but I know, and you know that I know, that you were directly responsible. I'm asking you how many others you have actually *killed* by your own hand.'

'It's not so many,' I said.

'*How* many?' said Dave.

'About thirty.'

'*About* thirty?'

'Thirty-two. No, '*three*.'

'Thirty-three would be the taxi driver I ran past earlier in the quiet street round the corner, I'll bet.'

'You should have seen how much he wanted to charge us for the fare.'

'I'm not judging you,' said Dave. 'I'm your friend. Your bestest friend. The fact that you are a serial killer does not affect our friendship.'

'Nor should it,' I said. 'It has nothing to do with our friendship. Have I ever condemned you for being a thief?'

Dave shook his head. 'You killed Captain Runstone, didn't you?' said he.

'I did.' I sighed. 'He was the very first – no, second, actually. He caught me in the restricted section of the Memorial Library. He was drunk and he tried to interfere with me.'

'Self-defence,' said Dave. 'You'd have got away with that one.'

'Oh, I didn't mind him interfering with me,'

I said. 'I quite liked it. But his breath smelt rotten.'

'You'd have gone down,' said Dave. 'You were wise to keep quiet. But what about all the rest?'

'I don't know,' I said. 'It was just here and there. People upset me. They make me angry. I hit them. I don't mean to. Something just comes over me, or into me, or something, and I'm not myself, I just do it. There was the labourer, once, on a building site, where Mother Demdike's hut used to be. He was a homophobe. Something came over me. I lost my temper. Stuff like that.'

'Well, I'm your bestest friend and I would never grass you up, as you know. It's your thing. It's the way you are.'

'It's my daddy's fault,' I said. 'I've read a lot about this sort of thing. An abused child becomes an abusing adult. It's in the programming.'

'Yeah, right,' said Dave. 'But I'm not judging you. All I'm saying, and this is the whole point of this conversation, you love Sandra and so you should put Sandra first. And if that means sacrificing a few young, nubile, attractive women to acquire their bodies as replacements, then you should consider it. You would be doing it for your Sandra. The benefits for yourself would of course be secondary.'

'Yes,' I said and I nodded thoughtfully. 'You have a good point there.'

'Of course I do,' said Dave. 'And I took the liberty of placing the dead cabbie in the boot of his cab and helping myself to the keys. So, if you wish to acquire the nubile young woman later, I'll be more than pleased to give you a hand.'

'You're a real friend, Dave,' I said, putting out my hand for a shake. 'I've wanted to talk to people about the bad things I do, but I know they'd only freak out and tell the police and then I'd have to go to prison and I don't want to go to prison. I'm really glad we could talk about it. It's good to have a friend like you.'

'Of course it is,' said Dave, shaking my hand. 'I'm your bestest friend.'

And so we drank some more champagne.

And we chatted about the good old days and we buddied up once again and I thought to myself what a wonderful thing real friendship is and how you can't put a price on it. Which is probably why the rich and famous, for all the money they have to squander, never have any real friends.

Dave nicked another bottle of champagne and we took to drinking that too.

And, of course, when you drink a lot of champagne and you're in the company of your bestest friend you do tend to talk *too much*.

'I talk to the dead every night,' I said to Dave.

'Now, why doesn't that surprise me at all?' Dave said in reply. 'You've finally taken to drugs, then, have you?'

'No, it's not drugs. I really do talk to the dead. On the telephone.'

'Yeah, right,' said Dave.

'No, really.' And I told Dave all about FLATLINE. *All* about FLATLINE.

'Bowls of bleeding bile!' said Dave when at last I was done with my telling. 'And this is *true*?'

'*All* true,' I said. 'All of it.'

'And you haven't got caught?'

'Barry and I have it sewn up.'

Dave shook his head and he shook it violently. 'You are in big trouble,' he said. 'And I mean the biggest.'

'Eh?' said I. 'What are you saying?'

'I'm saying,' said Dave, 'that I've heard about this. In the nick. I met an old boy in there – he'd been in for years – who told me about the FLATLINE thing and I didn't know whether to believe him or not. But if you've actually spoken with the dead, then it must be true.'

'Who is this old boy?' I asked.

'His name is Terence Trubshaw.'

'I've heard the name,' I said. 'He was a bulbsman. Mr Holland told me about him. He took a day off. It was wartime. They banged him up for forty years.'

'He didn't take a day off. He found out about the program. It wasn't called FLATLINE then. It had a secret operations name. Operation Orpheus. He was a Greek mythical bloke who went into the underworld.'

'I knew that,' I said.

'Well, it was part of the war effort. They had all kinds of weird secret operations back then. Because the Nazis had contacted aliens from outer space who were supplying them with advanced technology so they could win the war. Be a puppet world power run by the aliens.'

'Get real,' I said.

'It's true,' said Dave. 'Well, according to Mr Trubshaw, it is. The allies had to produce something pretty special, so some bright spark came up with the idea of contacting the dead by scientific means. The theory was to interrogate German officers who had been killed in the war. German officers who knew stuff, like secret information that the allies needed. They had this bloke who could impersonate Hitler's voice. They managed to tune into the dead by using certain radio frequencies and mathematical calculations and the impersonator interrogated the dead officers and got all their information and that's how the allies really won the war.'

'And Mr Trubshaw told you that?'

'He found out. Memos that he shouldn't have seen got put on his desk by mistake and he read them.'

'Oh,' I said. 'And how did he get found out about the memos?'

'He said that the entire telephone exchange is bugged. There's secret cameras and microphones everywhere. Well, there would be, wouldn't there, if it was a secret operations HQ in the war? And apparently all this stuff still goes on secretly. And the British government goes on pulling the same scam. When someone politically important overseas dies, or is assassinated, they call them up on this FLATLINE hot line, impersonating their Prime Minister, or King, or suchlike, and get secret information out of them, which is why Britannia still rules the waves.'

'But it doesn't rule the waves,' I said. 'There is no British Empire any more.'

'Oh yes, there is,' said Dave. 'England is really the ultimate world power, because we alone have the FLATLINE technology. England might not seem to be the power controlling the world, but it is.

249

It's all a big conspiracy. It's the biggest secret.'

'Well,' I said, 'thanks for sharing that with me.'

'Gary,' said Dave. 'Gary, my bestest friend. Don't mess around with this stuff any more. Leave it alone or you are going to turn up missing. This is a big deal here and you could be in *really* big trouble.'

'Yes,' I said. 'I appreciate that.'

'Run,' said Dave. 'Run now. Tonight. Don't go back.'

'Where can I run to?' I asked. 'I don't have any money. Where would I go? And anyway, just hold on here, I've been doing this for months and I haven't got caught yet. Maybe they don't have all the bugs and cameras any more. After all, they are a bit free and easy with the technology. Letting their operatives call up their dead grannies and suchlike.'

'They've all signed the Official Secrets Act. They know what the penalties are.'

'Yeah, but . . .'

'Get out,' said Dave. 'Run. This is big. It doesn't come any bigger.'

'Yes,' I said to Dave. 'You're right about that. It really doesn't come any bigger than this, does it?'

'No,' said Dave. 'It's huge. It's world-sized.'

'Yes,' I said. 'It is. I've been going about this thing all the wrong way.'

Dave made groaning noises.

'No, really, listen. Barry and I have been doing "biographies", dictated by the dead. That's what the launch party here tonight is for. P. P. Penrose dictated his life story to Barry.'

Dave laughed. 'Not to *you*, then? What a surprise.'

'Cut it out,' I said. 'I admit it, I didn't have the nerve to talk to him. But think about it, Dave: if the dead are willing to talk, they might be willing to talk about *anything*. We were just thinking biographies, but that was Barry's idea. You've given me a better idea. What about all those dead criminals, like, say, pirates for instance? They might be prepared to tell us where they buried their treasure. And not just criminals. Leonardo da Vinci might tell us where he hid his last notebook. Michelangelo might tell us about the location of a few missing masterworks.'

'Hitler's mob probably had all that lot,' said Dave.

'Yeah,' said I. 'And a whole lot more. There must be tons of hidden booty that only the dead know about. I don't know why I never thought of this before.'

'Because you weren't with your bestest friend,' said Dave.

'You are so right,' said I.

'And perhaps *you're* right too,' said Dave. 'Perhaps the fact that you haven't been caught means that there isn't any surveillance. I think that, together, you and I might pull off a very big number here.'

'The very biggest,' said I.

'Mind you,' said Dave, 'this will have to be between you and me. We daren't have any loose ends. No smoking pistols. No one but the two of us must know about this. Are we agreed?'

'We are,' I said. 'Anyone else,' and I drew my finger across my throat, 'no matter who they are.'

'Hello.'

I looked up and so did Dave.

'Enjoying yourself?'

'Yes indeed, Barry,' I said.

Sandra drove Dave and me home in the taxi. I was far too drunk to drive and also too excited.

Sandra drove very well, considering.

Considering that she had to get used to the nice new nubile body I had rather drunkenly and lopsidedly attached to her neck. But she did very well and I rewarded her later with as much sex as I could manage, considering my condition.

I had to set the alarm clock for five and get up to dispose of the taxi. I didn't want anyone finding Sandra's old body in the boot, so I drove out to a bombsite in Chiswick and set it on fire.

It burned beautifully and I enjoyed watching it burn. I considered its burning to be a kind of phoenix rising from the ashes of my past. A new beginning. For me. For Sandra. And for Dave. I felt that up until now I had been going about things in all the wrong way. Well, not really going about them in any way at all, when it came down to it. I'd just been drifting along on a life tide, washed from one situation to the next, with all my attempts at finding a real purpose and making a real success of myself failing, failing, failing. This would be a new beginning. This, I felt sure, was my fate. And I smiled as I watched that taxi burn and felt warm and happy inside.

My enjoyment was temporarily spoiled, however, by a lot of noisy banging that suddenly came from the inside of the taxi's boot.

I knew that it wasn't the cabbie.

And I knew that it wasn't Sandra's headless bits and bobs.

So I suppose that it must have been Barry.

But it soon calmed down and stopped.

And the taxi was soon reduced to a charred ruination.

And so, although I had a terrible hangover, I went off to work at the telephone exchange.

With a big fat smile on my face.

20

Priceless, really, the way things turn out.

Dave didn't have a motorbike, but he was the first person to apply for the vacancy at the telephone exchange. For the night-shift bulb-booth operator. Which was still referred to as the position of tele-communications engineer.

I called in on Dave at a little after eleven p.m.

'You look a bit shagged out,' said Dave.

'I am,' said I. 'Sandra's new body is a blinder.'

'Can I have a go?' Dave asked.

'Certainly not. Get your own zombie.'

'Hm,' said Dave. 'When you put it like that, it sort of puts it in perspective. I think I'll stick with living girlfriends.'

'So, what are we doing tonight?'

'Well,' said Dave, 'I made a list of possibilities.'

'Yes?' I said.

'And then I crossed them all out.'

'Why?' I asked.

'Because I used my head,' said Dave. 'If you want to be a really great thief, then you have to use your head. You have to put yourself in the position of the person you're stealing from. Think, if I were *you* where would I, as you, hide the booty?'

'Go on,' I said.

'So,' said Dave, 'it occurred to me that we would not be the first people to come up with this idea. After all, FLATLINE, or Operation Orpheus, has been around since wartime. Don't you think that others before us would have thought of doing what we intend to do?'

'Yes,' I said. 'You're right.'

'I am,' said Dave. 'So, following the direction of this thinking, where does it lead us to?'

'I don't know,' I said. 'Where?'

'To the top,' said Dave. 'You'd have to go to the top.'

'To God?' I said.

'To Winston Churchill,' said Dave.

'What?' said I.

'Churchill would know,' said Dave, 'where all the Nazi booty went. He'd have got his Hitler impersonator to find out. So Churchill is the man to speak to.'

I shook my head. 'I don't know about this,' I said. 'We're not just going for Nazi booty here. We're going for *all* booty.'

'In recent history, the Nazis nicked the most. It's probably all in Switzerland in special bank vaults.'

'I'm getting out of my depth here,' I said.

'I'm not,' said Dave. 'Nicking is my business. Let me have an hour on the phone with Mr Churchill and we'll both be rich men. I've looked up his death date, like you told me you have to. I've got it here. Let's do it.'

'Well, I can't see any harm in that. Let's give it a go. Follow me.'

And Dave followed me.

We took the lift to the seventeenth floor. I picked the lock of room 23 and led Dave to the telephone box. 'Take as long as you like,' I said. 'Dial in his full name and date of birth,' and I explained to him all the rest, 'and do your stuff.'

'Sorted,' said Dave and he entered the telephone box.

I dithered about outside. I paced up and down, then I sat and smoked a cigarette. Then I paced, then sat and smoked another one.

At what seemed a very great length, Dave emerged from the telephone box. And Dave didn't look very well.

'Are you all right?' I asked him. 'You look a bit shaky.'

'I *am* a bit shaky,' said Dave. 'I wasn't expecting to hear all that I just heard. That Winston Churchill is a very angry dead man.'

'Oh,' I said. 'Why?'

'He says that he was betrayed. He says that a secret élite is plotting to take over the world.'

'The British government,' I said. 'You told me that.'

'Not them,' said Dave. 'He says aliens.'

'Space aliens?'

'According to Winston Churchill. And who is going to argue with *him*?'

'Did he say anything about the booty?'

'Oh yeah,' said Dave. 'He said lots. Apparently there's a secret underground complex beneath Mornington Crescent tube station. All the booty is there. And all the rest of it. The real communications network centre.'

'For communications with the dead?'

'No, the aliens. The aliens who are us.'

'I don't know what you are talking about,' I said. 'But let me tell you this, Dave, and I'm sorry I didn't mention it to you earlier. You can't take everything the dead say as gospel truth. They have a tendency to make stuff up. They tell a lot of lies. I wouldn't take this aliens stuff too seriously if I were you.'

'I wouldn't have,' said Dave, 'except that it tied up with something that you told me years ago, when we were kids. Remember when you told me that you'd overheard those two blokes talking about human beings not really doing their own thinking? About their thoughts being directed from somewhere else outside their heads? About our brains being receivers and transmitters but not really brains that do thinking? Remember?'

'I do remember,' I said. 'Those two young men in the restricted section of the Memorial Library. One of them works here now.'

'And there was something about this at your daddy's trial, although it wasn't reported in the papers.'

'The Daddy must have known something about all this,' I said.

'He did work for the GPO,' said Dave. 'And you told me that he was on bomb disposal in the war. Perhaps he was part of the secret operations network.'

'Now, hold on,' I said. 'Are we going to get rich here, or not?'

'That sounds like the kind of question *I* should be asking.'

'Well, you ask it, then.'

'No,' said Dave. 'But I'll ask you this. What do you think *we* should do? We could go to Mornington Crescent and if there's anything valuable there that can be nicked I assure you that I can nick it. Or, and this is a big or, we could go to Mornington Crescent and try to find out what the truth of all this really is. What do *you* think?'

I thought long and I thought hard and it was a whole lot of thinking.

'All right,' I said, when finally I had done all the thinking that I could do. 'Let's go.'

'And do what?' asked Dave. 'One or the other?'

'Let's do both,' I said.

'OK,' said Dave. 'That's cool.'

Now, this wasn't going to be easy, because I worked the day shift and Dave worked the night shift and so I couldn't see how we could go together. And even if we *did* go together, how we were going to find what we were looking for, whatever *exactly* that was. I confided my doubts to Dave and Dave was, as Dave had always been, optimistic and up for no good. And, as he always had been, up to doing things at his leisure.

'You leave it with me,' said Dave. 'I have to do a bit more research with a few more dead men. I'll get back to you in a few days.'

'Don't you want me to let you into room 23 each night?' I asked. But that was a stupid question. This was Dave, after all.

'I'll let myself in,' said Dave. 'You go home. Give my best to Sandra, if you know what I mean and I'm sure that you do. And if we meet as we change shifts, just nod. Pretend you don't know me.'

'OK,' I said and I shook hands with Dave. I felt absolutely confident in Dave. After all, he was my bestest friend and he had never, ever, let me down. I trusted him. He was the only one I had ever owned up to regarding my homicidal tendencies. I'd never mentioned them to Sandra. Some things you just don't say to your wife although you would say them to your mate. It's a man-thing, I suppose.

So I went home and gave Dave's best to Sandra.

And for the next week I just nodded to Dave when I changed shifts with him, and he nodded back when he changed shifts with me. And then I found a note on the table of the bulb booth telling me to meet him on Friday evening at eight-thirty at the Golden Dawn.

So on Friday evening I togged up in my very bestest, put Sandra's head in the fridge to keep it fresh and stop her wandering about while I was out, and strolled off down the road towards the Golden Dawn.

It was a fine Friday evening. It smelled of fish and chips, as Friday evenings so often do, and there was still some sun left, as there generally is on a summery Brentford evening. And as I strolled along I wondered, quietly and all to myself, exactly what Dave might have come up with and where it might lead me and whether it might make me rich. Because I was warming more and more to the prospect of becoming rich. I felt that it was about time that I got what I knew I deserved.

It was all quiet and peaceful in the Golden Dawn. As quiet and peaceful as it had been the last time I was there. Which was more than six months before: on the night of my wedding anniversary, when Sandra had told me that she was going off for the caravanning holiday with Count Otto Black. I had Sandra wearing red now, by the way. I felt that she had mourned long enough.

But I'd actually quite forgotten about Eric the barman's threats to me. About how he said he'd grass me up if I didn't find out all about what went on in Developmental Services, because he had this thing about people's True Names and how some of the folk in Developmental Services – well, one at least: Neil Collins – didn't seem to have a True Name.

When I strolled into the Golden Dawn, and saw him standing there behind the pump, it brought it all back to me and I really cursed Count Otto for fouling up the orders I had sent him through the voodoo medium of Frank the invisible Chinaman, which caused him to butcher my Sandra instead of the blackmailing landlord.

I only mention all this in case you might have forgotten about it.

'Well, well, well, well,' said Eric. 'If it isn't my old chum the Archduke of Alpha Centuri.'

'Well, well, well, well,' I replied. 'If it isn't my *very* good friend Kimberlin Malkuth, Lord of a Thousand Suns. A pint of Large, please, and a packet of crisps.'

'I've been missing you,' said the barlord. 'For so many months now. You and I had an understanding, I remember.'

'Indeed,' I said. 'I've not forgotten. But I had a death in the family. My dear Sandra was cruelly taken from me.'

'Yes,' said Eric. 'I read about all that in the papers. Tragic business. Poor Lady Fairflower of the Rainbow Mountains. The world is a sadder place without her.'

I nodded and he nodded and then he presented me with my pint. 'But life goes on,' he said. 'We should be grateful for that.'

'We should,' I agreed.

'And the fact that you stand there before me means that you are now all grieved out and ready to face life without the Lady Fairflower. It also means that you have come to tell me all that I need to know regarding Developmental Services.'

'It does,' I said. 'Shall we step outside and discuss this matter in private?'

The barlord nodded and I smiled at the barlord.

A hand, however, fell upon my shoulder.

I turned and said, 'Dave,' for Dave's hand it was that had fallen.

'Not now,' whispered Dave in my ear. 'Wait until after closing time. You can do for him and I will do for the cash register.'

'You are, as ever, as wise as your years,' I whispered back. 'I'll tell you everything later,' I said to Eric. 'After closing, in private.'

'Right,' said Eric. 'And you see that you do. I'll lock up, then when I've kicked everyone out I'll let you back in the side door.'

'Perfect,' I said.

'Double perfect,' said Dave.

'A pint for Dave too,' I said to Eric.

'Indeed,' said the barlord. 'Always a pleasure to serve a pint to Barundi Fandango the Jovian

Cracksman.' And Eric once more did the business.

Dave took me over to a side table and we took sup from our pints.

'It has to be this weekend,' said Dave.

'What does?' I asked.

'Mornington Crescent. We have to go this weekend.'

'OK,' I said. 'But why?'

'Because I'm in too much danger of getting nicked and dragged back to prison. I'm working at the telephone exchange under a fake name. I'm a wanted man, remember. I told them that my cards and my P45 were being sent on by my last employer, but I think they're already becoming suspicious. I shall have to run this weekend no matter what. So we do it now, or we don't do it at all.'

'Seems reasonable,' said I. 'What is your plan?'

'Well, I've chatted with a lot of dead blokes this week and remembering what you said about them lying, I've been careful to cross-reference everything. I know how to get into Mornington Crescent and I have a pretty good idea of what kind of booty is in there. And it's *lots*. But there's something more. Something in there that frightens the dead and they don't want to tell me about.'

'Something that frightens the dead? I don't like the sound of that.'

Dave shook his head. 'You've had months and months at this, haven't you?' he said. 'You could have asked loads and loads of questions of the dead. You could have found out amazing stuff. Why didn't you?'

I shrugged. 'I've thought about this,' I said. 'Death

was my major interest when I was young. All I ever wanted to do was find out the point of it. I could never see the point, do you understand? I could see the point of life, but never death.

'I wanted to find out the truth. But when it actually came to it, when I actually found myself talking to the dead, I never had the nerve to ask. The first dead person I spoke to was my dad and he wanted to tell me something fantastic. But Barry cut me off and I never spoke to him again. I bottled out. I don't know why. I think it's because the living aren't supposed to know and I didn't want to know.'

Dave shook his head again. 'You're a real mess, Gary,' he said. 'Other people, given the opportunity that you were given, would really have gone for it. They'd have found out.'

'So, have you found out, then? The truth about everything?'

'No,' said Dave. 'I haven't. But that's because they wouldn't tell me. But I know enough to know where to look. It's all there at Mornington Crescent. And if you have the bottle to go there with me, we'll find out together.'

'I have the bottle,' I said. 'I'm not scared. I'm brave.'

'That's good,' said Dave. 'But you are telling me the truth, aren't you? There's no going back. When we do what I plan that we're going to do, there will be no going back. It's a total commitment.'

I sipped at my pint. 'What exactly are you saying?' I asked.

'I'm saying that this is the big one. For you and for me. If we don't do this, if we don't do the Big One, do it and get away, it will be all up for us. They'll get us, Gary. They'll catch me and drag me back to boring Strangeways. And they'll get you too. It's only a matter of time before they get you. You've killed thirty-three people. No, it's thirty-four now, isn't it? Counting Sandra's body-donor.'

'It's thirty-five, actually.'

'Thirty-five?'

'There was this smelly old tramp yesterday as I was walking to work. He asked me for money. He was so ugly. God, I've always hated ugly people.'

'Then I'm glad I'm so damnedly handsome.'

'You're not all *that* handsome.'

'But I'm not *ugly*.'

'No,' I said, 'you're not ugly, Dave.'

'Well, thank the Lord for that. So it's thirty-five and by the end of this evening it will probably be thirty-six.'

'It will *definitely* be thirty-six.'

'So it's time to be away. Do the Big One and away to Rio. We'll shack up with Ronnie Biggs.'

'I'll have to take Sandra. She can't manage on her own.'

'We'll take Sandra. It will be like Butch Cassidy and the Sundance Kid and the woman on the crossbar of the bike whose name no one can remember.'

'Why should anyone want to remember the name of a bike?' I asked.

'Was that some sad attempt at humour?'

'Possibly,' I said and I finished my pint. 'So what you're saying is that we pull off this huge Big One this weekend, then have it away on our toes to Rio.'

'If you're up for it.'

'I am,' I said. 'I'm absolutely up for it.'

'Good,' said Dave. 'I'm so very glad that you said that.'

I shrugged. 'Fine,' I said.

'No,' said Dave. 'I mean that I'm *very* glad. Because, you see, you can't go back to work at the telephone exchange, even if you want to. So I'm glad. All's well that ends well, or, we hope, will end well, eh?'

'Hold on,' I said. 'Slow down. What are you saying?'

'I was certain that you'd say yes,' said Dave. 'Which is why I'm here.'

'Yes, I can see that you're here. *What* do you mean?'

'I mean I'm here. I'm here *now*. At this minute, no one's manning the bulb booth, nor will do ever again.'

'What *do* you mean?' I asked once more, but with a different emphasis.

'Ah,' said Dave, cupping a hand to his ear. 'Listen.'

I listened and from the distance I heard the sound of bells. And sirens too, as well as bells.

'Fire engines,' I said.

'Yes,' said Dave. 'The telephone exchange is on fire.'

'It *is*?' I said. 'How do you know?'

Dave looked at me and raised his eyebrows.

'Oh,' I said.

Dave grinned at me. 'And when I say it's on fire,' he continued, 'I mean it's *really* on fire. *Someone* disabled the sprinkler system and emptied a whole load of petrol all over room 23. And barricaded the doors before crawling out of a back window. Oh, and really vandalized the bulb booth. Really badly. Nicked the bulb and everything.' Dave delved into his pocket and brought out the bulb in question. It was the XP103. 'Souvenir for you,' he said.

I took the bulb. It felt really weird in my hands. Like some kind of symbol or something. Something that meant something, but didn't, but still did, or something.

I put the bulb down on the table. 'You torched the place,' I said slowly.

Dave just nodded and grinned some more.

'You torched the telephone exchange. But why did you do it? Why?'

'Well,' said Dave, 'I don't know about you, but *I* really don't want to work there any more.'

I looked at Dave.

And Dave looked at me.

And then we both began to laugh.

21

I've never been a pyromaniac. The wanton destruction of property has always been anathema to me. But Dave and I did leave the Golden Dawn to wander down and watch the blaze.

And it was a very good blaze. Much better than the taxicab. The telephone exchange really went up.

Dave kind of skulked in the shadows. And that was all for the best, because in the midst of the conflagration, when people were coming and going and fire-fighters were making free with their hoses, Mr Holland appeared on the scene and came up to me all in tears.

'This is terrible,' wept Mr Holland.

'It's a bit of a surprise,' I said. 'But that's life for you, always full of surprises.'

'But the bulbsman,' wept Mr Holland, 'that nice new chap who does the night shift. He must surely have perished in the flames.'

'Sad,' I said. 'That *is* sad. Oh, look at that.' Certain explosions came from the seventeenth floor and policemen told us to get back to a safe distance.

'Tragedy,' wailed Mr Holland. 'This is a tragedy. Oh God, this is so terrible.'

'Terrible,' I agreed. 'But life must go on, I suppose.'

'My life is finished.' Mr Holland sniff-sniff-sniffed and wiped his nose on his sleeve. 'That exchange was my life.'

'That is *very* sad,' said I.

Tears ran down Mr Holland's face. 'I know I've been hard on you,' he snivelled. 'I know you must at times have hated me.'

I listened to him but I didn't nod, even though he was absolutely right.

'But the exchange was my life. Workers are just workers – they can always be replaced. There's always more. But the exchange is everything.'

'*Was* everything,' I corrected him.

'Tragedy,' wailed Mr Holland some more. 'My life is over. I wish I could depart this vale of tears.'

'Come with me,' I told him kindly. 'Let's go somewhere quiet and private and discuss this.'

And so, as one might an old incontinent dog that had been the beloved family pet but was now making too much mess on the duvet, I put Mr Holland out of his misery.

It was a very quiet alleyway and when I was done I turned to find Dave grinning at me.

'You certainly take pleasure in your work,' he said.

'He made me pee my pants the first day I worked at the exchange,' I said. 'I don't know why I waited so long.'

'Because you're such a great humanitarian, probably.'

And Dave and I laughed again.

'I'll hole up at your place tonight if that's OK,' said Dave. 'Then first thing tomorrow we do Mornington Crescent.'

Now, OK, I know what you're going to think about what happened next. You're going to think that it was wrong and immoral and downright wicked. But it wasn't really.

OK, Dave and I went back to my place. We had had a few drinks and then we had a few more to celebrate the end of the telephone exchange. And I got Sandra's head out of the fridge and put it back on that nice, nubile, shapely young body that Dave and I had acquired from Harry's/Peter's world-famous night club. And then we got to joking around a bit. And I don't know who suggested it first – I don't think I did, because I love Sandra, so maybe it was Dave – but one of us suggested that it might be fun to have a three-some. And if it wasn't me, and I don't think it was, then I was probably swayed by Dave, who said that it wouldn't really be having a threesome with Sandra *per se*, because the body wasn't Sandra's anyway, so if I just stuck to the top end and he stuck to the bottom end, where would be the harm in it? And we could always get Sandra a new body if we really messed up this one. So where *was* the harm in it?

And I had had a few drinks. And Dave was my bestest friend. And I'd always wondered just what it might be like to do that kind of thing. And I'd read that the rich and famous did it all the time.

And so we did it.

And I really quite enjoyed it.

And I know that Dave enjoyed it. There was no doubt about that, because he wanted to do it again quite soon after and I was too tired, so he did it on his own. Which wasn't the same. But as he let me watch, it sort of was.

I don't know whether Sandra enjoyed it.

Because I didn't ask her.

We all woke up at around ten o'clock in the morning. Because of all the banging on the front door. Dave went to see what was going on and he came back quite quickly. He only said four words to me, but they were enough.

'Police,' said Dave. 'Back door. Run.'

I got Sandra up off the floor and we headed for the back door. We struggled off down the alleyway and made our escape.

'We're committed now,' said Dave, and I knew what he meant.

'So, what are we going to do?' I asked him, as he opened up the rear door of a white transit van.

'We're going to make tracks sharpish,' explained my bestest friend. 'I acquired this van yesterday. Get Sandra into the back and we're gone.'

I had a terrible hangover. And Dave was a terrible driver.

'I've never had enough time to practise properly,' he explained. 'I've never had one vehicle long enough.'

We bumped up a kerb somewhere and down again.

'Tell me about your plan,' I said. 'But tell me quite quietly because my head hurts.'

'I know how to get into Mornington Crescent,' said

270

Dave. 'So in theory I know how to get out again. But what's inside, that's a bit of a grey area.'

'But it's an underground station.'

'What we're after is under the underground station.'

'Watch out for that old bloke on the bike,' I said. 'No, never mind, it's too late.'

'You should have put on your trousers,' said Dave. 'You look pretty silly in your underpants.'

I had Dave stop off at a fashionable boutique and steal me some trousers. And then we were off again.

And then Dave and I realized just how hungry we were. So we stopped at a café, left Sandra to snooze in the back of the van and went off to get some breakfast. And while we were having our breakfast I got a bit of a surprise. And just like all the other surprises I'd had, this surprise was an unpleasant one.

There was a television in the café and some kind of Saturday-morning children's show was on. I'd never seen it before, but it seemed to consist mostly of shouting. There were several presenters, a young-fellow-me-lad who looked as if he could do with a good smacking and a couple of sexy girls. They were all being terribly jolly and shouting good-naturedly and I was quite enjoying the show. But then the programme was suddenly interrupted by a special newscast.

I watched and I listened and my mouth fell open.

Elvis Presley was dead.

Dave tucked into his sausages and I pointed at the television and then I pointed at Dave and sort of croaking sounds came out of my mouth.

'Have you got bacon stuck in your throat?' Dave asked.

'Not . . . I . . . you . . . you . . .'

'Me? I'm fine, I've got sausage.'

'You . . . Elvis . . . you . . .'

'I'm not Elvis. Elvis has pegged it. Why have you gone all pale like that?'

I spluttered and coughed and got all of my voice back. 'You manking twonk!' I shouted at Dave. 'Look what you've done! Look what you've done!'

'I didn't do it. He probably died of hamburger poisoning, big fat pig that he was.'

'But you! You! You burned down the exchange.'

'Not so loud.' Dave flapped his hands about and nearly took his eye out with his fork.

'My passport to riches.'

'What are you going on about?'

'I've been waiting for someone like Elvis to die. So I could get them to dictate their life story to me down the FLATLINE phone. I'd have made millions out of Elvis. But you burned down the exchange.'

'Sorry,' said Dave. 'But how was I to know?'

'That's not the point. This is terrible.'

'No, it's not,' said Dave.

'It is.'

'It's not.'

'Is.'

'Not.'

I would have said 'is' once more, just to get my point across, but Dave was making a point of his own. Not with his mouth, but with his finger.

'Now, *that's* terrible,' he said. 'That's really terrible.'

I followed the direction of his pointing and its direction was towards the television screen. And when

I saw what Dave had seen, I had to agree that it *was* really terrible.

The face of Elvis Presley was no longer on the screen.

Instead was another face and it was *mine*.

'Gary Charlton Cheese,' the newscaster was saying. 'Aged twenty-seven. Wanted in connection with the arson attack on the Brentford telephone exchange, which it is believed resulted in the death of a telecommunications engineer who was working the night shift and the subsequent murder of Morris Holland, whose body was found this morning horribly mutilated. Police wish to question Mr Cheese regarding seventeen other so far unsolved murders, including that of Mr Eric Blaine, landlord of the Golden Dawn, whose body was also found this morning.'

'I didn't know you'd done him,' said Dave.

'Shut up,' I said to Dave.

'Chief Inspectre Sherrington Hovis of Scotland Yard is with us in the studio. Chief Inspectre, what information can you give us about Gary Charlton Cheese?'

'Hovis?' I said. 'Who's he?'

'A right shidogee,' said Dave. 'He's sent me down twice. Once he gets his teeth into a case, it's,' and Dave drew his finger across his throat, 'for the crim.'

'But how?' I spluttered a bit. 'How? Me? How?'

'Listen to the man,' said Dave.

And I listened to the man.

The man was an odd-looking cove. Thin as a bad wife's headache excuse, with a long and pointed nose of the style they call aquiline. He wore golden pince-nez and a four-piece suit of tweed. I recognized the tweed at once.

It was Boleskine tweed.

The very tweed that Lazlo Woodbine used to wear when he impersonated a newspaper reporter. Things like that mattered to me. Things like that also mattered to Dave.

'Note the four-piece,' said Dave. 'Enough said, I think.'

'The man knows his business and he *means* it,' said I.

The man was now talking to camera.

'Gary Charlton Cheese,' said Inspectre Hovis, in a fussy nasal tone, 'is a very dangerous man. If you see this man, do *not* approach him. And under no circumstances attempt to make a citizen's arrest. It is not my habit to compromise a homicide investigation by making a direct accusation against a suspect before he is brought before the due process of the law and stands trial. However, in this case I am going to make an exception, so damning is the forensic evidence against Mr Cheese – to whit, the new science of True Name Identification . . .'

'Eh?' said I.

And 'Eh?' said Dave.

'– that I have no qualms in identifying Mr Cheese as a serial killer. This man must be found and brought to justice.'

I looked at Dave. And Dave looked at me.

The newscaster looked at Chief Inspectre Sherrington Hovis. 'I understand, Chief Inspectre,' he said, 'that Parliament has passed a special Act to reinstate the death penalty for Mr Cheese. Is this correct?'

'It is,' said Inspectre Sherrington Hovis.

I looked at Dave once more. But Dave just shook his head.

'So great are this man's crimes against society,' said the chief Inspectre, 'that he cannot be permitted to live. Our investigations are ongoing and we expect to be able to tie Mr Cheese into over one hundred brutal killings.'

'One hundred?' I said.

And Dave whistled.

'Don't whistle,' I told him. 'I haven't murdered one hundred people. Nowhere near that figure.'

'The fix is in,' said Dave, turning his face to me. 'You're in the frame. He means to clear the London murder crime sheets for the last five years by stitching you up for all of them.'

'But I'm innocent,' I protested.

Dave raised an eyebrow to me.

'Mostly innocent,' I said.

'I think we'd better go,' said Dave. 'It's definitely South America for us. I'd best get on the phone to Mr Biggs and tell him we're coming.'

'I think we can forget about Mornington Crescent,' I said. 'Let's head for Dover.'

'Hold on there.' Dave made hold-hard hands-putting-ups. 'I don't have any money. Do you have any money? No, don't tell me, you don't. We can't get to Rio without many pennies in our pockets. It's Mornington Crescent or you might as well give yourself up. Or let me bring you in. There's bound to be a big reward.'

'You wouldn't?' I said.

'No, of course I wouldn't – you're my bestest friend. But we need big bucks and we need them now. And Mornington Crescent is the last place that anyone's going to be looking for you. Let's do the job, take the booty and flee these shores for ever. What do you say?'

I didn't hesitate. I said yes.

'That's sorted, then,' said Dave. 'Finish your breakfast, then I'll pay up and leave.'

'Oh, you're going to *pay*. This is new.'

'We don't want to call attention to ourselves, do we? We just want to behave as if we're perfectly normal people. Just like all the other people in this café.'

I glanced around and about. 'Dave,' I said. 'Dave.'

'What?' said Dave.

'Dave, we suddenly seem to be all alone in this café.'

Dave glanced all around and about also. In particular he glanced towards the cash register. 'The proprietor's gone,' he said. 'And all the waitresses, and the griddle chef too.'

And then we heard it. It came from outside, from the car park. I'd only heard it before in the movies and, I can tell you, it's much scarier in real life, especially when it's addressed to yourself.

It *was*, if you hadn't already guessed. A voice. A policeman's voice. And it was coming through one of those special police loud-hailers. Or bullhorns, as Laz used to call them. And anyone else too who lived in nineteen-fifties America, of course.

'Gary Charlton Cheese,' came through the police loud-hailer. 'We know you're in there. We have the place surrounded. Come out with your hands held high.'

'The format hasn't changed at all since the days of Laz,' said Dave. 'It's good to know that some things, at least, never change.'

'Very comforting,' I said. 'But how?'

'I suspect that the proprietor recognized you from your face on the TV, called the cops and quietly ushered out the patrons while we were talking,' said Dave.

Which explained everything, really.

'You have one minute,' said the voice from outside, 'before we employ the use of a short-range tactical missile and destroy the entire café.'

Another voice shouted, 'Oi, hang on, that's a bit drastic.'

This was the voice of the café's proprietor.

'Serves him right for grassing you up,' said Dave, who was now underneath the table.

'What are we going to do?' I asked him.

'Give yourself up. I'll forget about the reward. I'll even own up that I didn't die in your arson attack on the telephone exchange.'

'That's very big of you.'

'What are friends for?' asked Dave, which was probably a rhetorical question.

'We have to get out of here.'

'I can't see how.'

'Well, you wouldn't, not from down there. Come on, think of something.'

'You have thirty seconds,' came the police loud-hailer voice.

'It might not be him,' came the shouting voice of the café proprietor. 'In fact, now that I come to think of it, it didn't actually look like him at all. The bloke in there is a big fat fellow. And black, with dreadlocks. And one eye. That can't be him, can it?'

'Twenty seconds.'

'And a wooden leg. With a parrot on his shoulder.'

'Fifteen seconds.'

'It's been nice knowing you,' said Dave to me. 'Would you have any objections if I just ran outside with my hands up, before the tactical missile strikes home?'

I shrugged. 'No, I suppose not. I'm just sorry that we didn't have longer. We could have had one of those deep and meaningful conversations about the nature of friendship, with flashbacks to our childhood and stuff like that, like they do in the movies.'

'Ten seconds.'

'Shame,' said Dave. 'Sorry there's no time to shake your hand, but . . .'

'Five seconds.'

'That was a bit quick.'

'Three . . . two . . . one . . .'

And then there was this incredible explosion.

Half the side of the café came down. Chairs and tables rocketed towards us, borne by the force; pictures were torn from the walls; light fittings and fixtures shattered and toppled. There was tomato sauce everywhere. And mayonnaise, in those little hard-to-open sachets. And amidst all the force and the dust and the mashing and mayhem a voice called out to me. And the voice called: 'Come with me if you want to live.'*

I looked up and Sandra looked down, from the cab of the white transit van.

'Hurry up!' she shouted. 'My head nearly came off, driving through that wall.'

Dave and I scrambled from the rubble and scrambled some more into the transit. Sandra reversed it out at the hurry-up.

'Zero!' came the loud-hailer voice.

And then there was a *real* explosion.

---

*I know that this has now become a legendary phrase, uttered by the great Arnie Schwarzenegger. But, for the record, it was first uttered in that café in 1977.

22

I was really impressed with Sandra. That was genuine loyalty. That was love. That is what marriages are all about. And she drove very well for a woman. Especially a dead one. She managed to mow down at least three policemen as we left the car park. And a couple of civilians who were looking on.

Which served them right for being so nosy.

'I'm really impressed,' I said to Sandra, as she put her foot down and we sped away. 'That was genuine loyalty. That was love. That is what marriages are all about.'

'Sandra not do it for Masser Gary,' said Sandra. 'Sandra do it for Dave. Him great lover. Him has always been.'

'The woman's overexcited,' said Dave. 'She did it for *you*. She really did. Didn't you Sandra? You did it for Gary. Who won't put your head in the fridge any more. Or possibly rip it off and stamp on it, if he thought that you hadn't done it for him.'

'I did it for you, Masser Gary,' said Sandra. 'Sandra love Masser Gary.'

'That's the ticket,' said Dave.

'I'm upset by this,' I said to Dave, fishing a *London A–Z* from the glove compartment. 'Now, which way to Mornington Crescent?'

And then we heard the police sirens.

'Best put your foot down, Sandra,' said Dave.

'Oi!' I said. 'I'll order the zombie. Foot down, Sandra, *now.*'

'Sorry,' said Dave. 'No offence meant.'

'None taken, I assure you.'

They came up on us fast. But a transit is a transit and a police car is only a police car. We had one of them off the road at the roundabout and another into a row of parked cars soon after. Which left us only the helicopter.

'It's a helicopter!' shouted Dave. 'We'll never be able to lose *that.*'

'To the nearest underground station,' I said. 'We'll take the tube.'

'But we need a van for the booty.'

'We'll improvise when the time comes. To the nearest tube station, Sandra, and step on it.'

'Yes, Masser Gary,' said Sandra, bless her little heart. Charred though it was, in a burned-out cab in Chiswick.

Now happily for us, the nearest tube station was Earl's Court. And since there are loads of different lines that run through Earl's Court, the police wouldn't know which one we were getting on. So they wouldn't know which train to shut down in which tunnel. Which meant we were safe for now.

'Three singles to Mornington Crescent,' said Dave to the chap in the ticket office.

'Get real,' said the chap.

'Excuse me?' said Dave.

'Three singles to Mornington Crescent. Do I look like a complete twonker?'

'Yes,' said Dave. 'But what has that got to do with anything?'

'It has to do with the fact that Mornington Crescent station is closed for repairs.'

'Oh,' said Dave. 'Since when?'

'Since 1945.'

'You blokes on the transport don't rush yourselves with repairs, do you?'

'We're very thorough. We have the public's safety always in the forefront of our minds.'

'OK,' said Dave, 'what line is Mornington Crescent on?'

'The Northern line,' said the chap.

'And what's the nearest station to it, on that line?'

'Euston,' said the chap.

'Three singles to there, then.'

'Righty right,' said the chap. 'But just one thing.'

'Yes?' said Dave.

'The woman with you, the one with the wonky head that doesn't seem to match her body . . .'

'What about her?' asked Dave.

'Why is she stark bollard naked?' asked the chap.

'She's a naturist,' said Dave. And he paid up for the tickets.

Yes, well, I suppose that I should have had Dave nick some clothes for Sandra when he nicked some trousers for me from the fashionable boutique. But I can't be expected to think of everything.

I must confess that we didn't exactly blend in with all the other commuters. People kept looking at Sandra.

And, frankly, I found that rather offensive. Blokes eyeing up my missus. I felt that I should take issue with them. Possibly make an example of one.

'Don't,' said Dave, who apparently read my mind. 'We'll change from the District line at Embankment. Then we'll travel with the driver.'

'Do they let you do that?' I asked.

'No,' said Dave. 'But we'll sort it.'

At Embankment, we changed onto the Northern line. We got into the first carriage and Dave knocked on the driver's door. 'Inspector!' called Dave. 'Could I have a word?'

The driver opened the door. We pushed our way into his cab.

'Get out!' shouted the driver. 'You're not allowed in here.'

'Deal with the driver, Gary,' said Dave.

'Aaagh!' went the driver. 'It's Cheese the psycho killer. I saw you on TV.'

I dealt sternly with that driver. And then I turned to Dave. 'He recognized me,' I said.

'That's hardly surprising,' said Dave.

'Yeah, but no one else on the trains we've been on seemed to recognize me. How do you account for that?'

'I think Sandra might have distracted them.'

'Oh yeah. So what are we going to do now?'

'You're going to drive the train and stop it at Mornington Crescent.'

'But I don't know how to drive a train.'

'Sandra know,' said Sandra.

'You *do*?' I said.

'All middle-class girls taught how to drive trains at prep school,' said Sandra.

'Eh?' said I.

'In case society collapse. If revolution come. All middle-class girls taught everything. How to drive trains, run power stations, run government, everything.'

'I didn't know this,' I said.

'That because you working class. Working class know nothing. Get taught nothing at school. Kept ignorant, kept under control.'

'This is a bit of a revelation,' I said.

'It doesn't surprise me,' said Dave. 'Mr Trubshaw told me all about this conspiracy-theory stuff in Strangeways. He said nothing in society is actually what it seems. The whole thing is a big con.'

'I'd like to hear more,' I said, 'but the commuters will soon be banging on the door demanding to know why the train isn't moving.'

'You don't travel much on the tube, do you, Gary?' said Dave.

'No,' I said, shaking my head, and wiping the driver's blood from my hands.

'Well, trust me, the commuters won't notice any difference. Now, Sandra, drive the train to Mornington Crescent.'

'I'll tell her,' I said. And I told her.

There was something altogether weird about Mornington Crescent. As Sandra drew the train to a halt, Dave and I stared out at it. The lights were on, but no one was at home. Nor, it seemed, had anyone been home since the end of the Second World War. There were all these wartime war-effort posters on the walls, and others for Bovril and Bisto and Doveston's steam-driven wonder beds.

'What about the commuters?' I asked Dave. 'We can't let them all out here.'

'We'll leave through the driver's door, directly onto the platform,' said Dave. 'Why not stick the driver's hand down on the deadman's handle and send the train on to other parts?'

'But it might crash,' I said.

Dave raised an eyebrow to me.

'Sorry,' I said. 'I don't know what came over me there.'

We got out of the driver's door, I dumped all of the driver down on the deadman's handle and Sandra set the train back in motion. And we watched as the train gathered speed and left the station.

'There,' said Dave. 'Job done.'

'You're pretty quick on your feet, aren't you?' I said to Dave.

'Have to be,' said Dave. 'In my business, you always have to be thinking one step ahead.'

'If you're so smart,' I said, 'how come you're always getting caught?'

'Because,' said Dave, 'I may be smart, but there's always someone smarter. In my case it's Inspectre Hovis of Scotland. And that's now in your case too. So if we wish to outsmart him, we should *both* get on with the business at hand, rather than stand around here making chitchat.'

'Lead on, Dave,' said I. 'Take us to the booty.'

'Yeah, well, I don't exactly know the way from here. I sort of knew the way from a secret tunnel that Churchill told me about, but I don't think it's anywhere around here. We'll have to work this out together.'

'Fair enough,' I said. 'At least the lights are on. Let's go and explore.'

So we went and explored.

Mornington Crescent didn't smell too good. It smelled musty and lifeless, as if no one had breathed the air there for years. Nor was supposed to.

'It feels really odd here,' said Dave, as we wandered down the big tiled corridors. 'Unworldly. Do you know what I mean?'

I nodded. And I remembered too. All this reminded me of something. Something I'd felt a long time before. 'It's like those crypts,' I said. 'The ones I used to crawl into in the graveyard when I was a child. They felt like this. Like you weren't supposed to be in them. Which you weren't.'

'Station dead,' said Sandra. 'All dead here. Sandra know, Sandra dead too.'

'Don't go putting yourself down,' said Dave. 'You're more alive than half the people I know.'

'Thank you, Dave,' said Sandra. 'Sandra love Masser Dave.'

'What was that?' I asked.

'Sandra say, "Sandra love Masser Gary,"' said Sandra.

'Hm,' said I.

'There's a light up ahead,' said Dave. 'Big light. Big something, by the look of it.'

'Sssh,' said I.

'What?' said Dave.

'I hear people,' I said. And we crept forward. We emerged from the tiled corridor onto a kind of gantry at the top of an iron staircase. And we found ourselves looking down onto something that was altogether big.

'What the Holy big Jackus is *that*?' whispered Dave as he and I and Sandra stared down together.

It was big, and when I say it was big I mean what I say. It was like some vast aircraft-hangar sort of arrangement and there were . . .

'Flying saucers,' whispered Dave. 'Tell me that those aren't flying saucers.'

'I can't,' I said. 'They are.'

And they were. There was an entire squadron of them. Polished chromium craft. The classic Adamski shape. Discs with a raised central area, ringed around with little portholes.

'Well, I don't know what I was expecting,' said Dave, 'but I don't think it was this.'

'I thought you said that it was the Germans who had the alien technology in the war.'

'Yeah, but the Germans *lost* the war. Oh shug! Look at them.'

I looked and I saw. Little grey men with big egg heads moving around the flying saucers.

'Aliens,' I said. 'Well, I suppose that where you get UFOs you're bound to get aliens.'

'Sandra no want to see aliens,' said Sandra. 'Sandra scared of aliens.'

'Why do they scare you?' I asked her.

'We leave,' said Sandra. 'Leave now. Go back. Take Sandra back, Masser Gary.'

'We're staying,' I said. 'I want to find out what's going on here.'

'Sandra go. Sandra cannot stay.'

'Face the wall,' I told Sandra. 'Stand still. Dave and I will go and have a look around. Don't move until we come back.'

Sandra turned slowly and faced the wall.

Dave looked at me and I didn't like the way that he did it.

'Problem?' I asked.

'No,' said Dave. 'Nothing. What do you want to do?'

'You're the criminal mastermind; *you* tell *me*.'

'Creep down, have a shifty around, see what we can see, hear what we can hear, nick what we can nick.'

'Good plan,' I said. 'Sandra, stay.'

'Sandra stay,' said Sandra.

'Good girl,' I said. 'We won't be long. We hope.'

Dave and I crept down the iron staircase. It was a very long staircase and there were a lot of stairs, but presently we found ourselves at the bottom of them.

Dave looked back up the way we had come. 'We have a problem here,' he said. 'I can't see us being able to carry too much booty up all those steps.'

'There'll be another way out. Now, let me see, there's something we need if we're not going to be noticed.'

'Cloaks of invisibility?' Dave suggested. 'You are strong with spells today?'

'No, Dave. White coats and light bulbs, that's all we need.'

'Okey pokey,' said Dave and we set out in search of them.

Now, if there was one thing that I was certain of it was that, in places such as this, there is always a locker room where you can slip into a white coat or a radiation suit or something. At least there always is in James Bond films.

'Ah,' said Dave, pointing to a door. 'This will be the kiddie.'

I perused the sign upon the door. WHITE COAT AND LIGHT BULB STORE, it read.

'After you,' said Dave.

'No, after you.'

'No, after you.'

'Oh, please yourself, then.' And I pushed open the door and went inside.

And suddenly, for there was no warning at all, I found myself falling and falling into a bottomless pit of whirling oblivion.

Which is what Lazlo Woodbine used to fall into at the end of the second chapter of each of his thrillers, when the dame that done him wrong bopped him over the head.

Which might have been all right for Laz, but it certainly wasn't for me.

'Aaaaaaaaaaaagh!' I went.

And then things went very black indeed and that was that for me.

23

I awoke with undoubtedly the worst hangover I have ever had in my life. There is no mistaking a hangover. You can't pass it off as a migraine. It hurts like the very bejabers and there's no one to blame but yourself.

I made dismal groaning sounds of the 'I must have had a really, really good time last night' variety and felt about for that elusive something-or-other that folk with hangovers always feel about for when they awaken in this terrible state.

But then I became aware that I couldn't seem to feel about for anything, as my hands wouldn't move at all. I opened a bleary eye and viewed my immediate surroundings. At first glance they didn't look too good. On second glance they looked worse.

It appeared as if I was strapped into some kind of large chair. I tried to move my head, but found that I couldn't. I tried to move my feet, but this was not, as they say, 'a happening thing'.

I did some more glancing, just to make sure that the conclusions I had drawn from my previous glancings were not mistaken. No, it seemed that they were not.

I was in a small, rather surgical-looking room, with

walls to either side of me and a glass screen in front. And beyond the glass screen I could see another room, larger than mine and all decked out with rows of chairs. Upon these chairs I could make out a number of people, some of them strange to my eyes, but others most familiar.

Amongst the familiar persuasion, I spied out my mother, weeping into a handkerchief. And beside her my brother, whom I hadn't seen for nearly ten years. And there were several of my mother's friends. And there was a long thin man in Boleskine tweed: Chief Inspectre Hovis, he was. And there was Dave and sitting beside Dave, being comforted by Dave with an arm about the shoulder, was Sandra. She was dressed rather smartly in black and her face was well made up.

I began to struggle, as one would, and I *did*, but sadly to no avail whatsoever. So I decided that shouting would be the thing to do. But I couldn't shout because my mouth was gagged by what felt to be a strip of adhesive tape.

So I made ferocious grunting noises and struggled and struggled. And then a rather brutal-looking individual in the shape of a large prison officer appeared in my line of vision and menaced me with a truncheon.

'Shut it, loony boy,' said this fellow. 'Or you'll get one in the 'nads with this stick.'

I quietened myself, but with difficulty. I felt truly panicked. How had I ended up here? Wherever here was, it looked awfully like an execution chamber. And how come I had a hangover? I hadn't been drinking. I'd been falling. Oh yes, I remembered that – falling into a dark whirling pit of oblivion.

I confess that I was confused.

'All rise,' came a voice. And I tried but failed. 'All rise for the Honourable Mr Justice Doveston.'

And a chap in full judge's rigout mooched past me and moved beyond my line of vision. And now all the folk who'd risen on his arrival sat down again.

'Remove the prisoner's gag,' came a voice, which I assumed to be that of the Honourable Mr Justice Doveston. Great-grandson of the wonder-bed's creator?

The prison officer tore the tape from my mouth.

'Oooow!' I went.

'Silence in court,' said someone or other that I couldn't see.

'Let me loose,' I demanded. 'Set me free. I've done nothing.'

Now this, I know, was not exactly true. But these were the words that came out of my mouth. I couldn't seem to stop them at the time.

'Silence,' said the voice once again. 'Or you will be sedated.'

'What's going on here? Where am I? What are you doing?'

'Silence, for the last time. Officer, prepare the truncheon.'

The prison officer raised his truncheon.

'I'm cool,' I said. 'I won't say anything else.'

The voice said, 'Gary Charlton Cheese, you stand, or, rather, *sit*, accused of arson – to whit, the wanton destruction of the Brentford Telephone Exchange. And of multiple homicide – to whit, the murders of . . .'

292

And he began to read out a list. And it read as some litany of the damned. As damned as those on the list had been, at my hand. But the list went on and on. And name after name that I didn't recognize, of folk that I certainly hadn't put paid to, came one after another, after another. '. . . And Elvis Aaron Presley.'

'Elvis?' I choked on the name. '*I* didn't kill Elvis.'

'How plead you?' asked the voice.

'Innocent,' I said. 'Absolutely, uncontroversially innocent.'

'Oh dear,' came the voice of Mr Justice Doveston. 'I hope this doesn't mean that we'll be here all day. I have an urgent golfing appointment at three. Who represents the guilty party?'

'Guilty party?' I said. 'A man is innocent until proven guilty.'

'Don't be silly,' said Mr Justice Doveston. 'So who represents this vicious killer?'

'I do.' A lady now stepped into my eye line. And a very pretty lady too. She had a slim yet shapely figure, hugged by expensive black. And she wore, atop her head of flame-red hair, one of those barrister's little white wigs, which look so incredibly sexy when worn by a young woman but just plain stupid when worn by a man.

'Ah,' said Mr Justice D, 'Ms Ferguson. Always a pleasure to see you in court, no matter how lost your cause.'

'Thank you, Your Honour. I will represent Mr Cheese and it is my intention to prove to the court that, although Mr Cheese is guilty of multiple homicide, he is a victim of circumstance. A pawn in a game so great that it is beyond his comprehension. That a conspiracy exists, which, if the truth of it was exposed to the general public, would rock society to its very foundation. You spoke of lost causes, Your Honour. And indeed I have pursued many. But now I am privy to certain information, which I feel certain will—'

'Yes, yes, yes,' said Mr Justice. 'This all sounds terribly interesting. But do try to make it brief. Let's get it over by lunchtime, fry this villain and take the afternoon off.'

'Thank you, Your Honour. It is my intention to prove that a secret organization exists, possessed of an occult knowledge. This organization supplies the government of this country with information gleaned from certain sources that . . .'

'Are you sure this has any bearing on this case?' asked Mr Justice D.

'Every bearing. I will prove that although the hands that caused the murders belong to Mr Cheese, the mind that ordered those hands to commit those horrendous deeds was not the mind of Mr Cheese. The thinking did not go on in his head, the thinking came from elsewhere. From a distant point in the universe.'

I stared at Ms Ferguson and then I glanced towards Dave. Dave was giving me the thumbs-up. He mouthed the words, 'I've sorted it.'

'This all sounds very esoteric,' said Mr Justice D. 'And a less erudite and well-read magistrate than I would no doubt dismiss this line of evidence out of hand. But I like a good laugh and this nutty stuff has a certain appeal to me. As long as it's over by lunchtime, of course, and we can enjoy the frying. I've never seen an electrocution before and I'm really looking forward to it.'

'Quite so, Your Honour. I will try to keep this brief. Might I call the first witness for the defence?'

'As quickly as you can, yes.'

'Then please call Mr Reginald Boothy.'

'Call Mr Reginald Boothy,' called a voice. And presently Mr Reginald Boothy appeared. They sat him down in a chair facing me, which was decent of them, although after a glance or two at Mr Boothy I wasn't altogether certain. There was something distinctly odd about Mr Boothy. A certain unworldliness. I felt that here was a man who wasn't what he seemed. And what he seemed, whatever that was, wasn't what *that* seemed either.

Mr Boothy was tall and oldish-looking, and in his way was rather handsome. He had gunmetal-grey hair, decent cheekbones and a clipped gunmetal-grey beard. He looked a bit like a graphic designer. Because graphic designers always look like that. It's a tradition or an old charter, or something.

Mr Boothy wore a very dashing black suit cut to a design that I didn't recognize and was accompanied by two small and friendly-looking dogs.

The chap whose voice had urged me to be silent was in fact the clerk of the court. He stepped forward to Mr Boothy and placed a Bible into his hands. 'Do you swear to tell the truth, the whole truth and nothing but the truth?' he said.

'As much of it as I know,' said Mr Boothy. 'Which is some, but not all.'

'Good enough,' said Mr Justice D.

'No, it's not,' said Ms Ferguson.

'It will do for me,' I said. Because I recognized if not Mr Boothy, then at least his name. I'd come across it only once before in my life. And I'd never heard of any other Mr Boothy, for it didn't seem like a real name at all. The only Mr Boothy I'd heard of was the one referred to by Nigel and Ralph, the two young men I'd overheard in the restricted section of the Brentford Memorial Library all those years ago when I was a child. Was it the *same* Mr Boothy? Who could say? Not me.

'You are Mr Reginald Boothy?' asked Ms Ferguson.

'I am,' said Mr Reginald Boothy. 'And these are my two dogs, Wibble and Trolley Bus.'

'Quite so,' said Ms Ferguson. 'But I will address my questions solely to you, if you don't mind.'

'I'm easy,' said Mr Boothy.

'Splendid. So, Mr Boothy, am I right in assuming that you are the head of a secret underground organization, known as the Ministry of Serendipity, which supplies information to the government of this country and in fact influences every major decision made by the government?'

'I'm proud to say so, yes,' said Mr Boothy.

'Er, excuse me,' said Mr Justice Doveston. 'But, Mr Boothy, you are aware of what you are saying to this court, aren't you? You seem very eager to divulge secrets.'

'I'm easy,' said Mr Boothy once again. 'I know that nothing I say will go beyond these walls and, even if it does, no one beyond these walls will ever believe it.

296

That is the nature of a *real* conspiracy. Even if you own up to it, even if you can prove it, people, on the whole, will never believe it.'

Mr Doveston nodded, although I didn't see him do it. 'I wonder why that is,' he said.

'It's because it's the way *we* keep it, Your Honour. It's the way *we* want it to be.'

'This *we* being the Ministry of Serendipity?'

'This *we* being the powers that run not only this country but the entire world.'

'How exciting,' said Mr Justice D. 'But time is pressing on, so please have your say as speedily as possible.'

'Mr Boothy,' said Ms Ferguson, 'will you tell the court, as briefly and succinctly as you can, what *exactly* the Ministry of Serendipity does.'

'It co-ordinates interdimensional communications. Which is to say, communications with the dead.'

'Did you say the *dead*?' asked Mr Justice D.

'I did, Your Honour. If I might *briefly* explain?'

'Be as brief as you like, Mr Boothy.'

'Thank you, Your Honour. Back in Victorian times a scientific genius by the name of Nicoli Tesla invented a number of remarkable things: alternating current, the Tesla coil, for which he is still remembered today, and wireless communications. He sold out alternating current and wireless communications to the Thomas Edison organization. He was a genius, but not much of a businessman. Mr Tesla discovered, when he first perfected wireless communications, that his radio equipment was receiving all kinds of odd noises that he couldn't account for. He fine-tuned his apparatus and he found he could hear voices. These were not the voices of his employees testing his equipment. These were other voices. But as no other radio equipment existed on the planet, Mr Tesla was somewhat baffled by what the source of these voices might be.*

'He was to discover that he was listening to the voices of the dead.

'But his equipment was crude by today's standards and he could not tune it precisely. Tesla kept quiet about what he had discovered, for fear of ridicule. Before his death he was working upon the wireless transmission of electricity. It is said that he perfected it. His papers on that, however, are lost.

'His papers on his radio transmission received from the dead, however, were found shortly before the Second World War, languishing in the restricted section of the Miskatonic Institute in Arkham, New England, America. Happily, by an Englishman doing research over there. He brought them back to England. War broke out and the government enlisted every scientist in the country to help with the war effort. Our chap, the researcher, showed Tesla's papers to Churchill, who gave him the go-ahead.

'Mornington Crescent tube station was closed down. It had extensive storage areas beneath it and they were commissioned for the war effort. For Operation Orpheus, which was a project to communicate with the dead via radio. To interrogate high-ranking German

*This is absolutely true. You can look it up for yourself if you don't believe me. Try *Tesla: The man who invented the twentieth century*. You'll find it in the restricted section of the library.

officers who had died in action. To this end a gentleman named Charlie Farnsbarns, a music-hall entertainer, who specialized in impersonating Hitler, was called in. Mr Farnsbarns impersonated Hitler down the Operation Orpheus phone line to the dead. He was convincing enough for the German officers to pass on information that helped the allies win the war.'

'Incredible,' said Mr Justice D. 'But time marches on.'

'Indeed it does,' said Mr Boothy. 'And so does England. After the war, Operation Orpheus was not disbanded. It was too good to disband. It was such a winner. Every successive government pumped money into it. Numerous impersonators did their stuff. Some impersonated the Russian Premier, some the President of the United States, etcetera, etcetera, depending on which particular dead person we wished to glean information from.'

'This is – how shall I put it? – somewhat *sneaky*,' said Mr Justice D.

'That's the nature of covert operations, Your Honour.'

'Quite so. Please continue.'

'Well, Your Honour, back in the nineteen fifties, with radio equipment becoming ever more sophisticated, wavebands were being expanded. We discovered that there were wavebands within wavebands and others within them. It seems that there is an almost infinite number of wavebands. And when you tune into each of them, you find something there. Radio-wave transmissions are somewhat universal. If intelligent life exists somewhere in the universe, it inevitably stumbles upon radio waves. They are natural — part of the running order of the universe.

'The Ministry found that it was tuning in to life elsewhere in the galaxy. There were rumours that the Nazis had alien technology during the war, but this wasn't true. No alien has ever set foot on this planet.'

'That's a damned lie,' I said.

'Silence,' said the prison officer, raising his truncheon.

'But he's lying,' I protested.

'No, I'm not,' said Mr Boothy. 'When you entered the Ministry complex, you saw what you took to be aliens. But those weren't aliens. Those were underground hive workers. Intraterrestrials. There is an entire civilization living beneath our feet in the bowels of the Earth. The Ministry of Serendipity communicates with them. They share their technology. It all helps Britannia to go on ruling the waves.'

'This has now become seriously wacky,' said Mr Justice D. 'I think we'll fry the murderer and adjourn for lunch.'

'If I might just raise an objection to that,' said Ms Ferguson: 'I'd appreciate it if Your Honour would let Mr Boothy continue. His evidence is pertinent to this case.'

'Oh, go on then. Please continue, Mr Boothy.'

'Thank you once more, Your Honour. So, yes, we communicate with intraterrestrials and extraterrestrials, the latter being too far away to offer us much and we have yet to decipher much of their language. But, during the course of our communications and researches we discovered something quite mind-boggling.

We discovered the human-brain radio frequency.'

'And what exactly might that be?' asked the judge. 'Exactly and briefly.'

'We tuned in to the human brain. We discovered the radio frequency of thought. And we discovered that the thinking we think we do in our heads we don't really do in our heads at all. The thinking is done somewhere else in the universe and beamed into our heads on a radio frequency, unique to each individual on the planet.'

'What are you suggesting?' asked the judge.

'I'm not suggesting it, Your Honour. I'm telling you it, because it's true. Human beings don't actually think. Their thinking is done somewhere else and beamed to their heads, which are, in a word – well, two words actually – radio receivers, from a distant planet in the galaxy. We've even identified it through the use of radio telescopes.'

'So you and I aren't actually thinking?' said the magistrate. 'We're just puppet bodies being worked from afar?'

'In a word, yes.'

'Priceless,' said Mr Justice D, breaking down in laughter. 'Absolutely priceless. I'm so glad that I was here today to hear this. My chaps at the golf club will fall about over this one. Thank you very much, Mr Boothy.'

Mr Boothy grinned at Ms Ferguson. 'You see,' he said. 'I told you this would happen. When you called me to appear at this court, I told you that you were wasting your time. That no one would believe a word I said. Would it be all right for me to leave the witness stand now? My dogs would like to go walkies.'

'Not quite yet,' said Ms Ferguson. 'There are one or two matters I'd like to clear up.'

'Oh no, there aren't,' said the magistrate. 'I've heard quite enough.'

'But, Your Honour, there are certain matters here that need classification. Such as how, for instance, if all our thoughts are really occurring elsewhere in the galaxy, Mr Boothy is capable of even telling us.'

'Because,' said Mr Boothy, 'I have learned who I really am. I know my true name. I am Panay Cloudrunner, Ninth Earl of Sirius. This body is not my true body. My true body is many light years away, orchestrating the actions of this body you see here before you.

'And I can tell you all this because Mr Justice Doveston won't believe me. And do you know why he won't believe me? It's because his true self on a distant planet is pretending that he doesn't believe me. Because the secret must and will never come out. And although you're having a lot of fun with this, you, Lady Lovestar of the Golden Vale, daughter of King Elfram of Rigel Four, you know the truth of this anyway.'

'I am human,' said Ms Ferguson. '*I* am not orchestrated from afar.'

'Then there goes your defence for the defendant.'

'I mean to say that *I* am human. But *he* is a pawn, driven by the psychopathic thoughts of a distant alien life force that controls him.'

'Blumy,' I said. 'Is that it?'

'Indeed,' said Ms Ferguson.

'Well, all right,' said Mr Boothy. 'If the honourable

magistrate, Mr Justice Doveston, or, as I know him, or, rather, the entity that controls his corporeal form knows him, Damos Cluterhower, Laird of Carmegon Quadrant, Star King of Alphanor, would care to own up and confess that everything I've just said is true, I might continue and tell you the really nasty bit.'

Mr Justice Doveston laughed some more. 'Oh, go on, then,' he said. 'You're a real hoot, Panay, giving all this truth away to this lot. They'll all have to be silenced afterwards, the no-marks – you know how it works.'

'No-marks?' said Ms Ferguson.

'The uncontrollables,' said Mr Boothy. 'Those who cannot be controlled from beyond. I fear, Ms Ferguson, that you are one of those.'

'But you called me Lady Lovestar.'

'Because that is the entity who constantly seeks to control you. But she can't very often, can she? You see, the human brain *is* controllable. It is capable of receiving radio signals, the frequency of thought. But not *all* humans. Some, but not all. There will always be plenty who cannot be reached and controlled. Who will remain truly human. They are a real annoyance to us.'

'Oh yes?' said Ms Ferguson. 'And is the defendant one of these?'

'Oh no,' said Mr Boothy. 'He's just another puppet. A rather brutal being pulls his strings. Escaped from an off-world prison colony, a psychopathic megalomaniac Valdec Firesword, Archduke of Alpha Centuri.'

I took a step back in my seat. That was the True Name that Eric, the late landlord of the Golden Dawn, had bestowed upon me.

There was a lot of confirmation here.

'You see,' Mr Boothy continued, 'your defence of your client is quite justified. Absolutely correct. *He* is not responsible for his crimes, which are many. The entity that controls him is responsible. But he can't be brought to book, because he is 52,000,000 light years from here, beyond the Milky Way by a great distance. So Mr Cheese must take the rap. The court must condemn him to death. No doubt Valdec Firesword will find another brain to beam his instructions into as soon as this one is fried. Or at least until the galactic constabulary catch up with him.'

'It's a fair cop,' said Mr Justice D. 'Let's fry Mr Cheese and take lunch.'

'No, hang on,' I said. 'This isn't fair.'

'Why?' asked the magistrate.

'Because I'm *me*. I'm Gary Cheese. I know I'm me. I can feel I'm me. But if all the bad things aren't my fault, they've been caused because something out there somewhere in space has been getting into my head and making me do them, then it's not fair. It's not my fault, so I shouldn't fry.'

'Quite so,' said Ms Ferguson.

'Yes,' said Mr Justice Doveston. 'I do so agree. It's terribly unfair. It is terribly unjust. But it is the way things are. There are plenty of us, from elsewhere, running you lot by remote control. But we are outnumbered by those amongst you we cannot control. Some of them even infiltrated their way into the Brentford Telephone Exchange. Into Developmental Services. Some who were wholly human, who our over-talkative operative Eric identified to us, and we dealt with them. But the *status quo* must be maintained. We enjoy what we are doing. It is a great game, playing with humans. It is *the* great game. Our race loves the game. We don't want it to end.'

'You bastards!' I said.

'You bastards!' said Ms Ferguson.

'So you must die, Mr Cheese,' said Mr Justice Doveston. 'We must cut off the line of communication from the escaped psychopath Valdec Firesword. We'll try to catch up with him before he finds another human being to play with.'

'No,' I said. 'This isn't right. It isn't true. I *am* me. I know I'm me.'

'And I'm me too,' said Ms Ferguson.

'And *me*,' I heard Dave shout.

'It's of no consequence,' said Mr Justice D. 'I've heard all I need to hear. And as I knew it all anyway, it doesn't matter. Time is drawing on and all it needs is for me to pronounce you guilty. So, guilty it is. Will someone please pull the switch?'

'Can I do it?' asked the prison officer. 'Surely you know me, sir? I'm Caracki Maldama, honorary consul of Vega.'

'I knew your father,' said Mr Justice D. 'Go on, then. Pull the switch.'

And, what would you know, but what you know, he *did* pull the switch.

And he electrocuted me.

And it didn't half hurt.

And I died.

24

And then I was dead.

And then I remembered.

All those missing pieces from my life. All those times that it had seemed I'd slept through. Those were the times when I was truly me. Not possessed by some alien psychopath orchestrating my movements, beaming thoughts into my brain, making me his puppet, to kill folk as suited his whims.

I knew then that it hadn't been me who'd done those terrible things. It had been him: Valdec Firesword, Archduke of Alpha Centuri.

It hadn't been my fault at all. None of it. I was an innocent victim. And, it was quite clear to me, one of many, many, many others before me. Driven to extreme acts by the voices in their heads.

And now that I knew all this, it was too late. I was dead, and the thoughts of Valdec Firesword were no longer in my brain. I was dead and he was gone. Off to torment some other innocent victim of cosmic circumstances.

What an absolute frip shugger.

And oh dear, oh dear, oh dear. How much more of

it made sense to me now. How many times in my short life had I meant to do something positive? Something big. But hadn't. And why hadn't I? Because Valdec Firesword had altered my mode of thinking. Stopped me from being me.

I could remember it all now. All those missed opportunities. I'd had a hot line to the dead at my disposal. To the dead, who know everything. But had I asked them anything? Anything worthwhile? No, I hadn't. I'd wasted my opportunities, because he had made me waste them. He didn't want me to know the truth while I was alive, because I might have been able to fight him, if I'd known. To drive him out of my head and let myself be me.

I'd been used, used, used. I felt soiled, dirty, abused. And dead.

Dead, me, at my age! Only rock stars died at my age. And accident victims, of course, and murder victims. But it wasn't fair, for me to die, when I could have had so many happy years of my life still to come. Or could have if *he* hadn't been inside my head. But instead, I was dead, leaving behind me only an evil memory.

I could just imagine what the papers would be saying: SERIAL KILLER GETS JUST DESSERTS.

Or in the case of the *Brentford Mercury*: CHEESE ON TOAST.

And of course there would be no mention of what actually went on and was said at my trial. People would probably be partying in the streets, burning me in effigy.

This was all too much. I was angry, really, really angry.

Angry. And dead!

Dead angry!

Now, what you might be wanting to ask me is a question that I should have asked the dead when I had the chance, but never got around to, the question being: 'Just what is it like to be dead?' And, for that matter, 'Where is it?'

Both good questions, and pertinent. And I will answer them now.

What is it like to be dead? Well, I'll tell you.

It's empty.

That's what it's like to be dead. We never realize it when we're alive, but what we are is *full of life*. That's what it is, you see. We're all filled up with life. It bubbles through our veins and arteries; it jiggles about in our cells; it's in our hair and up our noses; it's all over us, inside and out. We're full of life. But when we're dead, we're all drained of life.

We're empty.

And I was empty. And where was I? Well, I'll tell you that. I was sitting upon the marble tomb bed of the late Mr Doveston, puffing on a post-life Woodbine and wondering how I would spend the day ahead.

Yes, that's where I was, or wasn't, depending on your point of view. I was there, I knew that; I could see it all around me. But I could tell instinctively that it wasn't the real McDoveston's marble wonder-bed. It was a kind of approximation, a dream landscape, if you will, made up of memories, but slightly fuzzy at the edges and all just a tad out of focus.

I suppose that we never look at things as closely as

we should when we're alive. But then, we're not expecting that we'll have to call upon these memories when we're dead to establish some kind of environment for ourselves to exist in.

I must have spent so much time at Mr Doveston's tomb that it seemed a natural place to recall when I died, so I suppose that it was the reason I was here.

Of course I'd spent a great deal more time in the bulb booth at the telephone exchange, but I had no wish to revisit *that* in the afterlife. And so I was here. And I wasn't alone.

I could see them, drifting about, wraith-like, pale and pasty. Other dead folk, and a lot of them.

I had no intention of sticking around here for too long. I'd finish my fag and take a wander home. To my memory of home. I wondered why this lot were hanging around in the graveyard. Some of them looked pretty ancient, by their costumes. Victorians, many of them seemed.

But as they showed no interest in me, I sat and puffed on my fag and pondered upon eternity and determined that it was going to be very long indeed and hoped that I'd find plenty of interesting and entertaining things to fill it with.

After I'd got the revenge out of the way. Oh yes, I was altogether certain about that.

I'd had my life taken from me because I had been manipulated into taking other people's lives from them. And someone, or some*thing*, or lots of someones and lots of some*things*, were going to pay for that.

I intended to get even.

'Be careful what you think.'

I looked up and saw her and she was beautiful. An angel, I supposed, for no Earthly woman ever looked as good as that. She conformed to all the average-male stereotypes of how-a-good-looking-woman-should-look.

Tall and blonde and shapely. Big blue eyes and tiny nose and mouth so large that you could stick your fist in it.

'That's not very nice, Gary,' said the angel.

'Was I speaking?' I asked. 'Or was I thinking aloud? And how do you know my name?'

'I know who you are and we can hear each other's thoughts here,' said the angel.

'I can't,' I said, cocking my palm to my ear.

'Well, you should be able to. Probably it will come in time and time we have here to spare.'

'But not to waste,' I said. 'Not for me. I have things that need doing, somehow.'

'You mustn't think like that,' said the angel. 'You'll end up like these.' And she gestured to the wraiths who drifted aimlessly about and paid her no attention, even though they really should have. Because she was an absolute stonker of an angel.

'You will become stuck,' said the angel. 'You must let go of any thoughts of revenge. Such thoughts will weigh you down and you'll be stuck here at your grave, for ever.'

'My *grave*,' I said. 'Here? I thought they'd probably cremated me and dumped my ashes in a dustbin at the prison, or something.'

'Whatever made you think *that*?'

'Well, it's what happens in the movies and in real

life, isn't it? Executed killers end up in unhallowed ground in the prison boneyard.'

The angel smiled. 'Your friend Dave nicked your body from the prison. Very enterprising of him, very brave. He thought you'd like to be buried here. He brought you here at night and slipped you into Mr Doveston's tomb.'

'Nice one, Dave,' I said. 'What a bestest friend.'

'You can't buy that kind of friendship,' said the angel. 'You should dwell on thoughts like that. And then you will be able to fly from here. To wherever and whenever. All the universe is here to be seen. It will take you for ever to see it all.'

'So,' said I, and I smiled. I did, I really did. 'So that's the point of death. I wondered about that when I was a child. I could see the point of being alive, to be aware of the world and everything around us. But I never could see the point of death. But that's it? What you're saying? When you're dead you can fly off and see all of the universe? Isn't that incredible? Isn't that utterly beautiful?'

And I thought about it and, as I thought, the terrible emptiness seemed momentarily to leave me. Or to change, as if, perhaps, I was filling up with something new: not life, but something even more marvellous than life. A kind of universality of being, that I was part of everything and everything was part of me. It was utterly wonderful and it made me feel that now nothing else mattered – nothing that I'd done or not done, nothing that I'd known. I just wanted to fly, to be at one with everything. To be eternal.

'So *that* is the purpose of it all,' I said.

'There is a purpose to everything.' The angel smiled at me. 'Especially death.'

'And these dead people here, these dead *souls*? They got stuck, did they? Because they had thoughts of revenge?'

'Or couldn't draw themselves away from their memories. They yearned to be alive again.'

'Shame,' said I. 'You might have mentioned this to them. It does seem a bit of a pity. Still, I suppose God knows his own business best. If He decided they should stay here, then there's probably a good reason for it.'

'God?' said the angel. 'What are you talking about? *God*?'

'Your governor,' I said. 'The big fellow. The bloke who pays your wages.'

'My wages?' The angel looked genuinely baffled.

'You look genuinely baffled,' I told her. 'You are an angel, aren't you?'

And at this the angel began to laugh. She laughed right in my face and all over me generally. And I remembered how much I'd hated people doing that. Especially Sandra.

'Oh, careful,' said the angel(?). 'Bad thoughts, heavy thoughts: wipe those thoughts from your mind.'

'Is Jupiter nice at this time of year?' I asked, rapidly changing the subject.

'Don't know,' said the angel(?). 'Never been there.'

'But you must get around a bit. After all, you are an . . . you know . . . Or aren't you?'

The beautiful being, whatever it was, shook its beautiful head. 'I'm not an angel,' she said. 'There aren't any angels, or, at least, none that I've seen. I'm just another dead person.'

I whistled. Loudly. The drifting wraiths paid no attention to my whistling. 'What a pity,' I said. 'I am *so* sorry.'

'Why?' asked the beautiful being. 'I had a good innings.'

'Good innings? But how old are you? How old were you when you died? Nineteen, twenty?'

'Ninety-eight,' said the beautiful being.

'Ninety-eight? You're having a laugh, surely?'

'Here, we look how we truly look,' said the beauty, 'no matter what we looked like when we were alive.'

'Oh,' I said and my hands slowly moved up to my face.

'Are you sure you want to?' the beauty asked. 'Are you sure you want to know what you truly are?'

My hands retreated at speed and found their way into my trouser pockets. 'I'm sure I look fine,' I said. 'In fact, I must look the same, because *you* recognized me.'

'True,' said the beauty. 'I know *who* you are. But it doesn't mean that you look the same. You must have noticed that now you're dead, things are the same, but different.'

'You're my mum,' I said, a look of enlightenment no doubt appearing upon whatever kind of face I had.

'Your mum isn't dead.'

'Oh no, I suppose not. I've rather lost touch with my mum. Then who? Sandra, is that you?'

The beautiful being shook her golden head and

rolled her eyes of summertime blue.*

'You young clodder,' she said. 'I'm Mother Demdike!'

Now, I have to confess that this caught me by surprise.

It did.

It really did.

But if *that* caught me by surprise, then what happened next and what happened after *that*, caught me by even greater surprise. And, as surprises had never been particularly happy things for me whilst I'd been alive, I suppose I should have had no good reason to suppose that they would be any better at all now that I was dead. So to speak.

And they weren't.

'I can't stay for long,' said Mother Demdike. 'I have a lot of bad memories and I don't want to dwell upon them here and find myself stuck. I just wanted to tell you that I don't bear you any malice for what you did.'

'And quite right too,' I told her. 'Because none of it was *my* fault. I was used. I was manipulated.'

'That is true up to a point,' said the hag who now was beautiful. 'You were not responsible for all of your actions later.'

'Never,' I said. 'None of it was my fault.'

'I'm afraid that is *not* true. The being that chose to use you did not choose you at random. It chose you because you were a suitable vehicle. The badness was already in you. You were already a wrong'n, Gary. A bad, bad boy.'

---

*Not to be confused with the Eddie Cochran song.

'I never was,' I protested. 'What makes you say such a thing?'

'I thought you could remember all of your life, Gary. All the missing pieces. All the pieces that it seemed that you slept through.'

'I can,' I said.

'So you're not, perhaps, blocking one or two of them out?'

'Why would I want to do that?'

'Because you *don't* want to remember what *you* did. Not what the being that controlled you did. But what *you* did, when you were young.'

'Oh,' I said. 'I know what you're talking about. You're talking about Mr Penrose. How I brought him back from the dead. Well, I am sorry about that and if I see him I will apologize for that.'

Mother Demdike shook her head. 'Not him,' she said. 'Before him. What you did to *me*.'

'To you?'

And then I remembered. Oh yes. I remembered what I'd done to Mother Demdike.

'I . . .'

'Say it, Gary.'

'I . . .'

'Go on.'

'I . . . killed . . . you . . .' I said.

'Yes,' said Mother Demdike. 'You did. That night in my hut. You said that I was hideous. Ugly. You said that you were doing me a favour. Doing everyone a favour. And you cut my head off and used my skull to mix up the herbs you needed to reanimate Mr Penrose. You said that at last I'd be useful for something.'

'Oh God,' I said. And I wept. I did, and the tears fell down whatever face I had. 'I did do it. I'm so sorry.'

'You were psychopathic from childhood. You were just the kind of person Valdec Firesword was looking for. He entered you moments after you killed me. You opened yourself up for him, Gary, once you had murdered someone by your own hand.'

And I wept some more. Like a child, like a baby. Because it does make you weep when you find out for the first time in your life, or in my case for the first time after you've died, that you're a psycho.

A thing like that can really upset you.

'Oh, I am so sorry,' I said with a sob.

And Mother Demdike smiled and patted my shoulder. 'I know,' she said. 'I knew that you would be. Which was why I came to see you. And to see the look on your face, of course.'

'When I found out what I'd done?' I blubbered.

'That *too*.'

'That *too*?'

'It was the *other* look I wanted to see. And I think I'm about to see it now. Oh yes, here it comes.'

I stared at her and I'm sure some strange kind of look must have come over the face I had. Because I could feel something altogether odd happening to me. Something really uncomfortable. Painful, in fact. Really, really painful. Something was pulling at me. Pulling in all directions at the same time. As if all the little bits of universality that had been filling up my emptiness were being torn right out of me again. And it hurt like crazy, it really, really did.

'Oooh,' I went, and 'Ow,' and 'Eeeek!' And I

316

clutched at myself and writhed from the ghastly pain.

'That's the look,' I heard Mother Demdike say. 'That's the look I wanted to see. But I can't stay to see more – I'll get stuck. Goodbye, Gary. Enjoy eternity. If you can.' And she laughed. And I saw her rise up before me and float off into the sky. Then my eyes crossed with all the terrible pain and I blacked out and tumbled once more down into that whirling pit of oblivion so often tumbled into by Mr Lazlo Woodbine.

And then I woke up.

I opened my eyes and stared up. At what? Surely *that* was my kitchen ceiling. And I could feel something. I felt cold, very cold. And wet. And horrible all over, really.

Then I heard this voice. And it was a voice I knew.

And this voice was joined by another voice that I also knew. And both these voices shouted a single word.

'*Surprise!*'

I turned my head and I stared through foggy, bleary eyes. And, yes, it was Dave. And, yes, it was Sandra. And they both shouted, 'Surprise,' once more.

And Sandra blew one of those plastic whistle things. And Dave popped a party popper.

'What?' I went. And I spat out something, lots of something. Dirt. Dirt? *Dirt?*

'Surprise,' said Dave. 'We've brought you back from the dead.'

25

It must have been a horrible scream, and a dreadfully loud one too. I'll bet it rattled the chimneypots. And, had it continued, it would probably have awakened the neighbours from their beds. But it didn't continue, because Dave rammed his hands across my mouth.

'Shut up!' he said. 'You'll wake the dead. Hey, wake the dead! Eh, that's a good'n, isn't it, Sandra?'

'That good'n, Dave.'

I fought to disengage Dave, but I didn't have much strength in me. No muscle tone, what with my heart not pumping and no blood reaching my muscles and everything.

'Easy, boy,' said Dave. 'I know this must have come as a bit of a surprise. But just compose yourself. You can thank Sandra later.'

'Thank Sandra,' said Sandra.

Dave lifted a hand from my mouth.

'Thank Sandra?' I said slowly, spitting out a bit more dirt.

'Her idea,' said Dave. 'Her idea to nick your body from the prison, bury it in Mr Doveston's grave, then reanimate you using that book you borrowed from the

318

library all those years ago. The one you used to re-animate Sandra. She was returning the favour.'

'Gary belong to Sandra now,' said Sandra. 'Gary call Sandra "Mistress Sandra".'

'I'll do no such thing,' I mumbled. Then I felt the pain and remembered just how the spell worked. Whoever reanimates a dead person has control over that dead person. As I'd had control over Sandra. And abused that control. 'All right,' I mumbled and spat this time as I mumbled. 'I know how it works. But it wasn't my fault, Sandra. You were at my trial. You know it wasn't *me* who did those awful things.'

'Gary belong to Sandra now,' said Sandra once more.

'No need to repeat yourself, you silly cow.'

'Sandra punish Gary if Gary cuss Sandra.'

'Tell her, Dave,' I said to Dave, as I dragged myself painfully into the vertical plane. Because it did hurt, I can tell you, every bit of it hurt. 'Tell her not to mess about with me. Not to order me to do things. Come on, Dave, mate, bestest friend.'

Dave shrugged and smiled. Rather stupidly, I thought.

'I'm not her boss,' he said. 'Her *masser*. She's her own woman now.'

'But, Dave . . .'

'Gary, kneel,' said Sandra. 'Kiss Mistress Sandra's shoe.'

'No,' I said. 'No.' But I did it. I had to do it. I was compelled to do it. I was helpless to resist. And I felt desperate, wretched, doomed and lost. All at one and

319

the same time. Eternity had been snatched from me. The beauty, the wonder, the magic.

'Silence,' said Sandra.

And I shut right up.

'Oh, come on,' said Dave to Sandra. 'That's a bit harsh. I'd quite like to hear about this flying around the universe business. And I'm sure your shoe is clean by now.'

'Not underneath,' said Sandra. 'Sandra step in dog poo earlier.'

'That's gross,' said Dave. 'Don't make him lick dog poo. Please, Sandra. I'll tickle your back later and pick the maggots out.'

'Slave can talk again,' said Sandra. 'Stop licking now. Finish licking when tell you.'

I looked up at Sandra and I don't think I had love in my eyes. And then I looked across at Dave.

'Don't look at me like that,' said Dave. 'Being looked at like that by a dead bloke is quite unsettling.'

'You want kick Gary's arse, Dave?' asked Sandra.

'No, I'm fine,' said Dave. 'Let's give him a nice cup of tea, or something.'

'A nice cup of tea?' I collapsed onto the floor. It was still the same lino and still in need of a sweep. I collapsed and I wept. Once more. Like a child. Like a baby. It was undignified but I was very miserable. 'Dave, reverse the spell, please. Send me back to my grave. Don't do this to me. We were bestest friends.'

'We're still bestest friends,' said Dave. 'But we need you. That's why I've brought you back.'

'I don't want to be needed. Please do away with me.'

'I thought you'd be pleased,' said Dave.

'Pleased to be a zombie? Who would be pleased to be a zombie?' I glanced at Sandra and Sandra wasn't smiling. 'Quite so,' I said. 'I'm sorry, Sandra. But it *really* wasn't me who did that to you.'

'No matter who,' said Sandra. 'Gary back now. Gary get Sandra new body. This one not good any more.'

'It is getting somewhat manky,' said Dave. 'I've got her all wrapped up in clingfilm under her clothes. She does need a new body.'

'Oh no,' I said, shaking my head violently. 'I'm not doing that. I'm not killing anyone. I don't do that any more.'

'Gary do what Gary told to do,' said Sandra.

'No, please,' I said. 'I spent half my life being told what to do, without even knowing it. I do know it now. Please don't do this to me.'

'Need new body,' said Sandra. 'Dave not want to play with this one any more.'

'Then, let Dave get you a new body.'

'No way,' said Dave. 'I'm a thief, not a murderer.'

'Yes, but you don't have to be a thief, Dave. You could fight the alien who controls your thoughts.'

'Oh, *him*,' said Dave. 'You mean old Barundi Fandango the Jovian Cracksman. He's out of the picture now.'

'What?' I sat on the floor and stared up at Dave. 'Your thoughts are entirely your own? Are you sure of this?'

'Sure as sure,' said Dave, helping me up to my feet. 'I sorted it.'

321

'But how?' I was very wobbly; my knees went knock, knock, knock.

'When you walked into that trap at Mornington Crescent. That door marked WHITE COAT AND LIGHT BULB STORE. I thought you were dead, so I legged it. But I didn't leg it far. All sorts of alarms went off and I hid and I saw them haul you out. You looked as if you were drunk or drugged or something. Some kind of nerve gas, I don't know. But I watched and I listened and I saw Mr Boothy and his dogs and he did one of those routines that the supervillains always do when they have the hero captured.'

'I don't remember,' I said.

'No, he said that you wouldn't. But he told you the lot and I overheard it. You heard some of it at your trial, but not all. A few important details were missing.'

'Go on,' I said, trying to remain upright.

'He thought you were a saboteur. You see, there are people, human beings, with no aliens controlling their actions, who know about FLATLINE, who've infiltrated it.'

'The ones with no true names,' I said. 'Eric the barlord, he knew about them. He told me about them. It got a passing mention at my trial.'

'Eric was a referee,' said Dave. 'Of this particular quadrant. The aliens have Earth divided up amongst themselves, so they can play out their games. They're not omnipotent: they don't know everything. Most of them don't know who's who, whether a human is being controlled or not. It keeps it all sporting. They fight their wars here, Gary. They do it by controlling some of us. Those who *can* be controlled. Those of us who have basic flaws in our character. Those of us who are weak. Who don't really know who they are. People like you and me. They play with us. They make us kill one another. The people you killed, you "randomly" killed: there was nothing random about it. The being who controlled you knew who controlled them. Every killing had a purpose. It was all part of their game, their sport.'

'But *they* don't die. When they kill one of us, the being that is controlling the person who gets killed, that being doesn't die, right?'

'Right,' said Dave. 'Because they can't die.'

'They're immortal?'

'No, Gary. They're already dead.'

'What?' I said. 'I don't understand this at all.'

'All the aliens,' said Dave, 'the whole lot of them, they're all dead. They blasted one another out of existence. Earth is now the last inhabited planet in the universe. When Operation Orpheus opened up communications with the dead it wasn't to just the human dead. Sometime in the late nineteen fifties, all the alien dead all over the universe tuned into Earth. Because the scientists discovered the radio frequency of the dead. But not just the human brain frequency: it's a universal frequency of *all* the dead, human or not. And once they'd turned on their tuned-in apparatus, it was a great big radio beacon and all the alien dead from all over the galaxies tuned right into it. And they found us. And they found that they could beam their thoughts directly into our brains. They didn't waste a lot of time doing it.'

'This is doing my head in,' I said. 'This is all too much.'

'Think of it as devil possession,' said Dave. 'Except that there aren't any devils. The devils are dead aliens messing about with living humans. It's about as feasible as anything else. The aliens may be dead, but they still hate one another. Alien racists are still fighting wars beyond the grave. They wouldn't be able to do it to us if we hadn't given them the opportunity.'

'So it can be stopped?' I asked.

'I thought you'd never ask,' said Dave.

'Well, can it?'

'I don't know,' said Dave. 'What do *you* think?'

'I think I want to go back to the graveyard. In fact, I *know* I want to go back to the graveyard. I belong dead.'

'Don't be a quitter,' said Dave. 'This is a chance for you to redeem yourself. You don't want to be remembered as a murdering scumbag, do you? Wouldn't you rather be remembered as the man who freed humankind from the menace of the dead aliens?'

'And you seriously think that any newspaper would print *that*?'

'The *Weekly World News* definitely would,' said Dave. 'And I think it would be a noble cause.'

'Oh yes,' I said. '*You* think. You said that you'd sorted the alien who manipulated you. How did you do that?'

'Easy,' said Dave. 'I told him to sling his hook. I knew his name: Eric had told me. I knew he was in my head. I knew that from listening to Mr Boothy talking to you. So I said, "Out of my head, mate. I know

324

you're in there. Go and screw up someone else."'

'And it was as easy as that?'

'Not quite,' said Dave. 'There was a bit of a fuss. I found myself thinking that I should give myself up to Mr Boothy, and lots of other dodgy things. I almost caved in, almost went mad. But I hung on.'

'Because Sandra save him,' said Sandra. 'Sandra know 'cos Sandra dead. Sandra stop Dave, save Dave.'

'Sandra thinks you should atone for all your bad behaviour,' said Dave. 'Even if it wasn't exactly your fault. Which is why she is going to despatch you to Mornington Crescent to destroy the receiving station.'

'The receiving station?' I said. 'This is new. What is the receiving station?'

'It's the line of communication between the dead aliens and us. You know about FLATLINE – it required technology. You can't just *talk* to the dead.'

'You're doing it now,' I said.

'You know what I mean,' said Dave. 'To a soul, if you like. I overheard Mr Boothy. The alien dead communicate to the living humans, control them, through the receiving station at Mornington Crescent. The one built for Operation Orpheus. Blow that up and you cut the line of communication.'

'So *you* do it,' I said. 'You're sneaky; you could do it.'

'It's dangerous in there,' said Dave. 'I might get killed.'

'Oh, I see,' I said, because I did. 'You've brought me back from the dead so I can get Sandra a new body and then go and risk, what? nothing, because I'm already dead, by blowing up Mornington Crescent and destroying the communications station that allows the dead aliens to control living human beings?'

'Nicely put,' said Dave. 'It's all so simple when you put it that way.'

I punched Dave right in the face. Which probably hurt me more than it hurt him. Which made me aware of just how much pain Sandra must go through, being a zombie. Yes, it was a lot of pain that I felt then. And also afterwards, when Sandra made me do certain things to atone for hitting Dave, which were so humiliating and degrading that I have no intention of mentioning them here.

'So you're up for the challenge, then?' said Dave. 'When you've finished doing *that*, which, frankly, I don't want to watch any more because it makes me feel sick.'

I just nodded my head to Dave.

Because Sandra had told me to nod it.

And because it's rude to speak with your mouth full.

26

OK. I know what you're thinking. You're thinking that this is all really far-fetched. You're probably thinking that it's ludicrous and foolish and that I'm just making it up as I go along. Well, frankly, I don't blame you. If anyone had ever told me a tale like this, I wouldn't have believed them. I would probably have punched them.

In fact, I might well have killed them.

But that was then, whenever then was, and this was now. And in this now, here was I, victim of cosmic circumstance, dragged back from an eternity of bliss and rattling along in the back of a knackered transit van in the company of a very great deal of explosive.

It was quite clear to me that a considerable degree of forward planning had gone into this operation. A lot of work had been done on the part of Dave and Sandra, before they brought me back from the dead.

I confess that I was slightly baffled. I'd never had Dave down as anything but dodgy. The thought of him caring a jam tiddly about mankind and wanting to play a part in 'saving the world' didn't seem to fit.

But then, love can do strange things to a man. And

it seemed obvious to me that Dave was in love with my Sandra. I don't know what it was about that woman that men found so attractive. Well, actually, I do because I had fallen under her spell. She was a very pretty girl, or had been while alive. And when it came to impersonating ponies, she was definitely in a class of her own. And I think that, even given everything – her infidelities with Count Otto and probably others – she was a *good* person.

But, like I say, here I was, rattling along in the back of another stolen van, *en route* for Mornington Crescent, thinking to myself that I'd rather be anywhere else but here. In fact, *everywhere* else but here.

At which point the extremely obvious hit me right in the face. And a plan of my own entered my poor dead head.

And, as it was an absolute blinder of a plan, it made me smile very much and feel rather happy inside.

A kind of blissful glow.

Which, of course, due to the nature of things, could not be allowed to continue for long.

'Stop van, Dave,' said Sandra. 'She do.'

'She?' said Dave, stopping the van.

'Sandra want body,' said Sandra. 'That body.' And she pointed out of the window. 'She do for body.'

'Oh no, please,' I said, cowering down in the back of the van. 'Please don't make me. Please.'

'Gary, fetch body now,' said Sandra. '*Now!*'

I will spare you the details and the horror. And as the horror is always in the details, these two are one and the same.

'Happy now?' I said, ten minutes later, as I wiped the blood from my hands.

Dave drove on and he cast an approving eye over the latest Sandra. 'It's a very nice body,' he said. 'It really suits you, Sandra.'

'Sandra know what Dave like,' said Sandra.

I sat and stewed in the back. My wife and my bestest friend. I now really hated both of them.

'You OK in the back there, Gary?' called Dave.

'Oh yeah,' I said. 'Never better.'

'Good lad.'

'You'll get yours,' I whispered. And I meant it.

When we finally reached Mornington Crescent it was around midnight. The good old witching hour. I sat in the back of that van, picking loose bits from my fingers and thinking that my life would have been oh so different if I'd been born someone else entirely. Someone destined to be rich and famous, perhaps. Rather than poor and notorious. But Casey Rahserah, or whoever it is, whatever will be will probably be.

'We're going down the secret tunnel,' said Dave.

'Oh, good-oh,' said I.

And down the secret tunnel we went.

After a prolonged period of secret-tunnel travelling, Dave brought the transit to a halt, got out, came around and opened up the rear doors.

'We're here,' he said. 'Time for you to do your stuff.'

'And my stuff would be what, exactly?' I climbed out of the van.

'Special mission,' said Dave. 'Sandra will tell you all about it.'

Sandra danced into view. She looked exceedingly sprightly with her nice fresh body. 'Gary take this,' she said.

'And what is this?' I saw what *this* was. 'No,' I said. 'I don't want to take that.'

'Take gun,' said Sandra, because this (and that) was what this (and that) was (or were).

I took the gun from Sandra.

'Gary go shoot Mr Boothy,' said Sandra. 'Shoot all intraterrestrials too. Gary do this.'

'I don't want to do this,' I told Sandra. 'I was a serial killer when I was alive. Now you're asking me to be one after I'm dead.'

'Not asking,' said Sandra. 'Commanding. Gary do what Gary commanded.'

'Yes,' I said. 'I'll do what I'm commanded.'

'Cool,' said Dave. 'And while you're at it, Sandra and I will set all this explosive down here. It will put paid to the entire complex. We'll have to synchronize watches.'

'I don't have a watch,' I said. 'I think it probably got melted when they fried me in the electric chair.'

'The prison guard nicked it,' said Dave. 'But I nicked it back off him.' And Dave gave me my wrist-watch. Which was nice, but it didn't make me hate him any the less.

'Thanks a lot,' I said.

'No problem,' said Dave. 'I have five past midnight. What do you have?'

'The same,' I said.

'Well, I'll give you until half-past. Do your stuff, then find your way to the tube station entrance. We'll pick you up there. I'll set the timer on the bomb for 12.31. OK?'

'Fine,' I said. 'No problems at all.'

'There is a problem,' said Sandra.

'Oh yes?' I said.

Sandra smiled. 'Sandra know what Gary plan,' she said.

'Plan?' I said. 'I don't know what you mean.'

'Do know,' said Sandra. 'Gary plan to let himself get all blown up by explosion. That what Gary plan. Be dead again. That what Gary plan.'

'I was planning no such thing,' I said.

But as you no doubt guessed, I *was*.

'Gary *not* do this,' said Sandra. 'Sandra *command* Gary not do this. Gary escape before explosion. Gary understand?'

I nodded my head. Dismally. Very dismally.

'I understand,' I said. 'I will do as you command.'

'Good,' said Sandra. 'Gary have much atoning for sins to do for Sandra.'

I ground my teeth. One of them fell out.

'Then, we're all set,' said Dave. 'Off you go, then, Gary.'

'I order zombie,' said Sandra.

'Sorry, Sandra,' said Dave.

'Off go then, Gary,' said Sandra. 'Follow Sandra commands.'

I nodded one more dismal time and set off on my way.

'Not *that* way,' called Dave. '*That* way.'

And I set off *that* way.

That way led me back to the gantry and all the steps down into the vast hangar where all the ranks of flying saucers were parked. If Sandra had been really smart, she would have ordered me to be really careful, to use the utmost stealth, and go undetected. But she wasn't *really* smart, so I just strolled down the stairs and whistled loudly as I strolled.

You'd have thought I was just asking to get caught and executed again. And you would have been right.

At the bottom of the staircase I encountered my first intraterrestrial, a small unassuming kind of fellow. He stared at me with his great black liquid eyes and I just knew that he'd raise the alarm and guards would appear from somewhere and capture me.

So I smiled at him.

And then I shot him dead.

'Damn!' I said, staring at my hand and the pistol. 'I really didn't want to do that.' And, believe me, I didn't. I'll throw the gun away, I thought. But I couldn't. I was compelled. I had been commanded. I was helpless to resist.

It felt really horrible, I can tell you. It's impossible to explain. I suppose its nearest equivalent would be hypnosis. And in a way that's sort of what magic is, an altered state. It's not a *higher* state; it's just a different state. But when *in* that state, *everything* is different.

And I suppose, as I strolled across the big hangar, potting off intraterrestrials and not cursing myself for doing it because I knew they needed potting off, but cursing myself for doing it because I had no free will in the matter, I realized for the first time in (and after) my life that I was a natural magician.

I had, after all, practised magic successfully. Not just by bringing Mr Penrose and Sandra back from the dead, but in other ways also. There was the matter of my father and of Count Otto – the matter of what happened to them before they died. The sniffing of swatches of tweed in the gents' outfitters. The outbursts of uncontrollable laughter. The Zulu king stuff and the dressing in robes befitting. And their obsession with the idea that an invisible Chinaman called Frank was driving them to distraction.

That was magic, you see. Very basic stuff, as it happens – sympathetic magic, voodoo magic, if you like. Creating an obsession in an individual. I was very good at it. I could tell you exactly how I made it happen. But I won't, because it's a secret.

'Stop,' said someone. 'Stop now.'

My gun was up and ready. But I stopped.

'Stop!' said Mr Boothy, for it was he. 'No more shooting. No more killing.'

I aimed my gun straight at his head. 'Sorry,' I said.

'Wait.' Mr Boothy raised his hands. 'Please wait.'

'For what?' I asked. 'There's no waiting left.'

'We should talk. You and me. Before you do this.'

I looked very hard at Mr Boothy. He stood before me, all slim and designer-stubbled, with his two dogs Wibble and Trolley Bus.

'You should at least look surprised to see me,' I said. 'I am, after all, dead.'

'I can see *that*,' said Mr Boothy. 'Do you think I'm stupid?'

'No,' I said, shaking my head. 'But you might at least look surprised.'

'Nothing surprises me,' said Mr Boothy. 'Surprises are for morons. Those in the know just know.'

I cocked my pistol. 'I have to shoot you dead,' I told him. 'I have no choice in the matter. I have been commanded to do so. But you *do* have it coming. You and your stupid boffins have been responsible for ruining my life. And not just mine. You really belong dead.'

'We should talk.' Mr Boothy smiled. And I'll swear that his dogs smiled too.

'No,' I said. 'It's time for you to die. But don't worry about it. Being dead is great. You'll love it. Just don't get in a big state when you're dead. Go with the flow. Let yourself drift. You can fly all around the universe for ever. That's the point of death, you see.'

'And you're telling *me* that. As if I don't know.'

'Uh?' I said. 'You *do* know?'

'Of course I know. Here.' Mr Boothy pointed to his chest. 'Put a couple of bullets here and then we'll talk.'

'Do *what*?' said I.

'Shoot me. That's what you came here for, isn't it?'

'Well, yes, it is, but—'

'Don't but me any buts, boy. Shoot me. Go on, do it. Get it out of the way.'

'All right,' I said. And I shot him. Twice. Right in the chest.

Mr Boothy just stood there. He put his fingers into the holes and then he licked those fingers.

'There,' he said. 'Now you've done your duty. You've followed your commands and got it out of the way. Shall we talk now?'

334

'I am perplexed,' I said.

'I'm dead,' said Mr Boothy. 'Like you.'

'I'm really perplexed,' I said.

'It's no big deal.' Mr Boothy shrugged. 'Or, rather, I suppose it is. You see, there's dead and there's dead and there's *really* dead. Would you like to come to my office and I'll tell you all about it?'

I looked at my watch. It was twelve-fifteen.

'OK,' I said and I followed him.

An intraterrestrial or two appeared before me on the way and I shot them when I saw them.

'Must you do that?' asked Mr Boothy.

'Sorry,' I said, 'but I must.'

'Never mind. Come on, then.'

He led me to his office. It wasn't much of an office. Nothing fancy. Just basic. A hat stand and a filing cabinet, a water cooler and a desk and a couple of chairs. It put me in mind of Lazlo Woodbine's office. But this didn't cheer me very much.

'Sit there,' said Mr Boothy.

I sat where he told me to.

'Drink?' he asked.

'I can't taste anything,' I said. 'But something strong would be nice.'

Mr Boothy poured me something strong. I think it was petrol.

'Bottoms up,' he said. And I drank what he had given me and he drank what he'd poured for himself. Then he sat himself down in the chair behind the desk, which wasn't much to speak of, so I shall not speak of it here.

'You're perplexed,' said Mr Boothy, patting a dog which had climbed up onto his knee.

'I am,' I said, patting his other dog, which was humping my leg.

'It's all been a terrible bols-up,' said Mr Boothy. 'Operation Orpheus. Everything really went wrong right from the start. We did get the information we needed that helped us to win the war. But then later, in nineteen fifty-nine, all this alien business kicked in and we didn't understand what we were dealing with or what was happening to us. By the time we did realize, it was all but too late. We did what we could, we tried to make reparations, but things got out of hand.'

'I am still perplexed,' I said. 'What do you mean by reparations?'

'Restoring people to life,' said Mr Boothy. 'Those who the aliens had killed in their games. Back in the nineteen fifties, the department, the Ministry of Serendipity, we investigated the possibilities of restoring the dead to life. Books existed, you see, in the restricted sections of the libraries. But I assume you know all about that, or you wouldn't be here now. You see, whenever someone important to us – a government official, or someone big in office – was killed, we used magic to restore them to life. But you know how chaotic that becomes. They fall to pieces. It's a real mess.

'But reanimation, for those killed in the course of their duties, was written into the standard work contract for the Ministry of Serendipity. My secretary reanimated me only hours after I'd been run down. And quite right too, because I'm important. But of course everyone involved had loved ones, and when one of them died they wanted them brought back to

336

life. It all grew and it got out of control. Did you know that there are towns in this country where the dead outnumber the living?'

I shook my head.

'Ever heard of Hove?' asked Mr Boothy.

I shook my head again.

'Well, believe me, it's a real problem. And I'm here heading up this Ministry. And now *I'm* dead.'

'You're lying,' I said. 'You gave evidence at my trial. You're being controlled by an alien.'

'You're so right,' said Mr Boothy. 'I *was* being controlled then. But I was *alive* then. I'm not now. You see, a knackered transit van ran over me outside the prison last week. It was making a speedy getaway. I understand that the woman who was driving the van had stolen your body from the prison graveyard.'

'Tough luck,' I said, though I couldn't disguise a smile. 'But about the dead aliens—'

'Listen to me, Gary,' said Mr Boothy. 'Forget about those dead aliens. Dismiss those dead aliens from your mind. They're not what you think.'

'Yeah, right,' I said. 'Dead aliens is what this is all about.'

'P. P. Penrose is what this is all about,' said Mr Boothy.

I scratched at my head. And bits of my head fell off.

'Careful on my carpet,' said Mr Boothy. 'I've just had it cleaned.'

'I'm going to shoot you again,' I said. 'Try to die this time, will you?'

'You've heard of P. P. Penrose, haven't you?' said Mr Boothy.

'My favourite author,' I said. 'I'm his biggest fan.'

'And you like all those Lazlo Woodbine thrillers?'

'Brilliant. I love them.'

'And what about the Adam Earth series?'

'His science-fiction books? They're rubbish. Everyone agrees on that.'

'Pity,' said Mr Boothy. 'Because you've been drawn into them. You're part of them. You and most of mankind.'

'Rubbish,' I said. 'Do you mind if I shoot you again? I feel compelled.'

'Help yourself. But mind the face. Don't touch the face.'

I emptied the gun into Mr Boothy's chest.

'Feel better?' he said. 'Did it help?'

'Not much, apparently.'

'Then let me continue. Mr Penrose died in nineteen fifty-nine, in a bizarre vacuum-cleaning incident.'

'I know,' I said. 'I went to his funeral.'

'I know you did,' said Mr Boothy, nodding his head and patting his dog. 'And did you read his biography that was published this year – P. P. Penrose: *The Man Who Was Lazlo Woodbine*, by Macgillicudy Val Der Mar?'

'Er, no,' I said. 'Although I did attend the launch party.'

'Yes, I know that too,' said Mr Boothy. 'You do turn up in the darnedest places. Well, had you read his biography you would have learned that Mr Penrose got really fed up with writing Lazlo Woodbine thrillers. He even tried to kill Laz off at one point.'

'In *The Final Solution*,' I said. 'He had Laz plunge to

his death over the Reichenbach Falls with his arch-enemy Montmorency.'

'That's right. But the public wouldn't have it. The public demanded *more* Woodbine. So he wrote the "Return" series.'

'It wasn't as good,' I said. 'But it was still brilliant. And certainly better than that Adam Earth rubbish.'

'Well, had you read the biography, you'd have learned that P. P. Penrose did not want to be remembered for the Lazlo Woodbine books. He really wanted to be remembered for the Adam Earth series, his science-fiction books.'

'But they were rubbish,' I said. 'The characters had all these stupid names like Zador Startrouser of the quilted codpiece, or whatever.'

'Yes, didn't they,' said Mr Boothy, with a grin. 'In fact, you'll find many of the so-called True Names – the names of the dead aliens who control humans – in those books. That's where the names come from.'

'You're telling me that real aliens adopted fictitious names?'

'No, that's not what I'm telling you at all. Something happened to P. P. Penrose, happened to him after he died. It turned him from being a sporting man and a good-natured novelist, who was merely a bit miffed that his science-fiction books weren't recognized as his greatest works, into a deeply embittered dead man. A dead man, it seems, who violently hates the living.'

'I wonder what might have done that to him,' I said.

'Probably being awakened in his grave,' said Mr Boothy.

'Oh,' I said.

'Yes, oh. He thought it all up, all of it. Invented the dead aliens who control the living. Gave them life from beyond the grave. He's responsible for it all. One man, but many now he's dead. He's all of those dead aliens, such as Valdec Firesword, Archduke of Alpha Centuri, that's you, and Lady Fairflower of the Rainbow Mountains, your wife Sandra: all thought up by P. P. Penrose. All characters from his books. That dead man has a remarkable imagination. And it's even bigger now, beyond the grave.'

'And you're telling me that all of this is down to him? The alien that possessed me and made me kill people, he invented this alien?'

'That's what novelists do: invent characters. Operation Orpheus gave a gifted novelist the opportunity to make his imaginary characters real. To let a dead man control live people. Let him project his characters into the brains of the living. It was an accident waiting to happen. We just didn't know it at the time.'

'So he did it to *me*,' I said.

'You were a fan,' said Mr Boothy. 'His greatest fan, you said. You were therefore susceptible to his ideas. Don't forget the word fan is short for *fanatic*. You've spent most of your life being a character in one of Mr Penrose's post-life novels.'

'I'm speechless,' I said.

And I was.

And I was made all the more speechless because I realized that it was all my fault. If I hadn't reanimated him in his coffin, he might never have done any of this. He was getting his own back on the living because of what one of the living had done to him after he died. It was all *my* fault.

I felt sick inside, I can tell you. I felt wretched. I wanted to blurt it all out to Mr Boothy; own up to what I'd done. But I didn't. Because you don't, do you? When things are all your fault you never own up. You deny. And if you can't deny, you make excuses. Or you simply refuse to believe it.

'I simply refuse to believe this,' I said. 'There are too many loose ends. Like, for instance, how come you know this. When did you find it out?'

'I found it out when I died. When the dead alien creation no longer controlled me. You must have experienced the same thing when you died. I have contacted experts in the field of this kind of thing. Reanimated experts, of course. We've pooled our knowledge. There's no mistake about it. Mr Penrose is behind all this. He's playing games with humanity. Role-playing games, based on the plots of his science-fiction books.'

I looked once more at my watch. 'Not for much longer,' I said. 'I have to go.'

'Oh, don't leave just yet.' Mr Boothy gave his dog some more patting. 'You'll miss the best bit.'

'Sadly so,' I said. 'I would have loved to stay and be part of it.'

'The big explosion, do you mean?'

'Well, actually, yes.'

Mr Boothy shook his head.

A knock came at his office door.

'Enter,' called Mr Boothy.

The door swung open and in walked Dave. And in

walked Sandra. Dave looked somewhat the worse for wear. He sported a big black eye. Sandra looked well though. Well, as well as she could.

Two men followed after Sandra and Dave. Big men, both, and carrying guns.

'Surprise,' said Mr Boothy.

27

'Well, well, well,' said Mr Boothy. 'If it isn't the woman who ran me over last week.'

'Gary shoot Mr Boothy,' said Sandra.

'Been there, done that,' said I. 'The gun's empty.'

'And who's this bruised fellow?' Mr Boothy asked.

'That's Dave,' said I. 'Hi, Dave.'

'Hi,' said Dave, looking dismal.

'And you were going to blow up this entire complex?'

Dave shook his head. 'Not me,' he said.

'Really?' said Mr Boothy. 'Yet I'm sure it was you I saw on the closed circuit television, driving the van into the secret tunnel. The same van that ran over me.'

Dave shook his head and said, 'No, it wasn't me.'

'I once thought of joining the police force,' said Mr Boothy. 'But a chum of mine said, no, don't do it, it's such a disappointment. Because criminals never own up, like they do in the movies. They never come clean, even when caught red-handed. They say, "It wasn't me," and "I didn't do it," and "I was two-places other at the time." So I didn't join the force. I joined the Ministry of Serendipity instead. And the irony of ironies is I've spent the last thirty years denying everything I've done to anyone who's accused me of doing it.'

'How very interesting,' I said. 'But I have to go now.'

'Why?' asked Mr Boothy.

'Because I don't want to stay.'

'But I can make you stay.'

'I think not,' I said. 'You can shoot me to pieces, if you want. And I'll thank you for it. But other than that, what? I'm dead, so what can you do to me?'

'Good point,' said Mr Boothy.

'Sandra go too,' said Sandra. 'Sandra dead, Sandra go.'

'Why does she talk like that?' asked Mr Boothy. 'All monosyllabic?'

'Because she's been undead for too long,' I said. 'Her brain is mush. You'll be like it soon and so will I.'

'Rubbish,' said Mr Boothy. 'The thinking processes remain unaffected.'

'Ssssh,' I said and I shushed him with my hands.

'Oh, I see,' said Mr Boothy. 'You . . . er . . .'

'You . . . er . . . what?' asked Dave, staring me pointy daggers.

'I just quietened her down a bit,' I said. 'She was somewhat over-feisty when alive.'

'Gary atone for sins big time when Sandra get Gary home,' said Sandra, which was rather too long a sentence for my liking.

Mr Boothy sighed. 'So what should I do with you?' he asked.

'You should shoot Dave,' I suggested.

'What?' said Dave. 'I'm your bestest friend.'

'You've been sexing my wife.'

'She's not your wife any more. You're dead.'

'That's a technicality.'

'It's a fact!'

'But *she's* dead too!'

'Gentlemen, gentlemen.' Mr Boothy held up calming hands. 'This isn't helping matters.'

'Stuff you,' I said. 'Keep out of it.'

'I think I have a solution to this that will satisfy all parties,' said Mr Boothy.

'Fair enough,' I said. 'Shoot Dave.'

'No, it's not that. You see, we at the Ministry would really like to clear up all this P. P. Penrose business.'

'What business is that?' asked Dave. 'And please don't shoot me.'

'I won't shoot you,' said Mr Boothy.

'Fine,' said Dave. 'Then I'm off. Goodbye.'

'I'll have you shot if you try to leave.'

'Fine,' said Dave. 'So what *is* this P. P. Penrose business?'

'All the dead aliens,' I said to Dave: 'they're not real. They're all the invention of P. P. Penrose. They exist in his dead imagination. They have a reality there and they're the ones who control the living.'

'Oh, that,' said Dave. 'I know all about that.'

'You do?'

'Certainly. I overheard Mr Boothy telling you all about that when he captured you.'

'But you never told *me*.'

'That's because I don't believe it. It is rather farfetched.'

345

I sighed. Deeply.

'May I continue?' asked Mr Boothy.

I shrugged. 'Please yourself.'

'Thank you. The problem of the late Mr Penrose really does need a final solution. I would never have known the truth about it if it hadn't been for Sandra here, running me over and killing me. I can't mention my knowledge to any live members of the Ministry – they're all under Mr Penrose's control. This is something I must sort out for myself. I feel that the best way to sort it out is to have a volunteer sort it out for me. Deal with the man, one on one, if you know what I mean.'

'I don't,' said I.

'Someone has to stop it,' said Mr Boothy. Someone has to assassinate Mr Penrose.'

'Assassinate him? Why don't you just shut down the FLATLINE connection? Shut off the power; put the phone down for good. What could he do? He'd be finished. It would be all over. No need for me to do any more bad stuff.'

'We can't afford to do that. Our link with the dead is far too valuable. We need the information the dead supply us with to keep us one step ahead of the rest. The British Empire needs it. Our government would be flailing about in the dark if we couldn't supply it with the dead's secrets. It's not the FLATLINE that's the problem, it's just that meddling Penrose. He has control of too many people and we just can't have him messing around with them and causing havoc any more. If he is eradicated, we will be back on track. He needs to be killed. We need him dead.'

'But he's already dead,' I said.

'I mentioned to you earlier that there's dead and there's dead and there's *really* dead.'

'You mentioned it,' I said. 'But as it didn't make too much sense, I ignored it.'

'He's out there,' said Mr Boothy, 'in the realm beyond death, constructing plotlines, inventing fanciful characters, playing his sporting games, projecting them into the brains of the living. This is not a good thing. This must be stopped. And the only way it can be stopped is by someone dead seeking him out and putting paid to him once and for all.'

'But you can't kill a dead man.'

'You can,' said Mr Boothy. 'You can with magic. Magic knows no bounds. If magic can restore the dead to life, then magic can also kill the dead. So, as I say, the Ministry has been looking for a volunteer. Someone brave who would take on the task.'

'And no takers, I suppose?' said Dave.

'Not so far,' said Mr Boothy. 'You see, glorious as being dead is, those we have reanimated are still keen to stay undead. I think it must be the good wages the Ministry pays and all the fringe benefits. Once people live again they are eager to keep on living.'

'I'm not,' I said.

And Mr Boothy grinned. A real big toothy grin — although he did have a couple of teeth missing and his tongue was somewhat furry.

'I rather thought not,' said he. 'In fact, I was absolutely sure of it when I watched you on the CCTV, strolling down the staircase, as if you wanted to get caught and killed again.'

Sandra glared at me. But then she hadn't stopped glaring since she'd learned about her 'dumbing down'.

'And I'm sure I'd be right in thinking,' said Mr Boothy, 'that you are a natural magician. And as it's all your fault anyway, I think you should sort it out.'

'All *my* fault?' I said. 'What do you mean?'

'Gary, this is the Ministry of Serendipity. It's a secret ministry, and secret ministries thrive on information, you know, like the CIA. Information is power. We have files on everyone. When you were brought to justice—'

'It wasn't justice,' I said. 'That trial was a travesty of justice.'

'All right, then. When you were brought to travesty of justice, we looked into your file. And we found all kinds of interesting things: old surveillance footage from the restricted section of Brentford library; surveillance footage from the home of P. P. Penrose; during his wake. It's all on film, what you did.'

'What?' I said. 'You have me on film? Outrageous! What an invasion of privacy.'

'Everyone is under surveillance,' said Mr Boothy. 'Everyone. Especially the rich and famous like Mr Penrose. You reanimated him in his grave. All this is your fault. It is extremely fortuitous that you should have turned up here today. You could call it fate. You are the volunteer that we have been looking for. Who else could it be but you?'

'I'm not an assassin,' I said.

'Gary,' said Mr Boothy, 'like it or like it not, you are a psychopath. With or without Mr Penrose's Valdec Firesword, Archduke of Alpha Centuri, in your head, you would have been a psychopath. It's not your fault, it's probably your father's fault.'

'It's definitely his fault,' I said.

'Which is probably why you did for him.'

'Let's not get into *that*,' I said.

'Well, be it here, or be it there' – Mr Boothy smiled and patted his dog some more – 'you are the ideal man for the job.'

'And when, I mean, *if*, I do this job, then I'm free? I can be dead and fly off around the universe for ever? I'm out of all this? I'm free?'

'Free as a bird,' said Mr Boothy. 'You'll have atoned for all your sins. Eternity will be yours to do with as you please.'

'Then I volunteer,' I said. 'I'm your man.'

'Gary *not* your man,' said Sandra. 'Gary Sandra's man. Gary stay here, serve Sandra. That what Gary do.'

I looked at Mr Boothy.

And Mr Boothy looked at me.

'Security guard,' said Mr Boothy, to one of the security guards. 'Kindly take Mr Cheese's wife down to the boiler room and toss her into the furnace.'

'No!' Dave shouted, and raised his fists. 'Hold on. Don't do *that*.'

Mr Boothy looked at me once more. 'Do you want me to have the security guard toss your friend Dave into the furnace too?' he asked.

I looked at Dave.

And Dave looked at me.

'No,' I said. 'Not really. Dave is my bestest friend, even though he's been . . . you know . . . with my wife. Don't bung either of them into the furnace. Let them go.'

'Nice one,' said Dave.

'Gary . . .' said Sandra.

'And in return, let *me* go,' I said to Sandra. 'Let me do this. Dave will look after you. Dave cares about you. I was never much of a husband, although I did love you. But I treated you badly and I should atone for what I've done. For all the bad things I've done. Maybe by doing this it will go some way towards making things right.'

Sandra just stared at me and I couldn't read her expression at all.

Dave said, 'Good luck, mate,' and put out his hand for a shake.

I shook Dave warmly by the hand. 'You are my bestest friend,' I said. 'You're an utter no-mark, thoroughly dishonest and untrustworthy, but I am proud to call you my bestest friend.'

'And you are a conscienceless serial killer,' said Dave. 'But you're my bestest friend too.'

And so we shook hands and got a bit dewy-eyed and trembly-lipped and patted each other on the shoulder and finally said our farewells. I reached out to give Sandra a kiss and a cuddle, but she just drew back, folded her arms and stamped whoever's feet she had upon the carpet. I think that, deep down, she still loved me. But women are funny creatures and don't always show their real emotions. ''Bye, then, Sandra,' I said. 'I hope you'll be happy with Dave.'

Dave and Sandra departed the office of Mr Boothy, leaving me behind. Sandra, however, didn't leave without a struggle, and one of the security men had to hold her mouth shut to stop her commanding me to do something unspeakable to Mr Boothy.

'That was rather touching about you and Dave,' said Mr Boothy. 'I've never really had a bestest friend. My dogs are my best friends. But it's not quite the same.'

'So,' I said. 'I suppose we should press on.' I handed Mr Boothy my gun. 'You'd best shoot me in the head. That should get the job done.'

Mr Boothy weighed the gun in his hands. 'I don't think this would work,' he said. 'Your body must be utterly destroyed. I think it would be best if *you* were tossed into the furnace.'

'Eh?' I said. 'No. That would really hurt. That's not a good idea. That's a really bad idea. I don't like that at all. The gun is the thing. One quick shot between the eyes. One—'

'The gun is empty,' said Mr Boothy. 'And we are in a hurry. Security guards—'

'No!' I shouted. 'No. Stop. Hold on.'

'Escort Mr Cheese to the furnace and—'

'*No!*'

'Bung him in.'

'*NO!*'

But damn me if it wasn't *yes*.

28

Can you believe that?

I mean, can you?

He had me thrown into the furnace.

If frying in the electric chair had been bad, it was a doddle compared with that.

That *really* hurt.

But it did get the job done and, there was no doubt about it, I was definitely dead again. And for good and all this time, with no Earthly hope for resurrection. Gone, reduced to ashes. No more Gary Charlton Cheese in the flesh. Only in the spirit. I didn't find myself back at Mr Doveston's tomb this time: I found myself nowhere in particular. A bit lost, as it happens. Just sort of drifting.

But it felt really nice. I didn't feel empty at all this time. There was a great deal of darkness around and about, but a light or two in the distance. I moved towards those lights.

As I moved on, the lights moved nearer. Big lights, two lights.

A car ran me over.

I picked myself up and dusted myself down and

chewed upon my lip as I surveyed the tyre marks over my chest. 'Not a great start,' said I.

But where was I?

It looked a bit like New York, but as I'd never been to New York I couldn't be sure. However, as I'd seen New York on TV and in movies, I could be sure. It was New York. But why New York?

I shambled along in a bumbling kind of fashion, like you do when you're lost, or drunk, or both. I didn't recognize any New York landmarks.

But then suddenly I did.

There was a bar up ahead – a New York bar, a Manhattan bar. A neon light flashed above it, spelling out letters that made up the name: FANGIO'S.

Fangio's bar, favourite hangout of Lazlo Woodbine. I bumbled towards Fangio's bar. Of course I recognized the cracked glass door. It was exactly as I'd imagined it, exactly as it had been in the books. And inside, the bar was all there, all exactly right. A man stood behind the bar counter, and he was a big man, a big *fat* man. This was Fangio, the fat boy barman. And seated upon the customer side of the counter, upon a chromium bar stool, sat the other man. He wore a trenchcoat and a fedora. He sipped on a bottle of Bud and munched upon a hot pastrami on rye.

The other man was none other than Lazlo Woodbine.

Fangio looked over at me as I swung in the door.

'Lordy, lordy,' said he. 'It's the elephant man.' I chewed upon my bottom lip and realized that it was a quite substantial bottom lip. And I remembered my encounter with the late Mother Demdike – how she'd said that, when we died, we each got the form that was *really* us. 'Ah, no offence meant, fella,' said Fangio. 'Looks ain't everything. Did the circus leave town without you? Why not have a drink? What'll it be?'

'Anything at all,' I said. 'Anything at all.'

'That's a bit vague,' said Fangio. 'We like to be specific here.'

'I don't care,' I said. 'Give me a beer. Give me a Bud.'

The guy in the trenchcoat (you note that I say 'guy' here, rather than 'man') turned to me.

'Sit yourself down,' he said. 'There's no appearance-code here. We're always grateful when someone breezes in to chew the fat. What's your name, buddy?'

'It's Cheese,' I said. 'Gary Charlton Cheese. And you are . . .' I couldn't get the words out.

'The name's Woodbine,' said Woodbine. 'Lazlo Woodbine, private eye.' And he added, 'Some call me Laz.'

'I would be proud to call you Laz,' said I. 'I'm your greatest fan. Well, the fan of your author. If you know what I mean, and I'm sure that you do.'

'Don't use my catch phrases,' said Mr Woodbine. 'And don't mention *him*. He and I do not see eye to eye any more.'

'I'm perplexed,' I said, as Fangio handed me my bottle of Bud. 'I mean, you're *real*. You're here. I thought—'

'That I was a fictitious character?'

'Well, yes.'

'That's because I was written up as a fictitious character. But I was once alive, like you were. So what

354

are you doing in this neck of the Manhattan woods?'

'It's a bit embarrassing for me to have to tell you,' I said, 'but I've come to kill P. P. Penrose. That dead man is wreaking havoc on Earth.'

'It's fine with me,' said Laz, for I could call him that. 'I hate the guy. He wrote up my cases then claimed all the glory for himself. Like I say, I was never a fictitious character. I was a real detective. He just changed my name.'

'Outrageous!' I said.

'And he had me killed.'

'*What!*' I said.

'I was going to expose him. He had me killed. Weirdest thing. Never saw it coming and me being Woodbine — well, Passing Cloud, actually; I'm half Cherokee from my father's side. This blind guy killed me. Blind guy from the circus. Count Otto Black's Circus Fantastique.'

'Oh no,' I said. 'My Uncle Jonny.'

'Small world, isn't it?' said Mr Woodbine. 'Everything fits together, eventually, doesn't it?'

'Where is he?' I asked. 'Mr Penrose. Do you know where he is?'

'In my office, doing his stuff: pulling strings, playing his sporting games.'

'Do you want to come with me?' I asked. 'Do you want to help?'

'Can't,' said Laz and he shook his fedora'd head. 'I'm stuck here, in this bar. Me and Fangio, we chew fat and talk toot. We tried to kill him, because we hated him so much for what he did. But if you hate, you get stuck. We got stuck here, but we make the

355

best of it. You go get him, kid. And here, take this; you'll need it.' And Laz pulled out his trusty Smith & Wesson and handed it to me. 'It's taken down a few bad guys in its time,' he said. 'One more won't hurt. Get the job done, kid, then come back here. I'll stand you a beer.'

'You can pay for the one he's just had, Laz,' said Fangio.

'We can discuss that,' said Laz to the fat boy.

I took Laz's trusty Smith & Wesson and stared at it. *The* trusty Smith & Wesson: what a collector's item. I was still a fan – I had no control over it. Once you're a fan of something or someone, you're stuck to it. I thanked Laz and waved farewell to the fat boy.

And then I left the bar. I passed down the now legendary alleyway, where Laz used to get into sticky situations, and found my way to his office. It was where I expected it to be, so it was no mystery how I found it.

On the partition door the words LAZLO WOODBINE INVESTIGATIONS were etched into the glass. I don't know what I felt. Nervous? Yes. Doubtful? Yes. Guilty? Yes, that too. It was all my fault, what had happened; what had caused Mr Penrose to behave as he had. But truth is truth is truth. He obviously hadn't been a good person. Not if he'd had Mr Woodbine, Mr Passing Cloud, killed.

But there was more that troubled me. Could I actually trust Mr Woodbine/Passing Cloud? I knew that the dead were notable liars. Perhaps I hadn't been told the truth. But I was really giving up on the truth. Perhaps there really isn't any truth, any ultimate truth. Perhaps the universe consists for the most part of half-truths and just plain lies. Perhaps there really isn't any real truth at all.

I knocked at the office door.

'Come,' called a voice.

And I entered.

It was the same office – the same office as that which Mr Boothy had occupied. Exactly the same. Behind the desk of this one sat an old gentleman clad in a suit of Boleskine tweed.

'Mr Penrose?' I said. 'Mr Charles Penrose?'

The gentleman stared at me, though he did not seem at all bothered by my obviously grotesque appearance. 'So,' said he. 'Someone who knows my real name, my True Name. And you would be?'

'Gary Cheese,' I said. 'Gary Charlton Cheese. You would know me as Valdec Firesword, Archduke of Alpha Centuri.'

'Oh yes,' said Mr Penrose. 'The maniac. But this is a bit of a surprise. I didn't expect ever to see you here.'

'It's fate,' I said. 'Everything fits together for a purpose. It's just that most of us never get to know what that purpose might be.' And I looked hard at Mr Penrose. He obviously didn't know that I was the one who'd woken him up from the dead and caused him to hate humanity so much. Well, if he didn't know, I wasn't going to tell him.

'And what is your purpose?' asked Mr Penrose.

I pulled out Laz's gun. 'I've come here to kill you,' I said. 'I'm sorry, but there it is. You are my favourite author and I'm your greatest fan. And I can't tell you just how incredible it is for me to meet you – if not in the flesh, then at least in the spirit. But I have to kill you, to stop you playing your games with humanity. All that has to stop now. But before I kill you, and I must, and I am sorry for it, would it be all right if I asked you a question? Something that I've always wanted to know.'

'Ask on,' said Mr Penrose.

'Thank you,' I said. 'The question is this: *where do you get your ideas from?*'

Mr Penrose made a groaning sound, deep in the back of his throat.

'So?' I said.

'Forget it, lad. If I knew where I got my ideas from I wouldn't tell you. And I do know, and it's a secret.'

'Like magic,' I said.

'Ideas *are* magic,' said Mr Penrose. 'So let's discuss the business of you killing me. What's that all about, then?'

'You know perfectly well what it's all about,' I said, waggling the gun at the famous author. 'All that beaming of science-fiction characters into people's brains: that has to stop.'

'Why?' asked Mr Penrose.

'Because it's not right.'

'People kill one another all the time, with or without my prompting. What's a few less people in the world?'

'That's a rather callous attitude. I don't think you're a very nice man. I thought you were a great sportsman.' I cocked the pistol.

'It's not very sporting to shoot an unarmed man,' said Mr Penrose.

'Sportsmanship doesn't enter into this,' I said.

'Well, it should. I've always given my characters a sporting chance.'

'You didn't give me much of one.'

'Oh yes, I did. You lost the game because you fell into an obvious trap. Imagine going through a door marked WHITE COAT AND LIGHT BULB STORE. Ludicrous.'

'Yeah, well,' I said, 'I was under stress. It had been a difficult day. And it wasn't me, was it? It was Valdec Firesword making me do what I did.'

'So if you had another chance, you'd do better, would you? Doing your own thinking, you'd win the game?'

'What game?' I said. 'What is the game anyway?'

'It's a role-playing game,' Mr Penrose explained, 'based on the plot from one of my Adam Earth series. An alien race is wiped out in a cosmic catastrophe, but their spirits are able to manipulate human beings. They're a competitive race, the aliens, and somewhat cold-blooded. They compete on Earth through their unknowing human hosts. It's survival of the fittest and the most intelligent. Eventually there will be only one of them left. That one wins the game.'

'And what's the prize?' I asked.

'Earth, of course,' said Mr Penrose. 'The winner will be the one who ends up controlling the entire planet.'

'That's daft,' I said. 'Just beam one of your characters into the head of the President of the United States and he's the winner.'

'Unsporting,' said Mr Penrose. 'Too easy. It has to be little people who can work their way up to become rich and famous. You had a lot of chances, you know. You were given the opportunity to communicate with the dead. That should have given you an edge.'

'If I'd known,' I said. 'But Valdec Firesword screwed it up, not me.'

'He never was too bright. Which is why he lost the game.'

'Who's winning at the moment?' I asked. 'Not that I'm interested.'

'I'm not going to tell you *that*,' said Mr Penrose. 'That would be really unsporting.'

'Well, it's neither here nor there. You're a dead dead-man.' And I levelled the pistol at his head.

'You can't do it, you know. You can't just shoot me here.'

'And why not?'

'Do you like this office? Do you really like it?'

'It's OK,' I said. 'It's nothing much to speak of.'

'So how would you feel about spending all eternity here?'

'I wouldn't be too keen on that at all.'

'No,' said Mr Penrose. 'And, frankly, I hate it. But that's what I'm stuck with. Because I'm stuck here. Because of what I've done. You'll be doing me a favour if you shoot me. I'll move on to another level. But you won't be doing yourself a favour. Your actions will cause you to become stuck here, right here, in this office, like mine have for me. Bad thoughts and actions weigh down the dead and stop them moving on.'

'Hm,' I said, scratching my head with the gun barrel and noticing for the first time just what a lot of head there was to scratch. 'A dead woman called Mother

Demdike explained that to me. This is a tricky situation.'

'I can't see any way out of it for either of us,' said Mr Penrose.

I stared at him and I scratched at my head once more. 'I think I can,' I said.

'Oh yes? And what do you have in mind?'

'Well,' I said, 'you consider yourself to be a great sporting man, yes?'

Mr Penrose nodded.

'Well, what if you and I had some sport? One on one and winner takes all?'

'I am intrigued,' said Mr Penrose. 'Speak to me of this sport.'

And so I spoke to him.

29

And that is the end of my tale.

'What?' I hear you cry. 'What?' What kind of cop-out ending is this? You can't end your tale here. You just can't.'

But I can.

I really can.

I could drag it out a bit longer. Because, in all truth, it hasn't truly ended yet. But then, it can't end. Because it doesn't have an ending. There is no end after you die. There is only for ever. A blissful for ever, with all the universe to explore. Not that I've started my exploring yet.

But I will.

I will, very soon.

Just as soon as I win the game.

I told Mr Penrose what I had in mind for us both.

It was simple and it was sporting. And he does seem to have a big thing about sportsmanship, that Mr Penrose. He's firm, but he's fair. I suggested that he give me a sporting chance, and considering all that I'd been put through, and being the sporting man that he was, I knew he'd take me up on it. He wouldn't be able to resist. And I felt certain that I would win, because I'd be calling my own shots this time. I would be in control of the situation. And I felt absolutely sure that ultimately I would triumph.

In essence this was my suggestion. He and I would both play the game. Against each other, and winner takes all. We had to work out a lot of rules that we both could agree on and this did take a lot of time. But we had time a-plenty, and when we had worked out the rules, and agreed that they were sporting and that any cheating would disqualify the player caught at it, we were both ready to play.

The game would be played in this fashion. Each of us would beam our thoughts into a living person of our choice. But it had to be an ordinary person of no particular consequence. No one rich and powerful. We would choose whoever we fancied, beam in and take control of that person. And it would be our secret. Neither of us would know who the other one was possessing, if you follow me. Then we'd go looking for each other and each would try to kill the other.

We both agreed that, as in the Lazlo Woodbine thrillers, it should end in a final rooftop showdown, with the loser getting blasted by the winner and taking the big fall into oblivion.

And, as I say, it would be winner takes all.

If I won, then Mr Penrose would be obliged, on his word of honour, to quit the game, taking all his created dead-alien characters with him, and for ever leave the world and its people alone.

And if *he* won, I would be obliged to leave Mr

Penrose alone to go on playing his games and I would be obliged to remain on Earth in a body of his choosing, which I suspected would not be a particularly appealing one.

So, having gone through all the rules to ensure that we both knew exactly how things were to be done and the game was to be played, and – here comes the clever bit – having persuaded him that he should remove all the other players (the dead aliens he had created that were mucking about with people's brains) temporarily, until we had completed our game, we chose our hosts and beamed our thoughts down.

And it was game on.

Now, for the afterlife of me, I didn't know how he caught me that first time. I'd beamed myself into the head of this young black guy in Tooting. He was into martial arts and weapons and in my opinion was a natural-born assassin. But he got run down by a woman shopper on the top of a multi-storey car park. Which I wasn't expecting.

'A woman shopper!' I said to Mr Penrose. 'What kind of body was that for you to choose?'

'It worked, didn't it? You weren't expecting it. And it was on a rooftop.'

'But how did you know it was *me*?'

'Aha!' said Mr Penrose, and he tapped his nose.

'That was unsporting,' I said. 'You forfeit the game.'

'No, I don't. I stuck to the rules. It's just that I neglected to mention that you can tell who's who.'

'How?'

Mr Penrose whispered – not that there was anyone around to hear – how.

'Oh,' I said. 'Yes, I suppose that's obvious. All right, let's make it best of three.'

'But you lost.'

'You cheated.'

'I didn't cheat. I just neglected to mention an important detail.'

'That's the same as cheating. That should have been written into the rules.'

'All right,' said Mr Penrose, 'we'll write it in.'

'And there's nothing else that you haven't mentioned?'

'Nothing,' said Mr Penrose.

But there were one or two other things.

So we made it 'best of three'.

And then 'best of five'.

I've kind of lost count now. I think we're going for best of thirty-three million, three hundred and thirty-three thousand, three hundred and thirty-three.

Between us, we're keeping down the population to a reasonably stable level, which is sound ecology, so I can't see anything particularly wrong with that.

I've had him a few times – a few thousand times, in fact. And I feel absolutely certain that ultimately I'm going to win.

I'm going to have another go at him tomorrow. But as it's New Year's Eve, we've both agreed to take time out from the game to party for the next couple of days. I'm looking forward to seeing in this New Year. I think 3012 will be a lucky year for me.

And this evening promises to be interesting too. I'm

currently inside the head of a quite remarkable-looking young woman. She's a window-dresser in a posh store here in New Brentford. It used to be called Rio de Janeiro, before the New British Empire changed it. The New British Empire runs all of the planet now and maintains world peace. Which is nice. Mr Boothy still runs the Ministry of Serendipity. I pop in to see him whenever I'm in England. He's holding up pretty well, what with all those advances in medical science and everything. He's the last zombie there is now. He had all the rest humanely despatched to foreverness. Including my Sandra, but it was right that he did. I like to surprise Mr Boothy when I see him. He always gets a kick out of seeing what body I'm currently in. I'm sure he'd like this one. She's not rich or famous or anything – Mr Penrose and I still stick with the rules – but she really is a beauty and I know, just know, she's going to get laid later by that handsome waiter who keeps giving her the eye.

I figure that it's worth experiencing life from every perspective, and over the last thousand years or so I certainly have. I'd like to say that there's nothing that a human being can experience that I haven't experienced. But it wouldn't be true. And thankfully so. There's always something new and that something new is always wonderful.

And I really am optimistic about the year that lies ahead. And I'm really sure that, OK, perhaps I won't win the game this year, because I still have a lot of catching up to do.

But if not this year, then next year, or the year after that.

Because I have no shortage of time.
Time is on my side.
I have all the time in the world.
In *this* world.
Because ultimately. And marvellously.
It's never, ever,

THE END

SPROUTLORE

The New Official

ROBERT RANKIN

Fan Club

Members Will Receive:

Four Fabulous Issues of the *Brentford Mercury*, featuring previously unpublished stories by Robert Rankin. Also containing News, Reviews, Fiction and Fun.

A coveted Sproutlore Badge.

Special rates on exclusive T-shirts and merchandise.

"Amazing Stuff" – Robert Rankin.

Annual Membership Costs £5 (Ireland), £7 (UK) or £11 (Rest of the World). Send a Cheque/PO to:
Sproutlore, 211 Blackhorse Avenue, Dublin 7, Ireland.
Email: sproutlore@lostcarpark.com
WWW: http://www.lostcarpark.com/sproutlore

Sproutlore exists thanks to the permission of Robert Rankin and his publishers.